Even when the lights are out, he can still see you...

Paul Holten's profession doesn't leave much room for doubt or conscience, but he's reaching his breaking point. The nightmares are getting worse, the jobs are getting harder to finish, and the volatile relationship with his boss Aaron is falling apart. Now faced with the possibility of an impending death sentence, Paul makes the fatal decision to run. Drawn into one hellish situation after another, he's forced to confront his dark past—and wonders if perhaps dying isn't the better option.

They had to get out of there—and fast—but he couldn't see a thing...

Jesus, it was dark.

It was disorienting in its completeness, in its total lack of light. In his lifetime, Paul had had his sight temporarily taken from him many times. Mostly by people who didn't want to be looked at or identified if—God forbid—something went wrong. But there had always been some degree of light leaking through the blindfold or a shift in someone's hand that was clamped tightly over his eyes, or the loose weaves in a rut-sack that was tied around his head. He'd always been able to see *something*.

This, however, was like the deepest part of the ocean. This was like having his eyes glued shut. This was what it meant to be blind.

The air grew colder and with that came the struggle to breathe. He didn't know if it was claustrophobia but it came pretty damn close. His chest hurt and his throat felt like someone was cramming cotton into his mouth. He tried to breathe more slowly, to at least calm the thundering in his rib cage, but the darkness around him fed the panic that was skating through his bones. The stones beneath his fingers were wet in some places and icy in others and, under his feet, things crunched and squeaked like he was stepping through snow and ice.

He *hoped* it was snow and ice.

Echoes came from all sides of him. It was impossible to decipher one sound from the next. He wondered if the people who heard voices felt anything like this. Just one gigantic ball of murmuring sounds and words that didn't make any sense.

There was a scraping sound behind him.

KUDOS for *Lights Out*

While the subject matter is more than a little uncomfortable, the book is extremely well written, riveting, and superbly crafted. – *Faith, senior editor*

Lights Out by Melissa Groeling is not for everyone, certainly not for the faint of heart. While it is a well-written and fascinating story, its subject matter is rather uncomfortable. The story revolves around Paul Holten, a professional assassin, who while growing up had been abused and forced to be a child prostitute. The story reaches a critical turning point when Paul rescues Ethan, a ten-year-old boy who reminds Paul too much of himself at that age. Determined to save the boy from the perverts who are abusing him, Paul takes Ethan and goes on the run, fleeing from assassins, his employers, and a mysterious Aztec shaman, all determined to kill him and Ethan both. Lights Out is a gritty, almost too honest story about the baser side of human nature and child abuse. The characters are extremely well-developed, three-dimensional, and are eerily real. As uncomfortable as the subject matter is, I found the book riveting and very hard to put down. – *Taylor Jones, Reviewer*

Wow! Lights Out by Melissa Groeling was certainly unexpected. As Groeling's debut effort was a YA novel, I was totally unprepared for this one. Lights Out is a hard-hitting, brutally honest book about pedophiles and child abuse, and the lasting effect this has on victims' lives. The main character, Paul is not a likeable man. He is a professional assassin, cold, hard, unemotional, and apparently without much, if any, conscience. But there is a vulnerability about him that really pulls you in. And while he is not the type of man you would expect to find a spark of goodness lurking deep inside, there actually is one and it is forced to the surface when Paul encounters Ethan, a ten-year-old boy growing up with the same kind of abuse and degradation that Paul suffered as a child. Lights Out is an enjoyable read, at least it was for me, but it is not exactly a comfortable one. The plot is strong, well-thought-out, unpredictable, and totally authentic. The story is gripping, and although its shines a spotlight on the depravity that humans are capable of, it also showcases the nobility that they can sometimes display. While I don't know that it is a book that I would read more than once, I am very glad that I read it the first time. – *Regan Murphy, Reviewer*

LIGHTS OUT

Melissa Groeling

A BLACK OPAL BOOKS PUBLICATION

Black Opal Books
BECAUSE SOME STORIES JUST HAVE TO BE TOLD

GENRE: MYSTERY/SUSPENSE/PARANORMAL THRILLER

LIGHTS OUT
Copyright © 2013 by Melissa Groeling
Cover Design by Nathan Mumper
All cover art copyright © 2013
All Rights Reserved
Print ISBN: 978-1-626940-88-8

First Publication: DECEMBER 2013

Published by Black Opal Books http://www.blackopalbooks.com

DEDICATION

To Mom and Dad
For everything you've given up
And everything you've given me.

To Nathan
For creating such an incredible book cover.

I created the sound of madness
Wrote the book on pain
Somehow I'm still here to explain
That the darkest hour never comes in the night
You can sleep with a gun
When you gonna wake up and fight
For yourself?

– Shinedown, *Sound of Madness*

CHAPTER 1

The barista hated coffee. He loathed the taste of it, the smell of it, and the sound of it—and yes, it did have a peculiar sound as it was slurped, poured, stirred, sweetened, and gulped by the gallon. He hated the bubbling, the churning, the nails-on-metal sound of beans being ground up. He especially hated the fancy names that he always tripped over while a fifteen-year-old punk with sleepy eyes, pimples, and a skateboard tucked under one arm could spout out a double-shot of espresso in a grande vanilla, no-foam macchiato, without missing a beat.

As the barista adjusted his apron strings, he earned another dirty look from John the Manager, whose shirt collar was soaked with sweat as the line of people at the counter doubled to four-deep.

Hell is coffee and I am in it, the barista thought as he turned to the huge metal sink to rinse out blenders, cups, spoons, and parts of something called an espresso machine that had gone belly-up about ten minutes ago.

A string of loud, colorful curses erupted from one of the tables. The barista looked over the counter to see the target muttering and swearing while wiping at the growing stain of spilled coffee down the front of his expensive suit. The barista froze in irritation, taking in the overturned cup and watching a stream of pale brown liquid trickle off the edge of the table.

Dammit.

The barista turned away, his hands clenching. His mind had begun to race with back-up scenarios when John the Manager's tomato-red face was suddenly inches from his own.

"Get him another coffee, black, no sugar. Can you handle that?"

Without a word, the barista's hands unclenched. His thoughts slowed and he carefully, methodically prepared the drink. He cast a nonchalant glance over the top of the now-defunct espresso machine and watched the target for a moment. A laptop was open on the table in front of him. Sunglasses were perched on top of spiky blonde hair that looked stiff enough to withstand a Kansas tornado. His eyes were as cold and clear as the weather outside, glaring up at the barista as he came over with the fresh cup of coffee.

"Here you are," the barista said with a friendly smile as he held it out to him.

The target threw a disdainful look at the offending coffee. "I wanted a latte."

"Espresso machine's down."

The target gave a grunt and grabbed the cup hard enough to send some coffee sloshing over the rim.

"Oops," the man sneered.

The barista calmly wiped his hand on his apron, watching for a moment as the poison was sipped. Satisfied, he turned and walked away. He took off his apron as he rounded the counter. John the Manager was at his side.

"What in the hell do you think—"

The barista tossed the apron at him. "Fuck you. I quit."

There was a moment of shocked silence then laughter and applause from his co-workers. He went for the door, where he paused for a moment.

The poison was fast-acting, tasteless, and would leave no footprint after death. He didn't have to wait long.

There was the shrill scrape of a chair sliding across the tiles, followed by a terrible gagging sound.

The barista swung the door open and went out into the cold sunlight, with the sound of a body hitting the floor trailing closely behind.

CHAPTER 2

Coffee? Coffee, Paul? Are you kidding me? I called you three different times and each time you were out getting a cup of coffee? You don't even *like* coffee."

Paul Holten hoped he looked innocent because he sure didn't feel it as he watched his girlfriend storm back and forth between the closet and the bed. A duffel bag, big enough to hold a baby elephant lay on the mattress in a messy nest of blankets and sheets. The bag was nearly full, bursting at the seams and the closet wasn't even half-empty yet.

Jesus Christ, he found himself thinking. *How did all of that even fit in my closet?*

It baffled him that even though he knew she was leaving for good this time, the only thing he could think about was the astonishing amount of shit that had accumulated from her presence. Clothes, make-up, jewelry, hairbrushes, shampoo, shoes, pictures, perfumes, her own sheets on his bed—her entire life was here and he was only now just noticing it.

She moved around him like a pissed-off hurricane. Her freshly washed hair hung damp and heavy down her slim back. Dry, her hair was a curtain of midnight, shimmering as if it held all the constellations of the universe. As it was presently, it appeared knotty and dull, like an old bear rug that had seen the best of the bottoms of everyone's shoes. But when she turned to him in a circle of aggravation and fury, she was anything but knotty and dull. Paul felt an unexpected pang in his chest at the fire in her green eyes.

He was going to miss her.

"Since when don't I like coffee?" he said, pushing for sincerity. "I love coffee. Can't live without it. And it's not like I didn't get your messages. I got swamped with work and I couldn't—"

She cut him off by holding up a slender, perfectly manicured hand. Then she resumed her packing, tearing her clothes so violently from the hangers that they swung off the rod and clattered noisily to the hardwood floor.

"Don't give me that. This has been going on for months. Every time I call you, you're out for coffee which is pretty amazing because for someone who loves it so much, I, for one, have never seen you drink a drop of it. You don't even own a coffee maker."

The disgusted look on her face was so acute he thought she would vomit all over the bed. When she spoke again, her voice shook.

"If you don't want to talk to me, if you don't want me around, all you have to do is say so. You don't have to play these stupid goddamn games with me."

"I'm not—"

"How long did you think I'd put up with this? What were you doing, waiting for me to reach my breaking point so you wouldn't have to be the bad guy and end the relationship?"

"I don't know why you're getting so upset," he said, rubbing at his forehead. "When I'm at work, I'm working. I can't just drop everything because you're calling me ten times a day. My boss rides my ass enough as it is."

"I do *not* call you ten times a day."

"Oh, okay, fine, yeah, you don't call me ten times a day. I got back to the office yesterday and there were eleven messages waiting for me and guess what? Half of them were from you."

She glared at him. "That's still not ten times a day."

"Kel, come on," he groaned. "You're being completely insane. I'm trying to be honest—"

"My ass," she snorted. "You're the best liar I know."

He mentally winced at her words. She went to the big oak dresser and swept all her make-up and other accessories into a bag that was nearly half the size of the bag on the bed. He watched her for a moment.

"So let me see if I understand this. You're leaving me because I don't answer your calls at work?" He made it a question which won him a scathing look over her shoulder.

"No. I'm leaving you because you don't care. You don't care about me. You don't care about this relationship. And I'm tired of doing the caring for the both of us."

His jaw flexed. "You know, I find that a little ridiculous seeing as how you were the one who was pushing so hard for this relationship in the first place."

She whirled around to face him. "And you weren't an active participant?"

"I told you that you were rushing things. After two weeks, you wanted me to say I love you. After a month, you insisted that we exchange keys to our apartments. Then after two months, you moved in. And don't think I haven't noticed the bridal magazines you've left laying around."

"There's nothing wrong with wanting to get married."

"After eight months? You think that's long enough to decide you want to marry somebody?"

"How long do you plan on waiting?"

"A lot longer than eight months. Maybe if we'd given things more time—"

"You're ridiculous. What's the big deal if I moved in after two months or two years? Does the timeframe really matter? You'd still be jerking me around."

"I am *not* jerking you around. Just because I'm not in a rush doesn't mean I don't want to be with you."

"A rush?" she repeated incredulously. "No, Paul, you're not in a rush. You're not in a rush to do anything. You just avoid the issue all-together."

"What're you—Jesus, Kel, are you making this shit up as you go along or what?"

"Forget it. I can't even talk to you about this."

"You could if you started making some sense."

She zipped her bag shut. "Doesn't matter. Even if we stayed to-gether, even if I started 'making sense,' you'd still find a way to screw it all up."

He gritted his teeth. "I'm not screwing anything up. You're the one leaving."

"If you gave a shit, you'd beg me to stay."

"I don't beg."

"If you cared about me, you would."

He rolled his eyes. "Give me a break."

Her hands tightened on the shoulder strap of her bag. "Give you a break? How about giving me a break? I'm the one who's had to put up your shit for the last eight months."

"You were welcome to leave at any time. No one was forcing you to stay here."

She went still, looking at him, her eyes wide. Paul's shoulders sagged a little.

"Kelly—"

"Forget it," she said, blinking rapidly as if to clear her vision. "Maybe someday you'll get it."

She slung the bags over her shoulder, the weight nearly toppling her. She pushed past him.

He followed at her heels. "What are you talking about? Get what?"

A sarcastic chuckle came out of her as she carefully made her way down the metal spiral staircase. God, he hated this staircase. In fact, he hated this entire loft apartment. It was cold, big, too modern with too much space and not enough furniture. The high ceiling was criss-crossed with track lighting which illuminated, quite spectacularly, how *not home* the place was, even after eight months of having Kelly around. The hardwood floors were always freezing. The overstuffed furniture, what little there was, was not as comfortable as it sounded and the exposed brick walls made it difficult to hang any artwork. Not that Paul had any artwork. Hell, he didn't even know what constituted artwork. But Kelly did and the few pictures she'd put up only intensified the fact that this life he was trying for was nothing but flimsy fucking window dressing.

"Life, Paul. You don't get life," Kelly was saying now. "It's not going to wait for you. Christ, you're not getting any younger. Maybe you should try growing up a bit."

"Are you serious? I have a job. I have my own place, my own car. How much more growing up can I possibly do?"

"You can't even commit yourself to a relationship."

"*That's* supposed to qualify me as a grown-up?"

Dammit, he *hated* this. He hated this as much as he hated the apartment. He knew and loathed the role of the typical male, diseased with commitment-phobia and an endless list of bullshit excuses for being the way that he was. But he played the part well and it was one of the few things he was good at.

Just ask Kelly.

She cleared the staircase, her heels sharp and final on the floor. She grabbed her coat off the back of the couch, struggling into it somehow without putting her bags down. Pulling on a white-knit cap, she tucked her wet hair up into it then headed for the front door. It was a heavy steel number that was bullet-proof. Not that she knew that.

"You're picking a great time to be purposely stupid, Paul," she said.

She started to jerk open the door when Paul reached around her to shut it. She fell back, her pretty face hard and unyielding. He took a deep breath and smiled, amping up the charm, trying to break the tension.

"I'm not being purposely stupid. I'm just..." he trailed off then said softly, "Come on, Kel, huh?"

But she was unmoved. She glared up at him, her eyes searching his. She wanted this to work. He could see it, the frustration and her rapidly dying hope. He could see that she was giving him one last chance to redeem himself, to come clean with her.

"Where do you go?" she demanded.

"What?"

"Why are there some days where you don't work at all but then all of a sudden, I won't see you for weeks at a time? Who calls you at all hours of the night and don't tell me it's work. You're a brokerage consultant, fine, but getting emergency phone calls at two in the morning? Even those crazy Wall Street assholes know when to sleep."

He stared down at her. His answer had to be good. It had to be flawless—an answer to end all answers, the one that would launch her back into his arms. And as badly as he wanted that, hell, it surprised him how much he wanted that, all he could do was look at her and lock up the words he wanted to say. She blinked hard then let out a harsh breath.

"Unbelievable." She threw the door open with an angry flourish. "Tell your next girlfriend I said good luck."

He followed her out in the hallway. The door swung shut behind him, making a strange-sounding *thunk*. A cold, desolate feel echoed along the cinderblock walls and the uneven concrete floor that stretched down to the opposite end of the hall where two large elevators stood waiting. The building used to be a factory or a warehouse. It was one of many places in the city that were converted into artsy, yuppie-style apartments. Although Paul was neither artsy nor a yuppie, he hadn't been too keen on the idea of moving in—not that he had a say in the matter. It was too isolated here, a harrowing echo of the secrets and shadows that made up the foundation of his life.

He hung back now, allowing Kelly to get a good lead. "Kel, wait," he pleaded. "I swear on the life of my mother—"

"You don't even *know* your mother," she snapped over her shoulder.

"But I will, I mean, I was thinking about tracking her down, maybe reconciling or something. Kel, don't leave, come *on*."

As if on cue, one of the elevators slid open and without stopping or hesitating, Kelly climbed in, nearly knocking over the person getting out with the huge sacks over her shoulder.

"Kel, please," he tried again. "I really think you're overreacting. I—"

His step faltered then stopped as the man who'd gotten off the elevator came toward him. Tendrils of ice snaked through his chest. With tremendous effort, Paul looked away only to see Kelly punch hard at the button panel inside the elevator. He opened his mouth to say something to her but every nerve ending in his brain was firing off as the man came closer, moving like a slow-creeping fog. His ankle-length coat spread out behind him like a pair of great dark wings. Paul felt his throat dry up.

He tried to focus.

"Kel?" he called out to her.

She didn't look at him. She folded her arms in front of her and bowed her head like the angel she was. A barely visible tremor passed through him and he felt the vice around his heart let go as the doors finally, *finally* slid shut. The hallway suddenly seemed a lot darker. He stared at the elevator, half-fearing, half-hoping it would open and she would emerge in tears, sputtering apologies, and wanting some heavy make-up sex.

But she wouldn't. Kelly had more pride than that. If only she knew how wrong she was. If only she knew just how faithful and loyal he'd been. She would pigeon-hole him, no doubt, and tell all her friends that he was just like the rest of them—an immature asshole. Paul found that that bothered him more than all the lying he'd done. Besides, if she came back now, she would definitely be dead.

The man in the dark coat came to a silent halt next to him but off to one side as if not wanting to obscure Paul's view. Paul let his eyes fall to the floor. He heard a soft chuckle. Feeling as if a heavy weight was crushing him, he slowly looked over and said, "Hello, Aaron."

CHAPTER 3

Aaron's grin was like a shark's, all teeth and just as cruel. It was at odds with the rest of his face. Eyes as dark and ingenuous as freshly churned soil, a choir-boy smile, long lashes, and dimples in his smooth cheeks, it was easy to mistake him for an eager-to-please college student. Soft black hair fell across his forehead, giving him a shy appeal that most people underestimated at their own peril. Paul had done it himself once upon a time and spent most of the last fifteen years of his life regretting it.

"Hello, Paul," Aaron said, his voice deep and relaxed like the rushing of water over rocks in a stream. "The bitch finally leave you?"

Paul looked away from him. "Her name is Kelly."

"Was, Paul, was. Past tense. I don't think she's coming back."

"What're you doing here?"

Aaron grinned at him, slipping his hands into his coat pockets. "I need a reason?"

"You knew she was here. You said you'd never come by if you knew she was here."

He shrugged, his eyes sparkling with their ever-present twinkle. "I knew she'd be on her way out."

His smug tone grated on Paul's nerves and he sucked in a deep, slow breath through his nose.

"How could you know that? We were actually doing pretty good."

"You thought the situation with Trina was going pretty good, too."

"That—was an oversight."

Aaron scoffed. "An oversight? In your line of work, Paul, an oversight can get you killed."

"Trina wasn't work. She was—"

"What?" Aaron interrupted. "A relationship? Please. When are you going to realize that you can't lead a normal life, Paul? You can't do what you do and have a little wifey at home, waiting for you at the end of the day with an apron on and a string of pearls. You're not cut out for it."

Paul looked down at the floor, at the mirror-shine of Aaron's black shoes.

"And I'll tell you," Aaron went on. "These last few months, you've been really off your mark."

Paul's head snapped up. "What?"

"You heard me. It didn't take me long to realize that it was because of this bitch you were shacking up with."

"I've performed every job you've given me to the best of my ability," Paul said with a strange sense of pride that left a residue of shame in the back of his mouth. "You know I have."

Aaron raised an eyebrow. "I do? Really? You drew attention to yourself with that little 'fuck you' scene at the coffee shop. You could've just walked out but no. You had to do some big, macho exit like some kind of a goddamn—"

"The manager was a dick."

"I don't care if the manager was a dick. You could've compromised everything."

"But I—"

"The only thing you've managed to impress me with lately is your willingness to finally get rid of Kaitlyn."

"Kelly."

"Whatever. You were with her for a while—"

"Eight months."

"Which is eight months too long and that much more dangerous."

"Dangerous how?"

"She would've pushed for marriage, Paul. Hello? Were you not paying attention? Can you imagine yourself being tied to someone? Can you imagine what would've happened if she found out what you do for a living?"

"I never would've let that—"

"It would've happened eventually, Paul. Believe me. You can only be careful for so long."

Paul stared down the hall at the elevator. Not for the first time he wondered what Kelly would've said or done if he had told her. She was smart, smarter than most of the women he dated. He wondered if she had it figured out even as she walked out the door. Maybe she had and she was only waiting for him to trust her enough to tell her.

But no. A fairy tale was all that was. No matter what the secret, no woman could ever forgive a man for keeping it from her. And truth only served to plunge him into a deeper pile of shit.

At this moment, with Aaron's presence choking him, Paul could only believe that someday, after she was happily married with a few kids and a house with a white picket fence, she would realize just how lucky she was that he was the way that he was.

Aaron's arm brushed his a second before Paul heard his voice hissed in his ear.

"Besides, you can't get married, Paul. You already belong to someone. Me."

And just like that, everything changed. The air between them thickened and chilled, as cold as the January wind that blew through the city. The twinkle in Aaron's eyes glowered into something that Paul had no words for. It gave Aaron a strange, half-dead look, like the face of a ventriloquist doll, half-alive but only when someone spoke for him. It was Aaron's true face, the one behind the illusions of friendship, that reminded Paul constantly of just how far beneath Aaron he was. The one that looked like he was wondering what Paul's insides would look like if he ever had the chance to lay him out on an autopsy table.

"You haven't forgotten, have you?" Aaron asked. "I would hate to have to remind you. Again."

Paul shook his head, every muscle in his body tense, waiting.

"Come on, let's go inside," Aaron said, spinning toward Paul's apartment. "You can fix me a drink."

For a moment, Paul stared at his back before following him in. He closed the door, staying near it in the hopes that maybe Aaron would take the hint and not stay long. He watched him wander about the place, coming to a stop at the windows that made up one wall, offering a spectacular view of the city. There wasn't much to see right now however. Obstructing the view was a sheet of white as snow poured relentlessly from the sky. Paul figured it wasn't nearly as cold out there as it was in here. Aaron's frame was dark and sinister against all that white. He turned to pin Paul with a look.

"Paul. A drink if you're not too busy."

Wordlessly, Paul moved away from the door and went into the kitchen. He took a bottle of bourbon from the cabinet and poured it neat into a crystal glass. There was silence behind him and his skin itched, knowing he was being watched. But when he turned around, he saw Aaron looking up toward the third floor loft. It had a balcony that overlooked the entire apartment and it was where Paul had slept before Kelly moved in. He wasn't sure why he preferred it over the master bedroom on the second floor. Must have something to do with paranoia.

"You know that's a good location to take someone out if they ever broke in here," Aaron observed.

"I suppose," Paul said with a nod as he handed the glass to his boss.

Aaron took a small sip and made a small sound of contentment. A small smile played tug-of-war with his lips.

"You really don't like me being here, do you?"

Paul pressed his lips together. "I didn't say anything."

"But you were thinking it."

"No, I wasn't."

Aaron laughed and it sounded like music in slow motion. "Paul, you are so terrible at lying. It's almost cute. But seriously, if you are in any way uncomfortable with my presence here, all you have to do is ask me to leave. Even though I *did* provide you with this place..." His voice trailed off.

"I don't mind having you here."

"It didn't seem that way when I first arrived."

Paul shook his head, feeling the skin along his spine crawl. "That was only because Kelly was still here and you said—"

Something flared through Aaron's eyes. "That I would stay away as long as the little tart was still here. Yes, I know that. But you were still bothered by my presence even after she left. Now why is that?"

"I—It didn't have anything to do with you."

"Oh, but I think it did. You didn't want me to witness another one of your spectacular attempts at trying to lead a normal life."

Paul shook his head. "No, I—"

"No?"

"No."

Aaron's top lip curled up and on anyone else's face it would've been a smile. "Are you sure? You seem pretty adamant about me not interfering with this existence that I provided for you. Am I right?"

Paul stared hard at a spot over Aaron's shoulder, his jaw muscles bulging. "No."

The word was squeezed tight, barely restrained from shaking. Aaron came toward him, his coat billowing. His shoes clicked sharply on the floor, purposely like a forthcoming nightmare. On instinct, Paul back-pedaled, taking two steps before trapping himself against the back of the couch.

"You forget who you're talking to, Paul?" Aaron murmured. "Do I need to remind you?"

Paul shook his head, two quick shakes. "No—no."

A sneer pulled one side of Aaron's mouth up. He moved closer. Paul arched his neck, trying to move his head back but Aaron stayed close, not allowing for much movement. He was about two inches shy of Paul's hulking, six-foot-five frame, but he seemed much bigger.

"There you go. Lying again," Aaron snarled, still in that quiet tone. "It doesn't make for healthy relationships."

Aaron grabbed Paul's chin with his left hand. His fingers were cold and burrowed into his skin hard enough to leave marks. When Aaron spoke again, each word was a hot whisper against his face.

"I saved you. I brought you back from that edge where you were too fucked up to realize that you were half a step away from going over. Do you remember where you've been? Do you remember what you've done?"

Paul shuddered as Aaron stroked his free hand down the center of Paul's chest. He wanted to shake his head but Aaron tightened his fingers on his jaw.

"No—"

"No?" Aaron repeated, his voice sinking even lower, growing more intimate. "No, what? No, you don't remember where you've been or no, you don't remember what you've done?"

His wandering hand dropped to Paul's belt. Paul's entire body jerked, automatically twisting away but Aaron pinned him to the couch and smiled. It was predatory.

"Aaron—"

"You do remember, don't you? You were a whore, Paul. You were fucking anything that moved for money, drugs, food. Anything that was offered, you took. What was it like? Huh? To be used and beaten? To be tied down, cut up, bled, for cash? You had a name for it, didn't you? Fuck-money, I believe you called it. How about it, Paul? Did you like it? Did you like it better than what I've given you? Did you like it more when you were treated like trash rather than a human being?"

Aaron took his hand away from Paul's belt and when he raised it to Paul's face, there was a knife in it. The flat of the blade trailed down the side of his face, dimpling the skin but not cutting. It moved over his neck, his collarbone, back down to his chest. Aaron played it over Paul's right nipple until it hardened. Paul squeezed his eyes shut, shame washing over him. Heat rushed up his neck as Aaron laughed delightedly.

"Well, well, maybe you do like it more."

Paul's eyes came open and they were wet and aching. "No." He swallowed. "No, I don't like it more. I don't."

Aaron's smile was as sharp as the knife in his hand. "Well, that's good, considering all the pain you went through. But I'm sensing a little bit of denial on your part, Paul. Maybe if you tell me what your favorite position was, I could—"

With a scream low in his throat, Paul slapped the knife away and shoved Aaron hard enough for him to stumble. By the time Aaron regained his footing, Paul had his .22 out and aimed at Aaron's chest.

His finger flexed on the trigger and the urge to pull it was so strong, his stomach cramped. Sweat cut icy paths down his back.

"Get the fuck away from me!" he shouted.

Aaron stood frozen in his tracks, the knife at his feet. His eyes twinkled. He didn't speak for a moment but when he did his voice was soft and sweet like fudge.

"It's all right, Paul," he said, his lips twitching with a smile. "Come on, it's okay. Everyone has that dark streak in them. It's nothing to be ashamed of."

"Shut *up*!"

"What're you going to do?" he asked, like he didn't have a gun pointed at his chest. "What do you think you can do? You think you can shoot me?"

Aaron began to walk slowly toward him, deliberately, his hands out to the sides. Paul's palms were slippery and he tightened his grip on the handle of the gun.

"Stop."

Aaron kept coming.

"I said *stop*!"

But he didn't until the barrel of the gun touched his chest, a couple of inches below the hollow of his throat. Aaron's eyes were deep, dark pools.

"Come on, then. I'm not stopping you. Shoot me."

Paul tried to calm himself, to think clearly. His throat constricted in frustration and his vision blurred. His shoulders were so rigid, they throbbed. Helplessness crashed over him as he met Aaron's eyes. The gun wavered and when Aaron moved one hand to cover the gun and gently push it down until it was pointed at the floor, Paul didn't stop him.

"Smart boy," Aaron said.

Paul let out a sharp breath, followed by another and another, feeling like he was hyperventilating. Aaron reached inside his coat and withdrew a thick manila envelope. He pressed it to Paul's chest. When Paul didn't move, Aaron let it fall to the floor.

"Work and payment," he said softly. He slid his fingers under Paul's chin and gently lifted his face. "Please stop trying to resist, Paul. You know you can't. You've been mine for too long. Fifteen years, if my math is correct. You can't survive out there without me. You need my…guidance, my counseling. Alone, you have no worth, I'm sorry to say. I always hate to remind you of that but you leave me no choice. Sometimes I think you *need* for me to remind you. But that's okay. That's what I'm here for. I'm here for you. I'll always be here for you." He slid back from Paul as if mounted on wheels. "But if you ever point a gun at me again, I'll cut out your heart." He picked up his fallen knife and left.

Paul stared blankly at the wall, the world swimming around him. As if in a dream, he holstered his weapon then bent to retrieve the envelope at his feet. He carried it into the kitchen. Slowly, he lowered himself onto a stool at the breakfast bar and looked at it, knowing it contained several bundles of one-hundred-dollar bills and a list of names and addresses.

These were people he never knew, never spoke to, and never saw until that last moment. It was all so familiar, so repetitive, as these faces blended with those from his past, who had paid to fuck him, beat him, bleed him, and cut him. It was a game, a nasty one with only Aaron at the board, making and breaking the rules…

ℰ✺ℰ✺

He liked the dark. It made it hard for the angels to see what he was doing. His shaking hands groped for the belt buckle that had flashed silver in the moonlight. He could feel the man's eyes on him even in the darkness of the car but he was careful to proceed as usual. It was what he was being paid for. He could get pancakes at the diner after this one was finished, with extra butter, too. His stomach rumbled and it sounded obscenely loud in the silence around them. He pulled back automatically when rough, calloused hands closed over his.

"No touching," he squeaked, trying for an edge of authority that most found so amusing, they tended to ignore it.

There was no response except for the tightening of the hands over his. He looked at where he hoped the man's face was. He could make out the faint outlines and the whites of eyes that seemed to glow in the surrounding darkness.

"Are you hungry?" came a voice that sounded like a melody was hidden inside of it.

It was first thing the man had said since he'd pulled up. He tried to pull his hands away. Panic laced through him when they were held immobile.

Not again, please, not again, he thought, the words chanting in a fever rush through his mind.

The man smelled of something expensive and almost-sweet. But he wouldn't let go his hands.

"Answer me," the voice said, this time with an edge to it.

He tried not to tremble. "Y–Yeah."

His hands were immediately released and before he knew it, the man had buckled him into the seat as if he were a child then driven to the nearest restaurant.

ברברב

Paul pulled himself away from the memory. He had been seventeen when he first met Aaron, already too old to be on the market and there were more nights than not when he was starving and desperate. Which was why he was surprised when Aaron's shiny black Excalibur pulled long side of him as he stood shivering by the curb, barely covered in ratty jeans and a tank-top that showcased his sunken rib cage. Paul had barely hesitated before climbing into that warm darkness and for the next fifteen years and counting, he was owned by something other than shadowed alleyways and parked cars with steamed up windows.

He sighed and ran a hand over his face. He looked around. It was so quiet. He half-wished Kelly was here, blasting that god-awful teen pop music shit she loved so much. In the time that Aaron had been in the apartment, it seemed like ages since she left.

"Life isn't going to wait for you."

He felt an ache in his chest, a feeling that he was wasting time. Guilt was quick to follow. Aaron had given him everything and this was how he repaid him? By wallowing in his own self-pity, crying that his life was wasting away just because some broad didn't like the way he was living?

Scowling, he tore open the envelope, letting the tightly-wrapped bundles of money spill out on the counter top. He unfolded the white notebook paper with the neatly typed columns of information. His fingers tightened on the edges of the paper and the letters and numbers blurred.

This was his life. This is what Aaron had given him.

Something that was treacherous, dangerous, and terribly aware of that piano dangling over his head, swinging by one fraying piece of rope. And when that rope finally broke, Paul often wondered if he would even bother to get out of the way.

CHAPTER 4

The wind was biting cold on the rooftop and the gray clouds were so low, Paul thought he could touch them. The snow had stopped but the wind was relentless, tearing through the white ski mask he wore. He'd tripled up on layers of clothing—two sets of long-johns beneath white ski pants; an undershirt; a thick wool turtleneck; a soft, thermal-lined white parka; three pairs of wool socks; two pairs of gloves; and white boots. He could barely move but he was warm and that was all that mattered.

Sprawling out on snow and concrete, he sucked in a lungful of frigid air and winced as it sank sharp teeth into his chest. Through the scope of the rifle, he could see into the windows of the low brick building across the street. He blinked his watery eyes, spying upon several different offices and the hard-working people they contained. He watched in mild fascination as a man bent over three lines of white powder on his desk. In another office, a woman talked frantically into the phone while next door, another was at the feet of her male superior. Paul watched as the man freed himself from his trousers and she, with an unhappy look on her pretty face, leaned over his lap. He ignored the prickle of discomfort along the back of his neck as he swept the eye-piece away, searching for Kathleen Young. Hers was the last name on the long list of people that Aaron had given him two weeks ago.

An office door opened and in she walked—thin, red hair bouncing, two chins wagging, crooked teeth slashing into a smile as she talked into her cell phone. She settled herself behind a desk that overflowed with papers and folders. She lifted the hem of her silk blouse and unsnapped the top two buttons of her pants, letting her round, blue-veined belly bulge free.

Ducking away from the scope, Paul plucked a bullet from the small case Aaron had given him specifically for jobs that would not require a large amount of ammunition. He hefted the bullet in his palm and stopped. He blinked down at his hand and swore under his breath.

"Goddammit."

Once again, Aaron had not listened to him.

Paul thought he'd made a pretty good argument in explaining to Aaron that the type of ammunition he held in his hand right now was useless. It wasn't suitable to penetrate glass or any other obstacle without throwing off the bullet's trajectory.

"Of course, Paul, whatever you say," he remembered Aaron saying in that grating tone like Paul was a kid trying to act like a grown-up.

He swore again, squeezing the bullet in his fist until he could feel it biting through his gloves. Now he was going to have to wait for her to leave the building. It was the only way to ensure a direct hit. Aaron probably wasn't going to like that but he wasn't the one out here freezing his ass off. He wasn't the one who had to compensate for substandard equipment. Ultimately, Paul didn't like the idea of shooting her in the middle of the goddamn street either but he didn't like the idea of missing even more so.

He slid the inferior bullet into the chamber then put his eye back to the scope. He watched as she continued to gab on her phone for another ten minutes. Then she glanced at her watch and got to her feet, more nimble than her bulk implied. Paul was patient as she closed her cell phone, buttoned up her pants, grabbed her coat and purse, then left.

He counted to fifty under his breath before spotting her in the lobby of the building, just inside the rotating glass doors. She was digging through her purse. Paul moved the scope away from her to assess her immediate surroundings. No one was standing around her so if the bullet kept going after tunneling a path through her cranium, there would be minimal second-hand damage. Gnawing on his bottom lip, he bought the scope back to the target.

She was standing outside now, the spinning doors moving sluggishly behind her.

And she was looking directly up at him, her eyes finding his through the scope of his weapon.

His heart catapulted into his throat.

Shit! For one incredible, breathless moment he was too terrified to move. A great weight seemed to press down on his neck and he could only watch helplessly as she seemed to smile at him, her lips twisting. He stared at her through the eyepiece.

She can't see you! There is no possible way she can see you!

A searing numbness that had nothing to do with the weather spread through his bones. He swallowed hard and it hurt.

Get out. Get out get out get out get out get out getoutnow!

When she didn't scream or point or make a run for it, he too-quickly settled his finger on the trigger. Aiming between her watery brown eyes, he shot her, not bothering to watch as she did a rather ungraceful death dive to the ground.

CHAPTER 5

He trudged down the hallway to his apartment. All was quiet except for his loud, hollow footsteps and his bags scraping against the concrete floor like bodies being dragged. He'd been gone for a week and a half, traveling all over the country in an effort to take care of every name on that goddamn list and he was *tired*. His bones ached, his eyes burned and his limbs felt shaky and unstable, largely due to the near-panic attack he had on that last job. Just thinking about it made him sick to his stomach.

Nothing like that had ever happened before.

Ever.

At least not while working. Sure, he had nightmares that would wake him up screaming and sweat-soaked, but in broad daylight? While he was looking through the scope of his rifle?

He didn't want to think about what that might mean. He couldn't. If he did, panic attacks or whatever the hell he'd experienced would be the least of his problems.

He let out a harsh breath and stopped in front of his door. He dropped his bags and dug out his keys.

Too bad Kelly's not around, he thought as he unlocked the door. *Could really go for one of her—*

He was halfway over the threshold when the soft muffled sound of a silencer went off. A split second later, a chunk of the wall exploded as a bullet tore into it, inches from his head.

Letting out a startled *shit*, Paul backpedaled out into the hallway and slammed the door shut behind him. There was a muted *thunk* as another bullet hit the solid steel door. He crouched down against the wall, swearing under his breath. His mind raced.

Who the hell—what—how? What did I do now?

An inappropriate sarcastic laugh resounded in his head.

Seriously, asshole? Pick something, anything you've done within the last fifteen years.

He winced as another *thunk* hit the other side of the door, followed by another.

Amateur. It had to be an amateur, he thought. *There's no way a pro would waste ammunition.*

He shook his head. Amateur or not, whoever the hell it was had gotten inside his place, his own fucking apartment, without him even detecting it. A chill ran up his spine. God, what if Kelly had been home? Would the intruder have killed her? Maybe raped her as he held a gun to her head or blown her face off as she sat in bed, painting her toenails?

A sour mixture of anger and relief spilled through his veins as more bullets attempted to make their way through the door.

Good thing she decided to leave me.

From a holster at the small of his back beneath his coat, he withdrew a nickel-plated, nine-millimeter Glock, a personal favorite. He held it in a two-handed grip and tried to think. He was willing to bet that the asshole was up on the third floor balcony. It was high up, offered a stellar view of the front door, and there was only one possible approach: the staircase. From the front door to the kitchen, there was an open space of about twenty feet. Since the kitchen was under the balcony, it offered the only cover. The hard part was getting there without being shot.

Shit.

Might as well go in with my hands up and my pants down.

He threw the door open and ran like hell for the kitchen in a rainstorm of bullets that erupted around him. He heard cracks and groans as they buried themselves in the floor, inches from his heels. A bullet whizzed by his ear, whistling before it shattered into the wall next to the front door. The splintering of plaster sounded like lightning in his ears, as if he was standing in the middle of a field during a monstrous thunderstorm. He dove headlong into the kitchen, tucking himself into a controlled roll. Pain sliced up his leg as he hit the base of the island in the middle of the kitchen. He sat up and saw blood soaking through the bottom half of his pant leg, blossoming out like a flower in superfast forward motion. He jerked the pant leg up and saw the bloody smear of torn flesh.

A bullet had grazed his calf. The wound didn't appear too deep but it still stung like a bitch.

Movement came from the stairs on his left. He moved without thinking, rolling to his knees. He scurried like a rat behind the counter as two bullets tore into the wood where his head had been just a second before. He huddled on the other side of the island, his breath whistling through his teeth.

Maybe this guy isn't an amateur, he thought.

He crouched on the floor and peeked around the corner of the island. It was a moonless night. Shadows encased the place, thick and solid. Vague outlines of furniture stood like huddling creatures, ready to spring on some unsuspecting prey. The only light was from the open front door but even that didn't reach far enough to illuminate the darkness. It was a palpable quiet, something he could touch. The air was charged with that readiness where he knew something was about to happen. He just didn't know when.

He strained his ears to hear a footfall, a swish of clothes, a soft exhalation of breath.

But there was nothing, not even a drop of sweat hitting the floor.

Soundlessly, he crept to the opposite end of the island and waited. He would wait out this son-of-a-bitch, wait till he made the first move and, sure enough, after a few moments something creaked overhead, then stopped abruptly as if the person realized instantly that the sound earned attention.

Paul crept cautiously to the base of the staircase and peered up. The stairs climbed into total darkness. Wasn't Hell normally in a downward direction?

He chewed on his lip. *Fuck it.*

He began to ascend as quickly as possible, staying close to the outer railing. He knew the asshole could hear him. Any minute he would unleash a hail of firepower and send Paul sailing to the floor below in all his bloody glory.

The thought made him increase his speed. He was taking a huge risk doing this, being out in the open like a deer charging a hunter in a field. It was stupid and novice, a Hail Mary, and it was certainly not how he was trained. But there was no other option. Pride kept him from running and anger urged him to blow this fucker away.

He made it to the second floor just as he heard a footfall on the steps above him. He eased back away from the staircase, plastering himself to the wall. Gun pointed straight out, Paul waited.

Come on, asshole, he begged, silently. *Come and get it.*

His fingers flexed around his gun and he blew out a long, quiet breath.

He waited. And waited.

The silence dragged into seconds then minutes, the echo of the creaking stairs long faded into the surrounding shadows.

Nothing moved.

No sound, only an answering silence to the silence that already waited. Paul searched the darkness. He valued himself on his patience, since his job required tons of it, but this asshole was putting it to the test.

Feeling himself growing restless, he moved along the wall, keeping his back to it. He went in the direction of the bedroom and bath. He stayed away from the balcony railing, lest his guest was peering over from the loft above him.

He came to the bathroom first and searched it. The bedroom was at the end of the hall. The door stood open. More shadows yawned beyond the threshold. He crept toward it, the hairs on the back of his neck standing on end. His eyes moved continuously, all around him. He tried not to think about the possibility of another gunman setting his crosshairs on him right now, ready to paint the wall with his blood. Swallowing hard, Paul held his gun out in front of him, figuring that even if he was killed, he could at least get one shot off and take this shit-bag straight to Hell with him.

A whispering sound jerked him around toward the railing, giving his back to the bedroom.

Bad move, he had time to think before he made out the length of a rope hanging from the other side of the balcony, sweeping out into the open, traveling down to the main floor.

What the hell?

He aimed at the rope. Then he realized what was about to happen a second too late as a large, black shape came swooping down like a mythological beast out of the sky. It came to a smooth halt directly in front of him. Startled, Paul fell back a step, his finger already squeezing the trigger. The dark figure swung close as if anticipating his move. Paul felt feet connecting solidly with his chest, knocking him backward.

A bullet exploded from his gun as his back hit the wall. The shot went wild, echoing painfully in his ears. The intruder leapt on him, forcing Paul against the wall again.

Paul felt his gun hand being grabbed in a clenching grip and he shouted wordlessly as it was slammed repeatedly into the wall until he had no choice but to let go. He flailed blindly, landing punches wherever he could. He swung a hard right but hit empty air. A booted foot in the gut forced him to his knees and another kick sent him skittering across the floor. Sputtering for air, he struggled to his knees but didn't get very far as hands balled into his hair. He reached up, grabbing for something, anything that might help him. His hand dug into cloth and he heard a winded *oof* from above him.

He'd grabbed the bastard's balls.

He tightened his grip and there came another strangled groan. Paul pushed to his feet. As he did, the hands left his hair, clawing at his vice-like grip around the family jewels. Paul leaned back, feeling the balcony railing behind him.

He swiftly grabbed the guy around the neck. In one fluid movement, he swung him around and gave him a hard shove over the railing.

There was a short scream then a sickening, crunching *thud.*

Paul collapsed to his knees, sucking in air, his mind reeling. "Jesus."

He looked over the railing and saw the dark, crooked lump in the middle of the floor. Blood, black as oil, crept across the floor, shining like a dirty mirror. He sucked in another deep breath, feeling his brain go fuzzy. He turned and slid down the wall until his butt hit the floor.

CHAPTER 6

Paul's jaw muscles bulged as he watched Aaron. He stood over the body, bunching his leather coat in his hands to keep the hem from sweeping into the large pool of blood that saturated the floor. Keeping his eyes on the back of Aaron's head, Paul tried for detachment but failed miserably. His skin felt cold and oily like a fish. His clothes stuck to him like wet paper. He breathed heavily through his open mouth as he wiped at his bullet-grazed calf with a damp cloth.

Despite Paul's barely coherent tale over the phone of what had happened, Aaron arrived at his door with no questions. He came armed with three large men in black pants and navy-blue jackets. They were pushing carts full of buckets, mops, disinfectants, huge rolls of plastic, and duct tape. Paul half-expected his apartment to be flooded with the police and nosy on-lookers but then belatedly remembered the sound-proofing system that Aaron had installed before Paul became a resident here all those years ago.

Aaron was, as always, thinking ahead.

Now he stood motionless at the edge of the blood pool, looking down at the corpse like a diver from the top diving board. He hadn't moved from that spot for the last twenty minutes, forcing the cleanup crew to work around him. It was strange. Aaron never bothered with the dead. Normally he would storm in, demanding details and answers and everything but Paul's heart on a silver platter. This time, however, he'd come through the front door without a word, taking in the scene with a calm indifference that had Paul more worried than if he'd come in screaming and pissed off.

Without turning around, he addressed Paul quietly, "He could've killed you."

"He didn't."

"But he could have."

There was no anger. Aaron's tone was calm, murmuring, as if he was half-asleep. Unsure of how to respond, Paul continued to wipe at his wound. The sound of swishing water, mops slapping wetly against blood and other things filled the silence. The smell of cleaning chemicals stung his nostrils.

Finally he said, "I'm okay."

Aaron didn't answer. His silence was growing heavier by the minute. The one-sided staring contest that he was holding with the dead man was unnerving. It made Paul wonder.

"Did you—Did you know him?" he asked hesitantly.

Aaron finally turned to him, his face tight and guarded. "What makes you say that?"

"You're staring at him like you're...remembering things."

Wordlessly, Aaron stared at him. Paul stilled, his hand hovering above his wounded leg.

The sound of unraveling duct tape bit through the tension like a mouthful of teeth. Paul felt the bite in the back of his neck, digging into his spine. Then slowly like water draining from a broken glass, the tightness eased from Aaron's face, leaving behind a wistful, almost proud expression.

"Impressive," Aaron said, nodding slightly. "I've always prided myself on being hard to read. But not with you, Paul. Never with you."

He turned his head to look down at the body again. Paul followed his gaze. Standing, the corpse might've been five-seven, give or take an inch, although to Paul in their brief moment of violence, he had seemed like a monster. His broken body was clad in black cammies, black boots, and a black turtleneck, typical recon-wear. His face was ghastly pale in the light, edged in gray, lips parted in a gasp. He had a squashed nose, not from the fall, but from genetics and a buzz-cut of blond hair. Well, it would've been blond if not for the blood that stained it to a scab-brown color. Colorless eyes stared in unblinking disbelief at the ceiling. The cleaning crew had searched him and the weaponry lay across the low table next to the sofa. It was a remarkable array and Paul felt uncomfortable as his eyes trailed over the mini-arsenal.

Whatever this guy had planned was not the usual beer and pretzels.

Besides the silencer-equipped pistol, there was a Derringer, a serrated hunting knife, another blade that looked like a freaking scimitar about as long as his forearm, two icepicks, and a bundle of barbwire. Goosebumps popped along Paul's arms as he stared at the barbwire, its sharp edges twinkling like fangs. He caught Aaron watching him.

"You were careless."

"I was surprised."

"Careless," Aaron repeated. "He could've had your head on a spike."

Paul pushed away from the counter. He held up his pant leg so it wouldn't brush the wound and came up to Aaron's side, just out of reach.

"Who was he?"

It was Aaron's turn to look away as the corpse was rolled into several sheets of plastic. Paul waited, hearing the plastic crinkle and whisper like it was telling them secrets. He watched Aaron's profile, seeing the quiet struggle on his face. It was rare to see Aaron display so much emotion.

"Do you remember Edward Long?"

Paul's eyebrows rose. "The priest?"

Aaron nodded. "If I recall, his death was a strange re-enactment of the death of Christ." The look he gave Paul was sly. "Do you remember?"

Paul hesitated then nodded.

Aaron's dry chuckle filled the space between them. "Revenge is terrible, isn't it, especially when it doesn't go your way? Look at this. Every weapon here is the same as what you used on this poor bastard's father."

Paul sputtered. "What?"

Aaron grinned at him. "The Father, the Son, and the Holy Spirit."

Paul shook his head, confused.

Aaron explained. "This sack of shit is one of the many products of Edward's...liaisons. Quite disgusting if you ask me, his extracurricular activities, but I think you effectively put a halt to his spreading more bad seed. Wouldn't you agree?"

"How...I mean, why...how do you know?"

Aaron shrugged as he once again stared down at the body. "You never know when something's going to come back to you. Retaliation is inevitable, especially when a man has so much...off-spring running around."

Paul shook his head again. "But it was so long ago. How—"

"Oh, come on, Paul," Aaron snapped, impatiently. "How long did you think it would take before someone decided that it was time to return the favor? What you did to Edward Long was highly publicized. Hell, *everyone* that you take care of for me is highly publicized, not to mention well-deserved although no one will ever say that out loud. Ultimately, it was only a matter of time before one of Edward's spawn tried to balance the scales."

"But why would they even bother? They had to know what kind of man he was, the things he did—"

"Please," Aaron scoffed. "The man was a legend. He donated enough money to this city to get his name carved into every plague on every wall in the front of every government building and then some. He had orphanages built, he got half the homeless population off the streets. You really think anyone would've believed that he took his compensation in the form of little boys and girls?"

"No one ever said anything? Nobody ever came forward?"

Aaron gave him a look. "Given your background, Paul, I'm rather surprised you would waste your breath on such a stupid question."

Paul felt sick. If this guy could find him, after so much time had gone by, how many others could? How many other sons, daughters, brothers, nephews would try and blow his brains out? He and Aaron never discussed the possibility of retaliation. Aaron had never bought it up and Paul had never questioned it. As far as Paul knew, his identity didn't exist. His files were long gone after his parents had been killed. He was just another missing person.

Until now.

"How many others will there be?" he muttered aloud.

Aaron raised an eyebrow. "What?"

Paul looked at him, forcing words from his mouth that he would never say under normal circumstances. "How many others will try and kill me? How many others will be waiting for me in my apartment? How many times am I going to have to do what I did tonight before someone finally succeeds? This is...Jesus Christ..." His voice trailed off and shook his head.

"Do you think I would let that happen?"

Paul blinked. Aaron's intense stare pinned him like an insect.

"Do you think I would let that happen to you?"

There was a subtle shift in the air and it felt like a rubber band being stretched to its limit.

"No. I mean, well...I don't...Look, this guy found me, right? I mean, how easy is it going to be for someone else?"

Wrong thing to say. Bad, bad, bad, Paul had time to think before Aaron was suddenly in his face, anger hissing through his words.

"You think so lowly of me? You think for a second that I would allow someone to take your life as easily as you take theirs? You think that I've never thought about that? Don't you fucking think that I would tell you if you were in any potential danger?"

"That's not—"

"After all the years I've looked after you, cared for you, taught you *everything*, you doubt my devotion to you?"

He moved forward and Paul immediately began to retreat.

"Aaron, I didn't mean that. I'm just—"

The words stopped in his throat as his back hit the wall and Aaron moved in on him, his dark eyes like bottomless pits. He kept his voice soft, making the fury in his voice more apparent.

"What? You're just what? Concerned? Worried?" A horrible sneer transformed his face. "Scared?"

"Aaron—"

"Do you need to hear me say that I'll always protect you, Paul? Do you need to hear me say that I would fight to keep you safe? Poor thing. Do you want me to tell you I love you, too? Maybe give you a kiss on the forehead and tuck you into bed?"

He laughed and the sound of it sliced into him. Paul felt his cheeks burn as the cleaning guys snickered. He stiffened as Aaron curled a hand around the back of his neck and pulled him close. His fingers were fever-hot.

"Your life is mine, Paul," he snarled. "Everything about you, everything that makes you who you are is because of me. Do you really think I'd give up something of mine without a struggle? Something that belongs to me? Do you think I'd let someone take you away from me? That I'd *let* someone else have the pleasure of taking your life when I could take it whenever I wanted?"

Paul stared down at him, too bewildered to speak. Aaron's eyes sparkled deviously and he smirked up at him like a grown-up who'd gotten the best of a little kid who didn't know any better.

"Does that make you feel safer? Does that put the monsters under your bed at ease? Oh, Paul. So scared, so lost. Jesus Christ."

He pushed Paul back into the wall with snort. He turned and went back to the corpse that was now wrapped neatly in plastic and duct tape. Paul stayed where he was. He swallowed a few times, trying to find his voice, but stopped when Aaron suddenly came back over to him. Something dangerous slid into his eyes as he reached up to Paul's face. He flinched as Aaron laid his hand gently against his cheek.

"I think it's time for me to show you just how truly special you are to me, Paul," he whispered, his words sucking all the light from the room.

"I—"

"Shhhh," he whispered, his thumb brushing across Paul's bottom lip. He smiled softly and it held an overpowering darkness. "I'll show you, since you need to know so badly."

Giving Paul a soft pat on the cheek, Aaron moved away from him. He left with the cleanup crew and Paul didn't move for a long time.

CHAPTER 7

Paul shifted his weight from one foot to the other. His black Cherokee idled behind him, sending a fog of white exhaust into the glaring headlights that were the only light source in the silent, cold world of one a.m. The flat plains around him were laid out in complete darkness. Snow swirled around his feet. He hunched farther into his coat. Christ, it was cold. He could wait in the car, but he always got antsy whenever he was stuck in an enclosed space. So he paced outside, hearing Aaron's voice in his head, advising him not to be late.

He bounced up and down on the balls of his feet, muttering under his breath, watching his surroundings even though he couldn't see a thing. He hadn't slept since the murder attempt at his apartment and it showed with his heightened sense of paranoia, not allowing him to go out unless he absolutely had to. Then there was Aaron wanting to meet him in the middle of nowhere…

Two circles of light appeared in the distance. Paul immediately stopped pacing, slipping a hand inside his coat to touch the Glock in his shoulder holster. It felt strong and reassuring under his fingers. As the headlights drew closer, he wondered again why Aaron had suggested meeting out here.

To kill you was the obvious answer. But he knew that wasn't it. If Aaron was going to kill him, it wouldn't be so obvious. It would have to be the most complicated, fail-proof plan ever designed and it would never be in the middle of the night. One of the few things Paul knew about his employer was that Aaron got a little nervous in the dark.

Gravel and snow crunched and flew as a white van that Paul didn't recognize careened to a stop next to his car. He automatically moved to put his vehicle between himself and the van. The passenger door opened and Aaron slinked out, wrapped expensively in a lined leather coat that fell to mid-thigh. Leather gloves covered his hands and a fancy-looking scarf was knotted beneath his chin. His shoes chewed noisily across the ground as he came to a stop, mirroring Paul's position on the other side of his car.

He greeted him with a warm smile. "Hello, Paul,"

The knot in Paul's back refused to loosen. He nodded a greeting then said with forced nonchalance, "Not exactly your style." He gestured at the van.

Aaron gave it a glance over his shoulder. "You don't like it?"

"It's different."

Aaron stared at him, his dark eyes resembling pots of ink. "Different. Funny you should mention that."

Paul waited, his hand never leaving his gun. Aaron strolled around the car, sniffing delicately in the cold.

"I want to run something by you. Get your opinion, if you don't mind."

"Yeah?"

"Yeah," Aaron nodded, his eyes sparkling with amusement.

Paul pressed his frigid lips together, the knot in his back working its way to his stomach.

Aaron blinked innocently up at him as he came to stop beside him. "You've been working for me for how long? Ten, eleven years?"

"Fifteen."

"Ah, right. Fifteen. A decade and a half. I can't believe it's been that long."

Paul watched him.

"And in those fifteen years, what have I given you?"

"What do you mean?"

Aaron cocked his head to one side, a condescending smile tugging at his lips. "What have I given you? Think back now. It's a lot."

Paul felt himself bristle at his tone. "You mean...You mean, like..."

Aaron rolled his eyes. "What have I given you, Paul? How have I turned your life around so that you didn't wind up dead?"

Paul shifted his weight. He wasn't in the mood to have this discussion in sub-zero temperatures.

"Aaron—"

"Oh, am I boring you?"

"No. I—"

"You got somewhere more important to be?"

Paul sighed inwardly. "Of course not."

"Good," Aaron spat, the amusement fading in his eyes. "Now. Fucking tell me what I've given you."

"You gave me a place to stay," Paul muttered, looking at the ground.

Aaron leaned forward, putting one hand behind his ear. "I'm sorry, what?"

"A place to stay," Paul repeated, louder this time. "Food, clothes." He hesitated. "A second chance."

"A what?"

Paul felt his face heat up despite the cold. Why couldn't there be an attempt on his life *now*?

"A second chance," he said, louder this time.

"Right," Aaron sneered in satisfaction. "A second chance and are you thankful for it?"

Paul looked at him. "You know I am."

"Do I?"

A cold ball of uncertainty settled in Paul's gut. He searched Aaron's face but was met with a brick wall. Aaron moved closer to him.

"Get your hand out of your coat, Paul."

The words were quiet but held a world of warning.

"Paul."

Slowly, he eased his hand away from his weapon until his arm hung straight at his side. His fingers bellowed from the loss. Aaron studied him for so long that Paul thought he'd fallen asleep with his eyes open.

"I'm not sure anymore if you're grateful for everything I've done for you. How can it be when you come here armed? How can it be when you've made it perfectly clear that you don't trust me?"

Paul felt the blood leave his face. "I never—"

"Yes, Paul, you did. You don't trust me to take care of you. You don't trust me to protect you and I find that rather…disconcerting."

Paul's mouth moved soundlessly before he stuttered, "Aaron—"

"But I trust you, Paul. Do you know that? I trust you. I trust you with my concerns, my requests, my work, my money. I trust that you will return to me every time I send you out and you do return. Every single time. Yet you don't trust me. At all."

"That's not true," Paul tried to say.

"How can you say it's not true? I think we've reached a point in our relationship where we can be honest with one another, don't you think?"

Paul nodded weakly, his heart slamming in his rib cage.

"I believe we've come to a crossroads," Aaron went on, suddenly linking his arm through Paul's like an overeager prom date.

"Yeah?"

"Absolutely," Aaron said as he began walking, practically dragging Paul in step beside him. "I think you need to know just how much I trust and value you. You need to know how much I care for you and that without you, nothing would be the way that it stands now. Perhaps, knowing this, you can learn to build some trust in me."

"But I do—"

"No lies, Paul. I think we need to do this. I want to do it. I've tried so hard with you and nothing ever seems to be good enough. It's time to reach for something higher, something greater."

The closer they got to the van, the more Paul wanted to dig his heels into the ground, like a screaming child on his first day of kindergarten.

"Aaron, you don't have to do anything. You've done enough—"

"No, no I haven't. I don't want to fail you, Paul. I don't think I could ever let you live if I did."

Paul stopped. Aaron walked ahead to the back doors of the van. As he put his gloved hands on the handles, he turned back with a smile that made ice drip into Paul's bloodstream.

"You were right before, you know, about this van not being my style. But it was the only way to guarantee that the meat would arrive in pristine condition."

Paul furrowed in brow in confusion. *Meat? What meat? What the hell is he giving me? Lamb? Beef? Maybe some chicken thighs?*

With a triumphant grin, Aaron pulled the doors open. Paul immediately took a quiet step to the side, trying to see around the open doors. Aaron reached inside.

"Come here. Now," Paul heard him command under his breath.

His puzzlement turned to horror when he heard a sound of scuffling, followed by metal clanging and being dragged over a hard surface. Goosebumps appeared on top of the goosebumps that were already scattered along the back of his neck. There came a whimper, pitiful and pain-filled like an animal caught in a trap. Then two small feet hit the gravel and Paul felt the world drop from beneath him as Aaron came back into view. He had his hand wrapped securely around the frail, bare arm of a boy who looked no older than ten.

For a moment, all Paul could do was stare. Then slowly, his brain started to whirl and scream and the air in his lungs dissolved into sand. Aaron grinned and in the uneven light, he looked like a hawk that just cornered a juicy meal.

"Ah, I can see you're speechless!" he laughed. "When I saw him, I knew he was perfect for you." He grinned mirthlessly down at his small prisoner then back up at Paul. "What do you think?"

Paul blinked against the searing heat in his eyes. His tongue felt like it weighed a ton.

"What...uh, what—" He stopped, cleared his throat, and tried again. "What is this?"

A joke. Please tell me it's a joke.

Aaron laughed again and it was mocking and cruel and Paul suddenly thought of the sweat-and-come-stained mattress that a gang of three had kept him on for two days.

"Do you like it?" Aaron asked.

'You like this? Huh, you little whore? You greedy bitch, huh?'

He was drowning. The iron shackles around his brain sprung open, unleashing a terrible onslaught of thoughts and images that had been a lifetime ago. He struggled for a stable piece of his mind and thought he might vomit all over the ground.

"Paul? Christ Almighty, you feel like answering me some time tonight?"

His skin jumped and crawled as he focused, focused on this...person in front of him.

"Yea...um, yeah, Aaron, I...it's...I'm not sure what—"

"Try and keep up, will you? This—" He gave the bony arm a shake. "—is Ethan. Why don't you come over here and say hello?"

Paul didn't move. He wasn't sure if he could.

"Aaron, a...kid? This...you think..."

That this is the kind of person I am?

"What? What's the matter?" Aaron's dark eyes were wide and innocent. "You don't like him? I picked him out just for you." He frowned down at Ethan as if it was somehow his fault.

"What...What am I going to do with him?"

As if you don't know the answer to that.

Aaron's smile was positively feral. "Oh, I'm sure you'll think of something. Hey! Maybe you can compare notes."

The remark hit home and Paul felt a biting anger through his nausea.

"I mean, granted, he's a bit younger than you were when you first started out, but he's definitely been doing it for a while. Just ask Vince."

"Vince?"

He jerked his chin toward the van. "My driver."

Paul's eyes went to the vehicle and then back again. "I thought you said this was something pristine."

He felt only a small nudge of satisfaction when Aaron's smile wilted at the edges.

"Well, I had to make sure I was getting my money's worth. I couldn't very well acquire him without a practice run. I did that once already and you know me, Paul, I hate repeating myself."

Paul stared at him. *What did I do?* he wanted to scream. *What did I do that would make you do this to me? What didn't I do? Is this what you think of me?*

His hand itched to grab his gun and shove it into Aaron's smug little mouth and see how much he would talk then. Or maybe he should just pistol-whip that shit-eating grin right off his face.

"I am not a baby-sitter," Paul said, surprised at how calm he sounded, despite the trembling in his bones.

"Oh, you won't need to baby-sit," Aaron said. "He's very independent and docile, too. Like a lamb, really. An absolute pro at stress relief and that's what you need, isn't it, Paul? Something to help put your mind at ease?"

The air threatened to choke him. "I don't—I don't need it, Aaron. I don't…want it."

The look on Aaron's face could've frozen gin. "Are you sure?"

Paul nodded, although it was more like a muscle twitch.

Christ, I am a dead man.

"Oh. Well." Aaron's lips pursed. "I'm so sorry, Paul. I didn't realize you were so picky. If you don't want this, I'm sure I can come up with something else."

I don't doubt that. Something probably ten times worse, although I'm not sure what could possibly be worse than this, Paul thought to himself.

"In the meantime, however," Aaron went on in a barely constrained voice. "I'll just take our little friend here back home. I'm sure he misses his daddy, don't you?"

His eyes never left Paul's, boring holes into his skull.

Paul felt a vice clamp around his chest at what Aaron was implying. The kid was somebody's property. If he was brought back, whoever owned him would know he was rejected and then the shit he would be in for not doing his job…

Against his better judgment, Paul let his gaze fall to the boy. Aaron's abrupt laughter sent shame slicing through him. He gave the kid a shove.

"Have a closer look. Maybe it'll help sway your decision."

Ethan slid in the snow, his worn Converse sneakers unable to keep him from skidding to his knees. Paul could see how filthy and torn Ethan's pants were, how threadbare the tank-top that hung on his too-thin frame. Paul thought he saw finger-shaped bruises on his bare shoulders. He swallowed against the sickness in his throat, focusing on the small blond head instead. Despite the worn clothes, the kid's hair was surprisingly clean and looked finer than silk, a color so pale, it was almost white. It fell in long, uneven layers around his face that Paul couldn't see until, at last, Ethan lifted his head. The look in those big, shining gray eyes hit Paul in the sternum like a solid right hook.

He was still at that age where he looked androgynous, which appealed extensively to the crowds made up primarily of twenty-somethings who weren't entirely sure about their sexuality, as well as the married forty-year-old husbands who secretly wore their wives' underwear. Those were the dangerous crowds. Those were the ones full of the most anger and the most pain, eager to take it out on somebody else and envious because that somebody else could be what they wanted to be.

So thin, he thought as he studied the bitten pink lips and the ribs that poked through the white, white skin of his torso.

Paul tore his eyes away. His chest ached. The cold air made it swell until he thought it would burst. Aaron was still laughing like a maniacal clown and shaking his head at him. With a painful grimace that was full of the taste of that afternoon's lunch, Paul suddenly knew why Aaron had chosen this kid.

He looks just like me.

CHAPTER 8

It was a reminder.

This small, scrawny, starving whore was nothing but a goddamn memento, a knick-knack, a fucking souvenir with a nice engraved message at the bottom, *To Paul: look at what you used to be. Look at what I've saved you from. Look upon this and be grateful.*

"So. Come on, be honest. What do you think?" Aaron purred as he slung an arm tightly around Paul's shoulders. "Not bad, right? Probably not what you were expecting, huh?"

They both stared down at the kid, who was still on his knees, his eyes now cast downward as if the weighty stares of two grown men were too much to handle. But Paul knew it was nothing more than a submissive gesture. This kid definitely knew what was going on.

"You know," Aaron said, speaking directly into his ear. "I thought at first you might be a little freaked out by this. But then I thought, Why would he be? It's not like this is new territory, right? It's not like you don't know the way the game is played. But you know what the real reason is behind this?"

Paul shook his head numbly as Aaron curled a hand against the side of his neck. He clawed frantically for his control as he was forced to look into Aaron's eyes. He saw his own pits of hell reflected back at him.

"I want you to be happy, Paul. I want you to have a fulfilling life without having to watch your back every time you leave your apartment. I want you to get through at least one night without nightmares."

Paul tried to pull away but Aaron held him close, crooning in his ear like a dove.

"There, there, easy. Easy now. Listen to me. You need to do this. I want you to confront your demons. I want you to cleanse yourself. I don't want you to ever have to second-guess me or any move I make. I want you to take this opportunity to learn how to trust me, to trust us. If you need me to say it, I will. That's what I'm here for, Paul, to help you become a better person." He sighed, running his other hand down Paul's face until he cupped his cheek.

"Take this gift, Paul. Take the kid. Use him the way you were used and clear out all those doubts that are rolling around inside your head, huh? What do you say?"

The world was tilting and the wall of blackness that was rushing toward him was solid, complete, and welcome. Surely, Aaron wouldn't be too enraged if he fainted at his feet.

But then something caught his attention, something that pulled him away from the venomous ramble that Aaron breathed into his ear.

There was a mark around Ethan's ankle. A band of skin about an inch thick around was dark and raw-looking.

The kid had been shackled.

Paul's insides congealed and amidst his brain's frantic screams, he made a decision that jarred him down to the very core of his being.

"All right, all right. I'll take him."

Ethan's head came up instantly, his eyes wide, searching Paul's face with a look that made him feel dirty and ashamed. Paul steeled himself, wrapped his turbulent emotions in iron, and looked at Aaron's pleased grin.

"Ah, good. Good, Paul. I'm so glad. Honestly, for a moment, I didn't think you would. You looked like you were going to puke a few minutes ago."

"It...I mean, I'm just surprised, that's all."

Aaron laughed and clapped Paul on the shoulder. Aaron went over to the kid and squatted down next to him. Ethan was shivering hard from the cold, his hands balled up into tight little fists as Aaron ran a hand up his back before clamping down onto the nape of his neck. His fingers encircled his throat perfectly. Paul tasted bile in the back of his throat as Aaron nuzzled a small ear, bringing his lips close.

"Hear that, little Ethan?" he murmured. "Paul's going to find some use for you. For how long? Who knows? I paid rather handsomely for you, my boy. Let's not disappoint, hmm?" His fingers tightened. "You remember what happened on the way over here? Hmm? Do you?"

Ethan tried to nod, his small mouth forming the word *yes*. Aaron's grip didn't allow for much else.

"Good. Keep that in mind while you're here, then maybe your snow-white ass won't get ripped apart too badly." He gave the kid a push and he fell to one side.

Aaron smirked as he rose to his feet and came back to Paul's side. There must've been a look on Paul's face because Aaron paused.

"What?"

"Nothing."

"Then what's with the look?"

"Aaron, it's freezing out here and the kid's practically got nothing on. What good is he going to be if I have to cut his limbs off because of frostbite?"

The laugh that came from Aaron was abrasive and he shook his head like Paul had just told a good joke. "All right, Paul, look, have some fun, okay? I won't call you for a few days or anything. I'm sure you'll want to use that time to revel in this little guy's maximum potential."

With an affectionate pat on the shoulder, Aaron started toward the van. Paul watched him go.

"Hey, Aaron?"

He turned. "Yes?"

"Thanks, you know, for everything."

Aaron sneered at him. "When I see you next, Paul, maybe you won't be such a pussy, huh?"

It was one last slap to the face. Paul didn't move until the van was out of sight. Even on his worst night he had never felt as abandoned as he did right then. He tried to swallow but his throat felt like it was wrapped in sandpaper.

Faint scuffling made him turn. Ethan stood about five feet from him, shaking like a leaf in the wind. His lips were turning blue.

What are you doing? his brain roared at him. *Are you completely mental? It's a kid! A kid who's as fucked up as you are! What is wrong with you? You can't do this! There's no freaking way you can survive this!*

Paul pressed his lips together, turned away, and vomited.

CHAPTER 9

When he finally got himself under control, Paul straightened to his feet. He wiped his mouth with his sleeve and sucked in some deep breaths. The world had temporarily stopped spinning. He put his hand on the hood of the car for balance. Ethan's gray eyes were steady on his, purposely free of any expression. As much as Paul was loath to admit, he knew that look well. He knew this kid had learned the same way he'd learned to hide his emotions, to act like nothing fazed him. Nothing could be too perverted, too rough, too horrible for him to do because he'd seen and done it all. It wouldn't be until he was alone that he would tremble and shake and puke and cry.

'Use him the way you were used.'

Paul bit the inside of his cheek and gave himself a mental shake. There is no fucking way. No way. God, he couldn't…there was no way he could…

For God's sakes, just get him out of the cold.

The logic of that statement was so simple he felt a hysterical laugh bubble up the back of his throat. *Simple. Easy. Keep it simple and easy.*

He squeezed his eyes shut then opened them. "Come on," he finally said, his voice hoarse from vomiting.

He walked rather unsteadily to the passenger side of his Jeep and opened the door. A rush of hot air blasted him in the face. He looked behind him and saw that the kid had not moved.

"Come on," he repeated. *Or do you want to freeze to death out here? Although technically, it would probably be easier for you to die out here than at the hands of some perverted psycho.*

Ethan came forward slowly, his walk smooth for his age. His eyes never left Paul's face. His narrow shoulders, so thin like the bones of a bird, were tense and rigid and it wasn't just from the cold. He expected Paul to be rough. He expected Paul to be like Aaron and Vince. He expected Paul to maybe pass him around to his friends once he was through with him. He was expecting this to be a new, lower ring of hell and this very air of expectancy was making Paul feel violently ill.

I can't—I don't think I can do this.

He balled his hands into fists, much like the way Ethan had done.

Get him in the car. Get him where it's warm. Remember that? On the coldest of nights, you didn't mind being in someone's car because it was so warm and it bought that tingling feeling to your numb fingers. It was nights like those that you were thankful for any fuck, for any blowjob because you were warm.

He held the car door open. Ethan jerked slightly and something like a sigh came from his lips as the car's heat reached him. He scrambled in, no hesitation now. Paul shut the door behind him then cursed Aaron to hell and back as he walked to the driver's side and slid in behind the wheel. He nearly sighed too at the feel of hot air against his cold face. He ripped his gloves off and put his hands in front of the vents of either side of the steering wheel. He stole a glance at his passenger.

Ethan's bitten lips were twitching and his hair fell in a bright curtain as he tucked his chin against his chest. Paul cranked the heat up as high as it would go then unzipped his coat and struggled out of it. Ethan looked over immediately at the sound of cloth rustling. He watched from behind strands of blond hair as Paul thrust his coat toward him. The smooth expanse of one cheek that Paul could see was flushed cherry-red and his teeth were clenched so hard to keep them from chattering that Paul thought his teeth might crack.

'So help me God, you little piss-ant, you bite my cock with those chattering teeth, I'll knock every single one of them down your throat.'

Paul pressed his lips tightly together. "Here. Take it."

The kid flinched then blinked up at him, his eyes glassy and round, full of suspicion.

"Go on."

He sniffed and reached out one trembling hand. When his red fingers closed around it, his eyes moved to Paul's face again, gauging his reaction, expecting it to be snatched back. He nearly jumped when Paul released it. He moved slowly as he shrugged into it. Paul tried not to notice how unfathomably large the coat was around that fragile little body as Ethan grabbed the lapels and pulled them across the front of himself so that they overlapped. He tucked his face into the collar and shivered.

Paul stared out of the windshield, at a loss. He couldn't drive away, not with this kid in his car. Every ounce of his being was demanding him to stay put, to push Ethan back out into the cold, because if he drove off with him, he would be haunted forever. Worse yet, it would only prove Aaron's obvious theory that he was some deranged twisted ass-hat who liked fucking little boys.

Hands were suddenly in his lap, lifting up his shirt and pulling at his belt. He jumped with a yelp and looked down wildly at the small, efficient, cold-bitten hands undoing his belt and the snap of his jeans. Gasping in shock, he grabbed at the hands so roughly, he heard the kid bite back a cry of pain.

With his heart in his throat, Paul met Ethan's gaze. The boy was kneeling on the seat, face inches away with his little mouth wet and hanging open in a way that made Paul shove him backward. Ethan cried out as he hit the door. Sweat prickled his scalp and it was suddenly too hot. Paul snapped off the heat, barely noticing the sudden silence with the blood roaring through his ears. His hands gripped the steering wheel in a white-knuckled grip.

There was movement beside him. He looked out of the corner of his eye and saw Ethan kneel once again on the seat. He didn't move after that, just knelt there, waiting patiently like a small angel, hands folded neatly in his lap.

How did you get there? Paul wanted to scream at him. *What went so wrong in your life that you're trying to give me a blowjob after enduring God-knows-what in that van on the way over here, with some asshole's finger marks on your shoulders and—*

Something soft touched his hair. He felt little puffs of hot breath on the side of his face and he squeezed his eyes shut.

God...no...

A hand touched his thigh, small and sure. Paul felt something in his brain snap and he twisted around his seat so quickly that Ethan jumped, his eyes going wide. Paul snatched his hands, enveloping them in his own.

"No."

The word was like a bomb going off in a vacuum. Neither one moved for a space of heartbeats. He searched the kid's face, looking for a sign that he understood, trying to convey some message to him that this was not what he wanted.

Ever.

Paul was relieved when understanding flooded the smooth, young face and he released Ethan's hands slowly. The relief was short-lived however as Ethan took off the jacket with a movement that was well-practiced. Paul watched with growing horror as he began to undo his own jeans and shifted around on the seat to push them down off his hips.

"No!" Paul practically shouted.

Ethan froze, jeans halfway down his legs and Paul could see the flash of a milk-white thigh and a welt that covered it, the length and width of a belt buckle.

"God, just...no," he said again, his voice weak and trembling.

Ethan stared at him. Paul could see the confusion he was causing him and he couldn't find the words to explain. The kid bit his lip, small leftover tremors from the cold rippling through him. Paul turned away, running a hand through his hair. After a few minutes, he looked back over and saw that Ethan was still locked in the same position.

He was waiting for orders.

Christ.

"Pull—Pull your pants up. Put the coat on, okay?"

Ethan moved quietly and quickly and when he was fully clothed once more, he knelt on the seat, watching him. Paul could feel his flesh crawl and shrivel as Ethan made another move toward him.

"I said *stop!*" Paul exploded.

Ethan cringed, moving until his back was against the door. Paul smashed his fist against the dashboard.

"Goddammit!"

Aaron, you fucking asshole. How can you do this to me?

"Don't...Don't you like me?" came a small, quivering voice.

Paul looked at him. He wasn't sure if he was more surprised that the kid actually spoke or by the question.

"Just stay over there, okay?"

"But you...you like me, don't you?"

A kid.

A kid's small uncertain voice in the dark, in the shadows that no one saw. A kid with a voice as clear as small silver bells, as innocent as hot chocolate and as lost as anyone could ever be. Paul sank his teeth into his bottom lip to keep it from trembling. It took him two tries before he finally found his voice.

"Of course I like you," he murmured. "But I—I don't really know you."

"But you can," Ethan whispered with a voice that was full of things that were far too old for him to know about.

Paul wet his lips and Ethan must've taken that for an affirmative because he began to move toward him again.

"What do you say we go for some pancakes?"

The question had the desired effect and Ethan stopped, his eyes blinking wide. "Pancakes?" he asked, his white-blonde eyebrows rising.

"Sure." Paul nodded. "Don't you like pancakes?"

Ethan hesitated and Paul could see him trying to figure out what kind of game he was playing. "And then what?" he finally asked.

That was a fantastic question on so many levels.

Ethan's stomach chose that moment to make itself known, grumbling loudly. He immediately clamped an arm over the middle of his body and a look of horror came over his face.

"I'm not hungry," he said quickly. "I mean—I—I'm not hungry at all, really, I'm not."

"Your stomach's saying otherwise."

"But—"

"Okay, pancakes it is."

"But I don't want pancakes! Please, I'm not hungry!" he pleaded, suddenly frantic.

Paul was stunned at the desperation on the kid's face.

"Please," Ethan begged again, his small voice quivering.

Paul tightened his resolve. "Look...Ethan, that's your name, right?"

He nodded.

"Ethan, my name is Paul. You can call me Paul. Okay?"

Another nod, barely perceptible.

"Now, you're hungry. So we're going to get you something to eat. I'm not going to hurt you. Okay? No matter what happened on the way over here, no matter what you heard when that other man was talking to you, I am not going to hurt you. Do you understand that?"

Ethan swallowed hard. "But then...then why did you agree to take me?"

The question sent an ice pick through Paul's inner ear. "Because you want pancakes."

The confusion deepened in Ethan's eyes and he opened his mouth to say something but Paul beat him to it. "Put your seatbelt on."

He cranked the heat back up and put the Jeep in drive. Something inside him shattered as he stepped on the gas. It was going to take him a while to decide if that shattered something was a good thing or not.

CHAPTER 10

The smell of old grease, bacon, and Formica was all around them as a bouncy waitress named Stephanie showed them to a booth in the far corner of the diner. She couldn't have been more than seventeen judging by her energy at this ungodly hour as well as the milky smoothness of the backs of her thighs that Paul couldn't help but notice as he and his young companion trailed behind her like shadows.

He shot a glance over his shoulder. He didn't like having the kid at his heels but Ethan wouldn't move otherwise. He walked either directly behind Paul or off to one side, close enough to let anyone know that he was with him, yet far enough away to bolt if things got out of hand. Paul was mildly surprised that he hadn't bolted yet, but only mildly. Ethan had more experience than Paul had at that age and a lot more brains, too. He knew things would be ten times worse if he ran. His survival rate was only slightly higher if he played by the rules. He supposed he could've made this whole ordeal easier by getting the pancakes to go but he was in no hurry to bring Ethan home with him. The very thought made him break out in a cold sweat, even in the overheated diner.

Easy. It's just a kid. That's all. Just go easy.

The waitress obviously thought it was easy enough. She hadn't stopped babbling about how cute the kid was since they stepped foot in the door. Paul shot him another look, trying to view him from a female point-of-view. The coat sleeves hung nearly to the floor and the collar came up to his ears, his head and legs dwarfed by the enormity of the garment. He kept trying to push the sleeves up so he could finger-comb his hair back but the sleeves kept overtaking his little hands. Watching him struggle was almost cute, Paul supposed, if it weren't for the way his eyes kept darting around. He avoided Paul's gaze and minutely flinched as Stephanie reached out and ruffled his hair. Paul wondered what it was about women who thought they could touch any kid they felt like.

He thought of Kelly in that instant, remembered her mentioning kids once upon a time. He thought about calling her. Surely she would know what to do with a ten-year-old boy. But then he thought better of it.

Sure, Kel, I found him wandering the streets and decided to bring him home like a stray. Help me out, will you?

"You are just the cutest thing," the waitress cooed at Ethan, squatting down and resting her elbows on the table-top.

The skirt of her waitress uniform rode up dangerously high and Paul thought he saw a flash of lace blue panties as he slid into the booth across from Ethan, who knelt on the seat, the same way he'd done on the ride over.

"Look at those eyes," she went on with a goofy grin. "Such a beautiful gray, kind of like wolf eyes, you know? Ever watch the Discovery Channel? They have programs on every Wednesday night devoted to wildlife in the forests and woods and stuff, you know, and they had one about wolves and everything and I swear to God, it made me want to go out and find one. It'd probably be kind of like looking after a dog, I mean, wolves and dogs are pretty similar, right? Can't be that hard to keep one, right?"

Ethan's eyes flicked briefly to Paul and there was a flash of questioning in those eyes. It took Paul a minute to realize that he was silently asking for permission to speak.

Oh Lord. He gave an awkward nod. Ethan immediately brought his head up and looked at Stephanie, his little mouth twisting in what could only be construed as a smile, although it didn't quite meet his eyes.

"I like wolves," he said quietly.

Stephanie's smile was blinding. "Me, too! Hey, we have something in common, Wolfie. Do you mind if I call you Wolfie? It's a good thing, I promise."

He gave a shy nod.

"Well, Wolfie, you can call be Steph, okay? Don't call me Stephanie because only my mother calls me that and that's only when I'm in trouble. You don't get in trouble, do you? You seem like a nice boy, huh? You behave for your dad here, right?" She flashed her grin at Paul, whose blood froze at the implication. He couldn't quite get his mouth to work properly but her attention was already flitting back to Ethan.

Ethan's throat worked as he swallowed and an old look came over his face as he looked at Paul.

"Yes," he murmured. "I behave. I'm a good boy."

Paul cleared his throat. "Um...I think, I think I'm going to have some scrambled eggs."

To go with my scrambled brains.

Stephanie straightened to her feet with a hearty, "Sure thing" and jotted down his order on her pad. "Coffee, too?"

"No, thanks. Orange juice."

"Okay and for you, Wolfie?"

Paul watched in part-fascination as Ethan gradually came alive under her attention. His gray eyes sparkled and the longer she spoke to him, the more his smile seemed to transform into something real. He gave an awkward fidget that was so childlike, for a moment he appeared to be just that, rather than the piece of meat Aaron had gifted him with.

"Do you have pancakes?" he asked, blinking up at her with wide eyes.

"Of course we do. We have plain, chocolate chip, and blueberry."

"Can I have chocolate chip, please?" His voice never rose above a soft murmur.

Stephanie was practically melting in a gooey puddle on the floor. "Coming right up, sweetie."

She flashed Paul a quick smile before bouncing away.

Paul watched her hamstrings bunch and flex before reluctantly turning his gaze back to Ethan, who was now looking at him with that wary, shielded look once more. He had to give the kid some credit. He could turn it on and off like a goddamn switch. Looking down at the table top, Paul focused on a coffee stain that hadn't been completely wiped away. It was an uneven splatter the size of a quarter. The edges were darker and the middle was faded. Just a couple more passes with a wet rag and the entire thing would've vanished. But whoever wiped down the tables didn't apply enough pressure. It didn't seem to matter if the next person who sat at this table would see it. It didn't matter because there was only going to be more coffee spilled so what was the point in cleaning it up? Paul wondered if Ethan felt as stained as he did.

Feeling the kid's eyes on him, he looked up. Sure enough, Ethan was staring at him. If he was breathing, Paul couldn't tell. He knew enough about kids that they couldn't remain still for any length of time. There was always a nervous energy, a tension that propelled them to move, talk and touch...

'No, the way I showed you! Christ, how many times do we have to go through this? Maybe you should be paying me for a blow-job. You suck me off the way I want you to, not the other way around. I ain't paying you to use your own goddamn technique.'

Paul didn't want to think about how many hands Ethan had passed through before he was able to maintain this uncanny posture.

'People just like you,' Aaron whispered in his head.

Paul scowled at that. *What would you know, you fucking bastard?*

He closed his eyes for a moment, trying to pull his head together. He turned his focus away from the general fucked-up-ness of the situation and onto the fact that he was now stuck with a ten-year-old whore, who was taking it all in stride while Paul was having near-fainting spells and puking his guts out.

You're a little out of practice, buddy, he consoled himself. *You haven't been in this kind of situation since you were seventeen.*

"Are you all right?"

His eyes came open. Ethan was looking at him, a small frown line visible between his pale eyebrows. Paul started to answer but Stephanie suddenly reappeared with two tall glasses of orange juice.

"Here we are, gentlemen. Wolfie, I totally forgot to ask you before what you wanted to drink so then I thought well, what else could possibly go with pancakes but orange juice, right?"

Ethan's entire face froze as his eyes snapped to attention at the sight of the juice she had set before him. Paul could practically hear him salivating. Stephanie moved her head a little so she could see his face around the curtain of hair that had fallen in front of it. Her smile gave way to concern at his lack of response.

"Um," she said, before looking at Paul. "Is that—Is this all right?"

He nodded. "It's fine."

She was hesitant. "Oh, well, okay, um, your food will be out shortly."

Casting one last look at Ethan, she walked away. Paul looked at Ethan, who was watching the condensation drip down the side of the glass, his little mouth hanging open a bit. Paul squared his shoulders.

"Do you like orange juice? Or would you rather have chocolate milk?" he asked, his words sounding weird and torn from his throat.

Ethan's eyes came up quickly and he seemed ashamed at his reaction. Paul guessed that he probably hadn't had anything nourishing in quite a long time.

"No," Ethan replied. "No, this is fine."

"Are you sure? You can have chocolate milk or something else if you want."

Ethan looked as if he couldn't believe Paul was giving him a choice. Paul swallowed, telling himself to keep going, he was doing good, that he was okay, that he wasn't the sick pervert that Aaron obviously thought him to be.

Not yet.

Paul gritted his teeth against that voice and motioned for Stephanie, who bounded over immediately.

"Yes?" she asked, brightly.

"Could you get him a glass of chocolate milk?" Paul asked.

"Oh, of course," she smiled, starting to pick up the orange juice.

"No, no you can leave that," Paul said.

"Sure. One chocolate milk coming right up."

She beamed another smile at Ethan before walking away.

"Thank you," Ethan whispered.

Paul nodded and let his eyes roam around the diner. It was a fairly typical lay-out. Chrome and red vinyl booths took up one half of the narrow room while the long counter with its stools took up the other half. There were covered-cake platters featuring pies and doughnuts, coffee pots, a small glass cooler that held individual cake slices. Sets of salt-and-pepper shakers, ketchup and mustard bottles, and napkin holders were placed every few feet across the counter. There was also a long cut-out in the wall behind the counter where the cook was barely visible through a wall of steam. He could hear the faint crack and sizzle of eggs being broken open, of pancakes being prepared in nice, perfectly-round circles. They were the only customers in the place, which made it only a little easier to deal with the quiet presence sitting across from him. As if against his will, he met the kid's eyes again.

Ethan was still watching him. There was a strange look on his face, like he was resisting the urge to say or do something. He knew better than to ask for it. He probably thought he would get punished if he did.

You know it's bad when you're on the same thinking level as a ten-year-old, Paul thought miserably.

He gestured toward Ethan's glass. "Go on."

Ethan blinked at him, a flash of hope igniting in his eyes before he caught himself and fixed Paul with a carefully blank look. "But I—the…"

"What?"

"I'm already getting the chocolate milk…right?"

"You can't have both?" Paul asked, thinking of the kid's frail collarbones poking through paper-thin flesh. "Go on."

For a moment, Ethan sat there, then, slowly, so slowly he reached for the glass with both hands, eyes locked on Paul's face. Paul leaned back from the table.

At that, Ethan curled his fingers around the glass and, without hesitation, gulped down its contents. When the glass touched the tabletop again, it was empty. Ethan's chest heaved as if he'd run ten miles.

"Good?" Paul found himself asking, amused and unaccountably relived for the kid's temporary lack of control.

Ethan licked his lips, catching any last remnant of juice that might have escaped.

"Yeah," came the soft reply.

There was an undertone of satisfaction that made Paul want to ask him when the last time he'd eaten anything.

"Thank you, sir."

"Don't call me that," Paul said sharply.

Ethan looked at him, confused. "But I—I thought…"

"No. You call me Paul."

"But I'm…not allowed."

"Says who?"

"My—" he cut himself off and looked down at his lap.

"Your what?"

Ethan sucked in a deep breath, as if trying to remain centered. "Whatever you want," he whispered, eyes glued to his lap.

The submission in his voice grated on Paul's nerves more than he wanted to admit. It reminded him of too many rules, too many games, and too many places where he had thought that death would've been the better option.

"May I ask you a question?" Ethan asked suddenly, his voice a quiet hum.

"Of course you can," Paul replied, trying not to sound irritated.

"How…How long will you keep me?"

Keep me. Not use me, not fuck me, not beat me. But keep me.

"As long as I can."

Ethan little jaw tightened.

"Don't misunderstand me, kid," Paul went on. "I meant what I said before. I won't hurt you, not in the way that you're…" He almost said *used to* but decided against it. "But I'm not going to take any of your shit either. You'll be a guest in my house, okay? If you want anything, you ask. If you have a question, you ask. I don't want you crawling around like a dog that's been kicked too many times."

The hurt that flared up in those gray depths made Paul want to kick himself. Ethan should've been used to it by now, but judging by the look on his face, Paul supposed not. Even if he was a whore, he was still a kid.

A whore with feelings.

Paul didn't think things could possibly get any worse until the door of the restaurant opened and two rambling drunk men staggered in, yelling at the top of their lungs about a football game. He looked over the top of Ethan's head, noticing that he'd bowed his head, as if trying to disappear.

"I need to piss, Lou," one of them said.

"Then go or do you need me to hold your dick for you?" the other replied.

Snorting laughter, one of the men began to make his way down the row of stools, passing Paul and Ethan's table on the way to the bathroom. The man leered at him, slowing down to shuffle past his table, then moving on, casting glances over his shoulder as if expecting Paul to say something. The bathroom door squeaked as it opened, then closed.

"Yo, baby doll! What's a guy gotta do for coffee around here?" the asshole named Lou was yelling at the counter.

"No need for yelling," Stephanie said, coming from the kitchen, balancing plates of hot food on a tray. "I'll be right with you."

"Hey, this shit looks pretty good." He followed close behind her, weaving a crooked line as she made her way toward Paul.

She rolled her eyes as she set the pancakes in front of Ethan and the scrambled eggs in front of Paul. The man came up short and stepped on the back of her heel.

"Ow!" she grunted, turning quickly and shoving him back a step. "Will you back off? I said I'll be with you in a minute."

"Nah, no need," he slurred as he stepped around her. "I'll just take some of theirs."

He reached down and dug his fingers into Ethan's pancakes. Ethan flinched back into his seat.

"Oh, come on," Stephanie groaned. "That's not yours."

"What's not yours?"

Paul heard the bathroom door squeak open behind him.

"I'm hungry," Lou said around a mouthful of pancakes, shooting his friend a smile.

"Oh, yeah? What else they got?"

The other man was suddenly looming over Paul, reeking of whiskey and foul sweat. He sneered as he grabbed Paul's plate and fork and began to help himself.

"You guys better pay for that," Stephanie was ranting.

"Shut up, bitch," Lou said, giving her a shove that sent her stumbling back. "How're them eggs, John?"

"Not bad. Might be better with a side of this dumpling," he leered, tangling a hand through Ethan's hair.

Paul's hand shot out, grabbing the fucker by the back of the neck and slamming his face into the table once, twice, three times. He fell to the floor with a strangled, egg-choked gasp. Blood gushed from his nose.

"Hey, asshole." Lou blinked at him in surprise, pancake crumbs spewing from his lips. He lunged and managed to get his hands around Paul's neck and his disgusting breath in his face before Paul reared up out of his seat and smashed his fist into his face. He felt bone break.

Blood flew, painting the floor in a dotted piece of artwork. The man went limp in his grasp and Paul almost hit him again but let him slide to the floor, holding onto his face, blood pouring from between his fingers.

Silence followed. His heartbeat roared in his ears and it was only with the sudden lack of motion that Paul realized how hard he was breathing. He sucked in a deep breath and turned around to find Ethan wedged in the corner of his seat. His little mouth was hanging open and one hand was gripping the edge of the table top as if he could tear a chunk out of it.

"You all right?" Paul asked, hesitantly.

"Holy shit, mister." Stephanie was suddenly at his side. "That was…That was amazing. Are you like a cop or something?"

Paul looked away from Ethan's eyes, not sure if he could comprehend the look in them. He wasn't sure he even wanted to. He turned to the waitress.

"I think we'll get our food to go."

She gave him an awe-struck smile and he found himself wishing he felt as good as she obviously did.

"Whatever you want. On the house."

She hurried away. He glanced at Ethan from the corner of his eye and saw him staring at the smear of blood on the table. Then he looked back up at Paul.

For me? His eyes seemed to say. *You did that for me?*

No, Paul thought to himself. *For me.*

CHAPTER 11

The last time Paul felt this uncertain was his first night on the streets and faced with his first blow-job. He remembered staring at the man's cock like it was some kind of alien life-form because it simply kept growing larger the longer he stared at it. He remembered how badly he wanted to ask what he was supposed to do, until the man had said with a hungry smile, "You gonna stare at it or suck it?"

He also remembered throwing up violently afterward.

Currently, and he was thankful for this, the urge to upchuck wasn't strong. But his head was pounding so hard he popped six Excedrin. He glanced at his watch and saw that it was after three in the morning. He sighed, exhaustion swooping down on him, letting him sag against the kitchen counter. He pushed away his untouched take-out container of scrambled eggs.

He heard the water running upstairs. He glanced at the clock again. The kid had been up there for ten minutes. It had taken him less time to get through his stack of pancakes. He ended up wearing half of it in his haste to fill his stomach. Paul wanted to tell him to slow down or he was going to puke everything back up but the heavenly bliss that had come over the kid's face as he gulped as fast as he could chew, stopped him.

Sighing, Paul undid his ponytail, letting his hair fall freely around his shoulders. He ran his hands through it, his scalp groaning appreciation. He was bone-tired, his eyes full of sand, his mouth open in a perpetual yawn but yet his mind was racing.

Where the hell should the kid sleep? If he takes a shower, what is he going to wear after? The same shitty clothes he was fucked and beaten in? I don't think I even have enough food in the fridge to feed him. Hell, I can barely cook. I can barely make hot dogs without having the fucking things explode.

A sound came from upstairs, jerking Paul from his thoughts. He darted up the stairs, taking two at a time. He went quickly down the hallway toward the bathroom. The door was slightly ajar. The light was on and he could still hear the water running. Frowning, he slowly pushed the door open.

Ethan was at the sink's edge, pushed up on his toes, weaving his fingers in and out of the water coming out of the faucet. He seemed mesmerized by it, his hands moving back and forth, a small smile twittering across his lips. He alternated between the water from the faucet and the water that was filling the sink, dunking his arms in up to his elbows and moving his arms around like he was in a swimming pool. For a moment, Paul watched him, wondering if he should leave him to his little pool. But then he saw that the sink was already more than half full and rising fast. He cleared his throat.

Gasping, Ethan leapt back from the sink. His hands flew behind his back. Water sprang in every direction and he almost slipped in his haste to stand at attention.

"I'm sorry," he immediately said. "I was just...I mean, I—I was just cleaning up—for you."

Paul frowned and Ethan quickly bowed his head.

Water still poured from the faucet and the sound of it scratched at Paul's brain. He stepped into the room, reached over, and shut it off. Paul stared down at him. He looked odd standing in his bathroom. Hell, the whole situation was odd. If anyone had told Paul last week he'd have a ten-year-old prostitute in his bathroom, he would've laughed himself silly. But it wasn't funny. No sir, no laughing here. Staring at a fucked-up stranger with a chasm of years between them and suddenly the familiarity that this moment in time invoked was so habitual, so routine, it was like slipping on an old sweater. So much time had passed since Paul found himself in the same shit-poor situation that Ethan was in right now yet it was so easy, *too easy* to remember. It shouldn't be this easy. But it was.

Shifting his weight from one foot to the other, Paul looked around the bathroom. His eyes landed on the shower.

"Did you...Why don't you take a shower?" he asked hesitantly.

Ethan's head snapped up, eyes as wide as silver coins. "No!" he said quickly. "Oh no, I couldn't—"

"Why not?"

Little white teeth clamped down on his bottom lip. "Well, I—I...only if you want me to."

Paul squared his shoulders. *Come on*, he pep-talked himself. *You can do this. Just breathe.*

"Let me get you a towel."

He went back out to the hall closet, feeling his heart pound in his ears. He grabbed two fluffy blue towels that were each bigger than Ethan was. He went back into the bathroom to find Ethan already stripping out of his shirt. Paul walked briskly past him to put the tow-els on the rack near the shower. He slid aside the glass shower door and flipped on the water, sticking his hand under it until it got hot. Then he turned around and froze.

Ethan stood before him, looking down at the floor, hands hanging loosely at his sides. He was naked and Paul could see in all its harsh glory, his body that was a work of unimaginable pain. The circle of bruised flesh around his ankle was stark and ugly, book-ended be-tween the white of his flesh and the white tiles of the bathroom floor. Brown, lumpy circles, the size of cigarettes, dotted his chest, not to mention the finger-shaped bruises on his bony, narrow hips. Thin lines of pink and white crossed his abdomen, marks that looked healed while others looked scabbed over, more recent. His legs were slashed with black and blue welts and Paul could swear he could make out a belt buckle in the skin around his left knee. There was a strange patch of skin to the side of his groin, on his pelvis. It looked wrinkled, rough, darker than the rest of him.

Paul pressed his lips together and started for the door.

He knew what a skin graft looked like.

"You can join me, if you like."

Paul came to a halt. He closed his eyes briefly before casting a quick look over his shoulder. Ethan was still looking at the floor, his hair shielding his face from view. Paul drew a deep breath that tasted like blood.

"No. Just…no."

He left the room, closing the door behind him before collapsing against it. He swallowed hard, not sure if he wanted to vomit or scream.

'What's the matter? Can't suck cock and hold your breath under-water at the same time? I thought you were a pro, you little shit.'

His vision blurred and he stumbled to his bedroom. He put the light on and sat down on the bed seconds before his legs buckled beneath him. He stared blankly out the window. The sky was dark but the city skyline cut through it with sharp-edged shapes and lights that blinked on and off, like huge eyes, watching, accessing, waiting to see if he would act on what Ethan was so freely giving him.

No, not freely.

Aaron had paid for him. He had paid someone, an animal, a sick pervert, in exchange for being able to handle Ethan any way he saw fit. Paul couldn't believe this was happening. On some scale, it seemed ridiculous that he was right where he'd been over a decade ago, only this time he was witnessing it instead of participating. It sickened him to know that the game had remained the same, even if the faces had changed. His skin prickled unpleasantly as he became aware of Ethan standing at the foot of the bed. He was wrapped in a towel, his little hands clutching it to his waist. There was an air of anticipation around him, a waiting.

He was waiting for Paul to say the word. And with that word, he would drop the towel and climb onto the bed and...

Paul launched himself to his feet. "You can sleep here," he said, gesturing toward the king-sized bed.

Ethan's eyes flicked from the bed then back up to Paul. He took a step toward him. Paul took an immediate step back.

"I'll be on the couch downstairs."

He stepped around the kid and strode toward the door, feeling Ethan's eyes burn into his back. He heard a small intake of breath. Stopping at the door, he turned back around.

"What? What is it?" he asked, hating the anxious edge of his voice but *God* how he needed to get out of this room.

The look on Ethan's face was confused. "I thought—I mean, don't you—" He cut himself off then dropped the towel.

Paul exploded. "No!" he practically screamed, racing forward.

Ethan jumped with a small, startled cry and started to propel himself back, but Paul caught him by the arms, swung him up, unable to believe how light he was, like a bag of cotton balls, and deposited him on the bed. He snatched up the towel and roughly wrapped it around the small, bruised body. He fell to his knees beside the bed, grabbing the kid around the upper arms again and giving him a shake. Ethan cried out as his head snapped back. The cry pierced Paul's brain and beat him back from the edge that he'd been balancing precariously on since he first saw him.

He sucked in several deep breaths, forcing himself to loosen his fingers. He peered up into Ethan's frightened face, watching as fear and confusion warred with the stubbornness of knowing he had a job to do and that there was nothing and no one that was going to stop him.

"Listen to me, Ethan, just...listen to me, all right?" Paul said, trying to keep his voice steady. "I'm—I'm not going to do anything to you or...with you. All right? Nothing. I need for you to understand that because I am barely hanging on here."

Ethan's lips moved silently for a moment then he licked them and said, "But I...I just want to be close to you."

It was so rehearsed, so false that it made Paul's stomach cramp. He could hear the fear and self-loathing behind it.

Christ, did shit like that actually work?

You know it did and it still does.

"No," Paul said, shaking his head. "No, you don't. I know you think you have to, but you don't, okay? Not with me. I'm not going to do anything and I don't want you to do anything, either."

"But I know you want me to," Ethan replied softly as his eyes moved to a point over Paul's shoulder.

Paul clenched his teeth, just barely stopping himself from giving him another bone-jarring shake. "No. I don't. Why do you think I'm going to sleep downstairs?"

"Because you're playing hard to get."

Paul gaped at him. *Jesus Christ.*

"It's okay," Ethan went on in a quiet voice. "You know? It's okay to want me. A lot of people do, even when they say they don't. Some people just need a little…help, that's all."

Paul watched him like a frozen animal as Ethan raised his hands toward his face and leaned forward. Paul felt his breath push over his lips and it was like someone had stuck an axe in his side. He jerked back and Ethan's hands closed on air. Paul got to his feet, his stomach balling into a sickening knot of anger and fear. He glared down at Ethan until Ethan moved back a little, staring up at him, waiting to be struck or worse. His little Adam's apple bobbed as he swallowed.

"You're going to sleep in this bed tonight. I don't want you to leave this room until I come and get you in the morning. Do you understand?"

Ethan's eyes searched his face.

"Do you understand?"

Ethan nodded, still looking confused as Paul made for the door again.

"Why don't you want me?"

He stopped in the threshold and looked back.

"Because I don't need to hate myself anymore than I already do."

Ethan's eyebrows rose into his hairline.

Paul closed the door and went downstairs. As tired as he was, it took him a while to fall asleep…

CHAPTER 12

The sand was soft between his toes, soft like talcum powder, sifting beneath his weight as he walked. The air was clear but dark except for brilliant patches of white that were cracked with veins of black. The horizon was stretched out as straight as an arrow, simpering down into two stripes of purple and gold. Large shapes loomed overhead. They could've been trees but there wasn't enough light to be certain. There was a clearing that glowed faintly with dark blue embers. In the center was a large white rectangular piece of a wall with a square cut out in its center.

Kelly was painting the wall with a paint roller on a pole. Her white suit was smeared with paint so dark it seemed she was painting with the blackness of the night sky. The wall seemed to disappear piece by piece as she painted, the roller moving over it with a sound like car tires crunching over loose gravel.

"Kel?" he tried to say but no sound came from his throat. He tried to clear it but even that sound he couldn't make. "Hey, Kelly? Babe, what're you doing?"

She kept painting, her movements steady and smooth. The pop-crunch was getting louder. The wall grew smaller. He started toward her but then stopped and flailed as he sank ankle-deep into the ground.

"Kel!" he shouted, panicking as silence was his only answer.

Pop-crunch! Pop-crunch! Pop-crun—

She stopped suddenly and turned to look at him. Her green eyes glowed brilliantly but they were blank, empty, as if she were looking through him and not at him.

"It's over, Paul." Her voice echoed, dream-like. "It's over."

He fought to free himself but only succeeded in sinking to his knees. "What? What's over? Kel, come on! Help me!"

The ground broke open like a skin sore and he fell, screaming silently...

❧❧

"Shit!"

His voice exploded in his ears as he shot up then promptly fell off the couch. Paul grunted as he hit the floor, tangled in the blankets. The floor was freezing but it felt good against his flushed face. He groaned weakly, laying there for a minute before pushing himself up and squinting against the light that blazed through the windows.

"Oh, man," he moaned, dragging himself back onto the couch and throwing the blankets over his head.

The dream was already fading and it didn't take long before he was falling back into blissful sleep.

Something thumped to the floor overhead.

He shot off the couch, instincts kicking his sleep back. He grabbed his Glock off the coffee table and vaulted up the stairs. He was surprised to find the door to his bedroom closed. Surprised and pissed off.

Goddamn these assholes breaking in here. Again. Surely they have better things to do than—

He swung the door open hard enough to let it crash against the wall. "All right, assho—"

He froze in mid-sentence.

Jesus. The kid.

Paul sagged against the doorjamb in surprise, lowering the gun to his side.

"I'm—Jesus, I'm sorry," he stammered, raking a hand through his hair. "I—I'm—I forgot you were here."

Ethan stood beside the bed, watching him with a calm and expectant look, as if Paul hadn't just torn through the door and pointed a gun at him.

"I'm sorry," he replied quietly, his eyes never wavering from Paul's face. "I wasn't sure how else to get you in here without leaving the room."

"What?"

"You told me that I couldn't leave the room until you came to get me."

"Oh. Right. Well…do you need something?"

The expectant look in Ethan's eyes became almost playful. The tip of his tongue darted out to wet his bottom lip. "Do you?" he asked, the corners of his mouth twitching upward.

It was then that Paul noticed that Ethan was naked. In the unforgiving light of the morning, his body was on full display, right down to the last scab. Paul felt his brain short-circuit and before he could stop himself, he was charging the kid. "Put some clothes on right fucking now!" he barked at him.

Ethan backpedaled until he collided with the night table, his face a show of shock as Paul advanced on him.

"B–But I thought—"

"What?" Paul seethed, the veins pulsing in his neck as he felt the hold on his sanity unhinge a little. "What? What did you think? That I would change my mind about you in the morning?"

To his surprise, Ethan nodded. The urge to hit him tore down Paul's arm like a whiplash.

"Well, I haven't changed my fucking mind. Now get dressed and come downstairs to the kitchen. Goddammit!"

He all but ran from the room, slamming the door shut behind him. He leaned against it, trying to catch his breath. His body shook horribly and he stayed against the door until he was sure he could walk without falling. Staggering down to the kitchen, he wondered if it would be considered merciful if he killed the kid right now. Or maybe if he killed himself.

God, he couldn't stand it. He couldn't stand the way the kid looked at him, trying to get at him, to entice him, to reel him in with a body that had seen the worse of humanity.

'*Some people just play hard to get.*'

Paul felt his stomach lurch.

'*This won't hurt a bit. Here, just turn around...*'

'*Wait...*'

'*Shhh, just relax. If you relax, it won't hurt.*'

'*But—*'

'*There, that's it, just a little bit more, okay? Little bit—oh yeah, right there...*'

Paul clapped a hand over his mouth to stifle the memory. The fact that he knew exactly what Ethan was doing, and why, was horrifyingly revealing, creating a gateway to a time that Paul had been striving to forget about for years. Now it stood before him, as bold and as real as his reflection and just as inescapable. He knew with unshakeable certainty that Ethan would keep trying. He would always keep trying because that's what kids like him did. That's what Paul had done and it was all so easy because people lied.

All the time.

It was a cold, hard fact. Through experience and persuasion, it wasn't difficult to contradict them when they said they didn't want it because they really did or why else would they be in a dark car with a kid in the first place? Paul knew what Ethan saw when he looked at him. He knew that no matter how many people he beat up in a diner, it would only be construed as a customer protecting what he was paying for. Not because he cared. Not because he thought Ethan mattered but because Paul was making an investment. Trying to convince Ethan otherwise would be like trying to put a dent in a brick wall with his fist.

Paul put the safety back on the gun then slammed it onto the kitchen table. He tried to calm himself when he heard the patter of bare feet coming down the steps.

He's doing the only thing he knows how to do, he tried to tell himself. *You were the same way once.*

Unwillingly, Paul thought of the hard back-hand Aaron had delivered across his face the first and only time Paul had tried to initiate anything. The violence had been a strong and effective tool and it had thrived in their relationship, making it the toxic thing that it was today. Looking back, Paul was sure Aaron did it simply because he didn't know how else to handle it. At least he was partly sure. With Ethan, subjecting the kid to more violence was something that made Paul physically ill. Besides, the kid was so frail, one punch would probably break his neck.

Ethan appeared promptly and at attention on the other side of the island in the kitchen, head bowed. Paul stared at the top of his head, grinding his teeth. He was wearing the same dirty clothes from the night before. Paul wondered if he should take the kid shopping.

'*Shopping*? *How long do you plan on keeping him*?' Aaron's voice sneered in his head.

Paul pursed his lips, searching for something to say. Ethan didn't move a muscle as seconds began to tick by.

"I'm sorry," Paul blurted out. "I shouldn't have...I didn't mean to yell."

"No. It was my fault," Ethan immediately placated him, his head coming up slightly so he could look at him through the pale curtain of hair that had fallen in front of his face. "I should have waited until you—"

"No," Paul said, cutting him off. "No, I...you...there's no waiting, all right? There's no...anything. I don't want you doing anything. I told you that last night. Do you remember what I told you that?"

Ethan stared at him for a moment then looked down at the floor. Paul balled his hands into fists to keep them from shaking.

"Do you remember?" he pushed.

The kid made a funny gesture that was half a nod and half a shake of his head. Paul could see his jaw working.

"I—I didn't think you meant it," came the soft voice.

"I'm not a very good liar. Just ask my ex-girlfriend."

Judging by the look in Ethan's eyes as he looked up at him again, Paul could clearly see that this was not going the way he was used to.

"I don't understand, sir, what—"

"Do *not* call me that."

"But—"

"You call me by my name, Ethan. The same way I'm calling you by yours."

"I—I can't..."

"Why not?"

"I told you already," he said, a hint of pleading coloring his voice now.

"No, you told me you weren't allowed. That's not a reason."

"It's the only reason I can give you."

Paul skinned his lips back over his teeth. "Yeah? Well, it's not a very good one."

Ethan bowed his head, not answering. Paul continued to stare him, wanting to wait him out but knowing the stars would burn out first. He chewed on the inside of his cheek. Silence prevailed around them. Then he said,

"Are you hungry?"

Ethan shook his head.

"Bullshit. I'll make you some breakfast."

Ethan's head came up. "You don't have to. I'm fine. I can just watch you eat."

"I'm not hungry but you are. Aren't you?"

"I—You—You don't have to do anything for me."

"Well, I want to," Paul snapped at him.

Ethan moved forward. "I can—"

"No. You're not doing anything. Sit down at the table."

He complied, moving jerkily as if he wasn't sure that's what Paul really meant. With a deep breath that singed his lungs, Paul turned toward the fridge. He yanked the door open as he heard the scrape of chair legs against the floor.

"How about scrambled eggs?" he asked. "It's probably the only thing I can make without burning it."

"Sir, really, you don't—"

"Don't call me that," Paul interjected, shooting Ethan a glare over his shoulder.

"I'm sorry," Ethan said, staring down at the table.

Paul squared his shoulders, trying to relax the knot in his back as he went about preparing the eggs.

"You want cheese on them?" he asked.

"Only if you—"

Paul slapped some butter into the pan with more force than he intended.

"Do you want cheese on your eggs?"

There was a pause behind him and finally there came a meek, "Yes."

Paul swallowed back his frustration. He finished up the eggs in silence. He could feel the kid's eyes burning into the back of his neck and he tried his best to ignore them. Mentally taking a deep breath, he turned away from the stove with a heaping plate of cheesy eggs in one hand. He nearly dropped it when he saw Ethan on his knees beside his chair, hands clasped behind his back.

"What're you doing?"

Ethan stared up at him as if it were perfectly natural for him to be on the floor. "I'm waiting for my breakfast."

"Waiting for…what?"

'Whores don't eat at the table.'

'But how—how am I supposed to eat this?'

'The same way you suck cock. With your mouth.'

Paul slammed the plate down on the table, feeling something hot collide into the back of his eyeballs. The ground that had seemed so stable a few minutes ago began to crack beneath his feet. His teeth clenched.

"Get up," he squeezed out. "Get up and get in that chair right now."

Ethan's brow furrowed slightly. "But—"

"Now."

Ethan moved his head back, craning his neck and Paul realized that he'd moved closer to him without even realizing it.

"But this—this is where I belong."

'That's right, you little cocksucker. On your knees.'

Paul choked on the bile in his throat. "No. No, you don't."

"I always eat on the flo—"

His words were lost in a gasp as Paul hauled him up by the shoulders. He shoved him in a chair at the table and pushed the plate of eggs in front of him.

"You will eat at this table," he said, his voice shaking. "You will eat here, with a fork and a napkin and a glass of…what did you want to drink?"

Ethan stared at him, his eyes the size of saucers. His mouth moved but no sound came out.

"What did you want to drink?" Paul nearly shouted in his face.

"Wa-Water, please," he stammered.

Paul moved stiffly as he filled a glass from the faucet. He put it down with a *bang* in front of the kid, who jumped and looked up at him.

"I—"

"Eat."

For a moment, Ethan didn't move. Paul thought for sure he was going to push the plate away. But after several moments, he picked up the fork with barely trembling fingers. As he dug into the eggs, he met Paul's eyes.

"You won't tell, will you?"

Paul's knees ached and he sank down into a chair across from him. "No. No, I won't tell."

CHAPTER 13

Paul stuck the kid in front of the television while he went upstairs to take a shower. Fighting away the chills that Ethan's innocent statement of *'Want some company?'* had induced, Paul turned the water on as hot as it would go, huddling under it as if he were under a pile of fleece blankets on the couch. He waited for the steam to unwind the knots that were twisting mercilessly through his body but it only seemed to increase the pressure as though someone was standing on the back of his neck.

Dressing quickly in jeans and a long-sleeved T-shirt, he paused at the head of the stairs. He glanced over the side of the balcony, eyeing the kid as he perched on the edge of the couch. His back was to Paul but he could tell Ethan wasn't comfortable being left alone. The remote hung loosely in one hand while his other hand clutched the edge of the couch cushion as if it were a life-line. Paul raked his teeth over his bottom lip. He wiped his palms on his legs, feeling as unstable and volatile as the situation.

He sucked in a few deep breaths and went downstairs. Ethan immediately turned as he approached and stood up. Paul stopped in his tracks when he saw the strained look on his face.

Uh oh.

"Is there anything you would like me to do, sir?"

"I thought I told you to stop calling me that."

"I can't. You know I can't," he said, his voice soft but shaking around the edges. His eyes burned with desperate, gray light. "Please. Please let me do something for you."

"There's nothing I want you to do."

"Then why am I here?"

Paul flexed his jaw. Ethan took two steps toward him, his eyes pleading, his hand clenching around the television remote. It was unsettling, the way he begged. He did it as if he were begging for food, as if it were life or death. Paul had heard people pleading for money with that same lost hopelessness.

"Please," Ethan begged again. "Please. Is there something I'm doing wrong?"

"No."

"Are you not happy with me?"

"I—"

"Is there something I've done that has upset you? I—"

"No, no, you're fine."

"I'm not," he said, his little chest beginning to rise and fall rapidly. "I'm not fine because if I was, I would be—"

"Ethan, there's nothing I want from you."

"But I have to do something. There are—There are rules and I can't—I can't *not* do them and you—I have to do them, sir, please." He took another step forward, the confusion, the frustration, the near-pain on his face was sharper than a knife's edge and it flayed Paul's chest to bloody ribbons.

He tore his gaze away from those large, pleading eyes, feeling them dig into his brain. His gaze traveled down Ethan's small frame, from the too-prominent collarbones to the paper-thin shirt he wore and the dirty jeans then back up again. When he reached Ethan's eyes again, the storm in them had calmed. His grip on the remote loosened and the tension seemed to drain from him. He thrived like a flower in the sun under the perusal and Paul cleared his throat.

"I think I want to take you shopping for clothes."

Ethan, in the process of moving toward him, froze. "I'm...sorry?"

"Clothes," Paul repeated. "For you."

Ethan stared up at him, speechless. His head moved back and forth with a small twitch of his neck.

"I..."

"What?"

"I don't want any new clothes," he said in a halted tone as if he wasn't sure about what he'd just said.

"You want to keep wearing those rags?"

"Yes."

Paul almost smiled at the sudden stubborn set of his small jaw. Maybe this kid wasn't so lost after all.

"Tough shit. We're going. I'm going to get my jacket for you."

He turned away.

"Don't," Ethan implored him after a moment's hesitation. "Please, just don't. I don't need them."

Paul glanced at him over his shoulder. The storm was back in his eyes and this time it was deeper than before. Paul didn't have to see into his mind to see the anticipation of something horrible that awaited him if he left here with more than when he arrived.

"Yes. You do. You asked me if there was anything you could do for me."

Ethan pressed his lips together.

"And there is," Paul went on, fighting to keep his voice firm and level. "I want you to come with me to buy you some clothes."

"Why?" Ethan whispered, his world resting on that one word.

"*Why*?" Paul stared down at him. "Because the clothes you have on now are filthy and I don't want you sitting on my furniture while you're wearing them, all right? Is that a good enough reason for you?"

It seemed to calm him a little.

Without another word, he got his jacket and handed it to Ethan. He dug another out for himself and they left the apartment.

The drive to Wal*Mart was riddled with silence and tension. A few times, Paul looked over at the kid just to make sure he was still there. His hands tightened around the steering wheel. He knew that he shouldn't be doing this. He didn't even know why he was bothering. When the kid went back to wherever he came from, he wouldn't take the clothes with him. So why waste the time?

Because maybe if he didn't look like a whore, the whole situation would be a little bit easier to tolerate. You're about three steps away from losing your mind as it is.

You are full of shit, he told himself. *There's a real reason why you're doing this and you're too chicken-shit to face it.*

He shut that voice up right away.

He found a parking spot away from the store. He cut the engine and turned to Ethan, who huddled against the door, staring blankly out the windshield.

"I think it'll go faster if I go alone," he said.

"Of course," came the soft reply.

"I won't be long. You stay put, got it? Don't open the door for anyone."

"Yes."

Paul stared at him, wanting to ask if he liked anything in particular but then changed his mind. He cranked the heat up then left the car running, locking the doors behind him.

The cold wind bit at his face, blowing snow and ice around like chips of iron. His eyes watered and he quickened his step. The spot between his shoulders itched and he glanced back at his Jeep. He could barely make out the little blond head in the window and he wondered if he should've brought the kid in with him.

Too much attention, he reasoned. *Too much to worry about.*

The air inside the store was noisy and stifling. He unzipped his coat as he made his way through the crowds of people, feeling his nerves jump at the too-close proximity of so many bodies. He located the boys' department quickly by following the sound of shrieking children.

"Mommy!"

"I want that one!"

"I want it! Now!"

"Noooooo!"

His step quickened desperately. All around him, mothers were pushing shopping carts teeming with wild, snot-faced, red-cheeked children. Children who were reaching, reaching, reaching with grubby, grasping fingers. There were a few fathers in the mix, who shared sympathetic looks with one another as they caught escaping five-year-olds, who struggled to climb bravely from the prison-like confines of their strollers in an attempt to get closer to the racks of neat, brightly-colored clothes. The surrealism of his environment made Paul wonder if he was, in fact, still in some kind of warped sleep cycle. But if that were true, then the headache behind his eyes wouldn't be hurting this much.

In and out had been the plan. Surely shopping for a kid who wasn't his shouldn't be too difficult but it was proving to be the hardest, most confusing thing Paul had ever attempted. It was a vast sea of shining racks filled with pants, shirts, jeans, pajamas and coats, reasonably priced, Paul guessed, and boasting colorful themes, unrecognizable cartoon characters, and weird graphics resembling skeletons and lettering that didn't even seem like English. Where did anyone even begin in this quagmire of cheap fabric and complete disorganized chaos? More importantly, how did anyone shop for a child according to age? What if the shirt or pants didn't match because someone had a large three-year-old? What if someone had a six-year-old who wasn't the proper height as designed by the charts that labeled what each child, at a certain age, should be? He had half a mind to run back out to the car, drag Ethan in here and tell him to pick out whatever he wanted. Surely, he would know what would fit him and what wouldn't. But that would only raise suspicion, since the kid had nothing but an oversized coat, a dirty tank-top and a pair of torn jeans, looking like he'd been dragged in off the street…literally. And it was freaking cold outside. How would it look if he was walking around with a kid who was dressed like that when it was twenty below?

Paul sighed in aggravation as he moved to a somewhat less noisy section of the store, brushing through T-shirts, jeans, and coats for older kids.

Definitely older, he thought absently.

Ethan was not a child. At least not in the sense of a shirt with Sponge Bob on it. He selected a few plain T-shirts.

"Paul?"

He spun around and his eyes bulged. "Kelly?"

"Oh, my God," she said, smiling uncertainly, coming toward him. "How—How are you?"

He floundered gracelessly. The sight of her was like an arrow through his chest and his senses rose up to embrace her. Dark wisps of her hair had escaped from her ponytail, framing her lovely face. He could smell her expensive perfume, sweet and musky, knowing that if he put his nose behind her ear, that's where the scent would be the strongest. Her full lips gleamed with the pale pink lip gloss that he loved on her. It would taste like berries, he knew, and he licked his own lips as if he could taste it. The urge to do just that filled his heart like a balloon. Her eyes traveled over him and he wanted to dive into their emerald depths and never come up for air again. He flushed slightly under her gaze and the uncertain smile on her lips became more certain, more familiar. He wondered what she would do if he caught her in his arms and planted a nice big wet kiss right on her berry-flavored lips. He wondered if she would wiggle deliciously against him, push him away, or tug him closer. He wondered if she wore that lip gloss for anybody else.

"I'm—I'm okay, I'm good," he finally managed to say. "How are you?"

She shrugged, trying for nonchalance. But she kept smoothing her hair back from her face and Paul knew that was a sign that she was nervous.

"I'm good," she said, shifting her weight from one foot to the other. "I'm good. You know, hanging in, working."

He glanced down at the blue vest she wore over her clothes. "Here?"

She raised an eyebrow, her smile fading. "Every Saturday, Paul, or did you forget already?"

"Oh right, right," he said, feeling like a jerk. "Yeah, sorry, I—I forgot."

"Obviously."

"You, uh, you look good, Kel. You really do."

She rolled her eyes. "It hasn't been that long."

"Yes, it has."

She looked at him. Something unreadable flashed through her eyes and her brow furrowed a bit.

"You sure you're okay?"

"Yeah. Yeah, why?"

"You look…tired."

He bit the inside of his cheek. "Yeah, I…well, I haven't really been sleeping good lately. Work's been rough. I've been traveling a lot more and it's just…it's just hard to catch up, you know?"

Her lips pursed as if she were contemplating believing what he just said. A knowing sparkle gleamed in her eye. "Sounds like you need a vacation," she said.

"Yeah," he said, chuckling too loudly. "Yeah, I do, actually. A nice, long vacation with no interruptions."

She folded her arms over her chest but it wasn't a defensive gesture. It was coy, especially when she closed the distance between them, looking up at him through her long, dark lashes. Paul stared down at her, letting himself get roped in.

"My cousin still works for that travel agency," Kelly murmured, tilting her face up to his. "I'm sure he could get you some pretty good deals on some place…exotic."

The last word rolled off her tongue and he inhaled, her scent filling his head.

"Yeah?" he said hoarsely.

She nodded. "Yup. That is…if you want to. I'm sure you wouldn't want to go by yourself. Someplace exotic? You want to share that with someone, right?"

He nodded, his voice stuck in his throat as her fingers played with the zipper on his coat.

"I miss you, Paul," she whispered. "I really do. I thought I was doing the right thing by leaving you but now, seeing you again. I still want you. Do you want me?"

She pressed her body against his and he couldn't help it. He dropped the shirts that he held in his hands and reached out, gripping her waist and darting for her shiny, pink lips. Chuckling, she ducked at the last minute, stepping back out of his grasp.

He blinked at her. "I've missed you, too," he admitted.

She smiled at him and there were so many things promised in that smile that Paul was glad that he wore loose jeans today.

Suddenly the loud speaker blared to life from above them. "All associates please report to the front for cashier assistance. All associates please report to the front for cashier assistance."

The spell between them now broken, Kelly took another step back from him, her face flushed.

"Well," she said with an embarrassed laugh. "I guess that's my cue."

He rubbed at the back of his neck, trying to clear the lustful fog from his head. She leaned down to pick up the shirts that he dropped.

She shook them out and started to hand them to him when she froze. He frowned.

"Kel? Hey, you okay, babe?"

She stared at the shirts then slowly, she raised her eyes to his face. She looked like someone had just told her that the world was ending and she had ten seconds to live. In that instant, he knew with startling clarity, with dawning horror what she was seeing.

"Who are these for?" she asked, her lips barely moving.

A hot flush spread around his collar. "It's not…Kel, it's—"

"Who are you shopping for, Paul?

"I—"

"These are boys' T-shirts. You're in the boys' department. What possibly reason would you have to shop in the boys' department, Paul?" Her face hardened as anger threatened to take over all rational though.

"I wasn't—I was just looking—"

"Looking?" she cut in, her voice as hard as steel. "You were just *looking* through boys' clothes and just *carrying* some T-shirts around for what? Shits and giggles?"

"No," he insisted, squirming. "Look, it's not—"

"What? It's not what?" she spat at him.

Back to square one.

She threw the shirts at him. "Tell me what it's fucking *not*!"

He flinched, letting them drop to the floor. People within earshot turned to watch, whispering and pointing. She shoved her finger in his face, her pretty features trembling, her eyes glassy with tears.

"Tell me, Paul. Tell me that it's not what it looks like, that it's not what I think it is."

He reached for her. She stepped quickly back, cringing back as if his hands oozed with toxic goop.

"Don't touch me," she snarled. "You've got a lot of fucking nerve coming here, knowing that I would be here—"

"Kel, I forgot that you worked here—"

"Fuck you, you forgot. You forgot to tell me a lot of things, didn't you? Forgot to tell me where you going all those times you left in the middle of the night. Forgot to tell me who the hell calls you at all hours of the day. Forgot to tell me that you were taking care of some whore's child when you should've been with me!"

He groaned. "Kel, no, Jesus Christ, there's no kid—"

Except if you count the one that was given to me as a gift.

Kelly's mouth trembled as she struggled to keep her voice down. Tears trembled on the ledges of her eyelids.

"How old is he, Paul? How old? Ten, eleven? Who's the lucky lady you knocked up? Who's the lucky lady that you pay child support to every month? God, you are such an asshole! How could you not tell me? I can't believe this. What the hell is wrong with you?"

"I—"

"How could you not tell me that you're a father? What, are you embarrassed? Are you ashamed? How the hell can you be ashamed of your own kid? You are sick! You are sick and you need help. God, you need so much help."

She turned to walk away from him but he grabbed her arm and pulled her back.

"Will you let me explain?" he demanded.

She tore her arm away. "I don't want to hear it. I don't want to hear anything you have to say ever again. You stay away from me, you got that? And take care of that damn kid. Try not to skip out on him the way you've skipped out on me."

The small crowd of onlookers parted for her as she stormed away. Paul stared after her. *She honestly thinks I kept a child from her?*

The urge to laugh bubbled up the back of his throat. It was completely absurd and yet strangely true. He did have a child, only not until recently. He wondered how she would react if he took her out to see Ethan, who was, no doubt waiting patiently for his return. What she would do if he actually let him explain how it all came to be? Would she still walk away? Would she want to help? Would she even believe him?

Probably not. She'd walk away quicker than the first time.

Fighting back a nauseating mixture of frustration and hopelessness, he picked the clothes up off the floor. He felt sick and clammy, not to mention mortified at the amount of people who'd overheard their argument. He pushed through them, ignoring the dirty looks and the shaking heads.

"Typical," someone muttered.

"Can't trust anybody nowadays," someone else said.

"Everybody's got a past. Everybody's got secrets."

"People need to do background checks before they start dating somebody. It's the only way to be sure who the hell it is that you're letting into your life."

"Dude should've been on *Maury*."

"You *are* the father."

That was met with laughter and Paul hurried away from the department, clutching his armload of clothes. He paid for everything with cash and had the cashier cram everything into one bag. Zipping up his coat, he left the store, allowing the frigid air to clear his head. As he crossed the parking lot, he let out a small, bitter laugh.

Ridiculous. Absolutely fucking ridiculous. Could things get any more fucked up?

Then he saw the three kids by his Jeep.

His step slowed as he watched them press against the passenger-side window as if they were drooling over a coveted toy in a store window. As Paul neared them, he could hear their voices, taunting and cracked-through by puberty not yet finished and cruel in a way that only kids could be.

"Come on, Twinkie, open the door."

"We just wanna talk to ya."

"Let us in, ya little faggot. Fucking cold out here. Think you're better than us, sitting inside this car? How many dicks did ya suck for that jacket? Ya know Jack's gonna be pissed when he hears about this."

Paul felt the back of his brain itch when he heard that name but he didn't dwell on it; especially not when one of the kids popped open a pocketknife and began to tap it gently against the window.

"Open up, Twinkie."

"Come on, don't make us bust out the window of this nice automobile."

"You do that and I'll rip the money it takes to fix it out of your ass," Paul said, approaching them from the side, near the back fender of the vehicle.

They turned as one and Paul was momentarily stunned at the stark contrast between their hollowed, emaciated appearance and the harsh malice in their voices. They were older than Ethan, probably in their early teens. Scruffy-looking, yet clean, which meant they belonged to someone—most likely this Jack character. Again, Paul refused to dwell on the name. They were dressed against the cold better than Paul was with puffy parkas, gloves, tight knit caps pulled down low over their eyebrows, and baggy jeans that could probably fit two more bodies inside. Looking at each one of them in turn, Paul felt everything raging inside of him settle and quiet.

This he knew how to deal with.

"I'll thank you kindly for getting the fuck away from my car," he said.

"Chill out, mister. We're just saying hi," sneered the kid with the knife.

He talked with a slight lisp and looked like he was missing a few teeth. The two kids on either side of him fanned out, keeping their eyes on Paul. Paul slowly blew the air out of his body, his eyes flicking continuously from one kid to the other.

"With a knife?" he asked.

"Can't be too careful. Lots of crazy fuckers out here." This came from the kid on his right. He had the darkest eyes Paul had ever seen and the sporadic patches of hair on the lower half of his face suggested the attempts of growing facial hair.

"True," Paul agreed. "So why bother saying hi at all?"

Snow crunched underfoot to his left and it sounded closer than it should've been. Paul tossed his bag of purchases to the side while grabbing at the coat of the kid charging him. He caught a quick glance of ice-cold blue eyes and a partly-healed split bottom lip before he spun the kid around with practiced eased and yanked his right arm partway up his back. The howl that came from the kid was high-pitched and filled with surprise and pain. Paul twisted the kid's arm higher, feeling the bones shift to the point of breaking beneath his hand. He looked down and saw the small tire iron at the kid's feet. Banding his other arm around the kid's chest to keep him immobile, he addressed the other two, who looked torn between making a run for it and trying to work up the nerve to carry out what their friend couldn't.

"Why don't we try this again?" Paul said, calmly. "Why would you want to say hi to someone with a knife?"

"Jesus, take it easy, man."

"Put the knife away and I'll take it easy," Paul replied, adding some pressure on the wrist in his hand.

The kid rose up his toes. Paul could almost hear his teeth grinding together.

"Okay, okay," the kid with the knife said.

Paul watched him as he closed the blade and put it into his pocket. He looked at each one of them in turn.

"What's your name?"

The kid rolled his eyes. "You want to get acquainted now? Show me twenty bucks and I'll think about it."

"You're going to need a lot more than that when I break his arm."

"Oh, for—all right, all right, I'm Kyle. That's John and the one whose arm you're about to break is Gavin. Now will you get the fuck off him?"

"See that kid in the car?"

Kyle didn't even look. "What about him?"

"Do you know him?"

"Why the fuck would you ask me that?"

"Because of Jack."

Kyle's left eye twitched. "None of your fucking business."

"I think it is especially after...what's your name again? Gavin? Yeah, Gavin here tried to bash my head in with a tire iron. Now I'm pretty convinced that if I hadn't shown up when I did, you would've broken through my car window to get at Ethan—"

"Ethan?" John suddenly laughed and Kyle joined in. "Ethan? You fucking serious?"

"That's not his name?"

"His name's Twinkie, dude. Give me a fucking break."

"Why Twinkie?"

Kyle smirked. "You're fucking him, aren't you? You tell me."

Paul shoved Gavin away from him, sending him skidding to his knees in the snow. Kyle and John helped him to his feet. Seething, Paul snatched up the tire iron and stalked over to Gavin as he turned to face him. Gavin took a step back, cradling his wrist against his chest. Paul loomed over him, grabbed Gavin's uninjured wrist and slapped the tire iron into his hand.

"Get the fuck out of here," he hissed.

John pulled Gavin back but Kyle stayed put, staring up at Paul like he was contemplating something. Paul looked back at him. The moment stretched, filling the space between them with sounds of traffic, broken bits of conversation and the hush of the wind. Then Kyle's gaze flicked away. Paul followed it and saw him looking at Ethan through the window. Paul started to take a step forward but then Kyle's gaze returned to his. The malice that burned there was palpable and the *I haven't touched him* tasted sick and desperate on the back of Paul's tongue. He swallowed against it, knowing it was useless. He almost wanted Kyle to take a swing at him. Maybe it would stop him from looking at Paul with that disgusting gleam in his eye.

Kyle suddenly turned and walked away, his stride stiff but quick. He joined John and Gavin and they continued across the parking lot. Paul watched them until they were out of sight. A sense of unaccountable loss set off a niggling in his brain and the rage that he had felt earlier dwindled into a dull ache at the backs of his eyes. He retrieved his bag of purchases and got in the car. Chucking the bag into the backseat, he slammed the door shut, letting the silence ring in his ears. Staring out of the windshield, he felt his chest constrict beneath a heavy wave of anxiety. An edge of blackness began to eat at his peripheral vision until it felt as if a cloud of tiny black flies was engulfing his head. It was too thick, too heavy with air that he couldn't keep in his lungs. As much as he tried to tell himself that he'd forgotten that Kelly worked here on Saturdays, he really hadn't. He wanted to see her. He wanted to talk to her, to feel like himself again, to have the life he'd had before this magnificent shit-storm deposited itself on his head. Kelly had seemed almost…happy to see him too as if she'd been waiting for him. But like every other woman, she jumped to conclusions and instead of hearing him out, she walked away. Again.

'*How could you not tell me you're a father?*'

He wanted to laugh but couldn't muster up the energy. He looked over at Ethan who was carefully not looking at him. He started the car, clicking on his seatbelt. As they left the parking lot, he said, "Friends of yours?"

Ethan turned his face away. "Not really."

"But you know them?"

"Yes."

"Why do they call you Twinkie?"

The mention of the name made Ethan's head spasm a bit like there'd been a twitch in his neck muscles.

"You don't really want to know, do you?"

It was the most straight-forward answer Paul had received from the kid and in his shock he almost rolled through a stop-light. He hit the brakes and looked over at him. Ethan stared out of the windshield, his little jaw clenched tight. Paul looked away, deciding that no, he didn't really want to know.

CHAPTER 14

D inner time rolled around. Paul made sandwiches and he and Ethan ate in silence. The only noise was the hum of the washing machine which held Ethan's new wardrobe. After arriving back at the apartment, the urge to wear Paul down seemed to leave the kid altogether. He didn't say a word except a murmured, "Thank you" when Paul put a sandwich in front of him. He didn't look at him and his thin shoulders were slumped almost dejectedly. Paul watched him thoughtfully, wondering if Ethan was really giving up that easily or if maybe those three kids in the Wal*Mart parking lot had something to do with his current state of defeat.

Not wanting to dwell on it, Paul heard the washing machine stop. He left the table to put the clothes in the dryer.. When he came back to the table, it was like he'd never left. Ethan still sat across from him, eating slowly, as if savoring every bite. He didn't look up as Paul sat down. Paul had a weird idea that maybe the kid was mad at him. Or embarrassed.

Twinkie, the other kids had called him. It didn't sound like a name to be proud of.

At long last, the dryer went off. Paul rose from the table as Ethan swallowed the last bit of his sandwich. Not wasting a second, Paul ushered him up to bed with his arms loaded with freshly-washed and dried clothes. Paul tried to not to notice when Ethan discreetly stuck his face into the clothes on top of the pile, breathing in the scent of dryer sheets and warmth.

It was something Paul did all the time, too.

Christ.

When the bedroom door was finally closed with Ethan tucked away inside, Paul let the bone-deep exhaustion crash over him. His eyes began to close even as he toed off his boots and collapsed onto the couch.

Within minutes he was asleep.

The next thing he knew he was being rudely awakened by someone pounding on his front door. Frowning and cursing under his breath, he struggled off the couch. His joints popped and the muscles in his neck twitched painfully. He winced at the dry-cotton taste in his mouth and glanced at the clock.

8:03 a.m.

Jesus, he'd been asleep for nearly twelve hours and he still felt like he'd been hit by a truck. The knocking grew louder and more impatient.

"Somebody better be dead," he muttered.

He fell against the door as he fiddled with the locks and bolts. The knocking ceased as he gripped the doorknob. The silence was beautiful and he had a moment to think, *That's more like it*, before the doorknob began to turn in his palm. He blinked then felt the door push against him. Startled and more awake now, he slammed his shoulder into it, shutting it with a sharp click and engaged the deadbolt.

"Who the fuck is it?" he demanded through the door.

"Paul. I suggest you open this fucking door right now."

Fuck.

He threw a quick glance over his shoulder, looking up at the bedroom door.

"I'm not going to ask again," Aaron threatened through the door.

Paul took a deep breath, hesitantly undoing the deadbolt.

The door flew open, slamming back against the wall as Paul danced back to save his toes.

Aaron stormed in, his rage swooping out in front of him like a shockwave.

"Hey…Aaron, what—"

The words stuck in his throat as Aaron came toward him. His eyes flashed like black diamonds, his face thinned and void of any color until it looked skeletal. There was a reason why Aaron locked his anger in a carefully constructed box, letting it out only through cold smiles and cruel, biting words. Anything more had the power to make an atheist think about God. Paul tried to keep ahead of Aaron's determined stride but his back met the wall.

"What—" he tried again.

"Shut the fuck up," Aaron hissed in his face.

Paul's mind worked frantically, trying to think of something he might've done that would piss Aaron off this much.

"Would you mind telling me if you are in possession of a working brain?" Aaron asked.

Paul could only stare dumbly at him.

"From that expression on your face, I'm going to assume that the answer to that is a big, fat no."

"What happened? What's wrong?"

Aaron moved closer, crowding him against the wall, his eyes burning into his. "Oh, I see. *Now* you're concerned?"

"I—"

"*Now* you give a shit? *Now* you care about the consequences of your actions? Do you have any idea what you've cost me?"

"No, not really."

Aaron moved his head back, studying him. "No," he repeated. "Of course you don't."

His eyes suddenly moved over Paul's face, down his neck, his collarbone, chest, stomach and lower, in a slow, lazy perusal that made Paul's skin tighten. He shifted uncomfortably and the movement snapped Aaron's gaze back to his face.

"You seem tense, Paul. Is the little munchkin not performing as well as we'd hoped?"

"It's...he's all right."

"Just all right?" Aaron sneered. "I'm rather surprised. I was so sure he was money well-spent. Or do you just not shit where you sleep?" He jerked his head toward the blankets that lay crumpled in a heap at one end of the couch.

"I'm just...I'm giving him a break."

Aaron smiled, humorlessly. "A break? How nice. How about giving me a break, Paul?"

"Aaron, what did I—"

"Does the name Greene's Diner mean anything to you?"

"No."

Giving a curt nod, Aaron pushed away from him and started a leisurely pace back and forth in front of him.

"There was a disturbance there a few days ago, in the early morning hours. Two gentlemen, thoroughly inebriated according to a cute waitress named Stephanie, were acting rather crudely to a certain blond customer who was eating breakfast with his son."

"Oh. That."

Aaron fixed him with a look. "So you know what I'm talking about?"

Paul hesitated. "That—I—those guys were being complete assholes. It was after two in the morning, I was tired, the kid was on the verge of hypothermia and all I wanted to do was get some food and get the hell home—"

"The kid?"

"What?"

"Don't you mean the whore?"

Paul barely stopped himself from glaring at him. "Yes, the kid, the whore, whatever—"

"No, no, no," Aaron cut in, coming toward him again. "Not whatever. I didn't give you a *kid*. I gave you a *whore*. It might be in your best interest to remember that. I didn't give him to you so you could adopt him, for Christ's sake."

"Does it matter?"

"You're goddamn right it matters."

"We just stopped to get something to eat. What good would he do me if he was half-starved? Didn't you say you wanted your money's worth?"

Aaron's dark eyes flashed and in one fluid motion, reached into his coat and pulled out a gun.

Panic exploded through Paul's chest. "Aaron—"

"Well, well," he spat. "Getting laid seems to put quite a mouth on you, doesn't it?"

Paul eyed the gun then met Aaron's gaze. "No. I just—"

"What?" Aaron cut in again, closing the distance between them and shoving the gun under Paul's chin, forcing his head back.

Paul choked on his breath, his hands scrambling uselessly at the wall behind him.

"What the fuck are you thinking, Paul? What's going on in that itty bitty brain of yours? Come on. Tell me. You used to tell me everything. Remember? You never hesitated. And now what? I can't even read you anymore. I don't know what you're thinking, what you're doing. To be honest, it's making me a little nervous."

Paul tried to meet his eyes but Aaron only shoved the gun in harder, keeping his head back. He could feel Aaron's breath against his neck.

"And you know what happens when I get nervous, don't you?" Aaron's lips brushed the side of his throat.

It felt like dead fish.

There was a *click* as Aaron turned off the safety on the gun. Paul felt the bottom drop out of his stomach.

"Aaron—" he squeezed out. "Don't—"

Aaron took the gun away and dug his free hand into Paul's hair. He yanked hard, pulling Paul's face down to his. Being this close to Aaron when he was so mad, Paul was surprised he didn't smell sulfur.

"Yes," Aaron breathed against his lips. "Yes, you know what happens, don't you?"

His fingertips pressed into the back of Paul's skull, bringing him closer. A small strangled sound made its way out of Paul's throat as Aaron's mouth hovered dangerously close to his. He felt the gun trace a faint path across his chest to where his heart was thundering in his rib cage.

"You know *exactly* what happens."

The words pushed Aaron's breath into his mouth. A drop of sweat inched down the back of Paul's neck.

Jesus, don't. Don't—

Then Aaron released him, stepping back from him so quickly that Paul nearly toppled forward. When he regained his balance, Aaron was already leaving, closing the front door quietly behind him. He blinked several times, breathing hard. He stared at the door.

Seconds ticked by.

Then minutes.

Bit by bit, muscle by muscle, nerve by nerve, he let his body sag against the wall. He bought a shaking hand to his jaw. When he was sure he could walk without his legs buckling, he went to relock the door. It took a few tries since his hands wouldn't stop shaking. A prickling sensation raced up the back of his neck and his lungs squeezed and burned. The room tilted. With a small gasp, he put his hands on the door for balance and swallowed back the vomit that rose in his throat. Slowly he turned his head to stare out the window. The day beyond was gray and muffled with the onslaught of snow. The city was barely visible, like a fuzzy blanket had been thrown over every-thing. He felt a jolt in his heart.

White. Blank. Empty.

Like him.

Like his life.

'And you know what happens when I get nervous, don't you?'

He squeezed his eyes shut, shaking his head as a torrent of emotion ripped through him.

Denial, fear, rage.

Each one spiked into him like a blow of both heat and ice, pain and numbness, power and weakness that stroked a willingness to both ac-cept what Aaron was saying and reject it. He'd been taught to embrace that he would never become more than what he was already. Broken into a million pieces then built up by someone other than himself. Al-ways judged and ruled by anyone but himself and always at the price of all that he was worth. His whole life was about power and none of it was his. Every movement, every thought had never been his, every dollar he'd earned was at the expense of a life. A life that amounted to countless other lives over the years.

And for what?

The question jarred his eyes open and for one crystal-clear mo-ment, he knew and it was the surest, most solid thing he had ever known. The most concrete thought that he ever possessed and one he could call all his own.

A deadly thought but one nonetheless.

It was the only way.

Aaron would kill him. He was sure of that.

He can try. But he won't succeed. He trained me too well.

He squared his shoulders and pushed away from the door. He headed upstairs to pack for the last time. He threw open the bedroom door and froze.

CHAPTER 15

The kid sat in the center of the bed, blankets piled around him like a cotton fortress. His hair was a tousled halo and the side of his face was marked with creases from the pillows. He had a white-knuckled grip on the blankets in his lap. Paul stared at him, feeling his hand begin to sweat against the doorknob. The stark morning light lit up the room and the inside of Paul's head like a thousand-watt bulb. There was nothing at that moment that could've made what was happening more real, more nerve-wracking. It was all suddenly as bare and noticeable as the finger-shaped bruises on the kid's shoulders.

"Is he coming back?"

The question echoed in the room like glass shattering on a hardwood floor. Paul unstuck his hand from the doorknob and took a hesitant step into the room. Ethan's eyes were glued to the bed, but the frail bones in his forearms moved as he clenched and unclenched his hands.

"I don't know," Paul replied. "Not at the moment anyway."

Ethan's shoulders seemed to sag and his head hung farther until his chin touched his chest. Paul moved toward his closet, keeping his eyes on the figure in his bed as if he were some deranged, bloodthirsty animal.

"But I'm not going to be here to find out," he went on. "And neither are you."

Ethan's head snapped up. Paul turned quickly to the closet doors and swung them open, the muscles in his back trembling under the weight of his own words. Staring incredulously at the clothes hanging in front of him, he hoped to find his brain hanging off a pair of jeans or dangling from a sweatshirt or maybe stuffed inside one of his boots on the floor. Because maybe he was as brainless as Aaron had suggested if Paul would imply *anything* that sounded like…*hope*.

Swallowing hard against the sand in his throat, he threw his duffel bag on the floor by his feet and began yanking clothes off hangers.

Just like Kelly, he thought bitterly.

As he packed, he could feel Ethan's eyes on the back of his neck. Ignoring it the best that he could, he turned away from the closet and went to the bed. He threw the bag on top of the blankets, shoved everything in and zipped it shut. He dropped to his knees and rummaged under the bed. The bed shifted above him and he looked up to find Ethan's face inches from his own. His eyes were big and uncertain.

"You're taking me with you?"

"Would you rather stay here?"

He paused then said, "Kind of."

Paul blinked at him. "Why?"

Ethan looked away, his fingers pulling restlessly at the corner of the quilt. Paul vaguely thought it was the one thing that Kelly had forgotten to take with her.

"Well, the bed…is nice and the shower—"

Paul straightened to his feet. Ethan immediately scooted back, gathering the blankets to his chest like he was suddenly shy.

"Look," Paul ground out through clenched teeth. "I'm glad you like it here. I like it here too. But if we stay, we're dead. Do you understand that?"

"If I go with you, I'll be dead anyway so it won't make much of a difference."

He said it so matter-of-factly that it took Paul a second to process it. "You think I'm going to kill you?"

"Not you."

"Who then?"

Ethan's eyes wandered away again, fixing on a point in the corner of the room. The blankets were pulled up to his chin now. Paul stared at his profile. In the back of his mind, he could feel time ticking away. He could feel it beating against the inside of his rib cage, urgently, inevitably, like thousands of butterfly wings. There was something alongside it, more like a thrashing of cat-o'-nine tail—the grim realization that they were each going to suffer the same fate at different hands, no matter if they stayed or ran. Aaron would, no doubt, grind Paul up and sell him as fertilizer. Ethan, on the other hand, would be put in an unmarked grave at a construction site and covered with concrete.

It sent a sickly jolt through his chest.

What a way to go, he thought to himself. *A lifetime taking orders and being led around by the balls and what do I have to show for it? Then there's this sorry-ass kid in front of me now who's barely been around long enough to put a dent in anything and all he's going to amount to is a six-foot-deep hole that no one's going to miss.*

The jumbled thoughts that were roller-coasting up and around his brain came to an abrupt halt. He'd never been good at doing nothing and he wasn't about to start now. If he'd learned anything from Aaron after nearly two decades, it was how to survive.

And this was no exception.

He'll make your death last forever. You'll be begging for it before he's done with you. True enough, Paul thought after a small mental pause.

He dropped to the floor again, pulling out a smaller black bag from beneath the bed. Squatting down on the balls of his feet, he unzipped it and began checking and double-checking the safeties on the guns, the buckles on the knife sheaths and the extra ammunition. Feeling Ethan's eyes on him, he deliberately pulled a K-bar blade from its thick, black sheath, holding it up until the light caught the edge, dancing along in a thin silver streak. Paul gripped it tightly. It felt good in his hand.

"You're really going to leave?" Ethan asked in a hushed voice.

Paul looked at him. "Yes. You coming or not?"

Ethan fumbled with the blankets. "But where will you go?"

"Haven't figured that part out yet."

Putting the knife away, he looked back up at the kid who was giving him a deep, searching look. An eternity lapsed between them until finally there came a quiet, "Okay."

Paul felt something loosen in his chest. "Get dressed. I'll meet you downstairs."

CHAPTER 16

The snow was practically a blindfold around Paul's eyes as he maneuvered his Jeep down the unplowed street. His hands were sweaty against the steering wheel and every now and then, he would bite his lip too hard and taste blood. The taste made him doubt but he didn't have the strength to turn around. If he went back, he was dead. Hell, if he stayed, he was dead.

'*You know what happens when I get nervous, don't you*?'

So either way the road he was on was leading him straight into the mouth of madness. Ethan was in the seat next to him, his eyes animated, almost happy. At least one of them was. Paul hadn't been able to shake the feeling of crosshairs on him since leaving his apartment. With each passing second, the feeling grew stronger until it felt like a brand was being pressed into the back of his neck.

With another quick glance in the rearview, he turned into a corner gas station. The tires slid in the snow as he stomped on the brakes. The Jeep skidded to a halt at a gas pump and the attendant approached cautiously, a blurred dark shape in the blinding rush of snow.

"Stay here," he said to Ethan. "I'll be right back."

Ethan nodded, his lips quirking in an almost-there smile. Paul groaned inwardly before climbing from the car.

Madness. Not to mention suicidal.

"Fill it up," he barked at the attendant before fleeing inside the gas station.

The air was stifling and dry, stinging his eyeballs, assaulting his nostrils with stale body odor and walk-in freezers. He was the only customer. The clerk behind the counter spared him a look then went back to the magazine he was leafing through. Paul hurried along the small aisles, grabbing snacks and drinks, his brain helpfully reminding him again and again that he was a fucking dead man. His fingers trembled and he dropped a bag of chips then a bottle of soda. He scrambled after them, earning an eye-roll from the clerk.

Paul stopped at a small rack of maps, considered buying a few of them to at least give him some kind of direction to head in. Running away wasn't the hard part. It was where he would end up that was worse.

"You seem lost," someone said from behind him.

The voice was clipped, husky and Paul would've ignored it if it hadn't been so taunting. Frowning, he turned around.

The woman who stood in front of him was stunning and cold, colder than the air outside. She was beautiful in that dangerous way that made men go broke, kill their wives, or take out absurdly expensive life insurance policies. And she stared at Paul like she wanted to break every single one of his ribs. The sight of her set off every alarm in his head. A second ago he and the clerk had been the only ones in the store. Now here she was, her strange, caramel-colored eyes focused on him so severely that it bordered on downright uncomfortable.

Nothing about her invited a reply to her comment. The smooth haughty planes of her face, the chocolate-brown of her hair that was swept back in a tight ponytail and the long red coat she wore with black stiletto boots all shouted, "No bullshit." She was eerily out of place next to a huge display of Frosted Flakes and a life-sized cardboard cutout of Tony the Tiger. Her hands were hidden inside her coat pockets. She was just beyond arm's reach but that did little for the fissure of awareness that went down his spine.

She was here for him.

Wow. That was fast.

Paul's first instinct was to drop her on the spot. But that instinct was dampened by the surprise that Aaron wasn't here to do the job himself. He'd always been very specific about what he would do to Paul if he ever left him. He would never give the glory to someone else, let alone a woman, even if she *was* gorgeous.

He's playing games, Paul thought to himself. *He probably thinks it'll get my guard down.*

"No, no, I'm good," he said to her, forcing himself to sound pleasant and non-threatening.

Her eyes never left his as he slowly maneuvered around a rack of potato chips, putting it between them. She moved with him. Her steps were gliding and graceful even with the needle-like heels she wore that pushed her to Paul's eye level.

"Are you?" she asked as if she could've cared less.

"Yeah. Why? Don't I look like I know what I'm doing?"

"Not really."

"That's funny. I feel like I know what I'm doing."

"Do you?"

"Yeah."

"Brave man."

"Am I?"

There was a flicker in her eyes and it took Paul a moment to realize that it was amusement. But it was gone as quickly as it had appeared.

"Yes," she said, her voice dropping even lower until she was practically purring. "You're out all alone when you know you're a wanted man. I'd say that's pretty brave."

He forced out a laugh that hurt his throat. "Or pretty stupid."

"And here I was trying to compliment you."

"You don't seem like the type to hand out compliments."

"You don't seem like the type to accept them."

Paul blinked. Something about this didn't feel right. His eyes flicked down her body to her feet then back up again.

"Who do you work for?"

An arching eyebrow twitched. "Will knowing make it easier for you?"

"Yes."

The ghost of a smile passed over her pale lips and Paul wondered where Aaron had found her. Her beautiful face gave nothing away.

"It's no one you know."

"Would you be offended if I said I didn't believe you?"

This time, one corner of her mouth nearly lifted. "You'll believe me soon enough."

"You know I won't go without a fight."

"I wouldn't expect anything less."

"I hope not."

Her mouth twisted slightly. A small crowd of people came into the gas station then, bringing a rush of cold air and noise. The strange woman chose that moment to move toward him, her steps steady and sure, her gaze unwavering. Paul held himself perfectly still, waiting. Someone brushed past him from behind but he didn't dare look away. Her eyes glowed like they were lit from the inside.

"I think I'd prefer a fight from you," she said, her voice nearly lost in the noise around them.

"You really want to do this in the middle of a public place?"

Minutely, her head tilted to one side. She studied him like he was an insect she wasn't sure if she should kill or not. "When has a public place ever stopped *you*?"

The uneasiness in his gut became painfully heavy.

"Tell me who you work for."

A little boy, no older than five, came streaking around the corner, giggling madly, darting between them hard enough to make them stumble apart.

"Michael! Michael, you come back here right now!"

A frazzle-haired, red-faced woman was not far behind. She pulled herself up short but still managed to shoulder-check Paul. He staggered back, his eyes torn from his adversary.

"Oh, excuse me, I just have to get him," the boy's mother began apologetically then cried, "Michael! Come here!"

The boy darted down another aisle, leaving his mother to scurry after him like a pet owner with a broken leash. Paul's heart gave a heavy *thunk* against his rib cage as he righted himself.

The woman was gone.

He blinked and turned in a circle, once, twice. There was no sign of her red coat, no creepy, caramel-eyed stare, just *poof*, gone. He let the snacks fall from his arms.

"Michael! There'll be no dessert for you tonight, young man!"

The boy was back, laughing like a loon, darting around Paul's legs. He heard the mother apologizing again and again but her voice sounded as if she were speaking through a metal pipe.

"...so sorry about this...gave him an extra cookie during snack-time today..."

Get out. You need to get out right now.

"...never doing that again...Michael!"

Another crowd of people came in, pushing Paul into action. Blindly, he went to the door, tripping over his scattered chips and bottles of soda. He shoved the door open and the frigid air took what little he had left in his lungs. Snowflakes and wind stung his eyes and he wiped at his nose as it began to run.

Something made him turn as the door swung shut behind him.

She was there again, standing next to the Frosted Flakes, watching him. Her eyes drilled into his skull, glittering like diamonds in the sun and the look on her face was ferocious and hateful. Paul saw his life in that gaze, saw it chained and captured like a beast, thrown into a cage and kept there for her own amusement. He suddenly wanted to shoot her, to eliminate this threat because, Jesus Christ, he wasn't even out of the city yet and already people were in his face, threatening to blow it off. But there were too many witnesses. Not even Aaron had enough influence to clean that up quietly. But Paul wondered if she wasn't coming after him for the same reason or if there was an entirely different reason altogether.

Brilliant white light enveloped him and he thought fleetingly, *Oh my God, I didn't feel a thing* before he spun around and saw a car screeching to a halt, headlights blazing, inches from his legs.

"Get the fuck out of the way, man!" the driver shouted.

Muttering a breathless apology, Paul staggered away, making his way toward his vehicle. He half-expected a bullet to shatter his spine.

He got to his Jeep on legs that felt like wet noodles, tossed money at the gas attendant, and dove behind the wheel, slamming the door shut behind him. He sat for a moment, breathing hard, his limbs jittery with adrenaline. The silence of the car soothed his ears and he tried to slow his breathing, tried not to think about how close he'd just come to…

Why didn't she do it? It's why she was here, wasn't it? Was she one of Aaron's? Or was she working for someone else?

Despite the frigid temperatures, the sliver of sweat that traced down Paul's spine was hot and quick.

"You all right?' someone asked from beside him.

He jumped and looked over to see Ethan kneeling on the seat. He was wrapped up in dark blue wool coat and a black knit cap that was pulled down around his ears. The coat as well as the clothes underneath fit him pretty good. Paul had thrown away the clothes that Ethan had arrived in. He'd wanted to burn them but decided that trashing them was a little less attention-grabbing.

Ethan's big eyes blinked curiously at him.

Paul wiped a hand over his face. "Yeah," he said, taking a few deep breaths. "Yeah."

He drove more recklessly than usual along the snow-slicked streets. The four-wheel drive was practically useless and he tried to tell himself to slow down or he was going to end up in a snow drift. But his anxiety was riding high and nothing would calm him until he put a few hundred miles or more between himself and anyone who was going to make a profit off of his head.

Such strange eyes, he thought to himself. *Like the chocolate-covered caramel candies that Mom used to like—*

His foot nearly slid off the gas pedal.

Jesus Christ, get a grip, man!

He blinked hard, trying to clear his head. He could sense Ethan's eyes on him but he stared stubbornly out the windshield, clenching his jaw.

The roads were nearly empty and he didn't have any trouble finding a parking spot in front of St. Christopher's Church. The tires skidded on the ground as he braked to a rough stop. He put the Jeep in park and let it idle.

Sucking in a few more deep breaths, he glanced out the passenger-side window, over the top of Ethan's head, to look at the old, stone structure. It had been years since Paul had been inside and it had definitely seen better days. But it was warm and it was friendly and that's what he remembered most about it. Ethan glanced out the window then met Paul's gaze expectantly.

"Are we going inside?"

Paul looked away, staring at the sweaty marks his palms were making on the steering wheel.

"No. Just you."

He could practically hear the puzzled look come over Ethan's face. "Why—"

"There are people inside who can help you. Who can keep you safe."

His words were met by a silence that stretched and stretched, threatening to snap like a rubber band.

"But—But I thought I was going with you."

"You're not coming with me."

"But you said—"

"I can't keep you safe, Ethan."

More silence.

The spot between his shoulder blades began to itch. He found he had to suppress the urge with some difficulty to simply toss the kid from the car. He had to keep moving. He had to get out of here. Trying to break the bad news as gently as possible was something he did not have time for.

'No! P–Please, you said you wouldn't do that! You promised!'

Paul choked on an inhale of breath. *Oh God. Oh holy Christ, where did that come from?*

His heart was suddenly racing in his chest all over again. Something was swimming through the dark waters of his mind, pushing toward the surface. He braced himself, trying to hold it back, to think of something else in order to stop what was going to come through and consume him.

Suddenly it was there.

He squeezed his eyes shut and he was back in that shadow-filled room, gagging on the scent of his own blood pooling beneath him, mixing with sweat and cum, some of it his and some of it belonging to…

ᏋᏝᏋᏝ

The blade bit into the flesh at the back of his thigh. The bonds that held his wrists over his head were vicious and sharp, making bloody bracelets as he struggled.

"You said you wouldn't, please, you said—"

"Oh, come now, pretty boy. It's a bit late to tell me you're not enjoying this."

The shame, the fear.

"You p—promised—"
"Did I?"
"You said you wouldn't!"
"I lied."
"Please!"

℃℃℃

"I said no!" His eyes flew open as his own voice exploded in his ears. He was back in the car, swallowing back the acrid taste of that memory. "It's better this way," he croaked, running an unsteady hand over his jaw. "It is."

Ethan stared silently at him. Paul looked away.

"I saw you."

Paul glanced at him from the corner of his eye. "What?"

"I saw you, what you did, at the diner. I saw the things you put in those bags when we left your apartment. It's safe with you."

"No."

"Yes, it is,"

"How do you know?" Paul demanded, his hands twisting over the steering wheel hard enough to rip out chunks of it. "How do you know I won't use any of those weapons on you?"

"You won't."

The steely resolve in his tone was unexpected.

"But how do you know?"

Ethan stared steadily back at him, a world of knowledge in his eyes, deep and fathomless. Then he turned toward the window. "We're the same."

Hearing it said aloud was the sucker punch that Paul didn't need. He wanted to shake his head, to give an absolute, without a doubt, fuck-the-world, *hell no*. It boiled in his throat but rose no higher. Closing his eyes, he leaned his head back against the headrest. He couldn't seriously be contemplating this. This was a death-trap. How far could he possibly get with a kid strapped to him? It was too noticeable, not to mention twice as dangerous and ten times more stupid. It practically shouted, *Come shoot me*! *I'm a big fat idiot*!

'We're the same.'

He wondered if Ethan had seen his parents get shot to death, too.

Something slammed into the car.

"What the fuck?" he exclaimed as Ethan was thrown across the center console.

Paul grabbed at him, pushing him gently but firmly back into his seat. Ethan crawled toward the passenger side window, pressing his face against the glass. "What was that?"

"Damned if I know," Paul said as he unbuckled his seatbelt. "Jesus Christ, can't even sit in a parked car without something fucking happening."

He twisted around in his seat, looking out of every window. It was nearly impossible to see. The snow was coming down with a vengeance and visibility was next to nil. He hadn't seen any cars driving by and he didn't think that a bike messenger would be out in this weather. Anyone slipping in the snow wouldn't have made that much of a noise if they had fallen against the car. From what he could see through the snow-covered windows, the streets and sidewalks were deserted.

He stared over Ethan's blond hair, holding very still, waiting for something or someone to reveal itself.

When nothing did, he swung the door open and stepped outside. His boots sank into about three inches of snow and the cold air robbed him of his breath. Ethan spun around.

"Where are you going?"

"Wait here." Paul slammed the door and stood beside the car, casting thorough glances up and down the street. Arching his neck, he looked up at the church in front of him. The small cross-shaped windows in the doors glowed softly through the haze of snow, inviting and beseeching to any lost soul. He let his eyes travel up and up until he could barely make out the steeple, hidden inside a swirling mass of snowflakes.

Snow crunched to his right.

He spun around. His hand was already inside his coat and on the butt of his favorite, never-leave-home-without-it, nickel-plated, nine-millimeter.

His ears buzzed when he saw the tracks leading around the back of the car. Paul's fingers made a surer grip on his weapon.

Inside the car, he could make out Ethan shifting in his seat. Paul's eyes flitted around like a squirrel's as he began a steady march toward the back of the Jeep. His boots crunched through the snow. The sound echoed like gunshots. There would be no element of surprise here. He would have to be fast and with no hesitation. A small part of him wondered if he was over-reacting. It could be just some idiot out, enjoying a prank in the snow and sub-zero temperatures. No harm in that, right?

Except for that woman at the gas station.

If there was one, there would be more to follow.

He rounded the back of the Jeep quickly, keeping low.

No one was there so he kept moving to the opposite side of the vehicle. The tracks kept going around the front of the Jeep now as Paul
came to a stop at Ethan's window. His small face peered up at him,
curious and blurred.

More snow crunched, this time from behind him.

Paul whirled around just in time to see a dark shape duck behind
the tail lights. He pulled his gun from its holster.

The exhaust from the Jeep swirled and ballooned from the vehicle,
into the street, onto the sidewalk, sifting through the air and snow like
ghosts who couldn't quite shape their former selves. It created an almost surreal atmosphere, forming a wispy circle around him, seeming
to cut him off from the rest of the city. Like a dream or a nightmare,
hiding the monster that was going to jump out and get him. The light
from the street lamps that could barely penetrate through the thick
snow illuminated the street in such a way that the buildings and trees
behind it were completely encased in shadows, making them appear
like backdrops for a Broadway play.

He listened. Shifting his grip on the gun, he crept around the back
of the Jeep.

The street was empty.

Fuck, he thought to himself.

He stayed at a crouch, looking around, watching, straining his ears
until he thought his head would explode.

The only sound was the soft blowing of snow falling to the ground.

Growing impatient, he took a few more trips around the Jeep,
searching as quickly and quietly as he could. He wasn't being nearly
as careful as he ought to be but if this fucker he was chasing around
his car like a moron was as cold as he was, maybe Paul would be able
to get the jump on him anyway.

He came up onto the sidewalk once again, walking around to
Ethan's side of the car.

His skin tingled.

Eyes were on him.

That was when he saw a shadow on the steps of the church.

He blinked and through the thick haze of snow saw that it was a
person. He blinked again, more surprised that he was actually looking
at someone.

He raised his weapon. "Hey! What're you doing—"

A tremendous force slammed into him from behind, driving him
forward, off-balance, to his knees in the snow. The gun flew from his
hand. He rose to a crouch and spun around but was barely able to raise
a fist before he was all but thrown against the side of the Jeep. His
shout of surprise was breathless as the air was punched from his lungs.

He caught a glimpse of the shadowy figure moving down the church steps toward him.

There were two of them, he had a moment to think before he threw a hard right and felt it connect.

He stumbled away. The world suddenly jumped as his legs were swept out from under him. His head struck the concrete and everything exploded in yellow and black stars. Snow leaked into his collar. He lay dazed for a moment before struggling to his hands and knees, with only the thought of being beaten and robbed propelling him forward, away from the edge of unconscious. He climbed shakily to his feet, his breath rattling unevenly in his ears.

Fingers gripped his shoulders and pulled him backward. He staggered, trying to keep his feet under him. The back of his head felt wet and he wasn't sure if it was snow or blood. He tried to focus, to see the faces of these sons-of-bitches who were going to grind him up and serve him out as food on a cow farm in Idaho.

Fuck you, Aaron.

He pushed and shoved as he was herded back against the hood of the Jeep. He craned his neck, trying to see through the windshield. But Ethan's face was lost behind the frosted, snow-covered glass.

So much for trying to keep you safe, he thought faintly.

A warm, heavy weight was pressing against his chest and he blinked upward to find an unfamiliar face filling his line of vision.

"Fuck—" Paul gasped out. "Fuck y–you."

Warm breath passed over his lips. Dark eyes, cold and black like marbles, were inches from his own.

"My pleasure," a raspy voice leered as Paul's coat was pulled open.

The collar of his shirt was yanked away from his throat. Pain engulfed his head as it was shoved back and held firmly in place by an unyielding hand beneath his jaw.

"Fucker!" he tried to say, struggling as the weight on his chest became heavier.

No way, no fucking way I'm having my throat cut like a goddamn pig!

There was a pinch at the side of his neck. A wave of heat washed over him. The edges of his vision blackened. His eyelids fought to stay open, to focus but they were drooping until finally, they closed…

CHAPTER 17

Snakes were crawling all over him. Slithering, bone-cold, scaly bodies sliding over his chest, down his legs, curling around his neck, and between his legs. So many, too many. Black ones, brown ones, green ones, yellow, some as thick as a bullwhip, others as thin as pencils. The weight of them was crushing and he couldn't sit up. Couldn't move, paralyzed, unable to sweep away the disgusting ooze of sliminess that covered his body. Panic clawed through him, erupting from his throat in a frenzied scream, only to have it choked off by a bundle of snakes taking advantage of his open mouth and—

꽃꽃꽃

Paul jerked himself awake, coughing around the scream that was locked in his throat. He batted at his chest and legs, swearing he could feel slithering, slimy things sneaking across his body. There was the sound of heavy, uneven breathing in his ears and it took him a second to realize that it was his own and it was echoing around him. He forced himself to stop flailing and took a few deep breaths, struggling to sit up.

A sick wave of nausea nearly pulled him back into unconsciousness and he fell to the floor. He stared up at the ceiling but couldn't see it. He couldn't see anything beyond the black spots dancing thickly in front of his eyes. He tried to take a few deep breaths but bile rose in the back of his throat. He rolled over onto his side, swallowing hard and feeling his head burst in three different places as the vomit found its way out of his mouth. He groaned, coughing and hacking, squeezing his eyes shut. A hand carded through his hair, pushing it back gently from his forehead.

'Shhh, that's it, baby, that's it. Let it come out. There you go.'

There was faint humming, a song, whispered words that sounded familiar and young and looked like innocence and sunshine. Cool lips pressed against his sweaty forehead and he caught a glimpse of beautiful auburn hair and bright blue eyes.

'That's my boy. That's my little man, that's it, almost done. I'll make you a nice bowl of soup when you're done. That'll be gentle on your stomach, okay? It's okay, sweetie. Mommy's here.'

His eyes came open on a scream that reverberated back from so long before and it sounded just as horrible as the day he'd heard it. He blinked several times, aware suddenly of his wet cheeks and the cold. But it wasn't a cold from outside, which bought back a faint memory of struggling with someone in the snow and feeling a needle puncture his neck, but more like an iciness that had settled in his bones, seeped through his skin, through the muscles and joints and took root at the very base of him.

He swallowed hard, wincing at the taste in his mouth and managed to push himself over onto his back. For a moment, he lay there, staring blankly as his mother's voice faded back into his subconscious. A chain rattled somewhere next to him, metallic and dragging. It echoed horribly, sending a fresh wave of hammers banging along the inside of his skull. He shook under the force of it and it took all of his willpower to crane his neck and find the source of the sound.

Ethan.

Paul blinked hard through the rough landscape of shadow and light. The kid's pale blond hair was like a beacon and he focused on that, feeling his mind click and his body awaken from its stupor. He moved slowly into a sitting position. The bones in his head protested and shifted and he bit his tongue on a cry of pain as he was forced back down to the floor.

"Goddamn it," he murmured.

He tightened his jaw and tried again, this time grabbing onto the bars to pull himself up and stay put. He stopped.

Bars?

He squinted and looked around, immediately wishing he'd remained unconscious.

He'd seen worse places. He'd been in worse places and knew the extent and purpose of such places. The room was barren, empty, so that it seemed to have caved in on itself to create something of its own. It was a whole other world full of forgotten stone, cold air, and hidden shadows. A world that seemed ancient, painful, and questionable, where no one bothered to find the answers. The air smelled wet and aged. It was quiet. There wasn't a sound. Not even the scratch of a mouse's claw on the stone floor. But there was the sound of Paul's breathing and it seemed magnified in the large room, as if the room itself was taking in oxygen. It took a while for his eyes to adjust to the dimness. The only light, soft and white as it was, came from electric lamps that glowed from deep narrow grooves set in the walls. They struggled to light up the room; just barely revealing the bottom half of a staircase against the far wall. Other than that, the darkness was thick and complete. Shadows stretched to every corner, across the walls and floor like oozes of black oil, creating a great, black mass, cloaking Paul's sight to near-blindness.

Great. What the fuck is this?

Suddenly, the lights brightened as if someone had turned up the wattage from a light switch. The dark was chased back but it did nothing to make the room any less bleak or to ease the feeling of dread in Paul's gut because now the light allowed him to see the opening in the wall next to his prison cell. A doorway was carved into the stone, low and dark like it was made for things with four legs instead of two. And then there was the drain in the middle of the floor. He fought back a shiver as he turned toward Ethan. It took him two tries before he was finally able to speak louder than a whisper.

Jesus, how long was I out for?

"Ethan?" he croaked. "Ethan, hey buddy. You okay—"

The words died on his lips.

The kid was in his own cage next to Paul's. Metal bars separated them and Ethan was huddled in the far corner.

He was naked.

A metal cuff was around one ankle. A length of chain ran from the cuff to a "D" ring set in the middle of the floor.

Paul stared at him, thinking of the first time he'd seen him, when Aaron had pulled him from the back of that van. There had been a band of raw, discolored flesh around Ethan's ankle, as if he'd been shackled.

Paul saw with despair and a flare of anger that the cuff was securely snapped around the same ankle.

"What the fuck—" he started to say then stopped, breathing deep. "Ethan? Hey, Ethan? You all right? Huh? You okay?"

His only answer was Ethan drawing his legs tighter to his chest and hiding his face against his knees. Faint tremors wracked his body.

Shit, Paul thought. *Shit, shit, shit. Christ, all I wanted to do was get this kid away from this shit. All I had to do was drop him off at that fucking church and he, at least, would've been marginally safer than he is right now.*

So much for that plan.

Gripping the bars with both hands now, he pulled himself to his knees, fighting hard against the rush of sickness that nearly knocked him flat. His brain seemed to lurch and spin with every move he made. Resting his head gently against the bars—he nearly moaned aloud at how nice and cool they were—he fumbled with the buttons on his shirt. His coat was gone and as he shrugged out of his long-sleeved shirt, he could tell that all the weapons that he'd had on his body were gone too.

Someone did a thorough search which was both a good and bad thing. It was good because it told him what kind of people he was dealing with. It was bad because it told him that he was dealing with people who knew what they were doing. Swearing under his breath, he slid his shirt down his arms and rolled it into a ball.

"Ethan? I'm going to throw you my shirt, all right? I want you to put it on, okay?"

No answer.

"Okay, here it comes. Heads up."

He tossed the shirt to him as gently as he could without jarring his head. The shirt landed on top of Ethan's feet that were crossed at the ankles like brittle angel wings.

Paul waited.

And waited.

The kid didn't move, didn't look up, didn't do anything. Was he even breathing?

"Ethan?" he said, then winced when the sound of his own voice sent a jagged knife of pain straight through his left ear. He carefully wet his lips and said quietly, "Ethan? Come on, man, talk to me. Dammit—"

"Save your breath, handsome. I doubt he'll answer you."

The voice snapped his head up and black spots immediately descended upon his vision. He grappled at the bars to keep himself upright, breathing deeply until he could see again. He gritted his teeth and looked around with watery eyes. It was hard to recognize it but it had to be Aaron.

Who else could it be?

Anger spread through him, chasing away the edges of the pain in the skull.

"All right, asshole," he spat out through gritted teeth. "Get yourself a set of balls and let me see you."

He waited, anticipated the burst of rage that would bring a promise of agony. And as much pain as Paul was in, he found that at this point, he didn't really give a shit. He was trapped in a cage like a goddamn animal, with a kid next door, shackled and practically catatonic. He would be damned if his last moments on this fucking planet where going to end in fear.

"Come on," he taunted again. "Show your face."

The echo of his voice seemed to take forever to fade and the silence that followed was thick and lasted for so long, he began to wonder if he'd imagined anyone speaking. He searched the darkness, blinking the cold sweat out of his eyes.

Any minute.

Any minute now and Aaron was going to explode. He was going to flip out, pull a knife, say a couple of harsh-sounding words and then gut him, let him bleed out slowly and then he would be forced to listen to him bitch and complain about what an ingrate he was as he lay dying.

"Come on, Aaron," he tried again. "Don't be a pussy."

A deep, rumbling chuckle that was decidedly *not Aaron* came from the shadows that cloaked the top of the staircase. Out of the corner of his eye, he saw Ethan cringe ever so slightly.

"If I wasn't Aaron," the voice said, amused. "Would you still consider me a pussy?"

Paul sagged against the bars. *Oh, man*, he thought then asked, tiredly, "Would you care?"

"Probably not. You don't really know me that well. Yet."

He squeezed his eyes shut. When he opened them, he saw Ethan peeking through his hair at him. His gray eyes were bright and alert and there was fear in them.

"What do you want?" Paul demanded, adjusting his grip on the bars.

He thought about getting to his feet. The stone floor was killing his knees. But he didn't want to take the chance of passing out again. Big black spots sat at the edges of his vision, just waiting for him to make a move.

"Would you like the short version or the long version?"

Paul blew out a slow exhale. *Wonderful. A comedian.*

"Short."

"Well, that's no fun."

"Look, as much as I enjoy this witty banter, there are some people here who are freezing to death."

"You're in jeans and an undershirt."

"Give the kid his clothes, asshole. And while you're at it, let him out of here. He's got nothing to do with this."

"You're sure of that?"

"Yes."

"But you don't even know what *you're* doing here so how would you know about the little guy's purpose?"

"What sort of purpose could a ten-year-old possibly have?"

There came a chuckle. "Oh, many, I assure you."

Paul ground his teeth together and he saw Ethan's fingers tighten ever so slightly around his elbows.

"I'm sure you can attest to that, can't you?"

It was something Aaron would say but now Paul was almost positive that this person wasn't Aaron. The voice certainly didn't belong to him. It held a musical quality, full of soft lilts and a deep smoothness that made Paul think of chocolate. There was an underlying bass to it that tickled along the skin like velvet and it cemented his question of whoever the hell this was, it was definitely male.

"Fuck you."

"There's no need for swearing."

"There's no need for any of this."

"Of course there is. Otherwise you wouldn't be here."

"What a fucking shame that would be."

"Aaron. He was your employer, correct?"

"He still is."

"You're not a very good liar."

"Do I look like I care?"

"Now, Paul, let's not play games."

"I'm not."

"That's fine because you're not good at that either. Is there anything you *are* good at?"

"Come in here and find out."

"Oh, nice and direct. I like that in a man."

Paul skinned his lips over his teeth. "Who the fuck are you?"

"If I tell you, will you cease the games?"

"Fuck you."

Another laugh came out of the darkness. He winced as it wreaked havoc on his skull. Footsteps, steady and sharp, descended the stairs. Paul snuck a quick glance at Ethan, who had managed to curl himself into an even tighter ball.

Hang in there, Paul wanted to say. *As soon as I'm done with this asshole, we're getting the hell out of here.*

He wondered vaguely when "I" had become "we."

A man stepped into the light in front of his cage.

Paul stared up into the dark, dark eyes that he remembered looking into seconds before he'd lost consciousness while sprawled across the hood of his car. The urge to laugh was suddenly overwhelming and he decided right then and there that the fates were cruel and that someone somewhere was having a joke at his expense.

This was it? This was the guy who bought me here?

The man looked like something out of a GQ magazine—one of those scrawny, emaciated boy-men who looked like they hadn't seen a meal or the sun in years. Thick, dark hair fell carelessly over his forehead, into eyebrows that arched as high as his cheekbones. He looked fragile, breakable, and so entirely not real that if Paul's head hadn't been feeling as if it was being split apart, he could've easily passed this guy off as a hallucination. But the contented, satisfied look on his face was very real. Paul could feel it inching along his skin like pricks of silver needles and he didn't like it. It meant that he was right where he should be. It felt familiar and disturbing all at once and it was beginning to unravel in the pit of his stomach.

Stay calm, he told himself. *Stay calm, find out what this guy wants, waste him if you have to, and then be on your way.*

Paul let his gaze wander over him. He was dressed in dark clothes, as dark as the shadows around them, making it seem as though his pale face and hands floated freely in the near-darkness. Paul remembered the strength of those hands, pinning him down as if he were a child. He saw them now as belonging to a pianist—gentle and graceful, fine-boned and easy to crush—not the hands of someone who could take a man of Paul's size down as easily as he had.

There had to be someone else involved.

Paul kept eye contact with him as best he could without moving his head too much. The man smiled at him with an intensity that burned the cold air around them.

"Not what you were expecting?"

"Not really."

"That's okay. I'm used to that. You, on the other hand, are much more impressive up close."

"You going to tell me what this is all about now?"

"I suppose but please. Don't get up." He produced a key and opened the door of Ethan's cage.

Paul's head cleared a bit as he watched the man stride across to where Ethan sat. He picked up Paul's shirt and shook it out.

"Leave him alone," Paul demanded, injecting as much authority into his voice as he could.

A look of amusement was his only response as the man laid the shirt gently over Ethan's knees, fluffing it out until it covered his feet. Ethan didn't move a muscle. Paul frowned then shifted restlessly as the man pivoted and came over to where Paul was sagging against the bars. He squatted easily on the balls of his feet, inches away from the bars and inches away from Paul. This close, Paul could make out a white scar that slashed across the front of the man's mouth at an angle. It started beneath his left nostril, cut across his lips, then disappeared into his chin like a long, white worm. Judging by its thinness, Paul guessed it'd been made by a knife and a sharp one, too. He raised his eyes from the scar, looking into those dark eyes, wishing he had the strength to put some distance between them. He tried at least to pick his head up off the bars, but he couldn't. He might as well have a shackle around his ankle, too.

"I can't leave him alone," the man said, his eyes moving restlessly over Paul's face. "He's more useful than you realize."

"Useful?" he repeated flatly.

"Yes."

"As what?"

"Your motivation."

Shadows played across the man's handsome face and the smile twisted into something calculating. Paul felt his insides jolt, as if trying to flee from the warm cavity of his body.

"No fucking way."

The man's mouth twisted like he was trying not to laugh. It made the scar stretch and move like a snake. "You're not even going to deny it?"

"Deny what?"

"That you are what you're paid to be."

"And what exactly is that?"

"A murderer."

Ethan lifted his face from his knees. Clenching his teeth, Paul looked the man in the eye. "Why would I deny it? It's the reason you bought me here, isn't it?"

The man's eyes glittered like black diamonds. "Well, your profession thrives on secrecy, doesn't it? Just so certain people don't try and take advantage of it?"

"You mean certain people like you."

He laughed and the sound echoed off the walls, making Paul wince.

"Exactly. But there's one small difference. I won't have to try very hard. You're going to help me whether you like it or not."

The certainty of his words grated down Paul's spine. "Don't count on it."

The man moved closer until Paul could feel his breath on his face. "Believe me, Paul. I am counting on it and if you care what happens to that little boy behind me, I have a feeling you won't waste too much of my time by refusing."

Anger pumped through him, hot and fresh and it allowed him to pull his head away from the bars. "I'm not doing anything for you," he seethed. "So don't waste *my* time by threatening me."

That got him a condescending smile. "Paul, come on now. Your time? Is it really that important? Where do you have to go? What do you have to do? Are you in that much of a hurry to die?"

Paul sneered at him. "You don't have the balls."

"Oh, I don't mean me. But your employer? Aaron? Do you really think you're going to survive outside of these walls for any longer than, let's say, twenty-four hours?"

"Twenty-four hours? That's all you're giving me? I think you're underestimating me."

"Says the man who can't even get to his feet."

Paul tried to glare at him but that was pretty useless, too.

"There is one thing I can assure you of, Paul. He won't find you here. No one will. No one knows where you are but that's what you were hoping for, wasn't it? When you decided to pack up your life and hit the road?"

"None of your fucking business," he spat through gritted teeth.

"Please, call me Jakob."

Paul grabbed at him through the bars, fed up and thoroughly pissed off. He got his hands clenched in Jakob's shirt and was hauling him forward to bash his face into the bars when Jakob rolled his eyes, *actually rolled his eyes at him*, and gave him a hard shove. His head snapped back and the dark spots rushed forward to overtake him…

∑∙∑∙

The trucks roared above them, making the concrete overpass weave and tremble. The night was cold, the ground colder as they huddled together, trying to keep warm. A fire coughed nearby, fighting futilely against the wind and the dark. Most tried to sleep but it was too cold and half-starved, half-frozen bodies trembled too hard to get comfortable.

Instead of sleeping, he watched the twitchy dude across the way, pacing nervously, pulling at his coat sleeves over and over again as he chatted up Melanie. There was a tattoo of wings on either side of his pale, pale neck that seemed to glow in the dim, flickering light.

When the van pulled up and the dude led Melanie toward it, he felt a maddening surge of jealousy. Not because she was lucky enough to get out of the cold for a while but because Melanie was his.

At least, that's what his thirteen-year-old brain told him even though she'd been hooking for the last two years he'd known her. But he watched after her anyway.

The dude was twitching too much and there was never any reason for a vehicle to come down here.

The van's side door slid open with a bang and two men jumped out. They overwhelmed her before she could back-pedal, grabbing her arms and throwing her inside.

The scream she let out was for him and he ran madly toward her only to be stopped by a knife in the gut by the man with the wings on his neck.

She kept screaming for him and the van was speeding away. Warm blood was gushing through his hands. Her screams grew louder, coming toward him.

So frantic.

So close.

ↄ৲৵ↄ

"Paul!"

He jerked awake with a gasp.

"Paul!"

It was right next to his ear and he jerked away from it. Cold stone scraped along his back and his hands flew to his stomach, half-expecting to find blood pumping out of his body.

Take me away from here.

He blinked up toward the sky and saw stone instead. He blinked again and rolled onto his side. The memory fell away with the sound of squealing tires and his own groan in his ears when he saw Ethan's little feet flailing and kicking as Jakob dragged him out of the cage by his hair and one arm.

"Paul!"

Ethan's cry of anguish pushed Paul to his hands and knees. Red tail lights disappearing into the night loomed in his mind as he grappled blindly for something to pull himself up with.

"Come on, little man," Jakob cooed to Ethan. "Let's give Paul a bit of shut-eye. I think he needs it, don't you?"

"Let him go," Paul tried to say but his voice came out in a dry rasp.

Jakob's dark eyes flicked to his and a delighted smile bloomed across his face.

"Hey there, handsome. Sorry, I didn't mean to shove you that hard."

Paul squeezed his eyes shut for a moment, trying to clear his head. Jakob waited patiently, watching him as he tightened his hold in Ethan's hair.

"You were making the most interesting sounds," Jakob said. "Were you dreaming?"

Paul's hand hit the bars and he latched onto them. Gritting his teeth, he pulled himself to his feet. The floor dipped beneath him. He kept a death-grip on the bars, using them as a guide to walk toward the front of the cage, closest to Jakob and Ethan.

"Let him go," he said, clearing his throat roughly.

Jakob raised a slim eyebrow. He glanced down at Ethan then back at Paul.

"Or what?"

"Or I'm going to break every fucking bone in your body."

Jakob pretended to shiver. "Oh, I'm terrified. That's a little hard to do if you're in there and I'm out here, isn't it?"

"Why don't you just let me out of here and see what happens."

"I'd rather not."

"Jakob. I'm telling you right now. I am not a person you want to fuck with. Let the kid go."

"But why? You're the one who wanted to leave him at that church. Why do you care what I do with him?"

A pained look came over Ethan's face a split second before a fist curled in Paul's hair and jerked him back from the bars. A strangled cry came from his throat as he stumbled and fell to his knees. His head was yanked back and he found himself staring into a face that jolted him. His mouth would've dropped open had it not been for the knife pressed to his throat.

The woman.

The one from the gas station.

Paul stared up at her in shock. *How did I not see that one coming?*

"Ah, I see you two know each other," came Jakob's voice.

Paul tried to look at him, but she had a firm grip in his hair, keeping his head back at an awkward angle. His hands flexed uselessly at his sides.

"I don't believe we've been properly introduced," the woman said in that low, purring voice.

Her strange, caramel eyes glittered down at him.

"Then allow me," Jakob said. "Irene, meet Paul. Paul, this is Irene. A stunning creature, isn't she? You wouldn't believe how many people underestimate her."

I can only imagine, Paul thought to himself.

"If you have any questions, she's the person to ask. She'll gladly take care of you while I take care of this little guy right here."

There came a whimper of pain.

Alarm shot through him when he heard footsteps walking away from him.

"No," he whispered.

"Paul—" Ethan started to say before there was the unmistakable sound of a hand slapping human flesh.

The sound echoed like a cracked whip.

"Goddamn it!" Paul tried to shout but the blade at his throat caught the scream in his throat.

He paused then reared up, feeling the skin on his neck break as the knife sliced through. He whirled, catching the woman under the chin with a sharp elbow. She fell back with a surprised cry. He ran forward, hands reaching for the open cage door, his vision already clouding with shadows as his battered skull protested the violent movement. He almost threw up again and the world tilted beneath his feet. But he caught a glimpse of Ethan, a speck of white in the midst of rapidly closing darkness, his face pinched with pain as he struggled against Jakob and Paul launched himself forward...

His legs were kicked out from under him and he hit the floor hard. The room flipped and twirled and he was lost in a void of darkness.

CHAPTER 18

Paul snorted air and a barely-suppressed scream as he vaulted out of a thick, dark hole of unconsciousness. Sputtering and choking, he immediately rolled to his feet even before his eyes were open. When he blinked them open, he squeezed them shut again as the room spun around him. But then he realized that it wasn't the room, it was him. Forcing himself to stop turning and breathe before he hyperventilated, he rubbed at his eyes and looked around. He was in a large bedroom that looked like it was carved from a tree. Everything was wood—the floor, the walls, the furniture, all made from dark, polished wood. The bed he'd been laying in took up one half of the room, a mattress teeming with pillows and blankets. Hurricane lamps glowed softly on the walls. The air was warm and smelled like sleep and pine.

Quite a difference from the cage he was in.

And then all at once, he was assailed with questions. Where the hell was he? Had he been transferred while he was unconscious? He was in a cell the last time he was awake and now he was in a cozy bedroom, sleeping it off like a bad hangover. Where was Ethan? Jakob? Irene? His head no longer felt like it was getting pecked apart by a gaggle of ducks so how long had he been out?

And where the hell are my clothes?

He glanced down at himself. He was only clad in his boxers. He cringed inwardly at the thought of Jakob or Irene undressing him. He worried even more so that he'd been at their mercy. That he still was.

Half-naked, with no weapons to speak of. He was a sitting duck.

If Aaron could see me now, he thought bitterly.

He turned toward the bed and saw at one corner of the mattress, that a pile of clothes had been left for him. His boots sat on the floor, the laces tucked inside. He frowned. Then frowned harder when he saw a sheathed K-bar and his Glock sitting on top of the clothes.

Why would they arm me?

He went over to the bed, eye-balling the room, half-expecting someone to step from the shadows. Hesitantly, he picked up the K-bar first, unsheathed it. The edge gleamed dangerously. He put it back then picked up the gun, checked the clip.

Fully loaded.

He did another quick scan of the room. It was so quiet. As the cliché goes, it was *too* quiet. There was a door to his left. Whether it was an exit, a closet or a torture chamber, one thing he knew with unwavering clarity that it certainly wasn't the way down the rabbit hole because he was already in fucking Wonderland.

He put the gun down slowly then got dressed. As he yanked on a pair of jeans, he prioritized his goals.

Get Ethan, if he could, then get the fuck out of here.

He pulled on his boots, a white T-shirt, and a long-sleeved green shirt. He pulled his hair back into a low ponytail then hid the K-bar in his right boot. Gripping his gun in his right hand, he made for the door. He stepped out into the hallway as quietly as he could. Like the bedroom, the hallway was all wood with a window at one end. The beginnings of twilight pushed against the glass and again the question of how long he'd been here went through his mind. He glanced left then right.

Letting out an even breath, he started down the hall, staying close to the wall. The silence was total and thick. It was so complete that he wondered if anybody else was home. His step faltered as the hallway opened into a staircase leading down. Cautiously, he went to the railing, flexing his fingers around his weapon. The room below was huge and open, lit only by a fire that roared in a massive stone hearth at one end. The high ceiling was criss-crossed with thick wooden beams and windows covered nearly every inch of wall space, offering a near-panoramic view of the encroaching darkness beyond. Furniture was sparse, the floors spotted with thick throw rugs. Firelight and shadows sprung around the room like tribal dancers. Paul leaned over the railing and listened for noise, voices, anything at all.

The only thing he heard was his own heartbeat in his ears. There wasn't a single aspect of this situation he could honestly say was working in his favor. Then he spotted the front door, seeming impossibly close, directly across from the bottom of the staircase.

Freedom.

He slipped quietly down the stairs, his back to the wall. He kept constant vigil around him, behind him, above him. The air around him was coiled, ready to spring, and he knew in the time that it would take for him to get to that door, something was going to happen. He could feel it building with every descending step and by the time he reached the bottom, the back of his neck was prickling so bad, it almost hurt.

Cold dots of sweat broke out in his palms as he peeked around the banister, toward the fireplace and then to the doorway that stood beside it. Beyond the threshold, the room was pitch-black but he had a feeling that it wasn't empty. The longer he stared at it, the more certain he was that someone inside was staring back at him.

He suddenly felt caught out, like a teenager busted by his parents after sneaking out to a party. The sight of all that blackness made him swallow hard. Paul had liked the dark once, before he realized the things that it hid. Presently, it made him back up a few steps and even though he was armed, he had a strong feeling that it wasn't going to help him. At all.

Something creaked overhead. The sound in so much stillness drew his eyes upward and he felt rather than saw something finally rush at him from the darkness.

Admittedly, Paul wasn't nearly as ready for it as he thought he would be. He heard rapid footsteps a split second before he was tackled to the floor. The gun flew from his hand, the breath from his lungs as he landed flat on his back. Gasping, he twisted around to his front, instinctively going after the weapon before it could skitter outside of his reach. His fingers brushed the barrel before an arm dropped around his neck like a steel noose, dragging him back. He gurgled, clawing at the arm.

He was dragged to his feet and he sent a hard elbow back, feeling it connect. The arm loosened and he shook it off and turned, fist cocked. He glimpsed a shadowed figure in the confusing dance of light and shadow and he swung hard. His opponent ducked at the last minute and lunged, taking Paul down to the floor yet again. He howled, kicking and flailing with his fists but it was like trying to fight smoke.

He struggled to flip them, to get this bastard beneath him but a heavy weight settled on his chest, pinning him to the floor.

"Get off me!" he shouted breathlessly, struggling.

Hands buried themselves in his shirt, bringing Paul up off the floor into a sitting position. Paul tried to wrench free, to get his feet under him but now the bastard was sitting on his legs.

"Goddammit, get off me!"

A trick of light illuminated his assailant's face.

Jakob grinned down at him, dark eyes wide with delight. "I didn't hurt you, did I?"

For a split second, all Paul could do was stare at him.

"I hope not," the man went on, smiling, the scar on his mouth twisting. "I need you in perfect health."

He spoke like he wasn't trying to pin someone down and he sure as hell wasn't dressed for it, either. He was wearing black pants, a dark dress shirt and a freaking apron pocked with bright lipstick marks that announced "Kiss the Chef."

Paul blinked.

"You really weren't going to leave before having some dinner, were you? I've been slaving away in that kitchen for hours," Jakob said.

"Get off me."

He started to push at him again but Jakob's hands were locked in his shirt, keeping him close.

"You must be starving. The roast beef is almost done. Do you prefer it on rye or white bread?"

"You stand up and move the hell away from me."

"I would, Paul, but if you want me to move away from you, you'll have to let go of me first."

Jakob's eyes sparkled with amusement. Paul flexed his jaw.

"Don't fucking play with me, asshole."

"Who's playing? I'm trying to be hospitable and you're calling me names."

"You call locking me up in a cage hospitable?"

Jakob's eyebrows rose in surprise. "You didn't like it? I would think you of all people would appreciate the irony."

A sound halfway between a growl and a scream came out of Paul's throat. He reared up, catching Jakob's chin with the top of his head. Jakob fell back with an *unh* as he toppled off of Paul's legs. Paul shot to his feet, had barely taken two steps when Jakob jumped on his back.

"Jesus Christ!" Paul bellowed as he staggered off-balance.

Jakob was definitely a lot heavier than he looked. *So much for being a scrawny, emaciated boy-man.*

Paul centered his body weight and arched his back, ready to fling him over his head and across the room. One step ahead of him, Jakob curled his arms around Paul's neck and both legs around his waist. Paul swung wildly to the left, right, then left again, trying to dislodge him but Jakob's legs were like iron clamps around his hips.

"Fu—Fucker—" he choked out, reaching back, fingers posed for eye-gouging.

He never had to actually gouge someone's eyes out before. He'd threatened plenty of people with the act but never gone much further than that. He figured it couldn't be any different than sticking his fingers into a rotten tomato. Jakob, however, had no intention of letting him test this theory as he sighed against his shoulder like a long-suffering parent.

"Oh, Paul, I hate to have to do this to you but you're not leaving me many options."

Paul shouted with pain as Jakob uncurled one leg and slammed the heel of his foot into Paul's right kneecap. Paul went down hard. The weight on his back lifted but he felt Jakob curl a hand under his jaw and pull, using it as a handle to bring him up to his knees. More pain laced up his thigh to his hip.

"Fuck—" he gurgled but promptly shut up when a knife settled against his throat.

"You've got quite an anger management problem, Paul," Jakob murmured, his lips brushing against his cheek. "Ever consider getting help for it?"

"Let go...of me," he said, wincing as Jakob pulled his head back farther until his neck stretched uncomfortably.

"You keep saying that and you keep ending up in more compromising positions."

"You're wasting your time. I'm not doing anything for you."

He felt the skin of his throat dimple around the blade's edge as Jakob added pressure to it. Paul's breath hissed between his teeth.

"Now is not a good time to grow a backbone, Paul."

His rage was blinding and in the back of his mind, Paul knew that Aaron would be so disappointed at his lack of decorum.

'*All of my hard work, gone in a fucking instant because you can't control yourself!*'

Gritting his teeth against the pain, he planted one foot on the floor and started to stand. The blade broke through the skin as thinly as a paper cut. It burned for a moment, like someone inserting a long needle. He found himself thinking that it was a well-cared-for knife and hoped that if he was going to die within the next five seconds, at least the weapon used would be a good one and not something pathetic like a butter knife.

"Stay down, Paul," Jakob commanded.

Like hell, he thought.

"Come on, Paul. I don't want to get your blood all over my brand new rug."

Paul's eyes flashed defiantly. "I don't give a shit—" The words ended on a hiss as the knife sank in deeper.

He could feel it, trembling close, a scant breath away from slicing into something major.

And I don't care! It'd be better than this! Better than anything that this asshole has planned for me—

So close.

Just a little bit more.

He continued to push upward into the blade. Blood began a slow descent down his neck, tickling horribly.

"Paul, stay down," Jakob ordered, his shit-eating grin faltering.

"Make me," he hissed.

The smile was gone now. "Down—oh, goddammit, Paul, why do you have to be so stubborn?"

He pulled the knife away suddenly and it made a wet sound like sucking thick fudge out of a chocolate truffle. Paul immediately shot to his feet, ignoring the screaming protest of his knee. He felt something shift then crack as he straightened it and he almost went down again. Biting back a grunt of pain, he whirled around, his fist already flying. But Jakob had dropped into a crouch and drove both fists into his gut. Paul doubled over, feeling the blood freeze in his face.

"Stubborn, stubborn, stubborn," Jakob was muttering. "Here I am, trying to be nice, making a meal for you, for Chrissakes, and you're fighting me the whole way. What the hell does a man have to do to get through to you, Paul, seriously?"

Another hit and Paul felt the side of his face explode. He hit the floor. His vision darkened then came back. A pained *groan* trembled from his mouth.

"So you've got a death wish, is that it? I mean, surely my company isn't that bad."

"I've had better," Paul coughed.

"You have to give me a chance here, Paul," Jakob said, his voice almost pleading. "First impressions are not always the best."

"They're usually pretty accurate."

"You think so? I think they're worthless. You don't really know anything about a person until they start to bleed."

Paul looked up at him. Something dangerous was sliding through Jakob's eyes, a pressure that thickened the air and bubbled on Paul's skin. For a moment, it seemed that Jakob was going to leap on him and shove that knife through his neck all the way down to his spine. But there was something holding him back, a restraint like those portraits of people whose eyes followed you around the room, clearly wanting something from you but unable to attain it. The fact that he was wearing an apron covered in lipstick marks only made the situation more unstable. Moving slowly, Paul climbed to his feet, trying not to wince as he put weight on his battered knee. It throbbed painfully with every beat of his heart.

"You're not going to make me change my mind," he said.

Jakob smiled and it looked disturbing in the firelight. He started toward him. "You have to let me at least try."

"It'll be a wasted effort," Paul said, backing away from him.

"You're underestimating my charm."

"Oh, is that what that is? Here I am thinking you were just trying to kill me."

Jakob laughed and it echoed disturbingly to the rafters. "Kill you? Oh, Paul. You'd be dead by now if that were the case."

He kept pace with him, sliding in and out of the shadows like a ghost. Paul watched him carefully, wanting to put enough distance between them so he could go for the K-bar he had in his boot.

"Well, hey, don't let me stop you."

"You want me to kill you?"

"It'd be better than anything you have planned for me."

"How do you know that? You won't even listen to what I have to say."

"Are you under the impression that I should after kidnapping me right off the street?"

"Well, I think you owe me that much."

"Owe you? What the hell do I owe you?"

"I saved your life."

"From what?"

Jakob raised a condescending eyebrow. "Aaron."

A painful buzzing noise filled Paul's ears. His mouth moved soundlessly for a moment.

"No," he croaked then cleared his throat and said more forcefully, "No, what the f—no, are you serious? I don't—"

"Oh, come on, Paul. Be serious for a moment, would you? How far did you really think you were going to get before Aaron caught up with you?"

Paul glowered at him.

"How long did you think you'd last? A day? A week? A year is probably pushing it. I'd give you two weeks, tops."

He felt mildly insulted. "I'm not an amateur. I would last a lot longer than that."

"Aaron has people everywhere, Paul. There is no possible way that you would've made it past the city limits."

Paul willed Jakob's head to explode in a cloud of gray matter, blood and bits of skull. His molars were beginning to ache from grinding his teeth together.

"I—"

"And even if you did make it by some miracle, are you seriously going to tell me that you wouldn't be sleeping with a gun under your pillow every night? Are you going to tell me that you would feel safe enough to settle down somewhere, put your feet up and never think about him or any of this ever again?"

"That was the plan—"

"Paul, this would be eating at you for the rest of your life. There would no way in hell you would ever be able to relax. The fact that

Aaron is even still breathing would be enough to give you an ulcer and you'd probably end up in an early grave anyway even without his help."

Paul skinned his lips back over his teeth.

"So," Jakob went on. "Aren't you glad I got to you first? I can assure you, I'm a much more pleasant person to be around than Aaron."

Paul clenched his hands. "I somehow doubt that."

He smirked. "Well, Ethan seems to think so."

"Ethan seems to think what?"

"That I'm a nice guy. Have you played with him yet? He has the most amazing—"

Whatever Jakob was going to say was lost in a rush of anger as Paul launched himself at him. They crashed into the wall. Paul listened with satisfaction as the air was punched from Jakob's lungs and the knife fell to the floor. Not that Paul would need it. Just fitting his fingers around Jakob's neck was enough.

"Sick," he spat. "Sick fucking bastard."

Jakob clawed at his wrists, his eyes wide and surprised, mouth gaping wide.

"Paul—" he tried to say but Paul squeezed hard, feeling the soft flesh give beneath his rampant fingers like a soaked sponge.

He could feel the quick hammering of the pulse against his palm, feel the rush of blood that was always so close to the skin and the tremors that shook down his arms as he put his shoulders into it, squeezing and pressing and squeezing until his vision tunneled and there were words coming out of his mouth that weren't making sense.

He knew he was going to kill him. He knew in that instant that nothing would stop him from doing it and he was all right with that. He could live with it because Jakob deserved it. There had to be some kind of restitution, some kind of revenge that would make all the faces and the hands and the sounds just disappear so he wouldn't have to wake up drenched in his own sweat anymore. So Ethan and all the ones before and after him could get some fucking sleep at night.

He was dimly aware of Jakob's struggles becoming less sharp, less powerful. That was when what felt like a length of pipe smashed into his kidneys, sending him back down to the floor.

There was a second thud beside him but he couldn't see anything through the white-hot haze of pain that wrenched across his lower back. He rolled over onto his side, trying to breathe. He squeezed his eyes shut, gritting his teeth so hard, he was sure they would crack. He tried to center himself, to compartmentalize the pain so he could get up and defend himself, just like Aaron had taught him but *goddamn, it hurt*. How the fuck was he supposed to compartmentalize when he couldn't even fucking breathe? He pressed his face into the floor. He tried not to whimper as he was shoved onto his back. Something cold touched his nose.

"I should put a hole right in the middle of your fucking face," a voice hissed from above him.

His eyes flew open when he heard the unmistakable sound of a bullet being lodged into the chamber. A strangled sound came out of his mouth as he found himself looking down—*or would that be up?*—the barrel of a sawed-off shotgun, held nice and steady, aimed at the center of his face. Irene stood at the end of it, her face tight and scarily angry. Her eyes shone like icy gold stones in the flickering light. She'd had a knife at his throat the last time they met and now she had some serious firepower aimed at his face.

Who knew I had such a profound effect on women?

He opened his mouth but no sound came out.

"Irene," came a scratchy voice next to him. "Irene, don't."

Jakob was slouched against the wall, his chest heaving. His apron was askew and Paul could make out the finger marks darkening his throat. He would've felt a surge of satisfaction if he hadn't been in so much pain. Irene inched the gun up his face until the barrel grazed the area between his eyes. He met her eyes, his kidneys pounding in perfect rhythm with his heart.

Come on, bitch. Do it. Do it.

"Irene, we need him."

"No, we don't," she said quietly, her gaze as steady as the gun in her hands.

"Yes, we do," Jakob insisted, bringing a hand up to his throat and wincing. "That's some grip you've got, Paul."

"Where's Ethan?" Paul squeezed out, his voice trembling.

"Paul—"

"Where is he?"

"He's unharmed."

"Bullshit."

"Oh, come on. I just said that to get a rise out of you. I wouldn't touch a child, for Christ's sake, that's disgusting. I prefer adults. *Consenting* ones," he added.

Paul clenched his jaw. Even after nearly getting strangled, Jakob was still as flippant as a spoiled brat.

"Where the fuck is he?"

A strange smile flitted across his lips. "What, *now* you care about him?"

"What—"

"When I found you—"

"When you *found* me?"

"—you were getting ready to dump him. You were going to leave him at that church."

"I—"

"So why do you care what happens to him now?"

"Paul?"

A new voice, with the force of light and the weight of solid steel slammed through his haze of outrage and pain. His eyes cut to the stairs and he felt his stomach plummet.

"Ah, impeccable timing, little guy," Jakob purred.

Ethan stood uncertainly at the bottom of the stairs, one hand clutching the banister in a white-knuckled grip. Paul blinked, wondering if he was just a desperate hallucination. But Ethan stayed right where he was, real and rather…clean. He wore a simple long-sleeved black shirt, jeans, and sneakers that looked so new, they probably squeaked when he walked. It was almost too hard to look at him. He looked like any normal kid in any normal neighborhood, ready to go outside and play with his little friends. A game of soccer or maybe ride around the block on his bike.

Normal.

Paul felt a pang in his chest. He slowly pushed himself to his knees, moving carefully with full awareness of the gun that was a millimeter away from his head.

"Cleans up well, doesn't he?" Jakob asked.

Paul looked from Ethan to Jakob then back again. "What—What is this?"

"Oh, I took the liberty of doing what you wouldn't," Jakob explained proudly as he used the wall to climb to his feet.

Irene backed up a few feet, gun still trained on Paul, who continued to stare at Ethan. The kid stared back at him. His hair was brushed back from his face, making him appear young and fresh. His eyes shone like newly-formed gray ice.

There was a squirming in Paul's brain that made him feel like he was missing something.

"And what is that exactly?" he asked.

"Taking care of your boy here."

Paul met his eyes.

Jakob began to laugh. It came out rough and he winced, swallowing delicately. "Paul, I swear on my life, I did not touch him."

"How do I know that?"

"Ask him."

"No. I'm asking you."

"You won't believe me anyway."

"Try me."

"I'm not going to bother. You're entirely too untrusting."

"Seeing as how you've taken me against my will, I can't say that there's any reason for you to be trusted."

"It was the only way."

"The only way? Are you—"

"It was the only way to get you to listen," he explained calmly. "You make it nearly impossible to have a conversation."

"That's what no usually means, asshole."

Jakob's smile turned condescending. "Are you used to people listening to you when you tell them no, Paul?"

His blood curdled.

"Besides," Jakob went on. "Saying no before you even hear what I have to say is rather rude. It might be something that you're actually interested in. Why don't you just hear me out?"

Paul shifted, tried to get to his feet but stopped as pain cracked across his back.

"You shouldn't be afraid to try new things," Jakob was saying. "You have to broaden your horizons, especially now since you're out and about and exploring new territories and such—"

"What the fuck did you think I was trying to do before you decided to kidnap me?"

"You were just trying to run and running is no fun, Paul. Eventually, everything catches up with you."

"How philosophical. Do you really think shoving a gun in my face is going to make me change my mind?"

It could've been the unstable light from the fire, but Paul could've sworn he saw a faint smile cross Irene's face. He thought he saw her finger tighten around the trigger, too.

"No. But a nice, hearty meal might. Come on. You must be starving. Irene?"

She didn't move for a moment, as if giving him one more chance to screw up. He stared back at her until she lowered the weapon and stepped around him, her high, thin heels clicking sharply on the floor.

"Paul, do you need help standing?" Jakob asked as he strode over to the pitch-black room, reached in and flicked on the lights. "Once you eat, I'll take a look at your back, make sure there's no internal bleeding. Irene can pack quite a punch if she gets mad enough, isn't that right, my dear? Anyway, you might need to rest for a bit to make sure you don't urinate blood or whatnot—"

"Just stay the fuck away from me."

Jakob looked indignant. "I'm only trying to help."

"Yeah, you're doing great so far."

"Well, if you would stop being so difficult—"

"So this is my fault?"

"You were trying to kill me."

"With good reasons."

Jakob sighed. "Ethan, would you please tell him that I did not touch you in any way that would be deemed as inappropriate?"

Ethan looked at Paul and solemnly shook his head. Paul stared hard at him, willing him to show that Jakob was just like every other god-damn pervert they both had the unfortunate luck of meeting. But Ethan's clear gray eyes gave nothing away. Paul couldn't help but feel somewhat betrayed.

"See?" Jakob gloated.

Paul looked at him then at Irene. Her face was in shadow now as she stood with her back to the fire. He moved gingerly to his feet, try-ing to straighten his body but stopping just short of a stoop as his low-er back refused to accommodate. His brain went fuzzy for a second as he tried to breathe past the pain.

"Are you sure you don't need h—"

"I'm fine," Paul spat out.

Jakob shrugged and went into the next room. Irene hovered at the doorway, waiting. Paul gestured for her to go in.

"Ladies first," he said.

"After you," she said tightly.

"Paul? Ethan? Come on, the food's getting cold," Jakob called out.

Paul stared for a second longer then broke for the front door. He nearly screamed as fire flung itself across the base of his spine and down the back of his legs and only sheer force of will kept him on his feet as he scooped Ethan up and flung him around so that he rode Paul's back much the same way that Jakob had earlier but without the choking part.

"Hang on," he advised as he half-ran, half-stumbled.

"Paul!" Jakob shouted. "Goddammit!"

The gun went off behind him, shaking the house on its foundation. He heard wood splinter next to his head as he fumbled for the door-knob.

"Paul!" Ethan gasped in his ear, his arms straining to hold on around his neck.

He didn't bother looking for his gun or going for the knife around his ankle. What the hell good would a knife do against something that could put a hole the size of a bowling ball in the center of his chest? His brain was screaming too loud for him to stop anyway and when he finally flung the door open, he expected to hear another cannon go off.

He darted outside, unscathed.

The air was freezing, pulling the air from his lungs with greedy, icy fingers. It was almost enough to make him turn right around and dive back into the house.

Almost.

He smelled snow, but he couldn't see anything. It was darker than hell outside. He groped in front of him and made for what he hoped were the steps. His feet slid and Ethan's arms tightened around his neck. He bit back a surprised *"whoa"* as he skittered down a small flight of steps and ended up thigh-deep in snow.

"Shit!" he bellowed.

He heard feet on the steps behind him.

"They're coming!" Ethan chattered out, his little body trembling against his back.

Without looking back, he took two and a half wobbly lunges when a force barreled into him, sending him face-first into the snow. Sputtering curses and chips of snow and ice, he rolled onto his side, half-aware of Ethan coughing and fighting to hold onto him. Paul struggled to his knees. He thought he could make out Jakob's face in the near-darkness and he punched him in the mouth, sending him flying backward. Paul scrambled to his feet or tried to but the snow was too deep and he was sinking ass-first, in very close danger of being stuck. He struggled to free himself, to at least get his feet under him. He heard wheezing, desperate noises coming from somewhere behind him.

Oh Christ, Ethan, hang in there, man.

His lungs were freezing and burning at the same time, his body beginning to shut down against the cold. His eyes watered, blinding him further.

Come on! Get the hell out of here! Move your ass!

But he could barely stand. He was digging himself a hole the more he tried to move. Snow leaked into his pants and down his shirt and into his boots, the feel of it nearly paralyzing him. It seemed to rise around him like the walls of an icy prism. He felt his hair freeze against his head and his nose ran to an icy stop on his upper lip. His breath puffed out in jagged, little clouds.

Come on, come on, COME ON!

The weight on his back was suddenly gone. Hands grabbed him under the arms and pulled him back. He howled in frustration and fought to free himself. He tried to shout but his words were lost in a teeth-chattering whimper.

He found himself looking up at Irene and he had a split second to think *here we go again* before she slammed the butt of the shotgun in his face...

CHAPTER 19

The claw hammers were huge. Cast-iron, gleaming in the light, ready to crunch through his head. He tried to get free, but there were hands holding him down and he couldn't get up. All around him, the hammers pounded on steel and metal, coming within inches of his flesh, so close that bits of metal like shrapnel broke off and became imbedded in his legs, arms, and torso. No one seemed to hear him as he screamed. The impossible noise drowned him out and moved closer as they pounded near his head. He jerked away, trying to put space between his head and monstrous weapons. But the hands shoved him closer and a hammer slammed him into him, through his skull, cracking it wide open, sending bits of bone splintering into his brain.

✷✷✷

Paul came awake with a gasp and a roaring headache that seemed to rip his head apart at the seams. He groaned or he thought he did but whatever sound he did make sent more pain catapulting through his skull. He bit back another groan, squeezing his eyes shut. His entire head pulsed with every beat of his heart; from the backs of his eyes to the tip of his chin, to the depths of his brain to the edge of his nose.

Slowly, deliberately, he opened his eyes and found himself in that bed once again. He lay in the center of it, on his stomach, weighted down by what seemed to be layers and layers of thick, warm-smelling blankets. His head rested wonderfully on a pile of chenille pillows and he wanted to rub his face against them like a cat but that was about the time when he realized he was naked. He immediately tried to twist over onto his back but his body seized up, every muscle trembling along his spine. His brain seemed to quiver within its confines. He swallowed hard, wincing at the metallic taste that coated the inside of his mouth.

Gradually, he became aware that there was someone sitting next to the bed. He blinked, trying to focus, and then an exhausted anger swept through him.

"Get—away from—me," he managed to rasp out.

As Irene's eyes met his, the memory of scrambling through the snow, trying to get away, morphed into her standing above him with the shotgun raised above her shoulder like a baseball bat. A stab of pain engulfed his head and as he shut his eyes against it, he felt the skin of his forehead tighten and pull. Raising a trembling hand, his fingers touched a bump the size of a freaking goose egg near his right temple. He tried to glare at her but it seemed to be a wasted effort. She stared calmly back at him, that pale gaze of hers piercing through his mind, probing.

"I suppose it's pointless to ask how you feel," she said with the same impassive look on her face.

Paul gritted his teeth, trying to relax his body before another wave of pain could dominate from his bruised kidneys. He had to try twice before he found his voice.

"Where's—Ethan?"

"He's here."

"Where?"

"The next room."

"Is he all right?"

"You nearly killed him after that little stunt you pulled."

"I want to see him."

"Soon."

"Now."

"You're making demands?" she raised an eyebrow.

"I'm not playing this game with you. Get me Ethan. Now." His body was tensing up and he bit back a moan as pain traveled through his back like butter on toast.

"Who's playing games?" she asked quietly. "You're underestimating me and Jakob, Paul. A mere bump on the head is nothing compared to what we can do to you."

"You can't—You can't use me if I have a concussion."

"You don't."

"How do you know? I could end up dead within the hour from internal bleeding."

His voice cracked on the last word. He licked his lips, trying to breathe slowly and evenly but then she smiled at him and it was damn near breathtaking. But it wasn't pleasant. It was more like a sneer. She dropped to her knees beside the bed, moving like she had no bones in her body, and bought her face close to his. He tried to move away but only found himself blinking back tears as the pain squeezed his lungs.

"You won't end up dead, Paul," she whispered. "We won't let you."

"I can make you wish you'd killed me."

"That's doubtful."

"I've been around the block a few times. I know a thing or two."

One side of her mouth twitched. "You haven't been around my block."

Black spots began to swarm around the edges of his vision. He tried to keep his focus on her but he could feel himself slipping. He shut his eyes against her harsh, beautiful face, feeling her lips brush against his cheek.

"We're not staying here," he whispered.

"Paul?"

His eyes opened and Ethan was suddenly in front of him, his small face regarding him solemnly

"Hey—hey, Ethan. You okay?"

He nodded, his gray eyes so close, trailing over the bruise on Paul's head.

"You sure? They didn't hurt you?"

He shook his head, his fingers picking at the blankets.

"Ethan, are you sure they didn't hurt you?"

"I'm sure," he said, chewing on his lip.

A small crease formed in between his eyes.

"What?" Paul rasped. "What is it?"

He hesitated, staring down at the blankets.

"You can say it, Ethan. Go ahead."

Finally those gray eyes lifted to meet his and there was so much anguish. He abruptly didn't want to know what Ethan was going to say but then he was saying it, "Were you really going to leave me? At the church?"

Paul let his head sink into the pillows, something like defeat crawling through him to curl tightly around his rib cage. Tremors ran through his body and this time it had nothing to do with the pain.

"Yes." He whispered the word, as if speaking it any louder would make it less painful. "I thought—I thought you would be safer there."

Ethan was silent for a moment. His fingers had gone still against the blankets. "I wasn't lying when I said that I would be safer with you."

Paul tried to shake his head. "No. No, you don't see what—you—did you see what happened before? With these people? It's dangerous, all right? This is no place for—"

"I'm not a kid," he interrupted softly. "I haven't been for a while."

Paul pressed his lips together, unable to argue. God, his head hurt.

"You know that, don't you?" Ethan asked.

He tried to find a suitable answer that would put an end to this madness but then Ethan's little face was replaced by Irene.

"You both would be safer here, Paul. Surely you understand that."

"You—You're not listening to me," he said, his speech beginning to slur. "This—"

"Oh, I've listened, Paul." Her mouth was a silky whisper against his cheek. He caught a faint whiff of snow and coconut. "I've listened and you know what I've heard?"

He squinted at her, trying to keep her in focus as he began to succumb to unconsciousness once more. "What?"

"A dead man."

A faint smile flickered over her mouth as he passed out.

CHAPTER 20

A dead man.

Paul awoke with those three words spinning through his head. His eyelids felt as if bowling balls were sitting on them and he forced them open with a groan that made his dry throat hurt. He tried to swallow and groggily pushed himself over onto his back, wincing at the tendrils of pain that lingered across the base of his spine. His head throbbed with a dull ache and the rest of his body generally felt as if it had been trampled repeatedly by a herd of manic buffalo. He supposed he should be grateful to be alive and in one piece, although it didn't make much sense that he was still alive. Whatever Jakob and Irene had planned, they needed him. Maybe he could play that to his advantage, like perhaps getting the fuck out of here.

He let his eyes wander around the room, lingering on the heavy shadows that gathered in the corners. It was quiet, still. Any second now he expected Jakob to appear, donning a chef's hat to match that ridiculous apron, spewing more of his bullshit or Irene, wielding another weapon to bash his head in with. But the cool semi-darkness peacefully ensued and for a moment, Paul let himself believe that there was nothing waiting for him beyond this room, that he really hadn't made the decision to run and put himself into an even deeper world of shit.

He sat up and shivered. A jittery sense of dread filled him, the kind that a claustrophobic person gets when the realization dawns that there's no way out of the small room that he'd been locked into.

He eased toward the edge of the bed, clutching the blankets in his lap, well aware that he was still naked. On a chair next to the bed was his duffel bag with his coat thrown over it. Surprised at the sight of it, Paul swung his feet to the floor then noticed that his bag full of weapons was nowhere in sight.

Dammit.

He rummaged for clothes, trying to tell himself that he didn't need any weapons. He could take care of himself. His bare hands were deadly enough.

Oh sure, like that's been working well for you lately.

Frowning, he dressed in a fresh pair of boxers, blue jeans, and a T-shirt. As he laced up his boots, his thoughts turned to Ethan.

Where is he? What are they doing to him while they wait for me to wake up?

He clenched his jaw, ripping his hair back from his face into a low ponytail.

Shit.

This was why he didn't want the kid around. This was why it was dangerous. This was fucking why he wanted to leave him at that church.

'I'm not a kid. I haven't been for a while.'

Yeah, no kidding, Paul thought as he went over to the door. *Maybe not a kid but definitely a bargaining chip.*

He put his ear to the door, listening for any sound beyond it. When he didn't hear anything, he pulled it open and stepped out into the hallway. His boots echoed with hollow, heavy thuds, alerting the whole damn house that he was coming and God help them, because he was. He searched the entire upper level, finding it empty before descending the stairs into the violet shadows of the room where he'd nearly killed Jakob. There was no fire in the hearth now. Without it, the room was cold and unwelcome. He moved to the center of the room, turning slowly, ears perked. He was unarmed, had a bull's-eye on his chest, and it was as good a time as any to get the hell out of there.

But how?

It was freeze-your-ass-off cold outside, night was in full swing, and he didn't have a clue as to where he was. He could be out in the boonies or in a totally different country. If he left without finding out his exact location, he would risk getting even more lost and freeze to death.

So how did I even get here? Snowmobile? Skis? Dog sled? Maybe I was brought here before the snow fell and there's a road nearby. Well, in that case, Sherlock, you're going to be waiting a while for the snow to be plowed.

He doubted Jakob and Irene owned a plow truck.

A sudden, muffled sound cut into his train of thought. He went still, sucking in a huge breath and holding it. He closed his eyes, straining his ears.

There it was again.

Long, high-pitched but muffled like a shrieking animal whose jaws were trapped in a muzzle. He went toward the kitchen, moving carefully. He stepped inside the doorway, listening, breathing evenly and deeply. The silence around him seemed to breathe with him.

He waited.

And jumped when the sound came once more. It seemed to linger this time. He moved farther into the room, trying to hone in on it. It grew louder and his step quickened. He felt along the wall in the near-darkness, his hand moving over cabinet doors and pantry shelves until he came to a corner. He hesitated then peeked around it. The corridor was long and narrow, stretching straight back. He spotted a door at the end, on the left.

The sound came again, louder than a few seconds before. He moved quickly down the hallway to the door, pausing briefly in front of it before grasping the doorknob and throwing it inward.

A piercing scream cracked around him like lightning, shattering the thick silence of the house. He leapt back, colliding with the wall. Wide stone steps led down, spiraling gently to the right before disappearing out of sight. The gray stones gleamed wetly in the lights that were set inside deep alcoves in the walls, casting narrow strips of light that stretched across the staircase. He had a horrible sense of déjà vu followed by an even more horrible realization.

Oh Christ! Ethan!

Another shriek, urgent and awful, ended in yelling. "Please! Don't!"

A man. It was a man yelling, his voice too deep for a child.

'*I'm not a kid. I haven't been for a while.*

Paul felt a quick rush of relief but if it wasn't Ethan, who the hell was yelling? He heard murmured voices, soothing and quiet, like the sounds a mother might make to a child who had awakened from a terrible nightmare.

A nightmare indeed.

"Christ! St–Stop!"

It wrenched him in the gut, echoing faintly up to him like a beast stalking him in the shadows, lurking, coming steadily closer and there was nowhere for him to go. His heart lurched in his chest. All at once, his brain started screaming at him to run, to shut the door, and just get the hell out of there once and for all because really, what was he waiting for? If he froze to death, who would really give a shit? It would be better than what was down there, although he knew it couldn't possibly be any worse than what was happening to that poor bastard at this very minute. He tried to breathe but the air was choking him.

It's not you down there either. You're not down there. You know you're not. Please…

Goosebumps rippled down his arms and he could smell his own sweat, his own blood, flinching as if he were there again, in that dark room in the back of his mind…

എൗൟ

A dark so solid he couldn't see the hand in front of his face. But the footsteps that moved slowly around him, he could hear that, just like he could hear the voices whisper to him so softly as if telling him a bedtime story. Then the fists struck his body, weakening him against the cat-o-nine tails that ripped into his back, sending him skittering away but not too far. The chain around his ankle held him fast.

'...*don't scream...*'

'...*you won't scream, will you?*'

'...*no, no, I won't...*'

'...*you know what will happen if you do...*'

'...*y–yes...*'

എൗൟ

He jerked back from the memory, squeezing his eyes shut, struggling for control. But it kept slipping away as more screams came from below, enveloping him so tightly, he could barely stay on his feet. Every muscle in his body quivered and trembled as he sagged against the wall, trying to get a hold of himself, trying not to get swept away by what lurked in his mind.

Another scream met his ears and he winced, balling his hands into fists until his nails bit into his palms. The urge to run was so strong now it made his stomach cramp. His legs shook with it, his mind screamed with it, as loud as the man below him.

Swallowing the hard lump lodged in his throat, he took a deep breath that stuttered in his throat when the scream that came next was abruptly cut off like someone throwing a light switch. Paul thought he heard the high, hissing *skish* sound of liquid hitting stone. The sudden silence that followed was awful. The air was alive, filled with pain, filled with a suffering that lived on the air itself. Leaning against the wall for support, the stones cool and wet beneath his fingers, he went slowly, waiting for his knees to give out. A heavy *thud* met his ears followed by a gritty dragging sound. His breath caught and he stopped, pressing into the wall for a moment, then moved on. A trickle of cold sweat ran down his spine and oh, how he wished he was armed.

For what felt like hours, he descended, following the twisting steps until finally, finally he came to the bottom. Another hallway, short and filled with shadows stretched before him. A faint glow lit up the far end. He moved toward it and stopped as the hallway opened to a small platform where more steps led down into a large open room. Glancing about, he felt a jolt of awareness.

He knew this place. This was where he'd first woken up after being taken from the church. This was where Ethan had been in a cage beside his, naked and shivering and unresponsive...well, at least this time he had some clothes on—

Paul stopped and blinked, realizing that he wasn't looking at a memory. That Ethan really was inside that cage.

Again.

He was huddled in one corner, his knees pulled to his chest, his face tucked down so that all Paul could see was his pale blond hair. There didn't seem to be any shackles securing him in place this time and the door to his prison stood wide open.

"Son of a bitch," Paul murmured.

Equal doses of anger and relief filled him like a breath of fresh air and he vaulted down the steps. He kept his eyes on the small form, willing the kid to look up at him, to move, to do something because he had a way out so why wasn't he taking it?

Paul didn't even notice the thick trail of blood that streaked across the floor until he was nearly ankle-deep in it. Biting back a curse, he stopped, the tips of boots inches from a gob of something that floated lazily along like a clump of leaves in a babbling brook. He choked back a gag at the violent smell, following the garish river of ghastly innards with his eyes as it trailed across the stone floor and vanished through the mouth of that pitch-black doorway, the shadows beyond it like theater curtains, shielding the stage from view.

"It was no one you knew."

He jumped as his eyes snapped to the cage adjacent to Ethan's.

The sight of Aaron staring at him through the bars nearly stopped his heart. An icy stillness screamed through his ears and he took a step back as if he'd been plowed in the chest with a wrecking ball.

"Aaron."

The name exploded in a soundless rush from his lips, his brain whirling, firing off scenarios, possibilities, excuses, lies, anything that would explain his presence here as quickly and painlessly as possible.

"Surprised to see me?" Aaron asked.

His voice cut through the still air in all its familiarity and danger, hissing undertones and intrusive sarcasm. It was a sound that made him want to run. It was a sound that made him want to fling himself down at Aaron's feet and beg for forgiveness. The old chains snapped at him. Something razor-sharp and hysterical clawed up the back of his throat. Letting his gaze fall to the floor, Paul struggled for coherency beneath the cement-heavy weight of Aaron's presence. His body seemed to have separated from his mind, packing its bags, under no obligation, and no note as to when it would return.

"Well? Nothing to say?" Aaron pressed, his eyes as deep and dark as ever, like black holes. "I figured you'd have plenty to say given your juvenile attempt to disappear."

Paul's tongue felt large and clumsy inside his mouth. "What...How...are you here?"

"The same way you are, obviously."

"You...They took you, too?"

"No one takes me, Paul. No one."

"So you're...here of your own free will? In a cage?"

"That is not what's important right now, Paul. What's important is you. What's even more important is you being *here*."

"I thought...I didn't think you'd find me."

Even without looking, he knew Aaron was tilting his head to one side.

"Really," he said flatly.

He tried to nod. There was a rustle of clothing and Aaron's voice, when it came again, sounded closer.

"You know how I feel about you, Paul. Why would you think, with all of my resources, with all of my power, that I wouldn't be able to find you?"

"You didn't seem very happy with me the last time we met," Paul ventured. "I thought it would be best if—"

"If you disappeared."

"Yeah."

There was a beat of silence. Paul slowly raised his eyes. There was a slight smile on Aaron's face as if Paul had done something inadvertently cute.

"If you tried to disappear after all the times that I wasn't happy with you, I would've kept you on a leash in my backyard."

"I thought you were going to kill me this time."

Aaron laughed and it echoed, empty and cold. "Well, that wouldn't be much fun, would it? Who would I have to entertain me?"

"I don't think you'd have any trouble finding a replacement."

"On the contrary, Paul, I think that I would. Not everyone has your...stamina."

Paul wasn't sure if that was a compliment.

"Aaron—I don't..."

Aaron gave a long-suffering sigh. "Articulate as ever, I see." He moved closer to the bars, closer to Paul and it took everything Paul had not to take a step back. "What were you thinking, Paul, leaving me the way you did? How far did you think you were going to get?"

He looked away. "I don't—know, I just thought—"

"That's the problem, you thinking. Nothing good ever comes out of that."

"What was I supposed to do?"

"What you always do. Nothing. Unless I give you the go-ahead."

Paul frowned down at the floor. "So I was just supposed to sit around and wait for you to kill me, is that it?"

"Well, I wouldn't say that. I was expecting more of a fight from you."

"So you *were* going to kill me?"

Aaron tilted his head to the side. "What do you think?"

Paul stared at him, trying to read past that blank, amused mask. "I'm thinking I need a straight answer from you for once."

"Not until you stop asking such asinine questions."

"It's not asinine if I want to know if you intended to kill me."

"Intended? As in past tense? What makes you think that my desire to kill you has passed?"

A chill ran up his spine. "You're—"

"The only thing stopping me is this cage, Paul. I would have to say you're pretty damn lucky at the moment."

Paul stared at him, the screams snapping off in his head like a thrown switch. In its place came anger surging through him like the tide. But this time, it felt…different.

Different in a way that was lighter, more solid, and not so weighted down by memories and hopelessness. It felt wholly acceptable, especially now that Paul truly realized just how little he mattered to this man. It was the proverbial kick in the ass, the punch in the gut that magnetized the sudden monumental shift in the dynamics of their relationship because Aaron was the one in the cage now.

However, there was still a small part of him that ached to know why he was so insignificant. Even after all of the bending and the breaking there wasn't one sliver of…affection? Respect? Care? Something that would lead Paul to believe that after all of their years together, there was maybe something that could resemble a friendship? Watching Aaron's eyes grow colder and the smile stretch wider across his face, Paul doubted it. There was nothing that Aaron would hate more than to lose the control and power that Paul would finally gain over his own life if he ever chose to leave him.

As if sensing his shifting mood, Aaron said, "It's a little late to be pissed off at me, Paul."

"No, it's not."

Aaron rolled his eyes. "What're you going to do, unleash fifteen years of pent-up aggression? I'm your owner, Paul, not your psychologist. I'm not going to stand here and listen to you whine about a past that's over and done with."

"It's not like there's anywhere for you to go."

Aaron regarded him silently for a minute. "Point. Well, all right then. Let's hear it. Let's hear how hard your life has been. Let's hear about how cheaply you had to sell yourself to get what you wanted, something that I gave you—"

"I have never sold myself cheap," Paul cut in, feeling the back of his neck grow hot.

Aaron raised an eyebrow, mocking him with a cruel smile. "Sure you have. Multiple times, in fact. All anyone had to do was offer you a hot breakfast and you were on your knees, willing to suck cock for free."

The *fuck you* that exploded from Paul's mouth came from his toes. "You don't know—You have no idea what I went through. What I had to do—"

"Oh yes, I do," Aaron spoke over him, his smile descending into a snarl. "I have an idea. I have a clue. I know because you told me. You cried and cried on my shoulder, spilling out every lousy thing that was ever done to you. Every horrible deed you had to perform to get some of that fuck-money you needed so badly. And what did you want in return, Paul? What did you expect from me? What did you see when you looked at me?"

Hope. Salvation.

"You trapped yourself, Paul. You're trapped inside your own nightmare and you want me to hold your hand—"

"No."

"And why should I when I've given you so many chances to turn everything around? When I've given you every opportunity to let go of all your shit, to become something greater, something better? I had such high hopes for you. Hell, I still do even if I want nothing more than to splatter your worthless brain all over this floor."

Paul clenched and unclenched his fists. "You—"

"It's no one fault that you're such a disappointment," Aaron went on as if he were the only one in the room. "It's no one's fault but yours. I can't say that your parents would be proud of what their only son has become because I'm sure they wouldn't be. Although, come to think of it, your father might be proud but that would only be because of the money you'd bring in. I doubt he would've cared too much about your emotional issues as long as it didn't interfere with his gambling problem."

"Shut up!" Paul screamed at him.

Aaron was already laughing. "For God's sakes, look at you. You can't even control your emotions. How the hell would you ever survive without me?"

"I would survive, goddamn you. I would make sure of it, you fu—"

"Oh, now, now, no need to stoop to name-calling. If you're so intent on surviving, perhaps you should get serious about clearing out all of those cobwebs that have taken up residence in your head. You know, just so you can start fresh and new. We wouldn't want the past dragging you down again would we, especially when you're to embark on a new chapter of your life?"

Paul glared at him, anger shaking through him, feeling pieces of himself dying inside.

"And even if by some miracle you do manage to carve out some pitiful existence, I'm sure you'll find a way to fuck it up," Aaron said, inspecting his fingernails.

"I won't—"

"Oh yes, you will. I know you too well, Paul. You won't be able to move on from this, no matter how hard you try. No matter what you do—"

"Yes. I will," Paul growled.

Aaron looked up at him. "Well, while we're waiting for hell to freeze over, why don't you do me a favor and get me out of here? I think I've been in here long enough."

Paul stared at him. Really stared at him.

Through the bars.

Locked in this cage.

And felt his anger ebb a bit. His spine tightened with another shiver of awareness, one even stronger than before. The expectant look on Aaron's face hardened as the minutes began to tick away and he became very still. A week seemed to pass before Paul lifted his foot, heavy and mindful of the blood on the floor, and took a step sideways.

Through the bars, Aaron's gaze was steadfast.

When Paul took another step, Aaron gently tilted his head, watching. Paul forced himself to take another step to the side and felt the breath lodge in his throat when Aaron suddenly moved with him, keeping pace with him.

"Paul."

The sound of his name was edged in razor-sharp talons and Paul flinched inwardly. He almost stopped. He almost turned back, following the sound of that voice but his eyes fell upon Ethan's small, curled-up form and it was the beacon that gripped him by the ears and pulled him closer.

He stepped over the thick stream of blood.

"Paul. Let me out."

The voice beside him slipped into his ear, like oily fingers, slick-sliding, curling, seeking, drawing him back to a place that was cold and desolate. His step faltered yet again. Despite the chill in the air, a single drop of sweat burned a trail down the side of his neck.

Don't do this. Don't you dare do this. There won't be a place in the world you can hide.

He could feel Aaron's thoughts inside his head. He opened his mouth to call out to Ethan but Aaron's voice battered in,

"Paul. Paul, look at me."

Panic began to form in the center of his chest and he tried hard to focus on Ethan but his body began to blur around the edges.

"Paul."

Paul let out a sharp breath, the blood pounding in his face.

"Let me out of here, Paul. That's why you came down here, isn't it? To let me out?"

"I…" The words stuck in his throat.

"That is why you're here, isn't it, Paul?"

Paul could swear he heard the sound of Aaron curling his hands around the bars, coming as close to Paul as he could. He could see him moving out of the corner of his eye.

"You seem conflicted," Aaron said, his voice quiet and taunting, smooth and cloying-sweet. "If you're not here to release me, then why are you here, Paul?"

Ethan snapped back into focus and Paul blinked rapidly, his heart ready to break out of his rib cage. He took a shaky step forward, his knees almost crumpling.

"Oh," Aaron suddenly laughed, dragging the syllable out like something perverted. "Oh, I see. Of course, yes. Your little slut."

It propelled Paul forward even as the ever-familiar shame crept along his skin.

"You've surprised me, Paul," Aaron said from behind him. "I honestly didn't think you had it in you to be so—nurturing."

Paul turned his head to the side, giving Aaron his profile as he hunkered down as quietly as he could next to Ethan. He could see small tremors going through him like those of a spooked animal and he curled more tightly in on himself when he sensed Paul near him. Aaron made a scoffing sound.

"Why do you do this to yourself, Paul? Why? Do you think redemption is so easily obtained? Do you think that little shit is going to appreciate your struggle? I doubt it. He may in the beginning but you know he's going to start resenting you. Eventually, everyone does. A hero is never a hero for long."

"I'm just trying to help him."

"No. You're trying to help yourself. You're trying to make sure this doesn't turn into another nightmare for you to fight with every time you close your eyes."

"It's too late for that," Paul murmured, staring down at Ethan's pale hair.

"Should I break out my violin?"

Paul's jaw flexed. "You were the one who gave him to me, remember?"

"Sure, Paul. Place the blame elsewhere. It makes life so much easier for you, doesn't it?"

Paul leaned toward Ethan, calling to him softly. "Ethan? Hey, Ethan?"

He reached out his hands but stopped, unsure if touching him was the right thing to do. He bit his lip when he heard Aaron snicker from behind him.

"Ethan?" Paul tried again.

Tentatively, he laid a hand on the back of Ethan's neck. His flesh was cool beneath his palm. Paul swallowed and gently lifted Ethan's head.

"Ethan? Hey buddy, you okay?"

His gray eyes were open but unseeing, staring off into the distance, looking at something not in this room. There was a smudge of blood on his cheek, bright and stark against the white of his skin. Paul pressed his lips together, a fine trembling coursing down his arms.

They made him watch. Whatever they did in here, they made him watch.

He swore under his breath. "Goddammit."

Biting back a snarl, he scooped Ethan up and straightened to his feet. Ethan made a small sound at being jostled and one hand curled into Paul's chest, latching onto his shirt. Paul spared a quick glance down at him and saw that his eyes were closed. He gave a shake of his head, feeling something hot burn at the backs of his eyes.

"We're getting out of here," he whispered. "You hear me? We're leaving. I don't think either one of us will be able to survive here."

A shiver went through the little body in his arms. He thought he felt Ethan nod against his chest. He clutched the kid tighter against him and turned around. He froze when he saw Aaron in front of him, still standing behind the bars but with a look in his eyes that made Paul think he wasn't. He took an unconscious step back at the black, unyielding stare, feeling it as something physically hitting him in the sternum.

"Let me out," Aaron commanded.

Paul swallowed with some difficulty. "I don't...I don't have a key."

"And if you did?"

Paul's mouth opened to respond but his pulse thudded into it and nothing came out. Aaron's face thinned out, his hands tightening around the bars until his knuckles were sharp and bloodless.

"You won't make it."

Paul shook his head.

"You can't," Aaron insisted with deadly certainty.

I have to try, he wanted to say but the look on Aaron's face burned away the words.

He turned away and felt something wrench apart in his chest.

"How did you know to come down here, Paul? Did our mutual friend, Jakob, tell you?"

Paul spun around. "What?"

Aaron smirked at him. "You have met Jakob, I presume?"

"What the fu—"

"Quite the charismatic individual, wouldn't you say?"

Paul gaped at him. "I—I'm not sure if that's the word I would use—"

"You don't like him?" Aaron's smirk deepened, twisting his face into something ugly. A sinking feeling hollowed out Paul's stomach. Then Aaron's eyes flicked over his shoulder a split second before a familiar voice drawled,

"You don't like me, Paul? I think I'm offended."

CHAPTER 21

Ethan went rigid in Paul's arms. Paul tightened his hold on him as he turned to find himself face-to-face with his own Glock. Jakob's face was behind it, unsmiling for once, his stare as black as the shadows around them. Irene stood behind him, cold and bored. Paul looked from one to the other then back at Aaron.

I don't fucking believe this, he thought to himself then demanded out loud, "What the hell is going on here?"

"Paul," Jakob said, his tone somber. "Be so kind as to hand the child over to Irene. The adults need to talk."

"No."

Aaron chuckled. "He's grown quite attached. It would be cute if it weren't so disgusting."

Paul shot a glare at him before looking back at Jakob. "You're not taking him anywhere."

"We haven't done anything to him, Paul."

Paul's back teeth began to ache from his clenched jaw. "You made him watch. Whatever the fuck you were doing down here, you made him watch."

"I'm sure he's seen much worse."

"Somehow I doubt that."

"And I'm sure you have, too, so why are you acting so surprised?"

Anger pulsed in Paul's temples and he realized his grip had tightened to the point of leaving bruises when he heard Ethan make a small whimper of pain. He forced himself to loosen his grip and without taking his eyes off the Psychotic Duo, he slowly squatted down.

"On your feet, Ethan," he whispered softly. "Come on, stand up. Get behind me and don't move."

Ethan hesitated then slid out of Paul's arms, standing shakily. He leaned against Paul's leg as Paul straightened up. The gun followed, nice and steady, centered on his left eye.

"I thought you said he wasn't capable of attachment, Aaron?" Jakob taunted.

"An error in judgment, I assure you," Aaron replied, folding his arms across his chest and leaning casually against the bars.

Paul leveled a stare at Aaron, trying to ignore the sting of betrayal that was rapidly gaining more pressure inside his chest.

"Any other errors in judgment that I should be made aware of?"

Aaron blinked lazily. "None that you need to concern yourself with."

"I beg to differ," Jakob replied. "If he's going to be working for us, I think it would be helpful to know everything that makes him tick. And even the things that don't."

"I am not working for you," Paul said flatly.

"Yes, you are."

"No, I'm not."

"Yes, you are," Aaron cut in.

"You go to hell," Paul swore at him. "I don't work for you any-more and I sure as hell am not going to work for these two assholes either."

"You really think you have a choice?" Jakob said, gesturing with the gun.

"I've had worse threats than a gun pointed at my face."

Jakob cocked his head to the side. "My, my. You've certainly come into your own in the short time you've been with us."

"Don't take all the credit," Aaron said.

"Oh, I won't. I think we owe a great deal to the little guy standing behind him."

Paul felt Ethan against the back of his right leg, a hot pressing weight, little hands gripping the denim. Paul leveled a stare at Jakob then at Aaron, imagining railroad spikes being driven through their heads.

"Who could've foreseen the hooker with a heart of gold?" Jakob chuckled.

"He's no Julia Roberts," Aaron said.

"True enough."

"But money well-spent."

Paul's gaze volleyed back and forth between them. "What *the fuck* is this?"

"This is an intervention, Paul," Aaron quipped.

"An intervention for what?"

"What all interventions are for. To help you," Jakob replied.

"I don't need your help," Paul squeezed out through gritted teeth. "I don't—"

Jakob suddenly moved, getting into Paul's face so quickly he didn't have time to back up. "Paul, don't fight us," he said quietly, his eyes earnest, almost pleading. "You know it won't end well if you keep this up."

"Don't pander to him, Jakob," Aaron said in a bored tone.

"I'm not pandering to him," Jakob said patiently. "I'm simply making him aware of his lack of options."

"Well, of course there are no options. You made sure of that from the moment you put me in this goddamn cage."

Jakob gave a condescending tilt of his head as he looked over his shoulder at Aaron.

"Now, Aaron. You sound like you're regretting our arrangement."

Aaron sniffed. "Of course not."

"What arrangement?" Paul demanded.

Jakob's eyes came back to his face and he smiled. Paul inched away from him.

"The child first, Paul?"

"No."

"Paul, this will go much quicker if you do as I say."

"No—"

"For Christ's sakes, just grab him. While we're still young?" Aaron snapped.

"Using force will get us nowhere," Jakob explained.

"Yes, it will," Aaron said impatiently.

Jakob shot Aaron another glance over his shoulder. "I can't imagine why Paul wanted to leave you in the first place."

Aaron's eyes hardened. "My business with Paul is none of yours. Get on with it, will you?"

"Quit talking like I'm not here," Paul snapped.

Jakob met his eyes. "Paul, come on. Just—"

"He's staying with me."

"I don't think that's a good idea."

"I don't give a shit what you think."

"Why do you care so much about him, Paul? I find it surprising, given the way you grew up."

"You don't know shit about the way I grew up."

"I know enough."

"Bullshit."

"Don't believe me?"

"Prove it."

"Where would you like me to start?"

"Wherever you think is necessary," he said snidely.

"Your parents were shot in front of you."

Paul blanched, the words charging into the room like a rampaging beast, uncontrollable and terrifying.

No one knew that.

No one but Aaron.

Something cracked inside Paul's chest. The compulsion to scream shot up the back of his throat like vomit and it took all he had to swallow it back down. Blinking slowly, he let his eyes find Aaron's but then Jakob kept talking and there was nothing Paul could do to stop himself from listening.

"You ran away from home with your father's brains splattered in your hair and your mother's blood on your shirt. What were you, eight? Nine? Even at that age you had some pretty good instincts."

Paul stared at him as the room began a slow, lethargic spin.

"It was a good move on your part, Paul. If you had stuck around, you'd be just as dead as Mom and Dad."

Just as dead.

In hindsight, that option was the better choice. Then he wouldn't be standing here, getting old wounds torn open, feeling memories and nightmares bleed out onto the floor. He wouldn't be seeing his father on his knees, begging for his life while the lives of his wife and son were forfeit because he would get the money, he would *always* get the money and Paul had hated him. Hated him for begging, hated him for getting them involved in a mess of his own doing. Hated him for not being able to keep more than twenty bucks in his pocket before the urge to bet it all grabbed him the way crack grabs an addict. Hated him for doing this to his mother who hadn't known just how far in the hole he'd dug them until the bullets blew her beautiful face apart. Even while she bled to death, twitching, gasping, faceless on the floor at his feet, his father still begged. He was still begging after his brain had been shot out across the room and Paul was running out of the door and down the street as far and as fast as he could.

The running had lasted for ten years.

Until Aaron.

Aside from him, Paul had never told a living soul what had happened and now Jakob was spilling it out like a candid ghost story around a camp fire.

He felt something warm and wet soak into the back of his shirt.

Ethan was crying. Paul could feel his chest shuddering with every breath he took as he tried to keep quiet. The shuddering was causing his own shuddering to kick-start but he wasn't sure if it was from anger or something else. He couldn't seem to grab hold of anything concrete.

"You don't—You—can't know—" he choked out, taking a stumbling step back as if putting distance between himself and Jakob could put distance between himself and the memories in his head.

Ethan moved with him, careful to stay out from under his feet. Paul automatically reached back to keep him close, gripping the back of his shirt.

"Oh, sure I do," Jakob said. "You ran for nearly ten years after that. Not sure if anyone bothered to look for you although I doubt they would've found you. You probably didn't want to be found anyway, did you?"

No, not really.

"But at least you were making good money. More money than your father ever saw in his lifetime, right? You were doing rather well for yourself. I'm sure with the right financial advisors you would've been able to invest some of that—what did he call it, Aaron?" he said without taking his eyes off Paul.

"Fuck-money," Aaron said helpfully.

Paul flinched as he met Aaron's eyes. *Damn you*, he wanted to shriek. *Goddamn you for this.*

"Ah, yes," Jakob continued, bringing Paul's attention back to him. "Fuck-money. Crude but accurate, but hey, money is money and I'm sure over time, you would've moved into a nice apartment instead of keeping house under an overpass somewhere."

Paul's breath trembled in his throat. "Shut up."

"Maybe get a car—"

"You—"

"Get a nice plasma TV, some running water—"

"Shut up."

"Once you stopped whoring yourself out, that is."

"God*damn* it, shut the fuck up!"

Everything exploded outward, coming out of his body in the form of a scream that was both tortured and animalistic. Shoving Ethan to the ground, he lunged forward, ducking and swinging a fist at Jakob's face before he had a chance to pull the trigger. He let out a triumphant howl as blood flew from Jakob's nose. Jakob fell back and suddenly Irene was launching herself at him, eyebrows drawn low. Paul caught her by the neck and shoved her, barely feeling her nails cut into his arms as she swiped at him. As her body made a gratifying sound when it struck the bars, he found it vaguely surprising that she fought dirty for someone who could handle a weapon so well. He spun around, anticipating another attack but only found Aaron staring at him. He stood back from the bars now, his face a carefully blank mask but there was a strange gleam in his eye. It pulled Paul away from his rage for just a second. He'd seen gleams in Aaron's eyes before and their presence was never a good sign. But this was something altogether different.

It was over. Well and truly over.

He turned away from him, this man who had been his mentor, his nightmare, his guide for so long, feeling the bond or whatever twisted, knotted thing it had been, break apart with a brittle snap.

He scooped Ethan up off the floor. He caught pale eyes widening in his tear-stained face and knew there was someone behind him. Without turning, he kicked his leg back, feeling his foot connect. He spun around to find Jakob doubled over. Movement came from the corner of his eye and he turned toward it, catching his face on Irene's fingernails. They ripped down his cheek, making him stagger back. He fell to one knee, off-balance. Adjusting his grip on Ethan, he started to rise, a voice in the back of his head, or maybe it was Ethan's voice in his ear, urging him to *Move it* before Jakob could aim the gun at him again.

Cold metal was suddenly against his head and he froze.

Too late.

"As much as I enjoy having you on your knees, Paul, this is getting tiresome," Jakob drawled from above him.

Paul looked up at him, noting with some glee that his nose lay at a crooked angle in the center of his face and blood coated his mouth and chin.

"Do you think I'm enjoying this?" Paul spat through gritted teeth.

Jakob chuckled then winced. "If your right hook is anything to go by, I should hope so."

"I'll enjoy it even more when we get the hell out of here."

Jakob smiled through the blood seeping out of his nose. The smile was dark and wet and he slid the weapon down Paul's jaw, hooking it under his chin and drawing his head back until Paul had no choice but to look at him.

"You know that's not going to happen, Paul."

"Says the guy with the broken nose."

"There are quite a few more bones you'll have to break if you want to get out of here in one piece."

"So put the gun away and let's get started."

Jakob's eyebrows lifted in amusement. "As soon as we put the child away, Paul."

Paul felt little stabs of pressure as Ethan's fingers sank into his arm. "He's not going anywhere."

Jakob leaned down into his face, digging the gun into the soft flesh beneath his jaw.

"Come on, Paul. You don't want *your* brains stuck in *this* kid's hair, do you?"

Paul glared at him. "You are a fucking asshole—no!" he shouted as Jakob suddenly wrenched Ethan from his arms.

He grappled for him, pushing to his feet but Jakob drove a knee into his gut. Wheezing, Paul collapsed to the floor. His eyes watered as he tried to breathe and he could barely make out Irene pulling Ethan, struggling and crying from the room.

"No!" Ethan cried.

"Let him go!" Paul tried to shout, his lungs burning.

"Hush now," Jakob whispered, hunkering down next to him, shoving the gun under his chin once more, this time with enough force to slam his mouth shut.

Paul winced as his teeth clacked painfully together. "Leave him alone," he rasped. "He—"

"Shhh," Jakob shushed. "It's time for the grown-ups to talk, Paul."

"There's nothing to talk about."

"Oh, sure there is." He carded his free hand over Paul's hair, almost lovingly, the way someone would pet a dog.

"I already told you. I am *not* working with you or for you. How many different ways can I say this?"

The smile he was given sent ice dripping down the back of his neck. "As many as you like," Jakob replied, his fingers skidding, feather-light, down the side of Paul's face, moving over the scratches left by Irene's fingernails.

Paul jerked his head away. Jakob chuckled and stood up.

"Come on, on your feet. Can't very well have a conversation with you sprawled out on the floor like this."

He lowered the gun with a knowing look. Paul slowly got to his feet, his knees creaking. He wrapped an arm around his mid-section, grimacing as he tried to take in a full breath.

"Sorry about that."

Paul glared at him.

Jakob stared back at him, waiting. "What, I don't get one?"

"One what?"

"An apology."

"For what?"

"You broke my nose."

"It'll heal."

Jakob rolled his eyes. "Neanderthal."

"I think we've wasted enough time with the violence and idle chit-chat," Aaron said.

Paul did not look at him but silently agreed. He kept his eyes on Jakob who seemed to bask in the attention of both men.

"Well, that could've been easily avoided if Paul wasn't so difficult. The least you could've done was warn me, Aaron."

"Jakob," Aaron warned.

"Okay, I get it," Paul said. "You're both in on this…whatever the hell it is that you've got planned. But if that's the case, why is he the one in the cage?" He pointed an accusing finger at Aaron.

Aaron raised an eyebrow at him.

Jakob chuckled. "Irene and I knew you two couldn't be in the same room without some kind of…restraint. Especially after everything that he's led you to believe."

Paul frowned. "Led me to believe?"

"Yes."

"And what has he led me to believe?"

"That he wanted to kill you."

The beats of silence that followed were loud enough to shatter glass.

"I thought we weren't going to tell him until he finished the job?" Aaron asked.

"Why wait?" Jakob shrugged. "The sooner we tell him, the sooner he'll get over his emotional turmoil and we can get down to business."

Paul blinked hard. "What?"

"You have awful timing, Jakob," Aaron said in a dismissive tone. "Truly."

"Hey, you're the one who said to get on with it so that's what I'm doing."

Paul's gaze volleyed back and forth, his eyes wide. "It…It was all bullshit?"

It was Aaron's turn to shrug. "I wouldn't say it was all bullshit. I was pissed at you, but as far as killing you? You are far too valuable. Much more than you give yourself credit for."

Paul's stomach twisted and he felt sick, like the one kid in a group of friends who didn't get the joke.

"Paul," Aaron said, his tone silky-smooth. "How could you ever think that I intended to kill you?"

Paul stared at him, slack-jawed. He didn't think his brain could handle any more surprises. He took a step back. "How can you ask me that when it was what you wanted me to believe all along?"

"But we've been through so much, Paul," Aaron said. "I thought for sure you'd see right through my ruse."

"Well, I didn't."

"No, you didn't. I'm exceptionally glad that you didn't because if you had, things would've become a lot worse for you."

"How can things get any worse?"

"You're alive, aren't you?"

"Not at the rate this conversation's going."

"Paul, I promise you. Nothing will happen to you, as long as you—" Jakob started.

"Do as you say," Paul finished for him.

"More or less."

"It would've been easier for you both to just kill me," Paul said stonily.

Aaron shook his head. "I doubt that. I trained you too well."

"You trained me to serve you. That's all."

"I've trained you to be the best. I don't expect you to be grateful in light of certain truths, but you can believe me when I say it was in your best interest."

"What the fuck do you even know about that?"

"Plenty. If I had told you about the plan with Jakob and Irene, you never would've gone for it. You never would've allowed yourself to be pimped out. It was easier for you and for your delicate mind to run, to believe that I was going to kill you."

"So you had me kidnapped. Along with a fucking kid?"

Aaron shrugged again. "I honestly didn't think the whore would still be with you by the time you were collected. But now that I see how much you care about him, I think he will be a good incentive."

Paul's jaw flexed. "I'm not doing anything that you have planned. This is some sick mind-fuckery and I'm not having anything to do with it."

Jakob smiled. "I think it's a bit late for that."

Paul turned to tell him to fuck off when Irene strutted back into the room.

"Ah, Irene darling," Jakob greeted her, taking her hand. "Is Ethan prepared?"

He kissed her knuckles. Her eyes sparkled with cruelty as they found Paul's.

"Prepared for what?" Paul demanded, his gut dropping to his ankles.

"Yes, he's prepared," Irene smirked.

"Paul? Be so good as to come with us, please?"

"Prepared for *what*?"

Jakob gestured for the stairs. Paul shook his head.

"Paul," Irene suddenly said. "The more you put up a fight, the longer he stays where he is."

"And where is he?"

Her smile could've frozen vodka. "Come upstairs and find out."

CHAPTER 22

With Aaron's jovial, "hurry back" ringing in his ears, Paul was taken upstairs, sandwiched between Irene and Jakob like the prisoner he was. Irene led the way, her posture ramrod straight and Jakob bought up the rear, keeping the gun at the center of Paul's spine. They were expecting him to attack one or both of them but in all honestly, Paul didn't have the strength. There was a heaviness in his head and in his bones. He felt like he was standing at the helm of a runaway train and the impact, when it came, was going to hurt.

A lot.

Gritting his teeth, he craned his neck to glance back at Jakob. "If you've hurt him—" he began in warning.

"We haven't hurt him, Paul," Jakob cut him off with exasperation. "We haven't laid a hand on him since you both have been in our care."

Not yet.

The words hung unsaid in the air, thick and very possible.

"Care implies that you give a shit."

"But we do."

"Not when you're shoving a gun in my back."

"This is merely a precaution, Paul. You've proven to be somewhat erratic."

"Were you expecting something else?"

"I was expecting what Aaron promised us."

"And what was that?" Paul said through clenched teeth.

"You. His best of the best, obedient and willing."

"Too bad that's not going to happen."

Jakob chuckled. "We'll see."

Paul dug his nails into his palms. They continued to climb the stairs in silence. It seemed to be taking an awfully long time to reach the top and Jakob unfortunately wanted to use that time to chit-chat.

"Your relationship with Aaron," he contemplated. "It's not what I expected."

Paul remained pointedly silent.

"I was expecting more of a 'yes sir, no sir' kind of thing. I mean, to hear Aaron tell it, he had you at his feet, eating out of his hand. But that's not entirely true, is it?"

Paul's molars grated together.

"I have to say, I'm glad for it, Paul. I was hoping we would have the opportunity to work with someone with a little…pizzazz."

Paul snorted. "Right. Pizzazz."

"No, I'm serious. If you were some mindless machine I doubt I'd like you as much. Although you'd still be very nice to look at."

"So glad you approve."

"I do. Very much so."

"Guys like me are a dime a dozen."

"Oh, I wouldn't say that. A guy with your kind of talent, not to mention your looks, is a deadly combination."

Paul felt the tips of his ears burn. Every inch of his being itched to turn around and bury his fist in Jakob's smirking face. And he was smirking. Paul could feel it burning into the back of his head.

"Even Irene agrees with me, don't you, my dear?"

Without breaking stride, she craned her neck to look over her shoulder. The corner of her mouth quirked up as she eyed Paul in such a shrewd manner that Paul felt his balls shrivel up. He glanced away from her, listening to the two of them chuckle. He began to mentally list ways of making them suffer slowly and painfully and by the time they reached the top of the stairs and trekked into the kitchen, his list had grown to sixty-three.

"Where is he?" he demanded as Jakob stopped him in the center of the kitchen.

Irene stopped before the doorway that led into the room where Paul had nearly strangled Jakob to death. Paul looked from one to the other. They were ignoring him and looking at each other.

Jakob smiled.

Irene didn't.

"Moment of truth," Jakob said.

Irene gave a slight tilt of her head then stepped to one side. Jakob gave him a nudge.

"He's in the living room."

Paul looked back at him, eyeing both him and the gun. Jakob nodded encouragingly.

He stormed into the living room.

The room was blinding white and it was only after his eyes adjusted to the brightness that he saw that it was full-fledged morning and it was snowing outside, so heavily that the wall of windows was completely whited out. Squinting against the harsh light, he looked around the room and promptly froze when he saw the steel cage sitting in the center of the floor.

Ethan was huddled inside on his knees, face to the floor, trembling so hard the wire mesh shook. The top of the cage pressed against his back and the sides touched his arms, pressing into his skin. It was a cage for a dog.

Paul's nails sliced into his palms. He turned slowly, trying to contain himself because the rage that iced through his veins was vicious and filled with teeth.

"Get. Him. Out. Of. There."

Jakob, who stood just inside the room, seemed to contemplate his words.

"I don't think I can do that."

"I'm not asking you to think about it. Do it. Now."

One corner of his mouth twitched. "No."

There was a slight rustle in the cage behind him. Like a heated touch, Paul could sense when Ethan's eyes found him.

He's alive. At least there's that.

But the pep talk wasn't working. Sure, the kid was alive but this whole situation was in the process of fucking him up more than staying in the game ever would. Paul leveled his gaze on Jakob. His nonchalance was fraying the last of Paul's nerves.

"Jakob," he said, a growl entering his voice. "I'm not going to tell you again."

"You might have to. I'm a little hard of hearing."

Paul took a step toward him, a lunge really but a tremendous force hit the back of his left leg and he went down hard. He immediately sprang back up but only got as far as his knees before he was pulled into a tight half-Nelson. Surprised, he reached back, digging his fingers into a thin but muscled bicep. He felt breasts at the back of his head.

Irene. Goddamn this bitch.

He started to push to his feet but her free hand was at the front of his throat, touching it with a knife that looked like it could slice through bone. He went still, air whistling through clenched teeth. He tried to inch his head away from the blade but it followed and Irene's hand on the back of his neck didn't allow for escape.

"Get...off me."

Jakob strolled closer to him, the gun swinging from his hand like a shopping bag. "You know what you have to do, Paul."

"Fuck you."

Jakob pursed his lips. "Nah. Maybe later. But for now—"

"I'm not doing anything for you!" he tried to shout.

"Shhhh." Irene's lips were suddenly next to his ear. "Don't shout. You wouldn't want to startle the puppy."

"You b—"

His words ended in a hiss as pressure was applied to the knife. He flinched as her fingers crawled up from the back of his neck to curl into his hair. Her mouth brushed, petal-soft, against his ear as she pulled his head back.

"You know what has to be done to make this easy for you," she whispered.

"No—" he tried to say.

"Yes," she countered, shifting her body until she was draped over his back like a cape. "Come on, Paul. You know he doesn't belong in a cage."

"I know that—"

"Then why have you put him there?"

His eyes widened. He struggled to turn his head, to look at her but couldn't without slicing his throat open.

"I didn't—"

"Yes, you did."

"No—"

"Yes. Every time you say no. Every time you refuse, you build the walls of that cage and put him in there." She smiled against the side of his face. "It's all because of you."

He jerked against her and cried out as the knife cut into his neck.

"Shhhh," she whispered again. "Quiet. Oh, see what you did? You're bleeding. You're willing to do *that* for him, Paul, but why not anything else? Hm?"

Something close to alarm skated down his spine as she nuzzled the soft skin behind his ear.

"Come on," she cooed. "Just say it. Say it and he'll be let out. Say it and he'll be free. You both will be free."

His eyes cut to the corners, trying again to see her.

Her mouth trailed down his cheek. "Do as we say and you'll never have to do anything you don't want to do again."

Paul's mind raced.

"It's only one thing, Paul," she went on, nibbling gently at his jaw.

He swallowed hard.

"Just this one thing and everyone will be happy. Happy and free. Isn't that what you want?"

"Yes," he couldn't help but say.

"Just one more, Paul. One more job. How bad can it be when you know what awaits you at the end?"

Freedom.

"It'll be so much better than running for the rest of your life," she continued, her lips leaving a warm trail back to his ear.

Her hair was soft against his face and smelled like flowers. She was so warm, her words even warmer, promising everything for one more job.

One more.

Just one more.

"That's—That's it?" he asked.

"Hmmm?" she murmured, her eyelashes fluttering against his cheek.

"Just one more job and you'll leave me alone? You'll let me and Ethan walk out of here?"

"Yes."

"You won't come after us?"

"No. Unless you want us to."

"And Aaron?"

She chuckled and the sound was filled with darkness. "He won't mind."

He frowned and this time when he tried to look at her, she let him, easing up on the knife but not the hand knotted in his hair. He met her eyes, their faces so close her breath pushed into his mouth. Her eyes were bright and drowsy as if she'd been drugged. But there was a keenness there that Paul was beginning to not underestimate.

"I want a guarantee," he said, this strangely intimate moment causing him to lower his voice to a whisper as well.

Her lips tickled his and for one heart-stopping instant, he thought she was going to kiss him.

"You have it," she said simply.

CHAPTER 23

I t took him nearly two hours to coax Ethan out of the cage. All the soothing words he'd repeated uselessly over and over again had fallen on deaf ears and Paul had begun to fear that the kid was locked so far inside his own mind that there would be *no* way to get him out. Then the small sounds had started, tiny whimpering noises like a kitten in pain. If there had been room, he was sure Ethan would've started rocking back and forth. The sounds were sharp, so knife-thin that Paul had wanted to break the damn cage apart with his bare hands.

By the time he'd crawled out and into Paul's arms, Paul was so drained, he could barely pick him up. Ethan clung to him, wrapping his legs around his rib cage and his arms around Paul's neck. With a sigh of relief and wasted adrenaline, Paul climbed shakily to his feet, banding both his arms around the quivering body. He could feel Ethan's heart pounding like a tiny fist and his face was wet as he shoved it into Paul's neck, as if trying to hide.

Goddammit, he thought for the millionth time that day. *None of this was worth it—*

"Paul?"

He turned to find Jakob watching him quietly. In the time that he'd left Paul to tend to Ethan, he'd straightened his broken nose—probably with a spoon—and bandaged it. The skin around it was puffy and purple.

Hope it hurts, you son-of-a-bitch.

"What?" he snapped.

"If you'll let me, I'll show you to your rooms. You both need some rest."

Paul frowned. "How long have we been here?"

"About three weeks."

Jakob's eyes were soft, filled with something resembling concern. Paul's frown deepened.

"Come with me," Jakob said.

Hesitating, Paul followed him up the stairs. He felt Ethan's arms tighten around his neck as he moved.

"Shhh," Paul whispered to him. "Shhh."

He glanced behind him as he was led down a series of corridors that never seemed to end. He tried to memorize their route but the exhaustion he'd managed to hold off was beginning to weigh heavily on his brain.

Jakob stopped in the center of a dead-end hallway. At the end was a huge circular window, filled with white from the snow beyond. It looked uncomfortably like the white of an eye that was rolled back into its head.

"Your room," Jakob instructed, pointing to one door. "Ethan will be across from you in this room." He pointed to another door across the hall. "Both rooms have their own bathrooms, fireplaces—"

"Fine." Paul glanced from one door to the other.

Jakob took a step forward, arms reaching for Ethan. "I can—"

"Back off," Paul immediately said, taking a quick step back.

Jakob froze, arms in mid-air.

"You can go."

"Are you sure?"

"Yes."

Jakob stared at him for a few moments then gave a curt nod and walked away. Paul waited until he was out of sight before heading toward Ethan's room. He put his ear to the door then swung it inward.

The room was dark except for the crackling fire in the hearth. Paul glanced around. It was comfortably furnished—a big bed that Ethan could get lost in, a large dresser, a few plush-looking chairs in front of the fire, and a door off to the right that led to the bathroom. Thick, heavy-looking curtains were drawn over the windows and when Paul shut the door behind them, he immediately felt enveloped in a warm, cozy cocoon. Stroking one hand over Ethan's back, he went over to the bed. He leaned over the side.

"Okay, buddy, here's the bed, right beneath you—"

He stopped when Ethan's arms tightened like nooses around his neck. His legs squeezed like they wanted to break through Paul's rib cage. He winced.

"It's all right, Ethan. Ethan? Hey, it's okay. I'm just going to set you down right here, okay?"

Ethan buried his face harder against Paul's neck, a small sound coming from his throat. Paul swallowed hard.

"I'm not going anywhere, Ethan. I'm just going to put you down on the edge of the bed, okay?"

But it wasn't okay. The kid pressed harder against him. Paul gritted his teeth, sliding his hands around Ethan's torso. His hands almost fit perfectly around his chest.

God, this kid needs to eat. He needs to rest. He needs…

"Ethan?" he tried again, keeping his voice low which made the cracking inside of it more apparent. "Ethan, come on, I'm not going anywhere, all right? I'm staying right here." He looked up at the ceiling, chewing on his lip. "Ethan, can you hear me, buddy? Huh? Come on, man, talk to me. Talk to me."

'If I wanted to listen to you talk, I would've paid for it.'
…gagging on the cock that was pushed into his mouth…

Paul shook his head, his eyes burning. He carefully gripped the back of Ethan's head, feeling more tears splash against his neck.

"Ethan?" he whispered. "Come on, let go of me, buddy. I'm not leaving you. You need…You need to lay down, all right? You need to rest. There's a bed here. You'll be able to sleep. You're tired, right? Huh?"

He didn't know how long he stayed there, whispering in his ear, telling him that everything was going to be okay, trying to believe it and failing. It felt more like he was talking to himself, telling himself that things were going to be fine but he didn't believe it any more than Ethan did. His legs began to burn, his arms deaden beneath the weight. He half-expected Ethan to start snoring, he stayed so still for so long, his limbs so tight around Paul's body. But then as the quiet around them settled and thickened to molasses, broken only by the snapping flames in the fireplace, slowly, Ethan began to relinquish his grip.

Paul stayed still, holding his breath. The kid pulled away, inch by inch, his legs loosening, sliding down until Paul leaned over the bed again and set him down on the edge. Ethan's frail arms lingered before falling away in jerky movements, fingers twitching as if unsure how to let go. Breathing a long sigh of relief, Paul went to his knees in front of him.

In the semi-darkness, the kid's pale eyes were huge, his tear-streaked face puffy and outlined in silver by the firelight. Strands of hair were stuck to his cheeks. Paul watched uncertainly as he braced his hands on the bed on either side of Ethan's knees and leaned forward, trying to catch his eye.

"Ethan?"

He was met with silence. He pressed his lips together, wondering if he should just physically maneuver the kid until he lay down.

"You should…uh, you should try and get some sleep," he said.

More silence.

"No one will hurt you in here, okay? I—"

"What if you don't make it?"

Paul blinked. "What?"

Ethan's throat convulsed as he swallowed. His eyes stayed on his lap.

"What if you don't come back?"

"Of course I'll come back. I'll be right across the hall—"

"No, I mean—from the job."

Paul's eyebrows rose. He hadn't thought the kid was lucid during that particular conversation. "You heard about that, huh?"

"I was two feet from you."

Paul almost smiled despite himself. *'I'm not a kid.'* "Right," he said, clearing his throat. "Well, I've been doing this kind of...work for a while. It's nothing I can't handle so you don't need to worry, oka—"

"What if something happens?" he said even before Paul was done speaking.

His little fingers twisted into the blankets beneath him and Paul could see his brow start to furrow.

Paul frowned. "Like what?"

"What if you change your mind?" he said so quietly Paul almost didn't hear him.

"About what?"

He hesitated then said, "Leaving."

"Leaving? Well, I kind of have to in order to do this—"

"No, I mean...I mean after."

Paul moved back. "After...Ethan, look I—" He stopped, staring at him. "You think I won't come back."

For you.

The unspoken words hung in the air. Ethan ducked his head down lower until his hair obscured his face, leaving Paul to gape at the top of his head.

"No," he said, his voice strangling him. "No, Ethan—"

Ethan turned his head away.

"I—"

"What if you don't come back?" the boy said again, his voice broken.

Paul stared at him.

ᕮᔑᕮᔑ

'But you promised! You promised you'd help me!'

'What the hell do you expect me to do? I can't just take you in like some kind of fucking stray animal.'

'But you said—'

'I know what I said but I can't!'

'Why—'

'I have a wife and three kids, for Christ's sake!'

'Well maybe you should've thought of that before you started paying me to suck your dick.'

∽∾∽

He grabbed Ethan by the arms more roughly than he'd intended but it had the desired effect. Ethan gasped, his head snapping up.

"Listen to me," Paul said around clenched teeth. "You listen to me and you listen good. I told you. I told you I was going to get us out of here, remember? Remember? I told you that. Do you remember? Huh? Do you? Do you?" he pressed when Ethan continued to stare mutely at him.

Ethan's forearms curled against his chest as Paul's fingers tightened around his biceps. He was vaguely aware of the muscles grinding beneath his palms but he wanted Ethan to understand. He *needed* him to understand.

"I meant it, Ethan," he went on, his words trembling. "I meant every word. I'm getting us out of here and this is what I have to do in order to accomplish that. Do you understand?"

Ethan's features trembled.

"I have to leave."

A small half-sob erupted from Ethan's mouth and he started to shake his head.

"No, no, no, listen to me," Paul pushed on quickly. "You cannot come with me, not on this job. But—hey, hey, look at me." Paul released one of Ethan's arms and took hold of his chin, pulling Ethan's face back to his. "Listen to me."

He forced himself to be patient, waiting for Ethan's tear-rimmed eyes to focus on him. When they did, Paul leaned in close until Ethan had no choice but to look at him.

"I *will* come back."

Ethan's eyes searched his. An eternity seemed to slip by until the tension suddenly left Ethan's body and he sagged back. Something flashed in his eyes that made Paul want to scream.

It wasn't belief in him or understanding.

It was resignation.

"I'm tired," Ethan said and pulled away from Paul's hands.

Paul released him with difficulty. He struggled to find something more powerful to say, something that would make Ethan believe him. But he came up empty. Ethan scooted back to the center of the bed, settling down into the blankets and mound of pillows. Paul stood up and started to turn away from the bed when Ethan whispered, "Stay with me?"

Paul turned back to him. Ethan curled up on his side, facing him, his face lost in the shadows now.

"Just 'til I fall asleep."

Paul pressed his lips together and pulled a chair over. He listened silently until Ethan's breathing evened out and his fists unclenched against the pillows as sleep took hold.

He stayed, watching a little longer than necessary.

Just in case.

Then he left the room, closing the door quietly behind him.

Rolling his shoulders to loosen them, he turned toward his own room and stopped.

Jakob stood in front of his door.

"Little guy all settled in?" he purred.

In two strides, Paul was in his face, crowding him back. Jakob simply stared up at him, his dark eyes twinkling.

"You touch one more hair on that kid's head and I will break every bone in your body."

"You can try."

"Why are you fucking with me?" Paul hissed. "You got what you wanted. Isn't that enough?"

Jakob pushed himself forward, forcing Paul to take a step back.

"No, Paul. It's not anywhere near enough."

"Bullshit," he snapped. "You won. You, Irene and Aaron. Congratulations. I'm going to do what you say like a good little puppy and then you will never see or hear from me again. So do me a favor. Until then? Stay the fuck out of my face."

Jakob smiled indulgently. "But I like you, Paul. I mean that. Our time together is limited and I don't want you to think that all of this is just because of some job. I want to establish some kind of relationship with you. I don't want you to feel used—"

"It's a bit late for that."

"But—"

"I'm doing this job and that's it, Jakob. That's what we agreed on."

A smirk pulled at Jakob's lips. "I bet it's killing you to say that."

"Are we done here?"

"Can I tuck you in?"

Not bothering to honor that with a reply, Paul simply stepped around him and started to open the door to his room when he felt a warm hand in the center of his back. He froze. Warm breath ghosted over his ear.

"It wouldn't hurt for you to be nice to me," Jakob murmured from behind him. "It actually might do you some good to have at least one person on your side."

Paul's jaw clenched as he turned his head to look at him. "And that one person is you?"

Jakob gave him a lazy smile. "Why, yes, actually. Or maybe you'd prefer Irene? My girl's quite taken with you."

"I bet. Get your hand off me."

The hand fell away but it seemed to leave behind a burning imprint.

"There's no need to be this way, Paul," Jakob continued. "It's true that you're giving us what we want. But keep in mind that we are also giving you what you want."

Paul's eyes burned holes into the door in front of him. "I hope you're not expecting a thank you."

The chuckle in his ear was low and breathless. "Wouldn't dream that big. But—" he paused.

Paul felt fingers twirl lightly into his ponytail. The goosebumps that popped up along his neck were unwelcome and itchy.

"There are a few things I have been dreaming about, Paul. Would you like me to tell you about them?"

Out of nowhere, he was seized by an old panic. The heat at his back, the pull of his hair at the nape of his neck, the biting fingers in his shoulders...

He blinked, long and hard. Something touched the shell of his ear and he jerked away from it, pushing into his room and slamming the door on the sound of Jakob's chuckle.

CHAPTER 24

Dawn approached cautiously, as if afraid. Paul didn't blame it. He didn't want to face the day either. He was showered and dressed by the time the sun peeked over the horizon, splashing coldly across the landscape of ice and snow that seemed to stretch for miles, broken only by the occasional scatterings of trees. He stood at the window and fought back a shiver. He couldn't believe how isolated the place was. No mountains in the distance, no animals darting through the snow. Nothing moved. Nothing breathed.

With a long exhale, he turned away from the window, rubbing his eyes. The sleep he'd gotten was awful, full of bad dreams and thoughts of fear and creeping paranoia. Having Aaron close by made it impossible for his mind to rest and the few times he had drifted off ended abruptly as an imagined scream echoed in the caverns of his consciousness, making him jerk awake, drenched in sweat, and clutching helplessly at the bed sheets.

Several times he thought he'd heard someone crying in the hallway but no matter how many times he went out to check, there was never anyone there. The surrounding shadows had laughed at him, the dying embers in the fireplace had mocked him, and by the time the sky had begun to lighten, he'd had enough.

Now he left the bedroom, squinting in the blazing light that poured in through the round window at the end of the hall. He crossed to Ethan's room. He knocked softly and when he didn't hear an answer, he quietly opened the door wide enough to poke his head through. When his eyes adjusted to the darkness, he saw Ethan's small form underneath the blankets. He was curled up along the edge of the bed, on the side closest to the door, as if not wanting to take up too much space while at the same time being as close to the only means of escape as he possibly could.

A breath Paul hadn't known he'd been holding came out of his lungs and he leaned back out to shut the door. There was no harm in letting the kid sleep. As long as he was up here and out of the way, he might be—

A hand landed on his shoulder.

Barely biting back a startled *shit* he spun around and found himself face-to-face with Irene. He took an immediate step back, feeling his shoulder blades collide with the door. She stared at him, her face its usual cool mask but her eyes sparkled with something that might've been amusement.

"Good morning," she said.

"Hey," he replied stiffly.

"Did you sleep well?"

He shrugged.

"And the boy?"

"Good. I guess, I mean he's still asleep."

She gave a slight nod. "It's probably best. We have a lot to discuss. Are you hungry?"

"I—"

"Follow me."

He hesitated, watching her walk away.

"Come on," she called impatiently over her shoulder.

When he still didn't move, she stopped and looked back at him. "What?"

"Every time I follow you, it usually leads to someplace bad."

She lifted an eyebrow. "It's breakfast and work. That's all."

"I have no reason to trust you."

"Yes, you do."

"And that is?"

"Currently, I'm not trying to kill you."

Paul stared at her. "Currently?"

The eyebrow came down. "Currently."

He followed her down the stairs, keeping his distance, watching her closely. She was dressed in dark cargo pants, tucked into fuzzy-looking black boots that came up to her knees and a black thermal shirt. There was certainly no place on her body that could hold a weapon, even the boots were skin-tight. But he'd been surprised by her before. If she looked unarmed, chances were she probably wasn't. He thought for a moment that Aaron would appreciate someone like her, both physically and professionally.

He started suddenly as if he'd been poked in the side. "Where's Aaron?"

A sound came out of her that resembled a chuckle. "Who?"

"Aaron? You know—"

"Oh, yes. Well. He's sleeping off a rough night."

"But where is he?"

She glanced back at him. "Around."

"Look, if it's not too much trouble—"

"Actually, it is," she said, spinning around and fixing her eyes on his face.

Paul stopped in his tracks.

"You have more important things to tend to," she went on, her husky voice dropping to a hiss. "And Aaron is not one of them."

His hands balled into fists at his sides. "Why don't you let me be the judge of that?"

A cold smile spread across her face. "I'm inclined to take your judgment with a grain of salt."

His lips skinned back over his teeth. "Look, I don't want to be here anymore than you want me to be. I'm sure I don't have to remind you that it was your idea to bring me here. You and your little boyfriend—"

"And Aaron. Don't forget Aaron."

His face flushed, words stuttering in his throat. She came toward him.

"What is it about your relationship with him, Paul?" she murmured. "Even after everything he put you through, after everything you found out, you're still concerned about his welfare. What does that say about you, Paul, when you can't even tell the difference between the truth and being completely fucked over?"

She was close enough now for him to touch her and he shoved his face into hers. "And I suppose you can tell me the difference since you've been fucking me over since I got here?"

Her eyes raked over his face. "I just might be the only one who hasn't been fucking with you, Paul. In fact, I would say that my actions toward you have been pretty straight-forward."

"Oh sure," he growled. "Smashing my face in, threatening to cut my throat. Sure. Very straight-forward."

She laughed and it was as cold as her smile. "I don't do nice, Paul. I can't. Not when someone responds so…adamantly to violence."

He almost hit her. "You don't know anything about me."

"That's true. I don't," she shrugged. "And I don't really care either. Now come on. My french toast is getting cold."

When she walked away from him again, it took everything he had not to pull her back by her ponytail and slam her face into the wall. He'd never met a woman who deserved to be hit but for this particular female Paul was willing to make an exception. He didn't think anyone would blame him either, except maybe Jakob.

Focus on the job, he chanted to himself. *Focus on the job then you can get the hell out of this nightmare.*

He trudged downstairs, trying to roll the tension out of his shoulders. He faltered on the last step when he saw the now-empty steel cage sitting in the middle of the living room floor. Gritting his teeth, he went into the kitchen as Jakob was setting a plate of hot scones on the long wooden table that took up half the kitchen. He glanced up with a ready smile, wiping his hands on his lipstick-marked apron.

"Morning," he said cheerfully. "Have a seat. I hope you're hungry."

Paul looked at the food and his stomach growled. It was a feast fit for a small army. Scrambled eggs, bacon, sausage links, pancakes topped with blueberries and strawberries, fresh cantaloupe, and honeydew sliced into perfect quarters, french toast glazed with sugar and syrup, and pitchers of orange and cranberry juice. He couldn't remember the last time he'd eaten and when Jakob gently guided him to a seat, he didn't refuse. Out of the corner of his eye, he saw Irene at the other end of the table, eating her french toast. He hoped she choked on it.

He helped himself to the fruit and eggs, taking care not to eat too quickly. He didn't need to show these bastards that he appreciated being fed even as his stomach screamed for bacon. He made a mental note to get a plate together for Ethan and take it up to him.

"So is Ethan still asleep?" Jakob asked as he sat down across from Paul and poured himself a glass of cranberry juice.

Paul swallowed the last of his scrambled eggs. "Yes."

"I can make up a plate and bring it—"

"I can do it."

"I can do it," Jakob insisted. "You're still eating—"

"I said I'll do it."

Jakob looked at him then sighed. "Okay."

Silence descended on the table, filled with the sounds of chewing, scraping silverware, swallowing, pouring, and, in Paul's case, barely suppressed moans of contentment. After what felt like hours of restrained gorging, he sat back, nursing his fourth glass of orange juice. He glanced up to find Jakob looking at him with something strangely like affection.

"Satisfied?"

Paul shrugged, shifting in his seat.

Jakob laughed. "It's okay. I know my cooking's good."

"You cooked all of this?" Paul asked skeptically.

"Don't look so surprised. Cooking is just one of my many talents."

'Can I tuck you in?'

Paul glanced down at the table top, feeling all of the food he'd just inhaled roil unpleasantly in his gut.

"Let's just get down to business, okay?"

Jakob gave a small chuckle as he got up from the table. Paul downed the rest of his juice, feeling Irene's eyes on him. It made his skin crawl. He forced himself to look over at her. A small smirk pulled at her lips, the kind a teenager would give his kid brother after jumping out of a closet and scaring the hell out of him. Paul's jaw flexed.

Jakob came back with a thick manila envelope. "Here we are."

Paul looked away from her. He ripped open the envelope with more force than was necessary and pulled out a glossy eight-by-ten headshot of a man that made Paul's feet go cold. He stared into the most haunting sea-green eyes he'd ever seen. They glowed so intensely, so fiercely that Paul felt the skin along his spine tingle. A heavy dark brow harbored them, setting them deep inside a bronzed, ageless face of sharp angles and stony edges. Paul stared at the photo, feeling a strange sense of relief that he was looking at this man in a picture and not face-to-face. There was a dangerous vibe here. A vibe that not even Irene could reciprocate. Tearing his eyes away with some difficulty, he looked at Jakob.

"His name is Chac Mool," Jakob said, returning to his seat across from Paul and folding his hands on the table in front of him.

Paul looked down at the picture again, felt the eyes probe into his brain. He put the photo on the table, resisting the urge to lay it face-down.

"What kind of a name is that?"

"An Aztec one."

"Aztec? As in human sacrifice-and-cutting-people's-hearts-out Aztec?"

"The very same."

"Do you plan on sacrificing someone?"

"No," Jakob chuckled.

"Then what do you want with this guy?"

Irene suddenly slid in next to him. Paul moved away from her a little. She didn't seem to mind or notice.

"Chac Mool is responsible for nearly eighty-five percent of all sacked burial sites, cities, and tombs in Aztec culture," she explained. "He's hired numerous specialized architects, archeologists, anthropologists, geologists, and other scientists who aren't interested in preserving ancient history to find and dismantle sacred monuments and tombs for the extraordinary amounts of jade and pottery that the Aztecs buried their dead with."

"Jade and pottery? What good is any of that to a dead person?"

"Like the Egyptians but uninfluenced by them, the Aztecs believed the dead travel to an afterlife, an underworld. For the journey, they would need food, things to carry their belongings in, and wealth, like jade, to offer the gods who would decide their fate."

"Like bribery."

"No, offerings. Jade was the ultimate treasure, valued even more than gold. It symbolized an almost-guarantee that their fate would be in the hands of goodness if presented with enough of it."

"Based on how much shit they presented to these gods?"

She frowned slightly at his choice of words. "Yes, and of course, how they lived their lives on Earth."

Paul rolled his eyes. "Look, as much as I appreciate the history lesson, you guys did tell me that there was an actual job involved."

"We're telling you this so you're prepared."

"Prepared for what? A fucking lecture? Just tell me what you want done and it'll get done, all right?"

Jakob leaned back in his seat as Irene seemed to turn to stone beside him. Paul's gaze volleyed impatiently back and forth between them.

"His living conditions are fit for a god," Jakob began.

"Jakob—"

"Let me finish," he cut in. "If we're sending you in there, you need to know what to expect."

"Fine," Paul said tightly. "Go on."

Jakob leaned forward again, his gaze intent upon Paul's face. "His living conditions are fit for a god and they are just as dangerous. No one has ever gone in and come out in one piece so the lay-out of the place is virtually unknown. What we do know is that it's huge and full of so much ancient history and artifacts, it's a museum curator's wet dream."

Paul watched a hungry gleam sparkle in Jakob's eyes. He had a feeling he knew where this one was going.

"So you're an...admirer of his collection," he said, injecting a bit of sarcasm into his tone.

Jakob smiled, flashing his teeth. "An admirer," he repeated, appearing to think that over. "Yes, yes I would say that."

"And you want to admire his collection up close and personally."

"Not the entire collection. Just one item." He dug into the envelope and pulled out a black-and-white photograph.

Paul took it from him, studying it closely. It showed a dark velvet pouch, sitting atop a small, square podium. The twined drawstring ropes that clinched the top shut were made of soft silk—Paul could tell by the way the light hit them. There was a piece of stone set in the middle of the pouch, roughly the size of a quarter. He peered more closely at it.

"Jade," Irene said, watching him. "The stone of the underworld."

"That's what you want?" Paul asked.

Jakob lifted his shoulders in a small shrug. "It's an added perk. What we want is inside the pouch."

Paul eyed the picture once more. "And what's inside of it?"

"Ashes."

Paul's eyebrow rose. "Of?"

"Someone of great power."

Paul's other eyebrow rose to join the first in a look of skepticism. "Are you kidding me? You want the remains of some dead Aztec ruler?"

Jakob nodded.

"How do you know the ashes are even in there?"

"They are."

Paul looked at the picture again. He wanted to ask what they intended to use it for but decided he was better off not knowing. He threw the picture down on the table.

"Fine. When do I start?"

Jakob blinked as if surprised. "Well...here, maybe you should take a look at this." He held the envelope out to Paul but he shook his head.

"I don't need to look at any more paperwork. I know what I have to get and that's all I need to know." He stood up.

Jakob stood up as well, holding the envelope between them. "Paul, I must insist. You need to know who you're dealing with."

"I can handle it."

"I'm sure you can. I don't doubt your abilities. But just humor me, all right?"

Paul glared at him. "I've been humoring you for a few days now and it's proved to be pretty damn pointless."

"Paul—"

He snatched the envelope from Jakob's hand and dumped everything out on the table.

Tax forms, insurance forms, receipts, real estate forms, airline tickets, everything that a paper trail could contain, it was here. A quick scan showed that everything was filled out properly, name, address, zip code, occupation which simply read "self-employed," salary made per year, how much taxes were taken out, how much he was refunded. If Paul was simply looking at this paperwork for no reason than what he was given, he would conclude that Chac Mool was a fine, upstanding citizen.

But then something caught his eye.

On every single form, under date of birth, there was an N/A. Paul rifled through all the documents to make sure he wasn't seeing things. "Weird."

"What?" Jakob asked carefully.

"There's no date of birth. No hospital, no town where he was born. I mean, you have all his information except for a birth certificate."

"Ah," was all Jakob said.

Paul fixed him with a look. "What aren't you telling me?"

Irene spoke up. "There never was a birth certificate."

Paul frowned at her. "Excuse me?"

"At least not that anyone ever found."

"That's ridiculous," Paul contradicted. "Everyone has a birth certificate. Even a fake one."

"No one has ever been able to locate it," Jakob said, quietly. "And if anyone ever has…well…" He hesitated. "See for yourself."

He shuffled through the paperwork until he came to a stack of pictures that were banded together. Paul took them from him and spread them out.

They were remarkably clear, so focused and sharp that it almost hurt to look at the shades of gray, white, and black, much like Ansel Adams' nature pictures. But these weren't photos of towering, snow-covered mountains or wind-swept deserts. These were jumbles of broken, mismatched puzzle pieces with large black blotches around them. Paul muttered under his breath, turning the photos around, his eyes trying to make sense of what he was looking at.

Then he stopped.

If a human being were to ever explode inside a phone booth, the picture that Paul was holding would be what it would look like. Chunks of flesh, bone, tissue, and thicker gobs clung to every available surface in a collage of gray and black Rorschach patterns. What he had first thought were lumps of raw hamburger meat were now bundles of bloodied flesh, torn muscles, and pulverized bone that splashed the walls, the ceiling, and the floor. He could make out an ear and he thought he could see something resembling a foot but he wasn't a hundred percent certain. He went to the next picture and saw a shot of a human head on a spike. The head had belonged to a man. Half-lid eyes, slack jaw, dark, ragged line around the torn neck. God only knew where the body was.

Paul bit back a groan of disgust and disbelief.

"Most of people in these pictures tried to steal from him or con him out of a valuable artifact, money, things like that. There were some who tried digging around in his files to see what they could blackmail him with. Basically anything that pertained to his privacy or his wealth won them a first-class ticket to—" He gestured at the pictures. "—that."

Paul shoved the pictures away. "You said you don't have a lay-out of this place, right?"

Jakob nodded.

"Do you know what kind of surveillance system he has?"

"The only surveillance is Chac Mool himself."

Paul burst out laughing. "This will be easier than I thought."

Jakob and Irene exchanged a look.

"Paul," Irene said sharply. "Perhaps, you are not understanding us—"

"I get it." He cut her off. "He's dangerous. Isn't that why you want me to do this job? So *you* don't end up splattered all over a wall like these poor sons of bitches?"

"Paul—"

"You're going to arm me, right?"

"Of course. We will give you your weapons when we get there."

"And Ethan?"

Jakob blinked at the subject change. "He will be fine here."

"You're damn right he will be." He turned away from them and put together a quick plate of breakfast for the kid.

He left the room with silence following him. He wasn't necessarily worried about the job or coming face-to-face with this Chac Mool. He was more preoccupied with why Jakob and Irene seemed almost concerned for his well-being. That made him worry more than any human body sprayed all over a wall.

CHAPTER 25

Night fall.

With Ethan's quiet, "Come back" burning in his ears, Paul followed Irene across the moon-splashed snow, moving low and quiet, like floating birds skimming over the surface of water. The snowmobiles were sleek and purred so silently, he doubted the wind would pick up the noise and carry it across the wide, open space. The night around them sparkled in silver and black. It was peaceful, cold, and silent and Paul wished there was time to appreciate it.

They rode through the woods. The dark trees were spread out enough that they could maneuver around them comfortably. Gradually, however they began to close in like a thick, line of soldiers. Paul and Irene had no choice but to stop. He climbed off the snowmobile, making sure it was in the shadows of the trees and slipped off his goggles. The icy wind was a slap in the face and his eyes immediately began to water. His breath puffed out in front of him. He was glad for the extra snow suit that Jakob just happened to have. Looking around, he saw that they were at the edge of a small clearing. Beyond it, a hundred yards off or so, was the house.

Except that it wasn't a house. It looked like a goddamn castle. It would've been better suited on top of a hill with banners blowing in the wind, waiting for the arrival of a king and queen with a peasant village spread below. But instead it was here, in the middle of an arctic landscape with not a soul around. It was a huge, dark stone structure, sprawling out and reaching up, up into the black sky. Paul let his eyes follow the spikes that decorated the top of the four towers that formed a perfect square. Narrow, arching windows blazed softly with light. The only thing missing was a drawbridge and a moat.

"He's in there all by himself?" he asked as Irene crunched through the snow to stand next to him.

She nodded. "As far as we know."

Paul turned his head to look at her, feeling that ever-present lump of frustration settle more solidly inside his chest.

"You do realize that there is a chance that this might fail, given your limited knowledge."

She returned his stare, her eyes dark but clear. "You won't fail."

He wasn't sure if he should feel elated at her confidence in him. "What makes you so sure?"

"You have someone waiting for you to return."

His jaw tightened. "If this Chac Mool character is as dangerous as you keep saying he is, no amount of sentimental thought is going to keep me alive."

"If you're good as Aaron says you are, you'll be in and out before Chac Mool even knows you're there."

"Are you really so concerned about my well-being that you'd rather I *not* run into this guy while I'm in there?"

"Why would you want to run into the person you're stealing from?"

"I don't. But you're acting like I won't be able to hold my own if I do."

"You won't."

"So let me get this straight. You think I'm good enough to steal something but not good enough to go head-to-head with some weird, off-the-grid spook?"

"That sums it up quite nicely."

"Do you have any idea how long I've been doing this kind of work?"

"A long time from what I've heard."

"Yes, a long time. I know how to handle myself. I don't need you or anybody else being 'concerned' about me or what I'm doing, okay?"

"Do I need to remind you of just how easy it was to take you off the street?"

As if he needed reminding. He was surprised that Aaron hadn't rubbed his face in it. But nevertheless, hearing it said out loud by this crazy bitch, of all people, made shame and anger burn hot in his gut.

"And do I need to remind you that if anything happens to Ethan while I'm gone, I will not hesitate to put a bullet in your head?" he said with a snarl.

A small smile tilted the corners of her mouth. "I'm aware of your feelings toward him."

"Oh, are you now?"

"Of course," she replied. "He's the reason we were able to get you with so little trouble."

Paul glared at her. "Do you think I can get to work now?"

She regarded him with quiet amusement before stepping past him and beginning a trek through the trees, keeping to the shadows. He followed her, hoping a mind shaft or a sink hole would open up and swallow her whole.

Through knee-deep snow they walked. In some areas, the snow was thigh-deep, thick and heavy. The air was silent. There was no wind, no chatter of night creatures, no serenity that came with being in the middle of nowhere. Everything was beautiful but empty, full but still and waiting, always waiting. Paul found himself looking up to find the moon but the black canopy of trees blocked the sky.

They came to another clearing, this one smaller than the first. Without a word, Irene swung her small backpack onto the ground and opened it. She took out a small shovel, made her way to the center of the clearing and began digging.

Paul watched her curiously. "We're digging our way in?" he asked.

She didn't answer and within a half hour, the shovel clanged loudly on metal. He jumped at the noise, making no move to help her as she put the shovel down and cleared away more snow to reveal a dirty manhole cover. It was set into the ground about three feet down. Irene wedged the shovel along the edge and pried the cover back. Paul expected a loud creak of some kind but the cover came up without a sound.

"This leads down into an old tunnel that Chac Mool uses to handle his work," Irene explained, straightening to her feet, barely out of breath. "As well as disposing useless…trash."

Paul approached the open manhole cautiously and squatted down. He peered into the hole, grimacing at the warm, putrid smell of mildew and dampness. A steel ladder led down into darkness. Irene handed him a flashlight. He swung the beam around, examining the ladder and the rocky floor below that seemed about fifteen feet down. Getting to his feet, he turned to Irene.

"Weapons?"

She picked up her pack and handed it to him, her eyes on his. He rifled through the bag, breathing an almost noticeable sigh of relief at the sight of his Glock, extra clips of ammunition and a few knives. He threw the flashlight inside and zipped the bag shut.

"If I'm not back in forty, you leave."

"No."

"You'll freeze to death out here."

She smirked at him. "Now who's concerned?"

Without another word, he slung the bag over his shoulders and descended the ladder.

About halfway down, he realized he was glad he wasn't claustrophobic. The dusky, warm darkness pressed down on him from all sides and he could feel the wall brush against him from behind. When his feet touched bottom, he dug out the flashlight and flipped it on. The sharp beam of light showed a small alcove in which he stood, its walls so close he wondered if this was what it felt like to be in that little fucking cage that Irene and Jakob had shoved Ethan into.

God help them if something happens to that kid while I'm gone, he thought bitterly.

The long, empty tunnel stretched out in front of him, dimly lit by bare light bulbs covered in wire mesh high up on the stone walls. He stared for a minute, watching, listening. Then he flicked off the flashlight and shoved it into his pack. He shrugged out of his heavy snow suit, hat and gloves, leaving them in a pile at the base of the ladder. Adjusting his black cargo pants and thermal black shirt, he took out his Glock, checking the clip before clicking off the safety. He shoved the extra clips and a back-up knife into his pockets and left the bag on top of the snow suit. Casting a brief glance up at Irene, he started off down the tunnel.

It was a straight shot. No turns, no doors, no places for someone to hide or jump out at him to catch him unaware. He took advantage of the poor lighting. Staying close to the walls that were more or less cloaked with heavy pockets of shadows, he crept from one pocket of darkness to another, quickly and steadily, stopping, then listening, moving ahead, stopping, listening, moving ahead again. It was repetitive, but at least the tunnel was warm.

A sound made him stop. He came to a silent halt in the shadows and let the air slowly ease from his body. A sliver of cold air curled around his neck, over his bare skin. He pressed his back against the wall, peering back down the way he'd come.

Nothing moved.

So what made me stop?

As if in answer, something scraped against stone, sending a high-pitched squeal echoing around him. The echo made it hard to pinpoint where it had come from.

Sweat trickled down the side of his neck. It felt like the temperature was rising. He moved forward, keeping his back to the wall.

The little hairs on the back of his neck stood up.

He wasn't alone.

He glanced around once more. Not seeing anything no matter how hard he looked, he swallowed back a flare of irritation.

Someone's screwing around, he thought.

He held his gun in a two-handed grip and kept going, even though he couldn't quite shake the feeling that something was keeping pace with him. He lengthened his stride then slowed automatically when through the shadows and light, he saw a heavy oak door at the far end of the tunnel. He would've been glad to see it if it weren't for scent of fresh blood and old raw meat suddenly clogging the air.

Shit.

Cautiously, he approached the door then stopped when, he saw something nailed to it, at about chest-level. He stared at it then his jaw slackened.

Like a fatty piece of pork, a human heart was pinned to the door by a huge knife that pierced it through the center. Streams of blood ran down the door, sparkling like melted rubies. The heart glistened red, white, and purple, shining and slick. The sight and the smell of it made Paul take a few lumbering steps back.

"Oh my God," he muttered, putting a hand under his nose.

He breathed deeply through his mouth several times, squeezed his eyes shut, then opened them, forcing himself to look again because maybe, just maybe he was hallucinating.

Nope. Still there.

He tried telling himself that he'd seen worse, done worse, and that organs outside of a body weren't as bad as seeing them inside of a body. But it was so…fresh.

That alone abruptly brought the world into immediate focus and he straightened away from the wall, readjusting his grip on the gun before it could slide from his sweat-slicked palms. Making sure to breathe through his open mouth, he looked over his shoulder. The far end of the tunnel was pitch-black and seemed to be watching him. Turning back to the door, he again eyed the bleeding, dripping mass of muscle in front of him.

He was being given fair warning. *Go any farther and it's going to be your heart on this door.*

He could see himself walking away. He could picture it perfectly in his mind as if he were actually doing it. How easy it would be. But he knew what was waiting for him if he returned empty-handed. Neither Jakob, Irene, nor Aaron had said anything about that possibility but Paul knew. He figured it was pretty awful if he couldn't readily decide if going back was better or worse than having his own heart join the one already nailed to this door.

Keeping his eyes averted, he reached out and eased the door open.

The suffocating stench of wet, rotting meat nearly bowled him over. He gagged at the power of it. His hand tightened on the edge of the door, frozen in mid-push as his senses were greased and lit up by the awful smell. He groaned silently.

A sudden feeling of awareness stole over him, like someone had settled crosshairs on the back of his head.

Moving quickly, he pushed the door open, catching it before it could slam into the wall. He closed it as quietly and swiftly as he could then pressed his back against it. He swept the gun around the room, eyes scanning instinctively for entrances, exits, and any position where someone could get the drop on him. Actually, that was what he normally would've done, except this time his brain couldn't even grapple with what he was seeing.

It was like he'd stepped into another dimension.

The room was huge. A cracked marble floor stretched from one side of the room to the other, right up to the impossibly high, dirt walls that rose to a ceiling cloaked in shadows. Obelisks rose far above his head. Every inch of them was covered with drawings and words of a language that looked older than time itself. They told a story that Paul couldn't even begin to comprehend, each displayed so vividly they seemed to leap through the air in brilliant splashes of blacks, reds, blues, golds, and greens. The air was warm and dry due mostly to the deep trenches dug into the walls. Fire filled them, casting flickering shadows across the room, giving it an appeal that was awe-inspiring, mysterious, and sinister. The light reflected off the dozens of cases that were set up through-out the room, each holding a relic from an age that was long-gone. The place could've passed as a museum if it weren't for the god-awful smell and the fire in the walls.

More curious than anything else, and reminding himself to breathe through his mouth, he stepped to the closest case and peered inside. The case itself was as high as his shoulders and about five feet long. Inside was a stone rack of human skulls. There must've been at least a hundred, smooth and brown with age, all flashing their empty eye sockets and skeletal smiles, arranged neatly in five rows. At first glance they appeared to be sitting on narrow rods of chiseled stone but upon closer inspection, it appeared that the rods were driven through the skulls, just under the base of the jaw so that the skulls didn't sit on the rack but rather hung from it.

Paul swallowed. The shadows from the flames played across the bony prominent grins, twirled around in the black eye sockets, jumped through the gaping mouths, locking them in a permanent state of emaciated hysteria. For a moment, they were staring back at him, screaming, shrieking to be let out, to be set free from this place so that they could be reunited with their bodies and finally, *finally* rest in peace. Jaws wagging back and forth, up and down, as if trying to speak around the rod that was gagging them—

He straightened quickly. He began to turn away when something at the end of the case, inside, caught his eye. Frowning, he took a few tentative steps and stopped.

Blinked.

At the end of the top row was a half-decayed head that still had its watery brown eyes intact, staring dumbly out as if unsure of how it got there. The lips were rotting, peeled back to reveal yellow teeth. Patches of dark hair clung to the top of the head. Brown crust that could only be blood stained the bottom of the case and the torn, almost frayed edges of the open neck. Paul knew enough about knife-work that whatever blade had been used, it had not been very sharp and the stone rod that pierced the flesh beneath the jaw was like a nail going through a thick pillar of wax.

Repeated chants of *holy shit* tumbled around in his head as he turned away. A trail of cold sweat made its way down his spine.

"Come on," he muttered to himself. "Come on, you have a job to do. Just focus."

He moved deeper into the room. Despite himself, he found himself practically wandering about like a tourist in a museum. There were displays of masks, sarcophaguses, pottery, stone chests spilling jade, beautiful feathers, obsidian and alabaster, stuffed exotic animals, some that resembled nothing he'd ever seen in a zoo. Behind some glass cases were enormous stone structures that were as big as a house, revealing more ancient language and artwork that depicted a confusing jumble of history and death. Things behind glass twinkled and gleamed, catching his eye then flinging his gaze to the next object until he finally became aware of how much time he was wasting. He shook his head at himself, feeling stupid and reminding himself of why he was here in the first place. Carefully, he maneuvered his way around glass cases until he finally found it.

The case was chest-high and sitting in the middle of the floor. Inside, the pouch was half-reclining on a bed of silk cloth. Paul bent down until he was eye-level with it. The black velvet looked incredibly soft, something that would slide easily under his fingertips. The silky drawstrings curled seductively down the sides, framing the stunning piece of jade that was settled in the center. It glowed softly, like it had a light shining from within. He stared at it, mesmerized at the brilliant green color gently broken by thin veins of white that wove through it. He had to admit, it was positively stunning, more beautiful than the picture he'd seen. He leaned closer until his nose nearly touched the glass. The longer he stared at the stone, the surer he was about the swirl in the center. He was shocked to find it moving and shifting, like the colors in a kaleidoscope. He leaned closer, letting it pull at him until it felt like he was standing in a field of swaying grass with the sun in his face and the wind riffling his hair. It would be so easy to fall onto his back and stare up at the sky, fold his hands behind his head and drift. And he would be allowed to drift because there was no fear here. No pain or troubles or worries. It was just him and grass and the smell of spring. He would be okay. It was perfect.

But there was something at his feet and, when he looked down, he saw that he was ankle-deep in blood.

He jumped, gasping. Blinking madly, he backed away. He wiped at his face, casting wild glances around him. Yes, yes, he was still here, right where he was supposed to be and not in some field.

He glanced down at the stone again and felt something tug deep inside his chest. He looked away, perplexed and out of sorts now. The gun felt clumsy in his hands and he wanted to put it down before he accidentally shot himself in the foot.

Then he caught a sparkle of red out of the corner of his eye.

He raised the gun quickly and spun toward it.

Then his jaw dropped.

Behind a wall of glass was a small stone temple. Broad steps led up to a rectangular structure with one opening that yawned into a void of blackness. At the base were two large braziers, empty and cold, but between them was a narrow slab of stone.

A body lay over it.

A nude man.

A nude, dead man if the gaping hole in his chest was anything to go by.

Paul lowered the gun and walked slowly toward it. Dread filled him like heavy water as he took in the grayish-white arms that were flung out to the sides, the legs sprawled like a dead frog's, back arched over the altar so the chest was easily accessible. Streams of blood poured down the torso, dripping to the ground.

And it was fresh.

The hole in the chest was big enough for two fists to go through, right under the rib cage.

Right where the heart should've been.

He rose up on his toes to peer inside the dark, glistening cavity.

He'd found the owner of the heart on the door.

The dead man's face was twisted in a frozen scream. Fingers were curled inward and there were little half-moon marks on his skin, where his nails had dug into his palms. Blood seeped from the tiny wounds.

Fresh blood again.

A sliver of cold touched the back of his neck and he spun, aiming wildly.

A man stood about five feet away, eerily silent, watching him.

CHAPTER 26

The photo that Paul had seen did not seem accurate. It seemed to take away something that was so obviously there in person, something vital, alive and extreme. Chac Mool's eyes were piercing, rivaling the jade stone that was on the pouch. They pinned Paul to the spot. The jumping firelight illuminated them in a way that made them shine with their own light. The shadows worked over the sharp angles of his face, deepening them until they looked like grooves in the earth. His black hair was cut short on the sides, but long on top, combed back from his high, bronzed forehead. He was dressed simply enough in black pants, a white button-down shirt, black dress shoes and no tie. The top button was open and for all intents and purposes, he looked like he'd just returned from a dinner party.

Except for the spear he held in his hands.

And the blood splatters on his shirt collar and the smooth expanse of his throat.

Quite abruptly, Paul had an epiphany. It was going to take everything he had to get out of here alive.

He aimed the gun at the man's chest.

Chac Mool's strong features softened in humor. "Are you going to shoot me?"

His voice rang with a deep resonance, booming with an authority and strength that would've caused a mass of worshippers to fall to their knees. It echoed deep inside, calling to the part in him that forced him into submission. Choice was taken away. Free will was obliterated and in its place was obedience and servitude, a mere step up from absolute slavery. But the slave in Paul was here under the orders of another master and it didn't matter if he felt strange and off-balance as he pointed a gun at this man. He had a job to do and it didn't include falling to his knees.

"Only if I have to," he said.

Chac Mool smiled and it was dazzling and white, cutting across his face like a bulldozer through the trees. It was unnerving, expectant.

"Cortez," Chac Mool said, his voice dropping to an eerie whisper that carried secrets and age like the artifacts around them. "Cortez in the flesh."

"Who—"

Then the spear was moving, darting toward him and smacking into his hands, hard enough that his fingers went numb. The gun slipped from his grip. Dumbstruck at the speed in which he was disarmed, Paul followed his weapon's descent to the floor. But then the point of the spear was under his chin, freezing him in place and shoving his head back. For a minute, he let himself breathe then his hands came up and knocked the spear away from his face. In the blink of an eye it was swinging back toward him. He ducked, hearing it whistle overhead. As he straightened, he lunged back, gaping as the glittering point bit into the floor where he'd been only seconds before.

Suddenly, he was swept up in a dance of dodging, lunging, ducking, and blocking as the spear swiped, sliced and stabbed at him in a confusing, blurred jumble of moves that took his breath away. If he had a moment, he would've admired the skill and speed that Chac Mool used to execute his moves. The quickness and fluidity of every step, every stroke was something Paul had never seen before and he had been in his share of fights over the years. But from the first stab of that spear, Chac Mool was already a step and a half ahead of him and it wasn't long before Paul found himself out of breath and beginning to panic as Chac Mool steadily and rapidly gained more ground and Paul was forced to constantly back away, giving up more and more as the spear nicked and sipped at his arms and torso, taking a bit of him at a time.

That spear, he knew, as he just barely jerked his head to the side in time as it feather-kissed his temple, was what kept him from inflicting any damage. It was at least five feet long, which kept Paul at that distance, not allowing him to move in and get within striking distance. The thought of getting closer wasn't appealing by any stretch but it was either that or find himself sliced to pieces like an onion.

Death of a thousand cuts, he thought grimly.

His skin jumped as he forced himself to stop trying to avoid the blows. He stepped forward. The action gave Chac Mool pause and Paul launched his attack, darting in quickly, fists raised.

When he saw the delight twinkling in those green depths, he knew he'd made a mistake.

Chac Mool dropped to a crouch and with a movement that Paul's eyes couldn't follow, swung the spear in a harsh, quick arc until it cracked against Paul's forearm. He howled as pain exploded through his arm and up to his shoulder. His eyes watered, blinding him and he nearly crashed into Chac Mool as he stumbled and lost his footing. Chac Mool simply stepped to one side as if getting out of the way of a passing pedestrian. Paul fell to one knee with a half-yell, half-groan. Squeezing his eyes shut, he tried to breathe past the pain but it only choked him as he cradled his right arm to his chest.

Christ, he broke my fucking arm!

Paul struggled to rise to his feet only to feel the spear at the back of his legs, sweeping them out from under him. He went down hard and nearly bit his tongue in two.

He shouted wordlessly, scrambling, trying to put space between them for *just a fucking minute* so that he could get his head straight.

He got as far as his knees before the spear point was back in his face, twinkling mere centimeters from his left eye.

"Do not move," Chac Mool hissed in a voice that was barely out of breath.

Paul's breath screamed through his lungs. His body shook and his face felt wet. The spear point was so close it was a blurred spot in his vision. The man stared down at him with a look of curiosity as if Paul was some interesting specimen he had under a microscope. Paul watched him. He wondered if he'd feel anything when Chac Mool shoved that spear into his eye. If he did, how much and for how long? Would he twist it up into his brain? Or would he simply corkscrew it until it came out of the back of his head? Or maybe—

"Why are you here?"

The question snapped Paul away from his thoughts and he blinked, trying to clear the sweat and tears from his eyes.

"I think you already know the answer to that," Paul started to say but barely got the first word out before the spear was under his jaw, angling his head up until he had no place to look but Chac Mool's eyes.

A sound that rivaled that of a dying animal crawled out of Paul's throat as the point broke gently through the soft flesh beneath his jaw, like a nail puncturing a tightly-stretched piece of fabric. His eyes widened as Chac Mool's own burned into his with a light that was scorching and booked no room for bullshit. As helpless as a pig in a slaughterhouse, Paul felt the skin of his throat stretch as Chac Mool added pressure, pushing until Paul's neck lengthened uncomfortably.

"Why are you here?" Chac Mool said again. "Hmm?"

Paul tried to come up with something that wouldn't cause his immediate death but every scenario ended the same way—with his headless body on the floor. Chac Mool asked, "Are you here to steal from me?"

Something warm and wet began to trickle down Paul's throat. Not that it made much difference. His entire torso was covered in blood, looking like it'd been put through a paper shredder.

"Yes," he said as best as he could.

"From my collection?"

Paul swallowed hard enough to hurt. "Yes."

"And what do you think of my collection?"

Paul winced as the spear inched deeper.

"Does it frighten you?" Chac Mool asked.

The more he spoke, the more Paul picked up on an accent. He couldn't identify it but it minced his words until they sounded like music, soft and hard, unkind and calm all at the same time.

"Yes," he answered, his voice quivering.

"Do you think you will end up like them?"

Headless and heartless.

"M—Most likely."

Chac Mool laughed. The sound of it was deep and smooth, like good chocolate. "And yet, knowing this, you do not beg for your life. Why?"

"I don't—I don't know—"

"Do you feel that your life is unworthy? Inadequate?"

Paul looked into those bottomless green eyes, feeling something tug at him, something that forced him to answer honestly. "Most of the time."

The laughter faded from Chac Mool's eyes, replaced by a look of calculated interest. "Do you doubt the value of your own life?"

Paul felt a sense of bewilderment at the question. It certainly wasn't one to be taken lightly, given the current situation but it seemed highly inappropriate anyway as he knelt there with a broken arm, bleeding from countless cuts all over his body and a blade at his throat. His existence, as shitty as it'd been, wasn't something that he wanted to talk about or even offer any insight on, especially with the end of it so close by.

"I—I don't know," he stammered.

Chac Mool cocked his head slightly to one side. "You must know. There must be something that you've done that has some value."

A sound came out of Paul that could've been laughter but it was more like a sob. "Not—nothing comes to mind."

Even as he said it, he thought of Ethan.

"Ah, you are lying," Chac Mool said with a satisfied smile as if he'd seen right into Paul's brain.

Paul could taste his heart in his throat. "No—"

"Do not lie to me."

"I'm—I'm not," he gasped. "I just—I don't think that I've done anything—"

"But you have."

"How do you—Why does it matter?"

"In order for your sacrifice to be significant, you must believe that you have worth, that your life as you've lived it is something to be valued. If you do not believe it, then it is simply a waste to remove your head."

Paul felt his hopes lift a little. "I—"

"But you have value or rather, you value something very important or you would not have fought me as you did."

"I was just trying to stay alive."

"You wish to stay alive but you do not value your life?"

"I—"

"Ah, I see. You fear the death itself."

Paul felt the skin on the back of his neck prickle.

"And as much as you fear it, you were more than willing to bring death to me?"

"I didn't—I was going to avoid it if I could. I was just going to—"

"Take what you wanted and leave? Hmm?" he interrupted smoothly.

Spots appeared in Paul's vision as more pressure was applied to the spear. When Paul could see again, he said weakly,

"That was the plan."

One corner of Chac Mool's mouth quirked up. "Your plan has failed."

"It certainly seems that way," Paul stated.

Something flickered in the depths of Chac Mool's eyes, something that hesitated. He suddenly stepped back, dislodging the spear point from Paul's skin. He grunted, sagging forward, catching himself on his good arm before he could crash face-first into the floor.

"Show me what you wanted to take from me."

Paul gaped up at him. "What?"

"Show me," Chac Mool repeated.

Moving slowly and keeping his eyes on Chac Mool, Paul climbed to his feet, swaying slightly. Chac Mool moved back, giving him plenty of space Paul glanced around, taking in the room in short, small glances as his eyes kept coming back to Chac Mool, not wanting to leave him for any great length of time. But Chac Mool stood there, waiting patiently for Paul to get his bearings, holding onto the spear that was tipped with his blood, looking as formidable as the warriors carved into the walls around them. Paul wet his lips and went slowly, painfully back to where the pouch sat safely encased in glass. He stopped in front of it as Chac Mool came up to the other side.

Chac Mool looked into the case and a furrow appeared between his eyes. Without lifting his eyes, he said,

"This?"

Paul nodded. Chac Mool stared at the pouch as if transfixed. Remembering his little trip into fantasy-land when he looked at the stone, Paul ignored it. He didn't need to be skipping down the Yellow Brick Road while his head was fair game. When Chac Mool finally raised his eyes, the look in them was disturbing.

"Why this?"

"What?"

"Why have you decided to take this?"

"I—It wasn't my decision."

Chac Mool raised an eyebrow. "You are not here of your own volition?"

He tried not to fidget but it was hard. "No…"

Chac Mool fixed him with a look that Paul couldn't quite read. "How much do you know about this object?"

He tapped a long finger against the glass. Paul's hesitation made Chac Mool's eyes harden to cold green glass. He began to slowly make his way around the case, prompting Paul to sidestep, moving to keep the case between them.

"You were sent here to obtain something that you know absolutely nothing about," he hissed.

"Well, that's not—that's not entirely true."

Chac Mool raised his eyebrows as if to say *care to elaborate?* Paul chewed on the inside of his cheek. He imagined a hole he was digging in his mind with a sharp wide shovel, flinging the dirt over his shoulder as easily as flinging back a bed sheet.

Deeper and deeper.

"I, uh, I was told that in your—in your culture, jade is the stone of the underworld—"

"Go on."

"And that inside the uh, pouch—are the ashes of—"

"Yes?" Chac Mool murmured, his eyes glittering dangerously.

The spot between Paul's shoulder blades began to itch. "Um—ashes of—of a dead Aztec ruler."

Chac Mool glided to a halt, his hand tightening minutely around the spear. Paul stopped as well. Chac Mool stared unblinking at him for a long moment then whispered,

"A dead Aztec ruler. And knowing this, you were going to take it anyway."

Paul stared at him, unable to dispute what he was saying.

"And you thought, 'What could possibly be so bad about that?'"

'*This will be easier than I thought.*'

Paul grimaced at the echo of his own words. Chac Mool grinned at him although it seemed more like a sneer.

"Yes. That is exactly what you were thinking. The ashes of a long-dead Aztec ruler. How useless. How cheap."

"I didn't—"

"But you didn't bother to ask, did you? You didn't bother to dig deeper because if you had, you would know that inside this case are not the remains of a ruler but of a power too magnificent and too complex for you to handle."

"What do you mean?"

Chac Mool's eyes bored into his. "Do you believe that death is the end?"

"Yeah."

"And if it isn't?"

Paul frowned. "Dead is dead."

Chac Mool laughed. The sound rumbled through the room like thunder ahead of the on-coming storm. "For some."

Paul's frown turned skeptical. "What are you saying?"

He really hoped that after everything he'd endured at the hands of this man, he didn't turn out to be some kind of nut.

"Look around you," Chac Mool continued.

Paul refused to take his eyes off of him.

"Go on. Look."

Reluctantly dragging his eyes away, Paul did a quick scan of the room.

"What do you see?" Chac Mool hissed in his ear, suddenly beside him.

Paul gasped, leaping backward but Chac Mool followed, his eyes burning like twin pools of green fire.

"Tell me what you see."

"Things, uh, artifacts, I guess. Paintings, weapons—"

"Yes, all material things," Chac Mool cut in. "Things that describe a culture that has unfortunately passed. Things that have been left behind not only as a tribute to the past but as an omen for the future."

"An omen?"

"Yes. A warning."

"About what?"

"Vengeance."

"So you're saying that something from this room is going to come alive and...kill me?"

"Who said anything about killing?"

"That's what vengeance usually implies."

"Do not mistake me. Killing will be involved but that is not the end."

Yup, definitely certifiable.

Chac Mool continued to stare at him, as if waiting for him to say something. When he didn't, Chac Mool gave him a strange half-smile.

"This does not interest you, does it?"

Paul considered lying then said, "Not really."

Chac Mool sighed and it sounded disappointed. "As I said earlier, Cortez in the flesh."

"Who the hell is Cortez?"

"Cortez was the man your history books say founded what is now known as Mexico. He was the man who expanded the Spanish Empire for the greater good of his people. His people and his people only. What your history books will not tell you is that the same man turned the Aztec tribes, who were already dwelling in Mexico, against the chief rulers of the Aztec community. He fought against the same tribes at the sides of the rulers until he saw the opportunity to overthrow the throne, to impose his religion and culture onto those poor, unsuspecting people. The tribes who fought relentlessly to uphold their sense of freedom and way of life, were overtaken, beaten down, broken, and then built back up to suit Cortez's needs. He was the one responsible for the fall of the Aztec Empire."

Paul looked around. "And what does that have to do with me?"

The force behind Chac Mool's eyes doubled and Paul almost backed up a step. "You do not care just as Cortez did not all those years ago. He did not care about the lives he was uprooting. He did not care about the destruction of a culture or what it would mean to those he wished to rule. Just as you do not care as you come into my home, seeking to steal something from me, something that is beyond your weak human understanding and you do not think of the repercussions that your actions will induce."

Paul didn't know what to say.

"But," Chac Mool went on, his voice dropping lower and lower. "If you do succeed in taking what you desire, only then will you know the consequences and you will wish for death."

Paul stared at him.

Chac Mool's strange half-smile widened. "And if she is merciful, she will give you death. Or you will suffer as she did."

"Who?"

"The power beyond death."

"What?"

Chac Mool came toward him.

"Wait a second, I don't—" Paul began, backing away. "I don't understand what you're saying. Who are you talking about? How do you know this will happen?"

"She came to me in a dream."

"Jesus Christ, *who*?"

Suddenly Chac Mool pitched forward with a strangled scream as if he'd been hit in the back by a hammer. Paul instinctively turned his body to favor his damaged arm but Chac Mool was already stumbling into him. Crying out in pain, Paul sagged beneath the weight and they both tumbled to the floor. He flailed, trying to get the weight off his arm. He pushed with his good arm, struggling to lift the man because he sure as hell didn't seem to be in any rush to get up—

Then Paul felt something warm soak his clothes.

"Shit!" he gasped as he looked down and saw blood blossoming like a huge carnation in the center of Chac Mool's white dress shirt.

An arrow had pierced his torso, the tip glistening with blood and bits of flesh. Paul frantically tried to keep Chac Mool's upper body from touching his, lest the arrow tip find its way into Paul's own chest. Chac Mool's face was slack and trembling. His mouth opened and closed soundlessly.

"Oh my God," Paul muttered.

Pain was deep and alive in Chac Mool's eyes and a croaking noise was coming from him as if he were trying to say something. Paul felt Chac Mool's body go lax little by little. He could feel the heart thudding hard as if it knew its time was up. Then it slowed like it was drowning, beating its fists against the underside of a frozen lake, trapped without air until finally, it stopped.

Paul blinked then blinked again. *What the hell just—*

Jakob's smiling face suddenly appeared over Chac Mool's shoulder. "Hiya, Paul!"

Paul gaped at him.

"Hope you don't mind a little intervention. You've been gone an awful long time so we decided to check up on you."

"Wh—"

"Oh, here. Let me help you."

He grabbed Chac Mool's shoulder and rolled him off Paul like a sack of beef. Paul struggled to sit up, pushing Jakob's helping hands away with a snarl.

"What *the fuck* is the matter with you?"

Jakob straightened, perplexed. He held a crossbow in one hand. It was already locked and loaded with a fresh arrow.

"What?"

"What, you didn't think I'd go through with it? You had to check up on me? I don't need a fucking babysitter."

Jakob cocked his head to one side. "No offense, man, but you looked like you were in need of a little back-up."

Paul winced as he got to his feet, swaying a little. "It was fine. I was fine, Jesus Christ."

"He was going to kill you, Paul."

Paul looked away, his eyes trailing back to Chac Mool's body. He lay like a broken doll, this collector of heads and hearts, blood pooling beneath him like a blanket.

"I was handling it," he bit out.

Jakob rolled his eyes, further aggravating Paul's nerves. "Sorry if I took your fun away but I wasn't about to let him finish you off."

"And why the hell not?"

Jakob flashed a shit-eating grin. "Because I'm not done with you yet."

The "fuck you" on the tip of his tongue was drowned out by the sound of breaking glass. He turned to see Irene gently lifting the black velvet pouch from its nest of silk with one hand. In her other hand was a mini-crowbar. The glass case lay shattered at her feet. Her eyes were riveted on her prize as she bought it close to her face, her fingers flexing into the velvet, testing its weight. For reasons he couldn't explain, seeing something so obviously important to Chac Mool in Irene's hand, made Paul uneasy. He didn't feel the triumph he'd expected or the urge to shout "Freedom!" He didn't feel like this horrible chapter of his life was finally over but rather it was continuing on, to some place altogether different.

A breathless whisper swept through the room, fading away on something that sounded like the last strings of a scream. Paul felt the hairs on the back of his neck stand on end. He sensed darkness and dread, an anxiety that brought everything around him into sharp focus. He suddenly felt like he was being weighed, measured, and judged, the empty eyes of the masks, the paintings, the skulls, all sizing him up and stripping him down to the blood, bones, and exhaustion that was snaking its hard fingers around his throat. The unsettling feeling that he was making a big mistake was suddenly something he couldn't shake. Feeling all the adrenaline abruptly leave him, he felt himself begin to sink to the floor.

Jakob was at his side in an instant, banding an arm securely around his waist.

"I'm fine," Paul muttered, trying to pull away.

"Come on," Jakob advised gently. "We're leaving."

"Let go. I can walk."

But then the floor dipped. A cloud of blackness began to drop over his eyes. He heard Irene talking about taking more artifacts with them and he tried to protest but his tongue felt like lead in his mouth. Their voices were getting farther and farther away. He unwillingly let Jakob take his weight and collapsed into unconsciousness.

CHAPTER 27

He was floating through shadows.
No control, no direction.
It felt good.

He wasn't sure if his eyes were open or if he was rising or falling. All he knew was darkness and he wasn't afraid of it. Then, as if he'd jinxed it, flashes of color cracked through the blackness. Images, faces, draped in shadows, loomed over him. Something heavy and wet was lifted away from him, replaced by something cool and soothing. Sound exploded through his ears and with it came pain. Pulling himself reluctantly through the dark waters of unconsciousness, he opened his eyes. At least he thought he did. All he saw was darkness with darker things moving around inside. Someone called his name and he turned toward it but fatigue wasted no time in pulling him back under.

When he came to again, it was from a deep, dreamless sleep. It took a few heart-stopping minutes to realize that the movements around the room were in fact shadows caused by the fire in the hearth and not the shadows in his dreams brought to life. He closed his eyes then opened them, trying to focus past the dimness of the room. He wondered how he got here, in this bed, so warm and sleepy.

It was almost instantaneous as the wall between him and his memories came crashing down.

Chac Mool.

Those fiery green eyes.

So close—so close, a kiss away from dying before Jakob swooped in like a goddamn superhero.

He gasped under the force of it, the last of his grogginess slipping away as he struggled to sit up. His teeth clamped down on his bottom lip in an attempt to hold in a scream as white-hot pain shot down his arm, forcing him back onto the pillows. Groaning like a wounded animal, he glanced down at himself and what little strength he had flitted away when he saw what looked like hundreds of papercuts scattered over his torso and arms. It was like half a dozen cats had decided to use his body as a scratching post. His right arm was propped up on a pile of pillows, the forearm encased with a short-arm fiberglass cast.

He winced at the sight of it, feeling as if Chac Mool was there again with that damn spear, casually and effortlessly taking his body apart a piece at a time.

"Paul?"

The tiny whisper from his immediate right almost sent him through the roof. He turned his head and saw Ethan next to the bed. The sight of him nearly knocked him breathless. It seemed ages since Paul had last laid eyes on him. His pale hair shone brightly even in the firelight. His small frame was hidden behind a pair of polka-dotted pajamas that Paul couldn't even use the brainpower to figure out where they'd come from. His gray eyes were riveted to Paul's face as if expecting him to disappear before his eyes.

"Hey," Paul said, his voice hoarse and cracked.

Ethan leaned over him, the tips of his hair tickling Paul's face. "Paul," he whispered again. "Is your heart still beating?"

Paul blinked up at him. It was such a strange question to ask. "Wha—"

A tremendous pressure punched the air from his lungs. Startled, he looked down to see a knife sticking out of his chest. Ethan's hand was wrapped around the hilt, twisting it.

Paul choked, eyes bulging, blood gurgling at the back of this throat.

Ethan's eyes were green, a bright flawless green like jade. "Don't worry," he whispered. "I'll stop it for you. You won't be needing it anymore."

He twisted the knife with more strength that any child should possess and the edge pierced his heart. Paul tried to scream as pain exploded behind his eyeballs.

"Hold still, Paul. This will not take long."

The voice hissed through his ears, sounding so incredibly wrong coming from Ethan's lips, the wide, white smile that sat on his face, hungry for his heart that was pierced like a knife through a piece of rare steak. He flailed, held down by claws that were clammy, cold, and dangerous. The pain, deep and intense, took root and he tried to shift away from it. But the more he moved, the deeper it settled. Blood filled his mouth, spilling out and down his chin.

"Paul! Paul, hey—"

His eyes flew open but he didn't remember closing them. Suffocation pressed through his body. Paul thrashed and jerked.

"Paul—"

Let go! Let go of me! Stop!

"Paul, calm down—"

No!

Then pain of a different kind, fresh and light, if there was such a thing, blasted through the awake/sleep darkness that had latched onto his mind and suddenly he could see.

"Paul! Wake up!"

The voice was loud, almost screaming and he cringed. Blinking rapidly to clear his vision, he found Jakob, half-sitting, half-laying on the bed next to him, hands gripping Paul's shoulders. He was looking down at him with an odd mixture of worry and frustration and if Paul had been in the right frame of mind, he would've enjoyed it. But his heart was pounding too hard and too fast, his mind in tatters as he tried to sort through it. He squinted, trying to focus, trying to speak but he couldn't get his lips to cooperate.

"Jesus," Jakob breathed. "Are you all right?"

Paul squeezed his eyes shut then opened them.

"You were dreaming," Jakob said, letting go of Paul's shoulders.

Paul began to sit up but Jakob immediately pushed him gently but firmly back down.

"Hey, easy. Easy now, you—"

Paul gritted his teeth on a scream as pain shot through his arm.

"Yeah, that," Jakob said.

Through watering eyes, Paul looked down and saw his right forearm in a short-arm cast and his torso—

He felt a jolt of panic. This was how he'd looked in his dream.

Except this…was he awake now?

"Am I—I—" The words came out in a confused jumble.

He couldn't help but flinch as Jakob softly brushed his hair off his sweaty forehead.

"Shhh," he murmured. "It's okay. You're fine. You were just dreaming."

Paul shook his head. "No—I wasn't, I—"

"Yes, you were."

"No, I—"

A surge of agony through his right arm cut him off and he couldn't stop the half-scream that spilled from his mouth.

"Shhh," Jakob whispered again. "Here you go."

He bought his fingers to Paul's lips, forcing two tablets into his mouth. Paul tried to shake his head but a glass of water was pressed against his bottom lip and cool liquid quenched the dryness in his throat. He pressed his head against the pillows with a gasp, water dribbling down his chin.

"Wha—"

"It's for the pain."

"No," he groaned. "I don't want—"

"Paul, you're hurt—"

"I don't care," he tried to say with force but it came out in a feeble rasp.

Jakob's hand touched his leg. "Paul, you have a fractured forearm. You need something to calm you and help you rest. You already scared Ethan half to death with all your thrashing and screaming."

Paul looked at him, defeated. "Oh, no—"

"Yeah."

"Is he—Is he all right?"

"I think so. I told him he could come back in when you were feeling better."

A pleasantly numb feeling began to sweep through him and he knew the pain medicine was already kicking in. But he didn't want to fall asleep just yet.

There were so many things to talk about.

So many things to do.

"Rest, Paul," Jakob murmured as if reading his mind. "We'll talk later."

Paul dropped into unconsciousness.

CHAPTER 28

The journey to consciousness seemed to take an eternity and when he finally managed to open his eyes, Paul felt nothing but a bone-deep exhaustion. Dreams had plagued him, crammed into his head, fighting for the spotlight. Dreams of darkness and jade-green eyes weighing him, examining him like a side of beef before slowly taking him apart. Dreams of his head on a stone rack, of his heart pulled from his rib cage. Dreams that made sure he would never want to close his eyes again.

Shuddering, he became aware that beneath the pile of soft blankets that anchored him to the bed, his entire body ached and throbbed with every beat of his heart. He blinked his eyes wide, struggling to keep them open as he looked around. The room was quiet, peaceful. The shadows in the corners seemed to understand his pain and left him alone. He took a deep breath, smelling the dying fire that was in the hearth. The electric lanterns on the wall kept everything to a nice, hazy glow. Would anybody blame him if he slept a little longer?

Then triumphant green eyes and fresh blood danced in his head and he forced himself to move. Wincing, he managed to inch his way up the bed until he could lean against the headboard. Just that small movement had him sagging against it, breathless.

He'd been on worse jobs. He'd fought against worse people; people who were desperate, lethal, and psychotic. But never with the intensity and power of his fight with Chac Mool. And it had been oddly…cryptic. Paul frowned, trying to remember the conversation before Jakob's appearance with a crossbow. Half of what Chac Mool had said was flat-out weird. It was an obvious rant of an overzealous member of a culture that had been gone for centuries—something that was made extremely apparent by the number of skulls he had in his possession. But while Paul had been told that Chac Mool was responsible for sacked burial sites and desecrated tombs, it was clear that greed wasn't what drove him. Everything he had was so beautifully stored and meticulously cared for. He spoke with a reverence, a rock-solid belief in the things around him. No, definitely not greed.

It was devotion.

Loyalty.

Allegiance to a time, a place and to a people that the rest of the world had forgotten.

But there was more to it than that. Something else was going on here. Paul could feel it dangling over his head like a scythe.

Something had been there, watching them.

Something in that room, holding its breath.

Waiting.

It was a panicked and horrible feeling and he made a mental note to ask the Dynamic Duo what they really needed that velvet pouch for. The door to his room opened.

"Hey there." Jakob smiled as he came into the room with a tray bearing a bowl of hot soup and a tall glass of water. "How are you feeling?"

The sight of him sent anger spiking through Paul and it was the last thing he needed.

"You got anything for pain?" he croaked out.

"Of course," Jakob replied, setting the tray down on the table next to the bed. "But first, you need to eat."

The smell of chicken noodle soup made Paul's mouth water. "I'm not hungry."

"Even so, you need to have something in your stomach before I can give you more pain medicine."

"I don't want to eat," he rasped.

"Yes, you do."

"No, I don't."

He raised his eyebrows as he picked up the tray and laid it gently across Paul's lap. "You're obviously feeling better."

"Jakob—"

"You have a fractured forearm, Paul. You need pain medicine, I understand that. But unless you want to pass out again after you take it, I suggest you get something in your stomach."

"How do you even know I have a fractured forearm? Did you take me to a hospital while I was unconscious? Did you take me in for x-rays?"

An annoying half-smile appeared at Jakob's lips. "You know I didn't."

"Then how do you know the extent of my injuries?"

"Paul, when are you ever going to learn to trust me?"

"Never."

Jakob's face changed and for a minute there was something close to anger. "Well that's rather unfortunate. It's only natural to reciprocate. I trusted you with this job. I trusted you to come back to me and you did and now I can't even get you to eat a bowl of my soup."

"I did this job because I didn't have a choice." Paul tried to shout but it came out as a dry, pathetic wheeze.

"Yes, but the second you were out that door you could've walked away. Once you left here, you could've just hauled ass on the snowmobile and put all this behind you. But you didn't. You stayed. All the way through to the end, I might add and you were nearly killed in the process."

Paul glared weakly at him.

"Now," Jakob continued. "I know it's not the pleasure of my company that made you come back. And it probably isn't Irene. She's not really your type."

Paul's left hand twitched and he glanced down at the tray in his lap. Eyeballed the bowl of hot soup and the handle of the spoon. As if sensing his thoughts, Jakob moved the tray back to the safety of the table beside the bed. Paul tried to strengthen his glare but it was obviously having no effect as Jakob settled on the bed, sitting down near Paul's propped-up arm.

"So what made you come back, Paul?"

Paul looked away. "I'm not answering your asinine questions."

"You have no reason to be angry with me."

Paul's eyes swung back to his, wide with disbelief. "Oh I don't, huh?"

"No."

"I have plenty of reasons to be pissed off at you."

"Such as?"

"Pick something. You wanted me to do a job for you. You went through great fucking lengths to make sure I agreed to your terms, only to send me out there with the intention of yanking it right out from under me."

"You're mad because I saved your life?"

"You interfered. I've been doing this for a long time. I don't need anyone watching my back."

Jakob shifted and Paul could suddenly feel his eyes on him like grasping fingers.

"Paul, you weren't in a good position. I saw you. Your arm was broken, you were bleeding so much, it was hard to pinpoint where all the blood was coming from and furthermore, you were unarmed. There was no way Chac Mool was going to let you walk out of there and you sure as hell were in no condition to fight him."

"So Irene left me there, came back to get you and the two of you rode to my rescue, all the while leaving Ethan here, alone, with Aaron. Good fucking thinking."

Jakob gave a dismissive wave. "Aaron is still under lock and key. Ethan was perfectly safe here."

That gave him pause. "He's still down there?"

"Of course he is."

Paul wasn't sure how to feel about that. "Where's Ethan?"

"Taking a nap."

"I want to see him."

"After you eat something." He held the spoon out.

"I said I wasn't hungry."

Jakob moved closer, leaning down into Paul's face. Surprised by the abrupt move, Paul could only stare up at him, not liking the way the shadows filled his eyes.

"Do it, Paul. I don't want to force-feed you, especially since you're already injured and all," he said quietly.

He took hold of Paul's left wrist and gently turned his hand over, placing the spoon handle across his palm. Paul tried to pull his hand away but Jakob's fingers tightened almost painfully.

"I'm not a child."

The shadows deepened in his eyes and Paul was immediately aware of how vulnerable he was.

"No, you're not," Jakob replies softly. "But I will treat you like one if you don't start doing what I tell you."

Paul stared up at him. "I did what you asked. You got what you wanted."

The corners of Jakob's mouth flicked upward. "That's not entirely true."

"What the fuck does that mean?"

"It means that our business with you isn't finished."

Paul's response to that was purely physical. "The hell it isn't! I'm not—"

Moving quickly, Jakob clapped a hand over Paul's mouth, forcing his head back against the headboard. His other hand pinned Paul's left hand to the bed before Paul could jab him in the eye with the handle of the spoon. Paul gurgled, struggling against him, knowing and positively hating that he was no match for Jakob in his weakened state. He thrashed and wiggled as much as he could. As if to drive the point home, Jakob crawled on top of him, moving fluidly and carefully as he straddled Paul's lap. Paul gurgled again, his eyes widening as Jakob smiled down at him, patiently waiting for him to stop struggling.

"Come on, take it easy, Paul. You don't want to wake Ethan, do you?"

Paul forced himself to still, his chest heaving.

"I'm just trying to help you, Paul. Okay? I'm going to feed you and then I'll give you some pain medicine. All right?"

Slowly, he took his hand away from Paul's mouth.

"Fuck you," he swore faintly.

Jakob's smile turned viscous as he slid the spoon from Paul's clenched fist that he held firmly against the blankets.

"Don't tempt me, Paul. You already know how much I like you."

Paul glared up at him. "This is bullshit. This doesn't change anything. I'm not doing anything more for you. I'm done. Do you hear me? *Done.*"

Jakob carefully reached over to spoon some soup from the bowl, his hand steady and slow. He brought the spoon to Paul's mouth. Paul turned his head away.

"Paul—"

"I can feed myself, goddammit."

"With one hand?"

"I can drink from the fucking bowl."

Jakob raised an eyebrow, the spoon unwavering beneath Paul's nose. He tried to ignore how good it smelled.

"I'm not going to have you slurping like some Neanderthal," Jakob said. "Now open."

Paul glared at him defiantly, refusing to budge. Then his stomach growled. Loudly. One corner of Jakob's mouth lifted. Paul's mouth watered as he smelled the sweet broth and the chicken beneath his nose. He felt his face grow hot as the edge of the spoon bumped lightly against his tightly-sealed mouth. Some of the broth sloshed onto his lips and he instinctively licked at it.

Groaning inwardly, he caved.

The soup burned deliciously as Jakob spoon-fed him like a goddamn baby. He knew his face was beet-red and he constantly shifted in mortification.

Christ, how had it come to this?

Silence settled between them as Jakob methodically and carefully fed him, every now and then patting his mouth with a soft napkin. Paul kept his eyes glued to a spot off to the side, refusing to look at him.

"I don't need you do anything else for us, Paul," Jakob suddenly said.

"Bullshit," Paul said around a mouthful of chicken.

"I'm serious. When I said our business wasn't finished, it's not for the reason that you think."

Begrudgingly, Paul looked up at him. "What do you mean?"

Jakob was silent as he spooned the last of the soup into Paul's mouth. He dabbed at his lips, his eyes lingering there as he tossed the napkin onto the tray. Paul's jaw clenched and he looked away. He felt Jakob's fingers around his left wrist loosen but not pull away completely.

"Are you thirsty?" Jakob asked quietly.

Paul hesitated then nodded. Jakob reached to the tray and held up two white pills for Paul to see.

"Pain meds," he said. "As promised."

He slipped them between Paul's lips and put the glass of water to Paul's bottom lip. As he swallowed, Paul saw Jakob's eyes on his throat, watching it convulse. Paul made an aggravated sound and Jakob took the glass away.

"Stop fucking doing that," Paul said.

Jakob's dark eyes twinkled as they met his. "What?"

Paul shook his head. He felt a warm numbness settle over him as the pain medicine took effect. He almost sighed in relief as the throbbing in his arm began to dissipate. His body uncoiled, sinking farther into the bed. Jakob smiled a little.

"You can get off me now," Paul said.

"If you insist."

He slid off his lap and settled next to him, stretching out on the bed which was only a little better than having him in his lap. Paul turned his head away.

"So are you going to explain what our unfinished business is or do you want me to guess?"

Jakob was quiet but Paul could feel his eyes on him and he fought not to shift beneath the touchable gaze. After what seemed like hours of silence, Jakob finally said on a quiet whisper, "My father repeatedly raped Irene when we were kids."

Whatever Paul was expecting, that certainly wasn't it. His head jerked around. Jakob's face was close, his eyes full of darkness, staring past Paul and into the dying embers that glowed at the bottom of the hearth..

"Irene and I used to play together all the time. When we first met, we were at that age where it didn't matter if your best friend was a boy or a girl. All that mattered was that you had fun and Irene…" His voice drifted. "She was fun, such a tomboy."

Paul blinked at him.

"We would find the highest tree to climb, the muddiest rock to tip over, the most untraveled bike trail. I had no idea what was going on every night she was over for dinner. I never suspected. I was just a kid. I had no idea, but my father—he would find ways to separate us."

Paul blinked again, watching him. Words caught in his throat as he saw the rare honesty on Jakob's face.

"He would have me do the dishes or take the dog out. Simple things. Things that I always did so it never occurred to me that anything out of the ordinary was going on."

Through the growing haze of the pain medicine, Paul wanted to say, *Why the fuck do I care about this*? but his tongue felt heavy and the look in Jakob's eyes grew more distant, more haunted. His tone softened and thickened and there was something close to pain in the slight downturn of his lips as he spoke.

"There were a few times where I would come back from walking the dog and Irene's eyes would be red and puffy. I thought it was just her allergies. She had them really bad and having the dog around didn't help. But that had never stopped her from coming over, so I didn't think anything of it."

"When did you start to suspect something?" Paul found himself asking.

"Probably around the time she started hanging out with me less and less. I would come home from school late sometimes and she would already be at my house, but then she would leave when I got there. She would leave and not say a word. It turned out that a couple of days a week, on the days that I would have to stay after school for detention or whatever, my father would pick her up from school. He would give her some bullshit line about how I wanted to talk to her and why didn't she wait for me at the house."

Paul looked away, trying to imagine Irene as a child and not as the cold, heartless bitch she was now. Tried to imagine her scared, with her nose running, her eyes watering as she was forced again and again, too young and too helpless to say no. He found that he didn't have to try very hard.

"I saw her bruises by accident. Bruises shaped like fingers around her wrists," Jakob went on. "She tried to brush it off like it was nothing. But by that time she was so far gone away from me, I couldn't get her to talk. And my father was getting careless, more arrogant in his pursuit of her, fucking her minutes before I would walk through the door. It only stopped because I came home earlier than expected one day and found him bending her over our kitchen table."

He heard Jakob take a deep breath and slowly let it out. "Blood was running down her legs and she was biting her arm to keep from screaming. God, the look on his face when he saw me in the doorway." He sighed. "From then on I felt responsible for her, like she was mine to protect. I don't know if it was guilt or something else, like I should've known, should've seen a sign but only in hindsight. Isn't that how it always happen? You see the signs that something is wrong only after the fact?"

Paul looked at him. Jakob was staring at him and Paul felt himself floundering a bit.

"It's the same way you feel about Ethan. You feel like you have to protect him, don't you? He's the reason you came back, isn't it?"

Paul looked away again. "Please don't compare your life to mine."

"I'm not. I'm merely pointing out the similarities."

"There are no similarities. I'm not trying to atone for anything."

Jakob leaned up on his elbow, facing Paul. "The hell you're not. But that's not what I'm talking about, Paul."

"Then what are you talking about?"

"Power."

"What?"

"The lack of power that we have over our own lives. That's the underlying similarity between us. None of us have had it for our entire existence. We wouldn't know what that feels like even if we had it right in front of us."

Paul pushed away an unwanted image of Aaron. "No one has control over their own lives, Jakob. Even if they think they do, there's always something that directs them. Something or someone."

"But what if we had that control? What if *we* had that control to direct the things and people around us?"

"Then we'd be no better than people like your father and Aaron."

Jakob gave a dismissive wave. "People like my father and your Aaron are weak. They want and they need and they take without any regard to the people who have to suffer for it."

"That's what control does, Jakob," Paul said. "It corrupts people. It makes them do things they would otherwise never do. If we had that control, we'd end up just like them. Or worse."

Jakob frowned at him.

"What?" Paul asked.

"You...surprise me."

"Why?"

"Because I would think you of all people would *want* control."

"I do. Just not over anyone else."

"But you know there will always be another Aaron, trying to get at you."

"I won't let that happen."

"How can you be so sure? Don't you want some sort of a guarantee?"

Paul sighed. "There are no such things as guarantees, Jakob."

Jakob suddenly leaned in close, his eyes sparkling. "What if I could give you one?"

Paul moved his head back against the pillow. "What—"

"A guarantee that no one will ever try to control you again. A guarantee that your life will be your own now until the day you're put into the earth."

Paul frowned, more than a little skeptical. "You're making my head hurt, Jakob."

Jakob laughed. It was low and full of dark things. "That's not answering my question."

"You wouldn't be able to offer anything like that. It's impossible."

Jakob's smiled deepened. "Oh, my friend, at this moment, the possibilities are endless. Rest now." He rolled off the bed in one fluid motion. "We'll talk more later."

"Wait. What about—"

"Don't worry, Paul. Just get some sleep. You've more than earned it."

CHAPTER 29

Unsure of how many days he'd been in bed, Paul forced himself up and into the bathroom. He was nearly blinded by the lights reflecting off all the chrome and slick, shiny tiles and he fumbled frantically at the light switch. When he had it at a dimmer setting, and he could look around without his eyes bleeding, he saw with a frown that there was no shower. Only a marbled bathtub that looked big enough for him to stretch out in and still have room. Had he been in a different situation, it would've been something nice to enjoy but looking at it now, all he could think about was how ridiculous he was going to look sitting in it. He gave a skeptical glance at the tray of shampoos and soaps that sat on the ledge above the tub. Not recognizing any of the name brands, he cringed, hoping there wasn't anything that smelled like flowers or fruit. Distantly, he thought of Kelly and her strawberry-scented shampoo.

He carefully undressed as the tub filled and he nearly gagged at the stench of himself. Most of the cuts on his torso were almost healed and even his broken forearm was pounding at a dull but persistent throb. After checking that the door was locked, he slowly lowered himself into the water, biting his lip on a gasp.

God, this felt good.

Keeping his right arm up on the edge of the tub, he leaned back, stretching his legs all the way out. He let himself soak for a few moments, breathing in the steam and the quiet. He forced himself not to think about anything, even though his thoughts were poised at the edges of his mind like battering rams. When his eyes began to drift close, he sat up and picked through the shampoo bottles and soaps on the tray, wincing as he read "Pleasant Peach" and "Refreshing Raspberries."

Then he found one that smelled like sandalwood and mint.

It seemed to take *forever* to get clean when he was doing all the scrubbing with one hand. His right arm twitched and spasmed as if it wanted to jump in and help and he had to practically pin it down to stop it from moving. He dabbed at the numerous cuts on his torso and tried not to remember. He rinsed himself off and climbed from the tub.

Drying off with a fluffy white towel that was hanging on the back of the door, he proceeded to dress.

Or at least, tried to.

By the time he managed to get his pants pulled up, his arm was throbbing and he was ready to scream in frustration. The only thing that kept him in check was the thought that Jakob would come running and Paul doubted that Jakob would have a problem with getting him dressed—or undressed, whatever the case might be.

You know he wouldn't have minded giving you a bath, either, snarked the voice inside Paul's head.

He left the bathroom, his hair hanging wet and heavy in his face, and he swept it back impatiently. Dressed in loose-fitting khakis and a long-sleeved black T-shirt, he sat down on the bed. He saw his wallet sitting on the night table and after thoroughly checking its contents and shoving it into his back pocket, he eyed his boots treacherously. He wondered if he was going to end up swallowing his pride and asking for help. How the hell else was he supposed to get his boots tied? His frustration grew and with it came the thoughts that he'd been trying to keep at bay. He thought about Ethan. He thought about the story Jakob had told him about Irene. Was it even true? It certainly explained a lot but the telling of it had seemed…calculated, like Jakob had been intentionally exploiting a shared loss of power and control over their lives for…for what exactly? What more could they possibly want from him? And then there was Aaron. Probably still locked down in that damn cage—

His thoughts screeched to a halt.

His ears perked.

The skin on the back of his neck pricked painfully.

There was a sound—faint, muffled but definitely *there*.

Paul blew all the air slowly out his body as he listened. The noise stopped suddenly. Then after a few seconds, it began again, higher-pitched this time, more urgent. He felt his breath quicken in and out of his lungs as he realized what he was hearing.

Oh shit—

A knock, soft and hesitant, came at the door.

He jumped, choking on a rather unmanly squeak. Hoping it wasn't the Dynamic Duo, he walked over and swung the door open. Empty space stared back at him. Then he looked down and felt a confusing jolt in his system that made it a little harder to breathe.

'He's the reason you came back, isn't it?'

The urge to slam the door shivered down Paul's arm, warring with the urge to hang his head with something like relief. The sight of that fair head and those wide, gray eyes was a blessing compared to the green-eyed demon-child who'd plunged a knife into his chest. He didn't need Dr. Freud to figure out the meaning of that dream.

"Ethan," he said, uncertainly reaching a hand toward him. "How are—"

"Paul? May I come in? Please?"

Ethan spoke with a quiet urgency. He looked jumpy and his little fingers worked hard at wringing the hem of his shirt, twisting it until Paul thought his nails would rip through the fabric.

He frowned. "Hey, hey, what's wrong?"

The muscles in Ethan's neck were stiff like he was afraid to breathe. "I—I'm sorry, I—"

"It's okay, it's fine," Paul assured him, his outstretched hand faltering between them. "What's the matter?"

Ethan hesitated. "I heard screaming."

Paul's balance nearly upended. "What? What did you say?"

"There was someone screaming."

"Screaming? Are you sure?"

Ethan nodded, his eyes never leaving Paul's face. He looked like he wanted to come closer but wasn't sure if he was allowed. Paul blinked then blinked again before motioning the boy inside the room.

"Get inside, come on."

The words were barely out of his mouth before Ethan was moving past him and into the room. Paul poked his head out into the hallway, checking one way then the other. He tilted his head, listening, but whatever he'd heard—*Screaming, you know it was screaming*—it had stopped. He went back inside, closed the door, and turned to Ethan, who stood awkwardly, still twisting his shirt in his fingers.

"Okay," Paul said. "You heard screaming."

Ethan nodded, his throat convulsing as he swallowed hard—loud enough for Paul to hear.

"Where were you when you heard it?"

"I was—I was coming upstairs and it—it was there. All around."

"Did you see anything?"

"No."

"Was it human?"

"What?"

"Did it sound like a man? Or a woman? Maybe an animal?"

Ethan's eyebrows pulled together in a small, pale knot as he tried to think.

"I think it was a man. It was deep or…well, it started out deep and then it—it kind of went…higher."

Uneasiness thickened across Paul's throat. "Do you—Do you know what direction it was coming from? Above you or below you or—"

"It was pretty far but it was still loud," Ethan explained in a halting tone. "It sounded like it was coming from below."

Paul's heart skipped a beat. He stared blankly at Ethan who stared back him.

"Are you—Are you sure?"

Ethan, noticing that something was wrong—God what *wasn't* wrong here?—began to back away. He gave a small nod.

Paul chewed on his bottom lip. His skin felt like it was ready to jump off his body and hide. Unless Jakob and Irene had gotten themselves another playmate, the screaming could only belong to one person.

Paul wiped a hand across his mouth, taking one shuddering breath after another, each one threatening to choke him. The thoughts in his head hovered and swooped down, loitered and came down again, crashing into him until he felt like he was drowning. He struggled to shove them away—the thought of Aaron screaming, the thought of him *scared* enough to do something he'd branded into Paul's training to never do—no matter what.

'Don't ever let them know that you're afraid. Ever.'

Movement caught the corner of his eye and he jerked his head around. Ethan froze as if stuck with a needle. Paul stared at him, hearing Jakob's whisper in his ear, *'He's the reason you came back, isn't it?'*

Stone-cold logic suddenly gripped Paul and kicked him in the face. He took a deep breath, desperately trying to scale back his thoughts and calm his quivering insides.

"Okay, look," he said. "Screw this noise, all right? My work here is done so we're getting the hell out."

Ethan said nothing, just watched him, waiting.

"Go back to your room and get whatever you need. Then you come right back here, okay? You come right back."

Ethan didn't move but his fingers began another twisting journey into the hem of his shirt. Paul stared at him, waiting.

"What? What're you waiting for? Go on."

Still Ethan hesitated. Paul skinned his lips back over his teeth, struggling for patience. "I'm not going anywhere, Ethan. I'm going to be right here waiting for you, okay? Now, please. *Go.*"

Ethan backed away then went from the room, not running but not walking either. Paul blew out a long breath, squaring his shoulders.

He's going to drag you under, slow you down. You might as well put a bull's eye on your back.

He searched the room, once again finding his bag full of clothes but not his weapons. He swore under his breath. He did not want to leave here unarmed. He turned and watched the door that Ethan had left open, realizing that his heart was slamming in his chest. His skin felt icy and covered with sweat.

You know it's him, came the feverish, inadvertent thought. *You know it's Aaron.*

Paul didn't think freedom could taste so sick. He never thought with it being so close, it would make him almost wish that it wasn't. It was too thick to swallow and he feared that Aaron would be right: that Paul wouldn't know what to do with it once he had it. He swallowed against the cotton-ball dryness in his throat and looked up when a shadow fell across the doorway.

CHAPTER 30

"Paul?"

The sight of Jakob conjured mixed emotions and Paul wasn't sure about any of them. Jakob seemed to be having similar problems because he remained half-frozen in the doorway, as if uncertain he should enter. His dark eyes were curious.

"Why are you out of bed?"

Paul blinked at him. "What?"

"And you're...dressed?"

"Yeah?"

"You took a shower?"

"There was no shower," Paul found himself admitting grumpily. "I had to take a bath."

Jakob's eyebrows rose into his hairline. "By yourself?"

"Well, of course, by myself. Who the hell else was going to do it?"

The unspoken *I would* was heavy in Jakob's eyes and Paul looked away, trying not to remember the complete mortification of being spoon-fed.

Jakob shook his head like a disappointed parent, his lips set in a tight, unhappy line. "You should've asked for help. You could've further injured yourself."

Paul bristled. "I didn't feel like waiting around."

Jakob kept staring as he moved into the room. Paul watched him then noticed the bag slung over Jakob's shoulder. "Is that mine?"

Jakob blinked and his eyes flashed with annoyance. He swung the bag off his arm and let it fall to the floor with a loud *thunk*. Paul nearly wept at the sound of his weapons knocking together.

Thank God, he thought, stooping down for the bag.

But Jakob moved in front of him, blocking his way. Paul straightened and took a step back.

"What?"

"Is that all you care about?" Jakob hissed.

Paul frowned. "Wha—"

"Your little toys, your useless weapons that you think for some reason are a fucking kind of extension of *you*?"

"What the hell are you talking about?" Paul demanded, unable to go anywhere but back as Jakob advanced on him.

The bed hit the back of his knees and he sat down quickly before he toppled over it. Jakob kept moving forward, bumping against Paul's knees until he had no choice but to part them. An unpleasant chill went down his spine as Jakob stepped into his personal space, his eyes flashing with a dark light. Paul's instincts screamed at him to fight, to push himself away because he *knew* what this meant. He knew the look in Jakob's eyes and it made his stomach flop over. It was the look that people got when they cornered something priceless. A thrilling knowledge that they have something that nobody else has, like some kind of exotic pet. A tiger, a shark, a chimpanzee—any animal that didn't require a trip to the local pet shop to buy a ten-pound bag of puppy chow. Animals that could never *truly* be trained because they were simply not made for domestication. Animals that could perform tricks, that could cuddle and enjoy having its tummy rubbed and even sleep at the foot of your bed, all the while fully capable of making a meal out of you.

Unable to stand the scrutiny, Paul started to stand up but Jakob raised his hands and buried them in Paul's hair.

"Hey—"

"Shhh," Jakob whispered and began to gently comb his fingers through the blond strands.

"Jakob," Paul began, trying to stand once more but Jakob tightened his hands against Paul's head, pulling sharply, keeping him in place. "Jakob," he said again, through clenched teeth. "What the f—*let go*."

"Let me help you," Jakob commanded quietly, moving in closer until nothing but an inch separated them.

"I don't—I don't need help. I'm fine," Paul tried to say.

He could feel the heat of Jakob's body against his inner thighs and he tried to move them away, farther apart, which only caused Jakob to move closer. Paul gritted his teeth in frustration.

"You can't pull your hair back with one hand, Paul and you certainly can't tie your shoelaces either."

It made perfect sense, it really did, but there was something too hard and possessive in Jakob's words, with his movements. Paul forced himself to blow out a slow breath when Jakob tugged on his hair, angling his head back. His fingers continued their slow slide from his scalp to the ends of his hair, moving gently through the knots, soothing like a masseuse. But Paul felt anything but soothed.

"Jakob, this—this isn't necessary."

"Yes, it is."

"No, it's not."

"Why not?"

"Because you're *petting* me."

Jakob laughed. It was a deep, twisted sound that matched the look in his eyes. "You don't like it?"

"Not really."

"Well, imagine how *I* felt when I walked in here to find you already dressed."

"What did you want me to do?"

"You could've waited for me," he replied.

Paul stared at him. *This is seriously getting to be too much.* "I was not going to wait for you. I'm a grown man. I can take care of myself."

Jakob pulled tightly at his hair, gathering it up at the base of his skull and tying it back with an elastic band. Jakob leaned back and Paul breathed a bit easier. Until Jakob leaned back in and placed his hands on Paul's legs, looking into his face. "I am very well aware of that, Paul," he leered. "But even men like you need some help from time to time."

He slithered down to the floor on his knees. Paul jerked back, his heart lurching into his throat.

"What're you doing?"

"Relax," Jakob purred, dragging Paul's boots over.

Paul flexed his jaw. Every nerve in his body was screaming with the urge to kick Jakob in the face and run. His fingers dug into the edges of the mattress.

"Don't even think about it," Jakob said quietly as he slid the left boot onto Paul's foot.

"What?"

"Kicking me in the face."

Paul glared at him. "I wasn't thinking that."

Jakob flashed a grin at him that was all teeth. "I can practically hear the wheels turning in that pretty head of yours, Paul. You were thinking about it."

Paul looked away. Jakob laced up the left boot, his fingers sure and graceful around the laces.

"No, I wasn't."

Jakob shrugged. "Doubt you'd get very far anyway with your injuries and all." He paused. "Although even when you were at your best, you still couldn't take me down." He grinned.

Paul flushed red, his nostrils flaring. "I can take you down and I have. It's not my fault Irene keeps swinging blunt objects at my head every time I get the upper hand."

"Excuses, excuses," Jakob murmured as he slid the right boot onto Paul's right foot and began to lace it up.

Paul tensed his leg, ready to jerk his foot away with a fervent, "Fuck you," when movement by the door caught his eye. Ethan was glancing around the edge of the doorway, a half-full plastic bag in his hands. His eyes were wide, questioning, and Paul's own eyes grew wide as he vaguely wondered what this scene must look like. If Paul thought he couldn't get any more uncomfortable, he was wrong. He gave a minute shake of his head. Ethan bit his lip and slid back out of view.

Jakob sighed, long and somewhat sad. He glanced up at Paul, his long white fingers curling around his right ankle like overgrown spiders.

"You know, it saddens me that you're still so eager to get away from me, even after all we've been through."

Paul swiped his tongue along his bottom lip then stopped when he saw Jakob follow it with his eyes. *Tread carefully.* "You knew this was coming."

"Yes. Just not so soon. I thought you would've waited until you were recovered more."

"I'm fine."

"You have a broken arm, Paul. That's hardly what I would call fine."

"I can manage."

"Can you? There's nothing around here for miles, Paul, not to mention that it's twenty degrees outside. You're not a hundred percent and yet you seem to think that you can handle anything that comes your way."

"That's because I can."

"You can't even get past me."

Paul pushed to his feet. Jakob rose as well, his gaze intense as he stared Paul down.

"A deal's a deal," Paul growled. "I did what you told me to do and that's it, you hear me? It's—whatever game that you're playing, it's over. All right? Over."

Something like pain shone in Jakob's eyes. "Is it me? Are you leaving because of me? Is it something I did?"

Paul gaped at him. "What—"

"Did I say something? Did I not say something? Come on, Paul, Jesus, I gave you everything I could. I saved you. I brought you into my home, for God's sake."

"Do you remember the part where you kidnapped me?" Paul exclaimed. "How about the part where you kept me in a cage?"

"It was for your own good," Jakob replied, raising his chin a notch. "I saved you, Paul. You know, deep down, that I did and you show more appreciation to a bag of fucking guns."

Paul stared at him, hearing the words from someone who seemed to be caught between a disgruntled housewife and Aaron. Feeling as if his brain was going to implode on itself, Paul scooped up his bags and went for the door.

"We're leaving."

"But—" Jakob said from behind him.

"No," Paul shot back over his shoulder. "This was the deal and that's fucking it."

He stepped into the hallway. His head buzzed painfully and the urge to laugh and vomit simultaneously crawled up the back of his throat.

"Ethan? Let's go, we're leaving."

The kid poked his head out of his room and relief lit up his little face as he saw Paul with his bags. He hurried to Paul's side, slowing slightly when he saw Jakob hovering in the doorway. Jakob's hands twitched as if he wanted to reach out and grab him.

"Paul, please—" Jakob tried, his tone pleading and it was suddenly so pathetic that Paul couldn't even look at him.

"Let's go," Paul said to Ethan and they started off down the hall. He could hear Jakob's quick steps behind them, could almost feel his shallow, panicked breaths on the back of his neck.

"Paul, you know you won't survive out there on your own."

"How the hell would you know?" he snapped as they hit the stairs. "I've handled far worse than this before."

Liar.

Paul clenched his teeth, trying to breathe past Jakob's desperation.

"That's doubtful. You've never run away from Aaron before."

Paul came off the last step and spun around so fast, Jakob stopped short on the step above him.

"You don't know anything," he spat at him. "Not a fucking thing."

"Yes, I do," Jakob replied softly.

"Give me a way out of here, Jakob."

"No."

Paul sucked in a sharp breath but he didn't miss the subtle twist of Jakob's hips as he answered, as if he were pulling something out of reach. Paul looked at him, waited a beat then dropped his bags and punched him in the face. Jakob fell back on the stairs in a graceless sprawl, crying out in surprise. Paul moved over him, awkwardly with one hand, patting down his pockets until he found a set of truck keys. Jakob grappled for them as Paul stepped back then hit him again. Blood splattered the floor.

"Goddamn you, Paul," Jakob swore, his voice coming out wet and full of pain.

Without sparing him a glance, Paul shoved the keys in his pocket, scooped up his bags and went for the front door. Ethan huddled close to his side, jitters coursing through his small body. When Paul wrenched the door open and the frigid air knifed into his lungs, he almost screamed.

He should've.

He wanted to.

But Irene probably would've taken it as an invitation to blow his head off. She stood on the porch like she'd been waiting for him, aiming a gun at his face, nice and steady, despite the freezing cold. Her breath puffed out slowly in little clouds, surrounding her head like a halo before dissipating. Her eyes seemed to glow as she glared at Paul over the gun, *his* gun.

His favorite Glock.

Paul blinked stupidly at the gun before flicking his eyes to her face. "Irene—"

"Where are you going?" she said, her husky voice almost amused.

"I—"

"You weren't going to leave without saying goodbye *again*, were you?"

"You—"

"Put your bags down and back up."

"Irene—"

"Now."

"Irene, the job's done, okay? Done. We are leaving. That was the—"

"Put your bags down and back up."

"I—"

She switched off the safety on the gun and the sound it made was loud enough to stop Paul's words in his throat. He stared at her. She stared right back. The hush of the cold and the oncoming night swirled around in an ever-tightening circle, constricting his chest like a claustrophobic person having an attack. He forced himself to take a deep breath. She moved forward until the gun was inches from the bridge of his nose. He shifted his body weight, wishing—*God, wishing*—that he'd taken a weapon from his bag before coming downstairs.

You are a freaking moron, he berated himself.

His eyes darted from left to right. He could feel Ethan behind him, shivering in the cold.

"Back up," she said again.

He licked his lips, wincing as the cold stung them. "Wait, just wait—"

"You might want to get the child out of the cold, Paul," she offered oh-so-casually.

The gun was ice-cold when it touched his forehead. He met her eyes and saw nothing that would save him. Nothing that he could reason with. Paul's stomach twisted. A scream flew up the back of his throat.

I am done here! Done, do you hear me? Just let me go!

The words hung on the back of his tongue like a thick gob of peanut butter. His vocal cords failing him, limbs uncertain as to which way to go as his brain responded to this dilemma with blanks and question marks. However, his lips parted, wanting to say something, *anything* but then Irene was shoving the gun hard against his forehead, pushing him back into the house. Ethan stumbled underfoot but righted himself as Irene stalked in after them and shut the door.

No—no—

Paul watched the door close, feeling the sound of it deep inside like a shot in the heart. His shoulders sagged and he let his bags fall to the floor. Irene kicked them out of the way. He looked at her, at her finger on the trigger and kept his hands in front of him. Maybe if she came closer to him, he could wrap his fingers around her neck and squeeze until her fucking head popped off.

"Irene," he said trying to keep his voice even. "Irene, we had a deal. Remember? We made a deal. Right in this very room. I did the job. I did what you told me to do. It's time for me, for us to leave."

"No need to get dramatic, Paul. I'm simply prolonging your inevitable departure."

That somehow didn't make him feel any better. "Why would you want to do that and what's with the gun?"

One corner of her mouth twitched. "Just in case."

"Just in case of what?"

There was a startling moment of ear-popping silence and Paul heard rather than felt the air shift behind him. Then he heard laughter. Cold, tingling laughter.

Even as he spun around, the sound of Ethan's cry was horrible and unexpected. He caught a flash of pale hair and then Ethan was sliding across the floor, coming to a crumpled stop against the wall.

"What the fu—" barely made it out of Paul's mouth before he felt a force ram up into his balls.

The world exploded in bright colors and zero sound as if everything had been sucked away in a vacuum. A noise came strangled and pained from his throat as he curled in on himself and collapsed to the floor. He gasped for breath, his ears tuning inward to his pounding heart, pulsing, echoing with, *ohGodholyshitithurts,* at every beat. Cupping his hands around his groin, he tried to push to his feet, feeling the danger around him like a fog, knowing that he had to get up and defend himself. Jesus, he might as well put his neck on a chopping block with the way he was laying about. But he ended up slumping to his knees again, unable to support himself. Through the haze of pain, he blurrily opened his eyes.

Jakob's smiling face floated above his. His blood-slicked mouth was moving but Paul was damned if he could hear what he was saying. He blinked long and hard, the air burning his lungs as he tried to put it to good use. Weak coughs sputtered from his throat and that was when sound suddenly exploded in his ears. He gasped, blinking up at Jakob as if he'd never seen him before.

"Paul, Paul, Paul," Jakob tsked, tilting his head to one side. "I swear, I think you antagonize me on purpose."

"You—ass—h—hole," Paul stuttered.

Something slithered into the dark of Jakob's eyes. Something unfriendly and there were suddenly glimpses of the maniac who would keep grown men in cages and children tied up like dogs. Not the caring, soothing, barely-there psycho whom Paul had inadvertently allowed to nurse him back to health. Oh, no. This was the man in all his insanity-rippled glory and Paul was hard-pressed to decide which one was worse.

Definitely bi-polar.

Jakob's eyes twinkled. "You, my dear boy, are a hard one to convince. Pleading doesn't work. Tears don't work. Apparently Aaron was right, as much as it pains me to admit. Violence seems to be the only thing that speaks to you."

Paul sucked in deep breaths. "F—Fuck—you."

Jakob's smile was dark and smug. "I've offered, pretty boy. You keep turning me down."

Paul shut his eyes, swallowing hard. His attempt to straighten to his feet was blocked again when his throbbing balls refused to let him move his legs. He bit back a groan and opened his eyes. "I'm not—staying."

Jakob rolled his eyes. "Jesus, man, you are one stubborn son-of-a-bitch."

"Could say—the same for you."

"Come on, Paul. What's it going to take, huh?" Jakob leaned into his face, his eyes raking over Paul like hot coals. "What's it going to take to convince you that staying is a *much* better idea than leaving?"

"What—fucking reason do you have for me to stay here?"

One corner of Jakob's mouth pulled up in a leer that was all heat and dark bedrooms.

"Having you on your knees is reason enough for me."

Paul sputtered.

"*And* you know that you'll be hunted," Jakob added.

"No one will be able to find me."

"Paul, I'm not sure if you're aware of this, but you're a hard one to ignore."

Paul looked away, wondering if he should try to get to his feet. Then Jakob asked, "Remember what I said about guarantees?"

Paul glared at him as much as he could. "Shove them up your ass—"

"Ah, ah" Jakob purred, cutting him off. "None of that now."

Paul stared helplessly up at him.

"I want—out."

The tilting of Jakob's head was disturbingly reminiscent of an eagle considering the squirrel caught in its talons.

"Paul," he said, speaking slowly now as if he was talking to a retarded child. "Do you remember what I said about guarantees?"

"Yes."

"Good," Jakob smiled slightly.

"Wait here, all right? I'll be right back." He walked away with a sickening spring in his step and disappeared into the kitchen.

Paul breathed deep a few times and started to climb to his feet. He heard the *click-clack* of Irene's heels behind him a second before he felt the gun on the back of his neck.

"Don't bother," she commanded softly.

Grimacing, Paul sank back down to his knees.

"Irene—"

"Shut up."

"Listen. Just listen—"

She pressed the gun in hard, until Paul could swear it grated against bone. "Shut. Up."

Paul balled his fists against his legs. Silence pressed down around them, hard and sharp. He tried again. "Is—Is Ethan okay?"

"He's fine."

"I—"

Jakob came back into the room, looking entirely too pleased with himself.

"Okay, Paul. I want to show you your guarantee. You said it was impossible, right? Well, wait till you get a look at this."

Irene backed off a little, the gun leaving his neck, but Paul could feel it hovering. Reluctantly, he looked up as Jakob came toward him.

The world slowed, stuttered, and almost came to a full stop. Paul's heart gave a painful lurch and the time between one breath and the next seemed like years. He gaped at the picnic basket in Jakob's hands, unable to look away, unable to do anything but listen to his heart pound agonizingly slow in his ears. In that long, breathless moment it takes for a tree to fall to the ground, Paul knelt there like a man at a vacant altar, praying helplessly for divine intervention. He stared at the basket, at the long shadow it threw across the floor, coming toward him like the crumbling edges of a bottomless pit. The quiet moved around him and he felt the hairs on the back of his neck spring up.

'*Door number one or door number two?*'

The gag was thick, hot, and wet in his mouth.

'*You have to choose. It'll make things easier for you if you do.*'

Paul's chest tightened. The shadows stretched and moved over the basket as Jakob bought it closer, weaving and hiding, revealing and shifting like a nest of snakes. He didn't want to know what lay inside. Good God, he *really* did not want to know.

'*I got it for you. Don't you like it? It'll look so good on you.*'

Laughter, hysterical and metallic, bubbled up the back of his throat. Taken out of context, this was completely ridiculous. It was a picnic basket. It was sunshine, parks, and checkered tablecloths. It was laughter and good times. It wasn't coming toward him in the middle of a room like a prowling beast, covered in shadows and bad, *bad* feelings. Not to mention that the bottom edges seemed awfully dark, as if something had spilled inside and saturated the—

He began to shake. The air in his lungs burned and he dropped his eyes to the floor.

'*Don't make me do this. Please, don't make me do this.*'

'*You have to. You must.*'

"Paul?"

Jakob's voice was close, too close. He could see the toes of Jakob's shoes but he refused, absolutely refused to look up.

"Paul, aren't you going to look at what I bought you?"

"No."

There was a pause then Jakob said softly, "But Paul, it's your guarantee."

Paul squeezed his eyes shut then opened them. His words trembled out of his mouth.

"I don't want it."

"You don't want it?"

Paul shook his head. A hand gripped his chin and forced it up. His bones rattled, a painful mix of anger, fear, and dread churning in a bubbling wave in the pit of his stomach.

"Why not?" Jakob demanded, his dark eyes regarding Paul with a look that one might give a puppy that had done something messy but cute. "This is what you need, isn't it?"

Paul steadfastly kept his gaze on Jakob's face, trying to ignore the basket that lurked just below his field of vision.

"I don't—" he tried to say again but Jakob shushed him, bringing his face entirely too close.

"Yes, you do."

This close Paul could see that whatever saturated the bottom of the basket was leaking onto the floor. It looked black and slick in the dim lighting. Paul thought he smelled meat and the coppery scent of blood. His teeth clamped together and his vision tunneled and his brain began to chant, *Bad idea, bad idea, this is a bad idea.*

And it was. It was so, so bad but his fingers, as shaky as they were seemed to *want* to know what lay inside. They seemed morbidly curious even though some part of his brain already *knew* what was there. Some part of him was already three steps ahead and screaming as his hands reached for it, straining to flip the lid up and back—

The lights went out.

CHAPTER 31

"Well shit," came Jakob's response from somewhere in front of him.

Paul blinked, yanked back into himself so quickly he lost his breath. He flailed a bit before staggering to his feet. "What the hell—"

Jakob put the basket on the floor and moved around him. The quick *click-clack* of Irene's heels moved away from him. Paul turned around and around, trying to get his bearings. Taking a deep breath, he closed his eyes then opened them, waiting for them to adjust to the dark.

"What the hell happened?" Jakob snapped from over to his right.

"How the hell am I supposed to know?" Irene snapped back. "The breakers are probably frozen."

"Oh, like *that* could happen."

"Well, what other explanation could there be?"

A shiver of rising panic went up Paul's spine. He took a few much-needed steps away from the picnic basket at his feet. Christ, he didn't need to trip over the damn thing and spill out whatever the hell was in there—*You know what's in there—waiting for you.*

"Where're my weapons?" he found himself demanding, his voice sounding thick.

Silence greeted his question. Then Jakob's quiet, "What do you need your weapons for, Paul?"

"Your power was cut. I want to be armed."

There was a pause. "Now when you say 'cut', do you mean 'on purpose'?"

"Yes."

Jakob laughed lightly. Paul gritted his teeth, eyes searching the dark shadows and seeing the outline of Jakob's form just a few feet to his right.

"Paul, we're in the middle of nowhere. I can assure you that no one knows you're here."

"You don't know that—"

"Stop being so paranoid." This came from Irene who was about ten feet in front of him.

"Give me my fucking weapons. Now."

He was glad for the dark. He could feel their eyes on him, as sure as the heat from the sun. Beats of silence passed and finally he heard Irene's heels move.

"All you had to do was say please," Jakob admonished.

Paul didn't respond. He bent over to grapple for the bag that was shoved at his feet. He pushed his hand in, his fingers closing on the first thing he touched, a sheathed K-bar. He slid it into the hip pocket of his pants. Another laugh came from Jakob, closer this time, as Paul grabbed another weapon from his bag. From the feel of it, he knew it was his Smith & Wesson and it was fully loaded. He switched the safety off.

"Paul, we're *fine*. Take a look out the window. There's *nothing* around here for miles and miles. It's perfectly safe—"

There was suddenly a series of soft noises, an odd combination of scraping metal, a heavy footstep on a wooden floorboard, and the soft whisper of the front door swinging open. The air was freezing as it rushed in, laced with fear and ice. The silence that followed was ear-splitting and no one moved, simply watched as the door bumped gently against the wall then stopped.

Right, Paul thought to himself. *Perfectly safe. Jesus Christ.*

The cold air breathed into the room, bringing darkness that expanded like great balloons of ink. He shivered, unsure if it was from the cold or the sight of the door opening by unseen hands. He straightened to his feet, balanced on wobbling knees. Slinging the bag of weapons over one shoulder, he backed up, putting some distance between himself and the door. He glanced at the windows. *What was the point of coming through the front door when a sniper could make the job so much easier?*

Personal. You know this is as personal as it gets.

He looked down at the floor, seeking out the shadow of the picnic basket. His throat tightened. *God, Aaron, I'm so—*

Hands lightly touched his back.

Paul jumped and spun around.

Ethan's blond head seemed to shine and Paul could easily picture the wide, gray eyes, the face upturned, waiting, questioning. Paul slowly exhaled, letting his hand graze Ethan's shoulder in acknowledgement.

Jakob's amused whisper bought his attention back to the door. "You expecting some company, Paul?"

"No."

"Then who the fuck is it?" came Irene's irate hiss.

Paul saw her darkened form move toward the door, the gun—*his gun*—out in front.

"Irene, don't," he hissed after her.

"Fuck off," she hissed back.

Something whistled through the air, high and quick. The hairs on his arms rose. There was quick movement—he could barely track it with his eyes. Then he heard a wet-sounding *thunk*. Irene's body flew backward and hit the floor.

Paul could barely make out something long and narrow sticking out of her chest. His brain leaped and for a moment all he could hear was the air rattling thick, heavy, and wet in her throat, her heels kicking and tapping out a staccato rhythm.

"Oh my God," Jakob whispered next to him. "What the fuck was that?"

"I don't know—" Paul started to answer.

"Irene?" Jakob called to her tentatively. "Baby, are you..." His voice trailed off followed by a burst of pure, escalating panic. "Oh my God, Irene? *Irene!*"

He ran toward her, sliding to his knees beside her, his hands grabbing at her as she gurgled and kicked against the floor.

"Irene, oh God, darling, no." Jakob was crying, his voice shaking with tears and pain. "No, you're okay. You're—Paul? Oh, God, Paul, help me, please!"

But Paul's attention was on the front door. The air shifted. The skin on his scalp prickled. He could feel the pressure building in his ears like he was sinking into water that was too deep.

Something was coming.

"Paul!" Jakbo cried out again. "Paul, what the fuck, man? Get over here and help me! She's dying!"

"Jakob, we've got to go. Now."

"Fuck you, I'm not leaving her."

"She's already dead, man, come on."

"I'm not—"

There was another whistling sound and Jakob's words ended on a small *unh*.

Paul didn't bother watching Jakob's body hit the floor. He whipped around and herded Ethan toward the steps that led up to the second floor. It was a bad move, he knew, but he didn't know where else to go. It was too fucking dark to see and there was too little time to weigh his other options. If there were any.

Ethan tripped on the first step but Paul held him upright and pushed firmly him along. He could've scooped the boy up and taken the steps two at a time—and he desperately wanted to. He could feel whatever it was growing behind him, pressing against his back like giant hands. But he couldn't do much with his arm in a cast, while trying to keep his bag on his shoulder and the gun, slippery with sweat, from sliding out of his hand.

From behind him, Jakob screamed. It was shrill, horrible and ended abruptly.

They bounded up the stairs. A gasping, clogging noise was following them and it was only then that Paul noticed that the noise was coming from him. They cleared the staircase, running into more darkness. Christ, it was darker up here than it was downstairs. Ethan slowed in front of him and Paul nearly went ass-over-tea kettle. Righting himself, he pushed the kid down one hall then another. It wasn't long before the idea set in that he might get them pretty fucking lost. Chest heaving, he looked around, swallowing hard. He could feel Ethan shaking beside him.

Whatthefuckwhatthefuck was screaming so loud in his head he almost didn't hear the kid when he whispered, "There."

"Where? What?" Paul muttered harshly. "I can't see—" He felt himself being pulled to the right then there was the sound of a door opening. "Wait, wait," he said, pulling Ethan back.

Paul took a small, hesitant step forward and nearly gasped when he realized that he could *see*. Shapes loomed out of the darkness and he saw a fire burning in a hearth, illuminating a bedroom that was like the one he'd stayed in.

Except for the manacles at the head of the bed.

Paul blinked.

Nope. They were still there and looked to be lined with fur. The bed sheets were tussled, half on the bed and half on the floor, the color of rich, red wine.

He'd found Jakob and Irene's bedroom.

He wasn't sure how to feel about that. He was torn between shuddering and rolling his eyes but then did neither when he thought that they were both dead downstairs. He swallowed past the dryness in his throat and looked down at Ethan. The kid's gaze was glued to the bed. Paul did not try to decipher the look on his face.

He quietly closed the door behind them and locked it.

"Come on," he whispered.

He began to search the room, the movements stabilizing his mind for the moment. Motioning Ethan to stay by the fire, he stuck the gun in the back of his pants. He found clothes in the closet; along with winter-wear which he dragged out and tossed on the back of an armless chair. He threw a heavy black parka to Ethan.

"Put that on," he commanded quietly.

Without waiting to see if he would do it, Paul went to the windows and jerked the heavy curtains open. The glass breathed coldness onto his face. The view was no different up here than it was from downstairs. The moonlit snow was still beautiful, stretching endlessly on a white-blue-silver canvas. The shadows were still deep and edged in violet. And there was nothing, absolutely *nothing* around for miles. He unlocked the window and threw it open, gasping at the cold air. He leaned out, his skin tightening painfully in the sub-zero temperature. Eyes instantly watering, he looked down at the ground, unable to gauge just how far up they were because *Jesus Christ* all he could see was white and he knew from personal experience that snow was not a cushioning agent. So jumping was out and climbing down using bedsheets as ropes like fucking Rapunzel was most definitely out, too. In the time that he would waste tying them off and lowering both himself and Ethan down *with one arm*, they could be killed ten times over.

Fuck.

He slammed the window shut, shivering. He threw open the bathroom door and flicked on the lights, squinting in the glare of white marble and chrome. Amidst all the eye-jarring brightness, the bloodsoaked clothes in the sink were incredibly hard to miss.

Paul stopped, his eyes frozen to the congealed mess that resembled coils of black-scaled snakes. The red smears across the countertop made it seem like an animal had been slaughtered. He immediately thought of the picnic basket—the fluid that had leaked through the bottom and the noise of something loose rolling around inside. He blanched, fumbling for the light switch. He hit it harder than necessary and backed out of the bathroom.

Aaron.

"Jesus," he mumbled.

Paul turned to Ethan. The kid's eyes were wide, but steady on Paul's face, and he looked lost inside the black parka. But at least he would be warm.

If you ever make it out of here.

Paul took a deep breath, trying to focus. His eyes swept around, forcing his numb brain to utilize everything in the room.

Come on, come on, come on. Find a way out. You'll be fine. Everything will be fine.

The pep talk cleared his head a little bit. But his hands wouldn't stop shaking and, as he put his bag on the ground, the hairs on the back of his neck stood straight up.

Time was running out.

"Okay, look," he said in a rush, shrugging into a coat that was similar to Ethan's.

It smelled like Jakob's cologne.

"No matter what happens, you stay behind that bed, all right? No matter *what* comes through that door, you stay down. You understand me? Ethan, do you understand me?" he pressed when the kid didn't answer because he was too busy glancing at the big bed that stood between the bedroom door and the wall.

After a moment, Ethan looked back up at Paul, his teeth chewing at his bottom lip.

"Go on," Paul urged him.

Something unreadable flickered over the kid's face before he turned away and squeezed himself in between the bed and the wall. Paul watched him then he slid the strap of his weapon bag over his head so that it crossed his chest. He pulled his gun from the back of his pants and checked the clip. Hugging the wall next to the door, he squatted down, flexing his fingers around his gun. He didn't bother putting his ear to the door to see if he could hear anything. His heart was pounding so loud, he was sure that whomever was on the other side—and he was damn sure that someone was—they'd be able to pinpoint him before he even turned the knob. His right hand reached out to the doorknob before he realized that it was still in a cast.

Damn it. Whoever was out there already had an advantage.

He put the gun on the floor and carefully, quietly turned the knob just enough to unlatch it. Then he picked the gun back up, stood, and used his foot to swing the door open as soundlessly as he could.

Pure darkness stared back at him. Throwing a quick glance back at Ethan, he saw the boy's eyes peering over the top of the mattress. Paul motioned for him to put his head down before easing his own out into the hallway.

A dark shadow rushed him and there was a loud *crunch* next to his head that wrenched his eardrum.

He jerked back with a shout.

He squeezed the trigger again and again, shooting at something and nothing as he flew back into the room and kicked the door shut. He backed away from the door, bullets blasting through it in a rainstorm of splinters.

Paul kept shooting until the gun clicked empty.

CHAPTER 32

Paul used to be a screamer. Even though those days were long over, he could still remember how good it felt to open his mouth and scream out all the pain, frustration, and insanity that was stacked up inside his chest like a crooked column of old library books. It had felt awesome, like pulling out a splinter. Most of the people he had been with liked it, too. It seemed to intoxicate them, knowing that they were unleashing so much pain, knowing that they were capable of it. It made them animals, man at his most base.

Every so often there'd been those who wanted him to be quiet, as if the bitten-back whimpers were somehow more powerful, more arousing. It was hard work, keeping the screams in, trapping them in the back of his throat until they burned. And when his path crossed with Aaron's, it was even harder because Aaron liked the quiet. He liked the restraint and he especially liked to test Paul over and over again. He'd once held Paul against the wall by his neck to see if he could feel a scream build in Paul's chest and catch it in his throat like a butterfly.

It had been an effective way to keep Paul quiet.

Now Paul's vocal cords threatened to snap at the force of the scream in his throat.

Fumbling, he dropped his empty gun, searching in his bag for another clip. His breath whistled in and out of his lungs. He felt blind and deaf as he somehow managed to reload.

"What was it—" Ethan began to ask, his voice a soft murmur.

"Ethan, you stay there," Paul replied just as quietly.

He blinked hard, looking up at the mangled door. The light from the fire played with the bullet holes, filling them with light, then shadow, then light again, making it seem like they were eyeballs blinking at him. It should've been ridiculous, except that it wasn't because there really was something standing outside that door, watching him. Something big and crippling. It terrified him in a way that Paul hadn't felt in a long, long time. Sweat trickled down his spine and he raised the gun, one-handed as he pushed himself to his feet. He leaned a hip against the bed to keep himself steady. Then he stepped to one side of the door, pressing his back to the wall.

Anybody home?

He bent his elbow until the gun was pointed at the ceiling and he nearly squeezed off a shot when he heard the sound of wood being twisted and snapped apart on the other side of the door. The sound of it was like ice in his heart. The back part of his mind knew it was the spear being wrenched from the wall. He'd seen it thrumming into the plaster, lit up by gunfire, before he'd slammed the door shut. He knew but it just wasn't *possible.*

No. No, it's not him. It can't be. It's not—

"Cortez?" he heard through the door.

Paul bit back a strangled scream. The muscles in his legs liquefied. *No—this isn't—*

"Cortez?"

Paul slid down the wall until his butt hit the floor. He turned his head to see Ethan peeking over the top of the bed again. The uncertainty in the kid's eyes pounded through Paul's veins, colliding viciously with the clammy fear that slipped its way up his spine.

"You—You're dead," he tried to say, his words rippling with disbelief.

There was silence for so long that Paul thought—*prayed*—that maybe he'd hallucinated.

"Am I?"

Paul bit his lip hard enough to draw blood. He turned his head to look up at the door, imaging too clearly those green, green eyes, white-hot, ferocious, and *alive,* but Jesus how could that be?

"I—I saw you—I saw you—" he managed.

"I told you, Cortez," came the voice again, powerful and invasive, squeezing Paul's muscles until they nearly burst. "Death comes to some. Not all."

"I don't—I saw you," Paul croaked. "I *saw* you die. I—I felt it."

"Did you?"

Paul gave a jerky nod although it was more like a neck spasm. Then he stopped when he realized he couldn't be seen. He didn't *want* to be seen. "Yes."

"Are you sure?"

Swallowing down a cold ball of hysteria, Paul said, "You had an arrow sticking out of your chest."

"Hallucinations can be caused by trauma and shock."

Paul shook his head. "I wasn't—"

"I'd just broken your arm, Cortez, not to mention you were bleeding quite profusely from various parts of your body. Whatever you saw—"

"No, I know what I saw. Jakob had the bow in his hand and the arrow was in—"

"Jakob had poor judgment. I think, by now, you fully understand that, yes?"

Dammit, I felt him bleed out. How the f—

"Don't you agree?" came the whisper-soft voice through the door.

"No. No, not really."

Chac Mool's chuckle prickled his skin, like the hissing kisses of a torrential downpour. "You sound like you need some convincing. Perhaps if we continue this discussion face-to-face—"

Paul sprang away from the wall, scrambling on his knees because he knew his legs wouldn't be able to hold him. He came to a stop by the bed, gun aimed. "You come in here and we'll see if you can survive a bullet in your brain," he warned.

"No one can survive such a wound, Cortez," the voice said oh-so-matter-of-factly. "Not even me."

"The fact that I'm even talking to you now makes me wonder."

"I'm very glad that you *are* talking to me, Cortez. I've been hoping to continue our conversation. We were interrupted rather rudely last time we met."

There was a kind of pleased humor in the man's voice and that was perhaps more chilling than his actual presence. He heard footsteps on the other side of the door, pacing back and forth, evenly and unhurried. Paul blinked hard and the desire to run began to worm its way through his legs.

Yes. Running.

Running the hell away from here.

And it seemed like a really good idea. Hell, it was the *only* idea because, due to this sudden shift of cosmic misalignment, he was irrevocably fucked.

"You were trying to kill me the last time we met," he said, his voice hesitant.

"Was I? I seem to recall thwarting an act of thievery."

"Just—tell me what you want, okay?"

There was a beat of silence and Paul's heart thudded into it.

"Where is it?"

The question came on a claw-edged hiss and Paul felt the power behind it like the calm wind before a hurricane.

"Where—Where's what?"

"Do not be so bold as to lie to me."

"I don't—I don't know what you're—"

"It was our topic of discussion, Cortez, until your friend, Jakob, made an attempt on my life."

Paul was about to say, "Yeah and from where I was standing, it was pretty successful," when he felt a jump in his brain as if someone had stuck him there with a cattle prod.

Oh Jesus.

Oh God, the ashes.

That little black pouch.

He stared wide-eyed at the door, mouth flapping soundlessly. "I—I—"

"Where?" Chac Mool demanded again.

Paul's mind reeled. "Shit," he whispered to himself then said out loud, the words catching around the edges of his dry mouth, "God, I don't—I don't really know. I—"

"You've misplaced it?"

"No—I—I mean, well, I don't know—"

"Do you know what I will do to you if you've lost it?"

Paul staggered to his feet.

'Things that have been left behind as a tribute to the past but also as an omen for the future.'

'An omen?'

'Yes. A warning.'

'About what?'

'Vengeance.'

Paul's fingers tightened around the gun, sure as hell certain that something was going to fly through the door at him now.

"I don't know where it is," he said weakly.

"Oh Cortez, you disappoint me. Jakob assured me that you would tell me where it is."

Paul mentally backpedalled. "Wait—*what?*"

"Dying men very seldom lie, Cortez."

A fierce pressure slammed into his chest. *God, Jakob, what did you do?*

"Well, he obviously did because I have no idea what you're talking about," Paul practically shrieked.

"Like I said," came the calm response. "Poor judgment."

Suddenly gasping for air, Paul pressed the side of the gun against his sweaty forehead. *Jakob, goddamn you, what the hell was this, one last fuck you before checking out?*

"I don't know where it is. If I did, you can bet your ass I would give it to you without any hesitation whatsoever but I don't—"

"Is there someone else in the room with you, Cortez?"

Paul paused and he spun around in time to see Ethan duck down behind the bed. Paul swallowed hard.

"No."

"I heard two sets of feet running away from me, Cortez."

"Stop calling me that."

"Stop lying to me then."

"I'm not—"

"Who is in the room with you?"

Paul faced the door again. "I—It's no one you know."

This was greeted with silence then came a thoughtful, "Ah. It is your worth."

"What?"

"We spoke of worth, Cortez, the last time we met. It was the reason you were fighting so hard to stay alive."

'*He's the reason you came back, isn't he?*'

Paul heard Ethan scuffle against the floor, heard his tiny fists tighten into the blankets that lay strewn across the bed.

"I don't know what you mean."

"Is it a child?" Chac Mool asked and Paul felt his pulse stutter. "The footsteps I heard were small, the strides short. They could only belong to someone of child-like proportions. And only a child could invoke such…self-preservation."

A tremor went through him. "It's not—"

"Why do you continue to lie to me, Cortez?"

"I—"

"I have not lied to you yet you seek to placate me like I myself am a child. I don't suppose you realize how rude that is?"

Surprisingly, Paul felt his cheeks heat up. "I—"

"Tell me about the child in the room with you."

'*I'm not a kid. I haven't been for a while.*'

Paul jerked the gun up to point at the door. "There is no child."

"Tell me," Chac Mool hissed through the door.

The gun trembled. Paul could hear soft, choked-back sobs from behind him.

"No lies, Cortez. They will only serve to make your death more necessary."

"Why do you want to know? What difference would it make?"

There was a faint scraping sound then the tip of a blade was gently worked through one of the bullet holes in the door. It turned around and around, corkscrewing slowly and curls of wood floated to the floor. Paul's mouth opened soundlessly as he saw movement through the hole and then a bright green eye appeared, settling on him like the crosshairs of a high-powered rifle.

Talking through the door to a supposed-dead man had allowed Paul to think that it wasn't really Chac Mool, but now that he was seeing those eyes, or rather, just one eye, it was something altogether different. His mind, which had struggled for what felt like an eternity to remain hinged, officially unhinged itself as he found himself staring into that endless green.

Bile burned Paul's stomach, making him dizzy. He heard humming, a tuneless melody and then realized that Chac Mool was talking, his voice edged in that strange rain-hiss. Paul struggled to focus through the screaming in his head that had picked up volume once again.

"My people worshipped Tlaloc. She was the god of water, lightning, and thunder. She and Huitzilopochtli were the most important and the most worshipped deities in Aztec culture. Huitzilopochtli represented life, the beginning of the Aztec as a people. Tlaloc represented water, the substance that would sustain that life. In order for the Aztecs to thrive, they made offerings and paid homage to those who had made their lives possible. Huitzilopochtli's worshippers were willingly sacrificed by the high priests, who removed their still-beating hearts from their chests."

Paul felt sick. The room began to sway.

"Tlaloc's worshippers drowned small children and infants in aqueducts, lakes, any body of water that they could find. It was believed that since children cried the most, their tears made the sacrifice more valuable."

Having an idea of where this was headed, Paul asked shakily, "What did their parents do?"

"They gladly handed them over."

"Their own children?"

"It was considered a great honor."

"Tell that to the children."

"Are you trying to make me angry, Cortez?"

"Look, if I—if I knew where those ashes were, would you let me—us—live?"

There was no hesitation. "No."

Paul tightened his fingers around the gun. "Looks like we're at a stalemate then."

He steadied his aim at that green orb and fired.

CHAPTER 33

His ears rang with the echo of bullets striking the door. He was surprised at how good the recoil felt in his hand, the squeeze of the trigger pulling at his forearm muscles like an old friend. He fired until the gun was empty. Without taking his eyes off the door, he reached for more ammo. As he slammed another clip in place, he heard rustling behind him.

"Stay there, Ethan," he ordered again.

The rustling stopped.

He pointed the gun at the door that now resembled the sheet that Charlie Brown wore on Halloween, and waited.

The air settled around him like dust as the minutes ticked by. The cracks and holes in the door were filled with flickering light and it was hard to tell if it was just shadows moving or something else. As much as he hoped that at least one of the bullets had struck Chac Mool, he knew that the man was in no way seriously injured. He was too damn scary to be killed in a barrage of bullets.

So the silence persisted. Paul listened to it. He listened for creaking floorboards or the heavy thuds of footsteps. The room held its breath as he slid forward.

The door flew open.

"Paul!" Ethan shouted from behind him.

Paul's eyes widened at the sight of Chac Mool, huge and terrifying in the doorway. There was a millisecond of stillness, then in a blur of motion Chac Mool's arm was cocked back and the spear that Paul knew all too well was ripping through the air. He rolled to the floor, squeezing the trigger again and again, knowing the shots were wasted but not caring. He heard the spear knife into the wall behind him and he said a quick prayer that Ethan had stayed down like he'd told him to.

Paul shot to his feet only to find those green eyes inches from his own. The gun was knocked easily from his grasp. Chac Mool grabbed him, toppling them to the floor. Paul was surprised to feel Chac Mool's hot breath against his face. He half-expected it to be cold or maybe not be there at all. But it was very real and so was he, his weight solid and dangerous, pressing Paul into the floor as if he weighed nothing.

"Where is it, Cortez?" Chac Mool hissed in his face.

Paul struggled beneath him. "I don't—I don't know—"

"You're lying again." Chac Mool grabbed Paul's jaw, his fingers strong and warm, holding his head still with barely any effort. "It won't be too hard for me to take your heart. And it will not require much effort to take your child's."

Paul's heart gave a painful lurch, causing Chac Mool to smile darkly. He pressed his other hand over Paul's chest.

"I've been hoping for a reason worthy enough to take it out of your chest." His eyes twinkled. "I believe I just found it."

Paul let his fist fly, watching it connect solidly to Chac Mool's cheekbone. His head whipped to the side then came back, his eyes flashing. The hand at his jaw tightened to the point of crushing the bones. But Paul reared up against it, hitting Chac Mool a second time, and then a third before a gun went off somewhere behind him.

Chac Mool flew back as the bullet struck him high in the chest. Paul twisted around to see Ethan kneeling by the bed, the Smith & Wesson on the floor in front of him, empty. The kid was shaking out his hands, his pale face set in a grimace of pain. Paul rolled to his feet.

Ethan glanced up at him then his eyes flicked to something over Paul's shoulder. Paul didn't even bother turning around to look.

"Go, go, go!" he commanded, urgently.

Ethan took off like a little blond bullet with Paul close behind. He didn't want to leave the Smith & Wesson but it was out of bullets and in the time it would take to load it, Chac Mool would probably have his hand wrist-deep in Paul's rib cage.

Out in the hallway, the shadows were thick and cold, swallowing them up so completely, Paul could barely see two feet in front of him. He felt Ethan's hands clench into the front of his coat, half-pulling, half-guiding him through the darkness.

"Ethan," he said, panting. "Ethan, do you know where you're going?"

In response, he felt himself being pulled to the left. As they turned the corner, Paul threw a quick glance back over his shoulder. The doorway of the room they had just left was lit up with firelight, looking like a yellow-white rip in a piece of dark fabric.

A shadow moved beyond the doorway.

Jesus Christ.

Paul let Ethan lead him through darkness that was blinding. Even with the certainty that Ethan guided them, even with the bag of weapons securely against his back, Paul could still feel something very close to fear in the back of his throat. He thought for a moment that he should be the one leading Ethan but the kid was uncanny and seemed to know exactly where they were going.

Paul thought he heard footsteps behind them. He felt himself being quickly guided around one corner then another, followed by another. The thick feeling in his throat was growing and he could barely swallow, could barely do anything with the jackhammering of his heart in his chest.

He looked over his shoulder.

There—a dark figure, moving against darker shadows, kept pace with them from about ten feet back. It stalked them, knowing how easy it would be to bring them down, to sharpen his claws on their bones.

"The stairs," Ethan suddenly whispered.

Paul stopped and saw that they were indeed at the top of the staircase. The room below was dimly lit by the moon-splashed snow beyond the windows and he felt his shoulders loosen a little now that he could see even if it was only a little bit. But then he saw what he was looking at.

Oh God.

He let Ethan pull him down the steps. Black puddles shown in the silver light and the air reeked of meat and blood. Two dark lumps lay sprawled across the floor and, as he cleared the last step, Paul heard something behind him.

He turned.

Chac Mool stared down at him from the top of the steps. He was cloaked in shadows but the shape of him was unmistakable. His eyes were luminous gems, hard and steady. Staring up at him, Paul again felt the calling in his bones to sink to his knees. But then Ethan was tugging at him and he allowed himself to be led to the front door.

He knew it was Irene's body he was stepping over because it was closest to the door. And the puddle beneath her was bigger. He swallowed hard and glanced back.

Chac Mool stood quietly at the bottom of the steps.

The door stood open and the blast of cold air at his back made Paul jump. Ethan stumbled underfoot. Paul reached out to steady him. The sound of their fumbling footsteps on the front porch echoed like thunder through the still night air. Wincing, Paul looked around and it was then that he realized his mistake.

He remembered the last time he was on this front porch, diving off of it with Ethan on his back as he scrambled through the snow, effectively digging himself into an icy hole. Irene had reached them in no time flat, even with those ridiculous heels on. If he tried running now, the snow would trap him again and, for Chac Mool, it would be like shooting fish in a barrel.

"Fuck," Paul swore under his breath.

He turned. Ethan huddled behind him, peeking out from around his hip. Chac Mool was at the door, a looming black shadow that made the cold burn in Paul's lungs. The air ignited with impending pain and death when Paul saw the sharp outline of a knife in Chac Mool's hand. Except it wasn't a knife. The blade was as long as Paul's forearm and the edges of it looked rough like the steel had bubbled when it was first forged.

Then Paul realized wasn't steel. It was stone.

He remembered the corpse arched over the altar, the hole in its chest looking torn and ragged. Like someone had simply hacked at the flesh instead of slicing it open to get to the heart inside.

Paul was pretty sure stone was never made to cut human flesh. His heart pounded in protest at the thought of being taken from its home. Licking his lips, he glanced around at the chasm of snow that stretched forever. His broken arm gave a painful twinge.

"I'll give you a head start, Cortez," Chac Mool hissed from the shadows of the doorway.

Even with the man's face obscured by shadows, Paul knew he was smiling. His jaw clenched and unclenched. Something that felt more than slightly hysterical clawed through his chest, working its way up as if it were a scream. He looked around again as if somehow the landscape would miraculously change into something more suitable to an escape. But the snow continued for miles like a frozen ocean. All that open land mocked him, taunting him with escape routes that were impossible. For a moment, but only for a moment, he considered launching himself into the snow anyway, calculating how far he could get before Chac Mool could get him.

Ten feet.

Maybe fifteen and that was only if Chac Mool didn't decide to throw that knife like it was a goddamn tomahawk.

Ethan shivered against his legs.

Chac Mool made a soft noise that sounded like a pigeon cooing. "Do not take this personally, child. Your death was assured from the moment we first met."

Ethan pressed himself hard against Paul's leg. Paul reached back, sparing a look down at him before bringing his eyes back up.

"Ethan," he rasped. "It's okay. It's okay, calm down."

The fear that came off the kid was palpable. Paul swallowed hard, mentally flailing as Chac Mool stepped out onto the porch, moving out of the shadows. Ethan's arm came around and grabbed onto the pocket of Paul's coat, pulling on it as if he could climb inside and get away.

"Paul," he whimpered.

He tugged harder, more desperate. Something fell out of the pocket and thudded to the porch. Startled, Paul looked down and felt his breath catch.

The black pouch lay at his feet, the jade stone winking maliciously up at him.

You've got to be kidding me.

A soft murmuring—words that Paul couldn't decipher—came from Chac Mool as Paul bent quickly to scoop the pouch up. He looked at Chac Mool who was staring at the pouch in Paul's hand. His face softened with reverence and something close to sadness. It was a look of worship, of peaceful joy and Paul was able to breathe easy for about three seconds before Chac Mool's face shut down again and fixed his glare back on him.

"Give it to me," he demanded quietly.

Feeling a bit more stable now, Paul took a deep breath. "I have every intention of doing that. But I want something in return."

Chac Mool's glare intensified, if that was possible. "You have the gall to ask for something in return for what is rightfully mine?"

"I'm willing to give this back to you. Doesn't that count for something?"

"It does not count when you're using it as a bargaining chip."

"It's not a bargaining chip. It's a fair exchange. Our lives for this."

Paul hefted the pouch in his hand, testing the weight, pressing his fingers into it. It was soft, the velvet smooth and cool. The contents inside sifted as if it were filled with nothing more than sand.

Ashes. Paul tried to ignore the cold shiver that went up his arm.

Chac Mool smiled and it was not pleasant. "You think your life is on the same scale of what's in your hand? I assure you it isn't."

Paul saw the certainty in his eyes and swallowed. "Maybe not. But nonetheless, it's still pretty important, isn't it?"

As soon as he said the last word, he could swear the man stopped breathing. His eyes seemed to burn brighter, drilling into Paul's skull with such ferocity, he thought his skin would sear. Beats of silence went by before Chac Mool snarled out, "Yes."

"So if I were to open this—"

"That would not be very wise."

"I doubt you could get to me in time."

"Do you really want to find out, Cortez?"

"No more than you want to see this upended all over the ground."

Chac Mool's lip curled and Paul was sure he was thinking of a hundred ways to make him suffer. But Paul stood firm. He had not gone through all of this shit just to end up on some nut-job's sacrificial altar.

"I will make it last for you, Cortez," he spat. "You will beg me to end it."

"Yeah, but will it be worth it if this—" He held up the pouch. "—is already destroyed?"

He could see the war in that finely-chiseled face, the pull of what he wanted to do versus what he had to do. It was odd but Paul understood that struggle. He knew the wrenching feeling when logic triumphed over screaming emotions.

"We'll both get what we want," Paul tried helpfully as if that would take the sting out of what he had just threatened to do.

One corner of Chac Mool's mouth quirked up. "That is doubtful."

Paul stared at him. Chac Mool stared back.

"Yes or no?" Paul persisted.

The look on Chac Mool's face changed to something that was almost amused and he shifted his weight as if he were settling in for the long haul.

"What kind of a man would I be if I let you go unpunished?"

Frustration swelled in the back of Paul's throat. "Look, I never wanted this damn thing in the first place. It was Jakob's idea to go in and get it—"

"Oh, Cortez," Chac Mool interrupted with a strange *tsking* sound. "Careful. You sound like you're copping out."

"I'm not copping out. I just want to get out of here."

Chac Mool gave an indulgent smile that made Paul's skin crawl. "It won't be that easy for you, Cortez. Not as long as your heart is still beating."

He lunged at him, his blade whistling through the air like a whip. Paul jerked back and then to the side as he felt the skin on his cheek split open. He cried out, shoving Ethan away. His lower back hit the railing. Chac Mool was on him in a second, his breath searing hot against the blood that splashed down Paul's face.

"Just like that? A simple exchange and everything will be set to rights. Like it's so simple?" His grin was a sneer. "That's the problem with Western thinking. You think that by simplifying things, you can somehow make amends. You think that by 'just getting out of here,' your problems will go away. You think you can taunt me with something *of mine*, in hopes of sparing your own life? Not so simple, Cortez, not so simple at all."

He snatched the pouch from Paul's hand and pressed the blade to Paul's neck.

"You're going to pay the same price that everyone before you has paid."

Paul flinched back as the flesh of his throat snagged on the blade. He stared into Chac Mool's eyes then sucked in a quick breath before digging his fingers into the bullet hole in Chac Mool's chest.

He wasn't really expecting a reaction. Maybe a raised eyebrow or a sardonic smile, perhaps a shrug of the shoulders. But a sound came from Chac Mool's lips that could only be a sound of pain. He jerked back as if he'd been shot again. Curling his blood-stained fingers into a fist, Paul sent a hard left hook into his face, knocking him to the ground.

Seconds. Precious seconds.

He pushed away from the railing, grabbed Ethan and ran into the house. He hoisted the kid up onto his hip and slammed the door, not bothering to waste the time fumbling in the dark for the locks.

"Paul—" Ethan gasped in his ear.

"Hang onto me," Paul panted.

Ethan's arms curled around his neck, his legs clamped around his ribs. Paul ran for the kitchen, cursing loudly as his feet squeaked and slipped through the blood on the floor. His foot caught something and he stumbled. Glancing down, he thought he saw an arm, Jakob's arm, stretched out as if reaching for him, begging for help. The front door crashed open.

"He's coming!" Ethan cried out hoarsely.

In the kitchen, Paul turned in a desperate circle. The counters were empty, the long table bare.

Goddammit, if I trapped us again—

Then he spotted the narrow hallway and the door at the end of it that led down below. He felt Ethan's arms tighten, felt a choked-off scream rise through his thin chest, and he knew that Chac Mool was in the kitchen doorway, filling the room like poison.

Paul vaulted to the door and threw it open. As he dodged through and slammed it shut behind him, a terrific force shook the door in its frame. Paul glanced over his shoulder at it, already descending the stairs.

The tip of the stone blade protruded from the center of the splintered door. Right about where Paul's heart would be.

He clutched Ethan tighter as he half-ran, half-skipped down the steps, catching himself against the wall a few times as his momentum threatened to pitch him head over heels.

"Almost there, almost there," he was muttering.

"Wh—Where?" Ethan asked, his voice trembling.

"I have no idea."

Paul reached the dungeon, tripped down those steps, eyes moving continuously for an escape.

But why the fuck would you come to a dungeon to escape, you fucking idiot?

There was nothing here but stone and steel bars. No way out but through the drain in the floor that even Ethan couldn't fit through and that low doorway that was pitch-freaking-black—

Paul bolted toward it.

It had seemed a lot bigger the first time he saw it. As he squatted down in front of it, he noticed that the top of the arching threshold barely reached his chin. Even Ethan would have to crouch down. Paul peered into the blackness. He could feel a faint, cold breeze, like a draft that ruffled his hair and he hoped that wherever this led, it would be outside.

"Okay, listen to me," he panted, as he set Ethan down. "We have to go through there. There's no other way, all right? I don't know where the hell this leads but it'll keep us moving and that's the important thing."

Ethan kept one hand balled into Paul's sleeve, as if afraid to let go. When he swallowed, it was nearly audible. "Jakob said—Jakob said this was how they took out the trash."

Paul looked at him in surprise. "When did he say that?"

"There was a man down here. Not the—Not the man you knew but another man. They—Jakob and Irene—they…" His voice trailed off.

Despite everything, Paul felt anger bleed into his bloodstream. He looked around the room once more, at the cages that now stood empty, the doors open and inviting, the floors bare and clean with not one drop of blood or one piece of a human flesh. But there was pain here. Pain and anger and while only a small amount was his, there was more from those who had been held here long before he ever set foot in this place. He could feel it against his skin, in his head like the air pressure rising. He could feel it radiating from the stones, bouncing the screams back and forth, absorbing the torment and the suffering and the blood. It was locked in the steel bars where fingers had grasped them in desperation, in fear, trapped and longing for a way out, for escape. It was kept here like wild animals, like bad memories that no one wanted to think about. If he survived this, he was going to come back and burn this place to the ground.

Paul took hold of Ethan's arm. "It's our only way out. I know it's dark and I know it's scary but just—just feel along the walls with your hands, okay? And keep moving. Don't stop for any reason, got it?"

Ethan looked at him, his eyes glassy, his brow furrowing in question.

Paul nodded. "I'll be right behind you."

CHAPTER 34

E than licked his lips like he wanted to say something. His eyes moved back across the room and he went white. Paul turned with a grimace, already knowing what or rather who he was going to see.

Chac Mool stood at the top of the stairs. Paul suspected that he was used to being in that position, high up and looking down at the lowly, unwashed masses. He could feel those eyes pierce right through his heart.

"Go," he commanded Ethan. "Go now!"

For a fraction of a second, Ethan hesitated then scurried into the tunnel, the thick shadows enveloping him like the mouth of a giant monster. Paul, sensing Chac Mool coming down the steps like a devastating tidal wave, dove in after him. Even at a low crouch, the ceiling skimmed the top of his head. He went as fast as he dared, his good hand on the wall, letting his fingers lead him.

Jesus, it was dark.

It was disorienting in its completeness, in its total lack of light. In his lifetime, Paul had had his sight temporarily taken from him many times. Mostly by people who didn't want to be looked at or identified if—God forbid—something went wrong. But there had always been some degree of light leaking through the blindfold or a shift in someone's hand that was clamped tightly over his eyes, or the loose weaves in a rut-sack that was tied around his head. He'd always been able to see *something*.

This, however, was like the deepest part of the ocean. This was like having his eyes glued shut. This was what it meant to be blind.

The air grew colder and with that came the struggle to breathe. He didn't know if it was claustrophobia but it came pretty damn close. His chest hurt and his throat felt like someone was cramming cotton into his mouth. He tried to breathe more slowly, to at least calm the thundering in his rib cage, but the darkness around him fed the panic that was skating through his bones. The stones beneath his fingers were wet in some places and icy in others and, under his feet, things crunched and squeaked like he was stepping through snow and ice.

He *hoped* it was snow and ice.

Echoes came from all sides of him. It was impossible to decipher one sound from the next. He wondered if the minds of people who heard voices were anything like this. Just one gigantic ball of murmuring sounds and words that didn't make any sense.

There was a scraping sound behind him.

Keep going. Don't stop. Don't turn around. Just keep moving.

His quads burned as he pushed himself faster. His guiding hand was sliding over solid ice now, smooth and painful. The air was freezing but there was an edge to it, a distinctive smell that he knew well.

Outside.

His heart lifted.

Then he hit a wall.

His breathing was loud in his ears or maybe it was just the echoing around him. Either way, he couldn't move forward. Frantically, he felt along the wall. His breath caught in his throat when he felt the crease of a corner then another wall to his right.

Boxed in. Trapped.

Another scraping sound came from behind him.

Panic clenched his heart as he looked behind him. The entrance glowed, a semi-circle of light that looked like a small sun setting into the darkness of the horizon. It seemed far away, so out of reach. But the crouched figure that was silhouetted against it was not so far out of reach. It grew bigger as it came closer, dodging smoothly back and forth in front of the light until it was blocked completely like the moon in front of the sun.

Paul's teeth chattered. Sweat froze on his brow. He turned back around. At least, he thought he did, Christ, he couldn't even be sure. Everywhere he looked it was the same.

All black.

Dark.

Echoing cold.

Then there was something up ahead.

An opening, an exit where snow shone pale and white and he could see the small outline of Ethan. With a hoarse cry, he shot toward it in a rapid, graceless sprawl of limbs.

Something scurried after him.

There was hot breath on the back of his neck. He thought there was a brush of fingers against his ankle. He kept his eyes on Ethan, on the snow even though he *hated* snow and when this was over, he was going to the beach, to the hottest beach he could stand. He was going to dig his toes into the sand and sit out in the sun until his skin fucking *blistered.*

At last, he was close enough to see Ethan's face, tight and red from the cold. He was crouched next to the tunnel, looking in, his eyes straining then widening when he saw Paul approaching at break-neck speed.

"Paul!"

Paul exploded out of the darkness, landing face-first in the snow. He gasped and shuddered as it went up his nose.

"Are you okay? Are you all right?" Ethan gasped, hovering over him.

Shaking with adrenaline, Paul pushed himself to his feet. "I'm okay, I'm okay," he wheezed. "Holy shit—"

He looked up, squinted against the coming dawn, unable to believe he was actually going to live to see another day.

A rapid scuttling sound came from behind him.

He spun around. The black mouth of the tunnel was like an empty eye socket against the white of the snow, frozen open, glaring at them in hate and spite. Something was moving inside, fast, and it was coming closer.

Okay, it's possible I won't *live to see another day.*

Ethan's jaw worked as he looked up at him. Paul swung him up onto his hip. He tried to ignore how the kid seemed to *fit* against him as Ethan immediately banded his arms around Paul's neck.

"Paul—"

"I know. I know. Give me a minute, okay?"

His breath streamed out in front of him in quick narrow clouds, lingering, before reluctantly floating away, revealing the small clearing in which they stood. The snow was pushed back so high that anything beyond it was hidden from sight. For one heart-stopping second, Paul thought he'd trapped them again, in more freaking snow, no less. But then his eyes were finally able to differentiate all the white-on-white and he saw an opening in the snow. It almost seemed like a doorway within the towering walls of snow on either side. It was narrow and purposeful, cutting a narrow swath through the winter landscape.

'This was how they took out the trash.'

His breath shook. It was clearly the only way out but that didn't stop Paul from looking for another escape route. This was a deliberate path. It was most likely made by Jakob and Irene and, if that was the case and Paul was fairly sure that it was then there was no way it was safe. It was here not for an escape and not for some kind of convenient way of getting to another part of the property. It was here for something else.

The trash.

The path went ahead for about twenty feet before curving to the left and out of sight. Where did it lead? What was on the other side? Was there some kind of body dump at the other end? Was there a Potter's field of people who had the unfortunate luck of crossing Jakob and Irene's path? Was there going to be a pile of frozen, eviscerated torsos and limbs, left out to feed the local wildlife?

Oh, for God's sakes, stop analyzing it and get moving! You're not safe here or did you forget?

The walls of white rose up around him as Paul finally got his feet moving. He breathed snow and ice. The hairs on the inside of his nose crackled painfully. The crunch of footsteps behind him made the air in his lungs turn to steel and he pushed himself into a half-jog, half-run. The path narrowed the farther he moved inside until the width of his shoulders caused mini-cascades of snow and ice to rain down in his wake. He had a sudden thought of *avalanche* and wouldn't that just be a bitch because then if Chac Mool wanted his heart bad enough, he'd have to dig him out first.

Ethan whimpered against his neck. Paul chanced a look over his shoulder. His steps stumbled then quickened when he thought he caught the edge of a shadow about fifteen feet back.

"Fuck," he muttered.

The corridor of snow went higher around him until the open sky above his head was the only thing that kept him from suffocating. His nose ran, coming to a freezing halt on his top lip. Years seemed to pass as he continued moving and it wasn't long before the frustration began to build.

Where the fuck does this thing end? I swear to God, if this leads back to the house—

He swallowed hard, his throat so dry he tasted blood. Trees, black and silent, arched overhead now, creating a skeletal canopy, a web of bony arms that only enhanced his growing fear of being led to another inescapable place. Glancing behind him again as he went around another bend, he thought he saw a flash of green eyes.

'See what happens when you run from me?' Aaron's voice muttered in his ear. *'See the deeper pile of shit you get dragged into because you think you can make your own decisions? You're dead, Paul. You might as well stop running. Save yourself some trouble, my boy, and just stop running.'*

Paul's eyes watered. It could've been tears. It could've been the cold, but then the path spilled out into a big open space and looming across the way was a large, dilapidated barn. It rose from the cold ground like a lighthouse in a fog above a stormy ocean, its walls sagging and the roof on the verge of caving in. Paul's heart gave a leap inside his chest and he broke into a full-out run, vaguely wondering if he was hallucinating the way a dying man would in the middle of the desert. His feet slid in the snow as he hit the large double doors, taking the brunt of it in his shoulder. The impact jarred his broken forearm and he clenched his teeth on a scream.

"Down, come on," he told Ethan breathlessly.

Ethan jumped down from his perch on Paul's hip, looking behind them as Paul yanked the barn door open enough for them to slip through. He flinched as the cold metal door handle took off a layer of skin on his palm. Sticking his head inside, he squinted at the dark interior.

The sky was slowly brightening and weak tendrils of early dawn leaked through the decaying walls of the barn. The floor was matted dirt, pocked with footsteps, drag marks, and tire tracks. Paul nearly let out a whoop of joy when he saw the black SUV. Ushering Ethan inside the barn, he slid the door shut behind them. Ethan ran ahead of him to the driver's side door and tried the handle.

Locked.

He turned to Paul with urgency brimming in his eyes.

Snow crunched from outside. A shadow moved beyond the barn door, steady and *alarmingly there.*

"Shit," Paul muttered then remembered the keys he had taken off Jakob.

Fingers half-frozen and nearly useless, he dug them out of his pocket, fumbling and nearly dropping them in the dirt and—*Jesus Christ*—who carried a key ring with eight identical keys on it anyway? The fourth one was the one that fit into the car door lock and the sound of it disengaging was the sweetest sound Paul had ever heard.

He yanked the door open and without waiting to be told, Ethan clambered inside. Paul dove in behind the wheel and slammed the door behind them. He leaned over the wheel, jammed the key into the ignition and started the car, wanting to cry when the engine rolled over.

"Get your seatbelt on," he said to Ethan as he shifted to put his bag of weapons on the center console.

The barn door suddenly slid open with a monstrous metallic screech. Paul jumped before going still. Ethan, in the process of fumbling with his seatbelt, turned into a statue in the passenger seat.

Paul stared through the windshield at the empty, open door, at the road ahead of him that led out of the barn, cleared and primed for his foot to hit the gas. His eyes slid away, moving slowly, methodically around the barn, listening to the blood rush through his ears. The hairs on the back of his neck were rising and he knew they were being watched.

"Where is he?" came Ethan's hushed voice from beside him.

Paul shook his head. The silence was prickly and sharp. He looked in the rearview mirror then the side-view mirrors. Nothing moved.

Go. You need to go right the hell now.

He put his hand on the gear shift. It was awkward doing it with his left hand but he managed.

That was when he saw him.

Standing next to his window.

Ethan screamed a wordless warning, effectively shattering the thick silence. Swearing loudly, Paul shifted the car into drive.

Chac Mool's mouth curved into a smile. Paul's foot came down hard on the gas. Tires squealed and plumes of dirt billowed behind them as they rocketed out of the barn. There was a horrible moment as the vehicle tail-spun in the snow but then traction grabbed hold and it straightened out. Paul twisted in his seat to look behind them, the scenery whipping by as he pushed the gas pedal to the floor. He fought to maintain a strong, one-handed grip on the wheel, but the tires skidded and shrieked, the car bounced off the snowdrifts like a Ping-Pong ball.

"Hold on!" he shouted as he took a turn too sharply.

The car slammed sideways into a bank of snow that was nearly as high as the roof. Metal screamed. Paul clenched his teeth, grunting as the force of the impact nearly sent him to the other side of the car. He righted himself and, without pausing, hit the gas again. The car shuddered before pulling away from the snow.

"Fuck!" he swore.

He jerked the wheel hard, forcing himself to ease up on the gas so the tires could grip the snow-covered road. He glanced over at Ethan, who was so quiet Paul thought he'd been thrown from the car. But he was still in his seat, clutching his seatbelt with a white-knuckled grip.

"You okay?"

Ethan turned his head to look at him, his eyes wide and shell-shocked.

"Ethan, are you okay?" Paul practically shouted at him.

The kid gave a small jerk of his head that Paul took as a yes. He shot a glance in the rearview, saw the barn getting smaller and smaller as they raced down the road. He sucked in a few deep breaths, his hand twisting hard against the steering wheel.

Looking out of all the car's windows in turn, he half-expected to see Chac Mool riding up on his noble steed, his weapon arched back over his shoulder, poised for his heart. But all he saw was snow and the empty road around them, the distance between them and this nightmare finally growing. But Paul refused to let up on the gas.

Somehow he trusted Chac Mool would find a way to catch up to a car going seventy miles an hour on a snow-covered back road. From beside him, Ethan was trying to see out the back windshield. When he spoke, his voice was trembling much like the way Paul's insides were.

"Are we safe now?"

Paul spared a glance at him, looked at his gray eyes that were hoping for the best. But Paul knew better and he thought Ethan did too.

"I don't think so," he replied.

"What're we going to do?"

Paul squeezed his eyes shut briefly, trying to relieve the burning that lay within. Christ, he was tired. Tired of running, tired of fighting, tired of trying to believe that his life was worth all of this trouble. Maybe he *should* just stop running. Maybe he should let Chac Mool have his way with his heart and his head. It'd be a hell of a lot easier than running because Paul knew, deep down in his guts, in his bones, that the man was not going to stop. He was not going to give up. And Paul was pretty damn certain that he would give up first long before Chac Mool ever would.

So why delay the inevitable? Let's pull the car over and let him come collect you.

Paul glanced over at Ethan, who was watching him. The look on his face was solemn, patient but cautious, like he was waiting for Paul to work it out.

Without a word, Paul pressed down on the gas.

CHAPTER 35

They bounced and slid along the silver landscape like a clumsy bullet, jarring down a twisting labyrinth of ice and snow-caked roads. The roar of the engine was ear-splitting in the silence of the early morning, cracking through it as easily as an egg against the steel edge of a frying pan. Snow rose high on either side of them, so close that the side-view mirrors carved out niches as they sped past. Numbness spread through Paul's limbs as the adrenaline left him. Ethan huddled in front of the heating vent in the dashboard. The heat was on full blast but it didn't seem to be making a difference to either one of them. Paul glanced in the rearview for the millionth time.

"All right," he said hesitantly. "First things first. We're going to find out where we are. Once we're done with that, we'll figure out the rest, okay?"

It wasn't much of a plan but it was a place to start. Ethan gave a weary nod. Paul could see the edge of a dark bruise high up on his cheek.

"He's not going to stop, is he?"

The soft timbre of Ethan's voice could barely be heard over the blast of the heater. Paul took a long breath, feeling a twitch in his eyelid. He rotated his shoulders, trying to loosen the knots in his back. "No."

A tiny furrow appeared between Ethan's eyes as he looked over at him. "Are you scared?"

"I'd be stupid if I wasn't."

Ethan blinked at him, giving him that strange, too-old, assessing look before settling back into his seat. "I'm scared, too," he murmured.

Paul glanced at him from the corner of his eye. A child psychologist would have a field day with this. Bonding over impending-death situations—a shaky but otherwise stable foundation for a budding relationship. He would've laughed if he'd had the energy.

"What about that man?" Ethan asked after a moment of silence.

"What man?"

"The man you knew."

Paul fought to keep his throat from closing up. "What about him?"

"Is he dead?"

He tried to use his elbow to steer so he could wipe at the sweat that suddenly popped along his upper lip.

'*Go on, Paul. Open it.*'

Aaron was dead.

He couldn't say it out loud but he was as sure of it as he was of his right arm being broken. And it didn't matter what Jakob had said about their little arrangement. There was no way Aaron went into this without telling anyone else about it. If something were to happen to Aaron, he would be sure to get his revenge, even from beyond the grave. The range of people who would come after Paul was going to be astronomical. He was only mildly surprised that he wasn't more afraid by the prospect of being a hunted man. If anything, he felt more annoyed, like this was just another item added to an already-long list of things to do before dinner-time.

Shifting in his seat, he stammered out, "Probably."

"Will you miss him?"

Paul clenched his jaw so hard he thought he heard his teeth breaking. "You should try and get some rest."

Ethan didn't move for a moment then Paul heard him shift around, trying to find a comfortable position before nodding off. Silence settled in. The tires crunched up the miles and the more the odometer clicked over, the better Paul felt. Well, not really better but more confident that as long as they kept moving, Chac Mool couldn't get them.

As they came over the crest of a hill, sunlight hit Paul square in the face. He winced, nearly missing a turn-off that led to a two-lane highway that was better cleared of ice and snow. He did not hesitate to floor it. The countryside whizzed past, a blur of white and green pine. He wanted to crack the window and take a whiff of the air but didn't want to wake Ethan. It left Paul feeling vaguely unsettled that he was putting the kid's needs before his own.

The trees gave way to farmland and soon civilization. He took the first exit, following signs for *"The best apple pie this side of the Mississippi."* His stomach grumbled, which bought his attention to the gas gauge. They were close to riding on fumes.

The road suddenly became rugged and gravely and the SUV bounced along, protesting against the rough treatment as Paul drove too fast over a battlefield of potholes. When the road veered right, the engine sputtered and Paul hoped they would make it to a gas station or maybe a diner or both. What he got was a town that looked like something straight out of a Dickens novel. Not that he'd ever read a Dickens' novel but he'd seen *A Christmas Carol* plenty of times. Scrooge had always reminded him of Aaron, except at the end.

Out of habit, Paul drove around, taking in the lay-out. He counted two traffic lights, a plethora of bed-and-breakfasts, a general store, a few restaurants that were relics from *Happy Days*, a post office, a gas station, and a hardware store that sold everything from nuts to appliances.

Black iron streetlamps still glowed in the early morning light and, beneath the freshly plowed snow, were cobblestones. Paul half-expected a horse-drawn carriage to gallop down the street. Shaking his head, he pulled to a stop at the curb in front of an establishment called Mel's Diner. He killed the engine and waited. After a full five minutes, he rummaged quietly through his weapons and took out a nine-millimeter. He loaded it then shoved it into the back of his pants. The K-bar was still in the hip pocket of his pants. He left it there then climbed from the SUV. Stretching his legs, he looked around. The still air was hushed, quiet, as if it knew the town's inhabitants were still sleeping. And they were probably were. Paul didn't see a single person moving around. Didn't all small towns get up with the sun?

Obviously not.

His boots crunched through the snow as he went around to the passenger side of the car. Seeing Ethan sleeping against the inside of the door, he carefully pulled it open and Ethan nearly tumbled out, jarring awake. He caught himself on the seatbelt.

"Wha—" he mumbled sleepily.

"You hungry?" Paul asked.

Ethan blinked at him then looked around, much in the same way that Paul had, before nodding. Ethan unbuckled himself before jumping out. They went into the diner and Paul was struck by a sense of déjà vu. He stopped just inside the door, breathing in the smell of grease, plastic vinyl and bacon. Ethan must've felt it too because there was a strange look on his face, as if he was trying to remember something.

"Hiya, folks!" a voice boomed.

Paul jumped. He felt Ethan move closer as a man poked his head in through the swinging door that led into the kitchen.

"Have a seat anywhere you like. I'll be with you in a jiffy."

Paul led Ethan to the counter. They perched carefully on the stools and waited in silence. He looked down at Ethan, watched him hunch into his coat, shivering as if he were still outside. Paul wanted to ask if he was all right but knew it was redundant. Of course, he wasn't all right. Neither of them were.

"So, good morning!"

Paul's hand twitched toward his gun as the owner of that boisterous voice made another appearance. He was quite possibly the jolliestlooking man Paul had ever seen. He was in his fifties, tall, not as tall as Paul but just as solid with dark, thick hair streaked with white. His face was so rosy it seemed he'd been out running in nothing but a T-shirt and shorts before coming inside. Blue eyes twinkled with good humor. His forearms were streaked with blurred tattoos that might've been impressive before age took its toll.

Dressed in a blindingly white, button-down shirt that strained over an extremely large gut—which made Paul think, *A bowl full of jelly*—a neat pair of black pants, and a grease-splattered apron, he very well could've been a relative of Santa's, perhaps his rebellious brother.

Paul nodded. "How're you doing?"

The man leaned against the other side of the counter, beaming a disarming smile full of joy and crooked teeth. But it faltered when he laid eyes upon Paul's face.

"Oh hey now, mister, what happened to you?"

"What?"

"Looks like ya got cut there or something."

Paul raised his hand to his face and winced when he felt the gash in his left cheek. Between the cold and running for his life, he'd forgotten about the sharp drag of pain when Chac Mool had pressed that wicked knife into his face, the way his skin seemed to get caught on it like a fish on a hook. The blood had dried to a frozen crust that ran down his face to the edge of his jaw. Flakes of red fluttered into his lap as he grazed his fingertips over it. Ethan had gone very still next to him and the man across the counter looked at him with a mixture of concern and curiosity.

"Ya might want to get that looked at," he said helpfully. "Hey, hang on, let me see if I got a first-aid kit in the back."

"No, that's not necessary—"

"Be right back. You two look over the menu."

He disappeared through the swinging door once again. Paul glanced down at Ethan. Before he could say anything, the man was back with a small white case with the familiar red plus sign on the lid.

"Here you go. Uh, don't suppose you want to tell me what happened," he said. "People're gonna be asking about a man with a bloody face coming in here for breakfast and I gotta tell them something."

He beamed a good-natured smile. Paul took the first-aid kit from him and set it on the counter, trying to smile back but he was too busy trying to come up with something that sounded reasonably plausible.

"Bet ya it was a hunting accident, huh?" the man guessed. "Am I right?"

"Well—"

"That's okay, you can tell me," he said with a laugh. "Lots of city folks come down this way, thinking they can rough it after seeing *The Deer Hunter* one too many times and they end up more banged up than my truck." He laughed again and it filled every empty booth in the diner. "But hey, no worries. I've seen people leave here with broken limbs so a cut on the face is nothing, really, and where the hell are my manners?" He wiped a hand on his apron and stuck it in front of Paul. "I'm Mel, owner and business entrepreneur of all things greasy and delicious and since it is the ass-crack of dawn, er, sorry there, young man." Mel nodded sheepishly at Ethan who was staring at him with a mixture of disbelief and awe. "I will be serving ya up with whatever you want. Maggie—she's my waitress on the morning shift—don't get her lazy carcass out of bed until nearly nine damn o' clock, which I don't see how that's even normal since most people are already work-ing by then."

Paul stared at him, waiting for him to take a breath.

"So what can I get you, folks? We've got everything and anything that you could possibly want, and if I don't have it, then you don't need it. How about you, little guy? Pancakes? I got 'em with chocolate chips. How's that sound?"

Ethan's eyes brightened and he looked up at Paul. For a second, Paul could see the kid inside. The actual child inside all the darkness. Paul's chest felt strangely warm as he nodded.

"Yes, sir," Ethan answered.

"Sir!" Mel boomed with a laugh.

Ethan shrank back a bit.

"Well, I'll be damned. Sir! No one's called me that since my old man passed away and that was twenty some years ago. You're a hoot, little man. Okay, chocolate chip pancakes it is." He turned laughing blue eyes to Paul. "And you, good sir?"

"An omelet with green peppers and bacon."

"Coffee?"

"If you don't mind."

"Not at all. Hey, Tony!" he hollered. "Get the grills going, will you?"

"I'm on it," came the answering shout from the kitchen.

Mel went down the counter and came back with a white coffee mug and a steaming glass pot of coffee.

"So where're you boys headed?"

Paul shifted in his seat. "We're just passing through, on our way home."

"Yeah? Where's home 'cause I'll tell ya what, you stay over there at old Edna's and you'll never want to go home again."

"Old Edna's?"

"Yeah. Nice little b-and-b around the corner, near the woods. It's quiet back there, peaceful if that's what you're looking for, and Edna makes one hell of a peach cobbler."

"Oh—"

"Now I'm not trying to disrespect your home or nothing but I'll tell ya. Lots of them city folks I was telling you about? They come from maybe four, five hundred miles north of here for a little R and R and then decide they want to stay here."

Paul took a tip of scorching coffee, not knowing what else to do.

"Now I know what you're thinking," Mel went on, barely pausing as he set a glass of ice water in front of Ethan. "City folks—in the middle of nowhere with no service on their little computers and their noisy U-peas or U-pords or whatever the hell those things are—"

"iPods," Paul couldn't help but say with amusement.

"Yeah, iPods," Mel said with a laugh. "Well, I'll tell you what. Those iPods don't mean dick around here. Sorry about the language, kid, but it's true. Don't get a lot of service out here but we're all the better for it, you know what I mean?"

Paul murmured agreement.

"People need change. It's part of the human condition. Like say, you can't have pancakes every day right? But you like them, don't ya?" He angled the question at Ethan who shot Paul a baffled look then gave a hesitant nod.

"Sure you do," Mel boomed. "But every now and then you've got to have eggs or maybe waffles. Dash it up a bit or else the pancakes'll get old and there's nothing worse than old pancakes."

"You sound like a real estate agent," Paul said.

Mel's eyes twinkled. "Can't blame me for trying. You both look like you could do with a little unwinding."

The statement hit closer to home than Paul was willing to admit. Before he could respond, Mel turned and yelled, "Hey, Tony! Did that order come in?"

"Which one?" came the muffled response.

"Be right back, folks and, you," he said to Paul. "There's a bathroom 'round back if you want to clean up your face. All right then?" he said before disappearing into the back.

Paul watched him go, blowing out a long breath. Ethan was eyeballing his water glass.

Paul nudged him quietly. "Go on."

Ethan went for it, his fingers sliding through the condensation on the glass. Paul let his eyes roam the diner and wished for just a second that he could believe what Mel had said about settling down and unwinding. Christ, what the hell did that even mean? He didn't think he could ever apply that word to his vocabulary.

Movement caught his eye and he turned away from Ethan just in time to see a figure move back behind the kitchen door.

No. There was no way Chac Mool could've caught up to us already.

But the warning bells going off in his head could not be silenced. Ethan, somehow sensing the change in him, peered up at him from over the rim of his glass.

"What—"

"Food'll be read in a few more minutes, gentlemen!" Mel suddenly appeared, holding the swinging door open with one hand. "Keep holding them horses!"

Paul looked at him, looked over Mel's beefy shoulder, because the figure he'd seen just seconds before was suddenly there, in plain sight and it wasn't Chac Mool. That alone produced a small amount of relief, which instantly evaporated into a freezing mist because in the depths of dark, dark eyes that bored into his head, he saw a reminder of Aaron.

Sneering, malevolent, gnashing his teeth, barely constrained in the face of Mel's cook. He was young-looking, maybe in his mid-twenties with closely-cropped brown hair and a smooth, angular face. Thin lips were set in a weird, twisting pout like he couldn't believe his luck.

Paul couldn't believe it either. Of all the places he could've stopped, of all the towns that were along the highway, there was someone waiting for him *here*.

In the early hours of the morning.

In Mel's Diner.

He figured he should've been better-prepared for this. Aaron probably had people in place long before he cemented his deal with Jakob and Irene. Paul slowly let all the air out of his body, watching carefully as Mel turned to the young cook and said, "Come on, Tony, can't keep 'em waiting any longer. When a man's hungry, a man's hungry and that cannot be reckoned with."

"Just waiting on the pancakes, Mel," Tony said, a cheery grin exploding across his face so instantaneously that it was like someone had snapped up a window shade.

"All right then," Mel said, stepping around him and going back into the kitchen.

He let the door swing shut. Tony remained where he stood, the smile gone, his gaze a deep pool filled with razor-tipped tentacles, reaching out to curl around Paul's throat and pull him down into its depths. One corner of his mouth twitched upward as the door closed.

Paul slid to his feet. "You need to use the bathroom?" he asked Ethan, not bothering to keep his voice down.

Ethan nodded wordlessly. Paul grabbed the first-aid kit then motioned for him to follow him into the men's room. It was small, square, and green-tiled, crammed with a sink, two urinals, and one stall. He checked the stall then turned slowly in a full circle. Ethan hovered by the door.

"You stay right here," Paul said quietly. "I'll come back for you."

Ethan's eyes widened a bit, confusion settling across his face. "Where are you going?"

"To the ladies' room."

Ethan's eyes widened even more. Paul could tell he wanted to say more but he didn't give him time.

"Lock the door behind me."

Paul left. He waited outside the door until he heard the soft *click* of the lock. Then he went across the hall. He could feel eyes on the back of his head as he shut the ladies' room door behind him. The room, he saw with some degree of disappointment was almost identical to the men's, minus the urinals and green tiles. The flowered wallpaper curled around the edges and the small bowl of potpourri on the counter looked like three-week-old bread. He went to the sink and turned the water on. The air was hot and smelled too heavily of the pine disinfectant that could never fully cover the stench of urine and body odor. He put the first-aid kit on the edge of the sink, ignoring his reflection.

He counted down slowly from ten.

By the time he got to five, the bathroom door opened, creaking softly. Paul looked into the mirror at Tony who came inside and locked the door behind him. He was small and wiry, dressed like the goddamn cook that he was, that Mel thought he was. His beady dark eyes narrowed on Paul's face and his smooth face broke out into a blank grin.

"Ready to go home?" he whispered, his voice slithering around the room like a wet snake.

"Mel's going to be a little upset to find out his cook won't be finishing his shift today."

"I would say that that kid will be even more upset to find he's going to be stranded here. Maybe he can earn his wages in blowjobs. I don't think Mel would mind."

Paul's teeth clacked together as if he'd been socked in the jaw. Then the man was moving, pulling a gun equipped with a silencer from the waistband of his white, grease-stained pants. Paul was already in his face, his elbow cracking into the man's nose. Tony fell back without a sound, blood spraying the air like paint. It didn't loosen his grip on the gun though. Paul darted forward, forcing him into the wall. He curled his hand around the man's wrist, pinning the gun to the wall beside his head. He pressed his cast. *This freaking thing is coming in handy even though it hurts like a bitch*—against the man's throat. Tony's dark eyes bulged.

"You're a dead man," Tony rasped out, blood pouring from his nose and into his mouth, spewing as he spoke.

Paul pressed his cast in harder, listening as the man choked. "Tell me something I don't know, asshole," he hissed.

He didn't see the fist coming from the side until he was staggering back with stars exploding behind his eyes. His hand was still curled around Tony's wrist, bringing him away from the wall. Tony struggled against him but Paul held on tight until his vision cleared. Then he changed his grip and broke Tony's wrist with a clean snap. The gun clattered to the floor, drowned out by a startled, mewling sound. Tony fell to one knee, cradling his arm. Paul scooped up the gun and aimed. His finger was pressing down on the trigger when the mewling morphed into barely audible words. Paul stopped.

"What?"

The man took a deep shuddering inhale before raising his head. He tried to sneer but it came out as a gurgle. "Christ, how low you've gone."

Paul's jaw clenched. "What do you know about it?"

Climbing slowly to his feet, Tony leaned back against the wall, wincing in pain. "You kill me and there'll be fifty more to take my place."

"So I should just let *you* kill me?"

"It would certainly make things easier for you."

"That's awfully considerate of you."

Cold laughter came from the ruined, blood-splattered face before him. "Take advantage of it, man. Doubt you'll be running into anyone else who'll be as nice as me."

"How long have you been here as Mel's cook?"

"Long enough to have the smell of grease permanently oozing out of my pores."

"Must be a turn-on for the ladies."

Tony scoffed but it was hard to do with a broken nose. "Ladies? In this town? Half of them don't even own a razor. You could braid beads into their armpit hair."

"A small price to pay for this particular job, I'm sure."

He let out another explosion of humorless laughter. "Absolutely. But faced with a chance to kill Aaron's prize student? Believe me, hairy women are definitely doable."

Paul's nostrils flared. "Guess I should be flattered."

"I would be. You'd be surprised how many people are searching for you."

"Aaron's got all his bases covered, huh?"

"And then some." Tony's wet, bloody smile turned sly, his eyes sparkling with a gleam like what could only be found in the faces of little old ladies who spread around juicy neighborhood gossip. "You really trying to leave the game?"

"Does that shock you?"

"A little. I mean, you trained with Aaron. The man's a legend. What's not to like?"

Paul tasted metal when he swallowed. "I wouldn't even know where to begin."

The smile faded. Tony's eyes narrowed dangerously. "You're an ungrateful dickbag, you know that?"

Paul's hand tightened around the gun. "Am I?"

Tony shook his head in disgust. "All that training, all that knowledge Aaron wasted on you. You know how many guys would've killed for even a fraction of what you have? The lifestyle, the money that Aaron gave you, some street-punk kid, who would only piss it all away fifteen years later?"

"I don't give a shit about other guys. I just know about me and the tight fucking leash I was kept on."

"Oh, boo-fucking-hoo. Aaron's the reason *why* you're as good as you are. He's the reason you're still alive. He's the reason you even made it this far, you fucking moron. And now you're here, and Aaron's in a hole somewhere because you got your panties in a bunch."

Paul stared hard at him. "What makes you think Aaron's in a hole?"

"Because you're here and he's not. Everybody knows he met up with those two fucking weirdos. Everyone knows that you were 'kidnapped' by them, too. So you do the math."

Paul smashed the gun across his face. "How do you know about Jakob and Irene?"

Tony spat blood and a tooth on the floor. His eyes blazed pure hatred, but he said, "Everything came out after Aaron disappeared. He told a few people about the little arrangement with the Dynamic Duo, you know, just in case something happened to him because, seriously, working with those two? They enjoy their jobs just a *tad* bit too much." He flashed a knowing grin that shone red and painful. "But I'm sure you already knew that."

Paul twitched as if someone had inserted an ice-cold needle into his ear.

"But don't let it eat you up," Tony went on. "That tight leash you mentioned before? Aaron kept you on it for a reason."

"And what reason is that?" he asked, his voice beginning to shake.

"To keep you deaf, blind, and dumb and to ensure your cooperation for this secretive fucking job that he wouldn't tell *anyone* about."

Chac Mool.

Paul licked his lips. "The job with Jakob and Irene."

Tony nodded. "Aaron insisted that *you* were the only one who could do it, which I and a number of others took great offense to, naturally."

Paul gave him a skeptical look. "You haven't been in this line of work for very long, have you?"

The look on Tony's face could only be described as a wet kitten trying to act like a lion. "Long enough to know a dead man when I see one. Your life isn't worth shit."

"Your life isn't worth much either if you were sent on this suicide mission."

Tony's tongue came out to swipe at the blood on his upper lip. "Maybe a month ago this would've been a suicide mission, but now? Knowing the way you tucked your tail between your legs and ran like a bitch alongside that little cocksucker out there? It's more like a mercy killing."

Paul's sweaty grip on the gun steadied. He pressed it against Tony's forehead.

Tony smiled but it wasn't pleasant. "See you in hell."

CHAPTER 36

Paul cracked the door, listening. Regardless of the silencer, it was still nearly two hundred pounds of human flesh hitting the floor. He slipped out and rapped his knuckles on the men's room door. It opened before he could drop his hand.

"Are you okay?" Ethan asked immediately. "What happened?"

"It's fine. I'm okay. Go back out there and start eating, all right? I'm going to clean up a bit."

"But—the ladies room?"

"I—it's—hang on a second."

He dashed back inside, grabbed the first-aid kit, and came back out. Ethan was frowning now.

"I thought the women's room would have better lighting for this," Paul said, gesturing at his cut cheek. "But it doesn't. So I'll just finish up in here."

He stepped around Ethan, who still stood in the doorway. Paul gently nudged him out, jerking his chin toward the restaurant area, where Ethan's pancakes were waiting.

"Go on," he insisted. "I'll be right out."

With one last, strange look, Ethan gave a hesitant nod. Paul watched him go, saw him glance over his shoulder at him a few more times, saw an unexpected flash of concern that made him close the bathroom door in a hurry. Once inside, he let his forehead hit the door with a hollow *thunk*.

He closed his eyes, waiting for his head to go quiet but Tony's words spun like an echoing tornado inside his cranium.

Tony. If that was even his real name.

Cocky little shit, wasn't he? Glorifying this line of work like it was a goddamn union job and how long had he been doing it? A year? Maybe less? Long enough to idolize the very people who would put him in the front lines like so much meat? Long enough to see Aaron, with blinders firmly in place, as if he was some kind of rock star? It was preposterous. Aaron keeping him in the dark was no surprise. What was surprising though was everything that went on without Paul's knowledge and it played out like some kind of high-school/soap-opera drama. The rumors, the assumptions, the finger-pointing, the whisperings, and the plotting—what Paul had previously thought—of his life being strung along by a talented and vicious pup-peteer—was now being orchestrated by none other than a group of mean-spirited teenage girls.

If teenage girls came equipped with firepower and in the disguises of diner cooks.

Paul opened his eyes, trying to center himself before staggering over to the sink. He ignored his reflection once again but he caught snatches of pasty-white skin that glowed sickly and dark half-moons under his eyes.

The beach, he thought to himself again as he cleaned up his face. *Definitely going to the beach and getting a tan.*

The cut looked worse beneath all the blood and dirt, like someone had set a hook into his cheek and dragged it down to his jaw. The anti-septic cream stung, bad enough to bring tears to his eyes, and he knew that it was going to scar if he didn't get to a hospital. But there was no time for that. Christ, he'd probably be gutted with a scalpel by some asshole Aaron had planted as a doctor. After taping on a few gauze pads, Paul shoved an extra handful of them into his coat pocket.

He went to the door and opened it just enough to see out. He heard Mel's voice, thundering easily over Ethan's soft replies and he could've sworn he heard the kid laugh. The sound of it froze him, sent a sharp edge of despair through his chest, because in all the time he had been with the kid, there had never been a moment that required a laugh, a giggle, or even a smile. And there it was again, delicate and hesitant like a baby bird, as if it wasn't sure if it should be heard. But it should be. It should be *heard* for Christ's sake. He was a *kid.* Kids were supposed to laugh. They were supposed to be *allowed* to laugh. Nothing was supposed to crush them into shit-kicked, obedient little robots where they earned their wages in blowjobs. They weren't sup-posed to be trapped on the depraved whims of someone who had too much time on his hands, too much money to spend, and too much of a capacity to spread misery and pain to an eleven-year-old.

Paul looked at the ladies' room door, seeing past it to the body that he knew was sprawled across the toilet in the last stall, with a glisten-ing red hole in the center of its forehead. But instead of Tony's slack face staring up from the floor, it was his own.

'You're a dead man. Your life isn't worth shit.'

It was time to move.

He opened the ladies' room door once again, reached in to lock it from the inside, shut it firmly, and then walked back to the dining room.

"Hey!" Mel greeted him with a grin. "We were wondering if we'd have to fish you out. 'Bout to send your boy in with my fishing rod."

Paul tried to smile as he lowered himself onto the stool. The steaming plate of food in front of him almost made him retch and he wiped a hand over his face. Belatedly, he realized he should've checked himself to see that there were no bodily fluids on him.

Shit, he thought.

He looked over at Ethan who was clutching a fork in one hand even though his food appeared to be untouched. His face was solemn now, watchful and Paul thought that maybe he'd only hallucinated hearing his laughter.

"Hey, son, you all right?"

Paul's eyes snapped up to Mel. "What? Oh. Yeah. Yeah, I'm okay. I'm—"

"I was just telling your boy about them cave tours they got up the road a bit. Old coal mines and such if you'd be interested in hanging around for the day. That is, if you're not in a big hurry to get on home."

Paul tried to keep his tone light. He half-expected a horde of breakfast people to come in, order breakfast, and then oh, look, one of them has to use the bathroom…

"Uh, thanks, but I think—I think we need to get going. Can we get this boxed up? Looks too good to go to waste."

"Sure, sure, of course you can." Mel flashed a sheepish grin. "Can't say I didn't try."

"You're doing a good job though," Paul said with a quick smile.

Mel laughed as he fished out two Styrofoam containers. "I missed my calling. Should've been a salesman or something."

"Sure did."

There was a pause and Paul's heart slammed into it.

"Hey, you sure you're all right? You don't look so good."

Paul could feel Ethan's eyes steady on the side of his face.

Oh, sure, I just shot a man in your bathroom. You might be a little short-handed today.

He cleared his throat. "Yeah, I'm, well, I, no actually I'm not. My arm, you see?" He pushed back his sleeve. "My arm's been giving me some trouble."

Mel hissed in sympathy as he boxed up their food. "Damn, that don't look good and you're probably right-handed, aren't you?"

"Yes, sir."

"Hunting accident? The same one where you scratched up your face?"

Paul mentally scrambled. "Uh, no." The weight of Ethan's eyes grew heavier. "No, I slipped on some ice a few days ago. Can you believe it? Landed wrong and broke my forearm clear in half."

"Dang," Mel shook his head. "Big boy like you landing on that poor arm must've been like a brick building falling on it. You taking anything for it? Broke enough bones in this ol' body of mine to know that a simple cast doesn't help much with the healing."

"Not really. Pain medicine makes me loopy and I need to drive."

"Right, right. Don't understand how they give you pain meds that you can only take at bedtime which doesn't really help you during the day. Don't these frigging doctors know that you've got to work?"

"Exactly."

"Well, all right then, boys. You take care now." Mel pushed the food containers across the counter along with the bill. "And you come back soon and visit. Those caves I was talking about, they're pretty interesting and they ain't like those cheesy tourist traps either. They're the real deal."

"Will do, and thanks," Paul said as he paid the bill.

He hustled Ethan out of the diner and into the SUV, doing his best not to stamp down on the accelerator and get *the hell* out of there.

CHAPTER 37

There was a gas station down the street and the SUV was gasping its last as they pulled up to one of two gas pumps. Paul practically leapt from the car, demanding that Ethan stay put.

"Have some of that food if you want," he snapped before slamming the door and jogging toward the small convenient store where a clerk cheerfully met him at the door.

"Morning, sir. How can I help you?"

The clerk looked like he was still in high school—tall and gangly with careless blond hair and warm brown eyes. He was shrugging into a heavy wool coat as Paul came in.

"Morning. Twenty, nope better make that forty on pump one," Paul said with a smile that hurt the flesh of his face.

"Sure, I'll be right out."

"I can do it—"

"This is a full-service station, sir." The kid grinned. "Just sit back and relax."

Paul stared at him for a minute then nodded. He went back outside, feeling the skin itch on the back of his neck. He slid in behind the wheel and watched as the clerk came out and went to the pump. The constant puffs of air that hovered in front of his face suggested that he was whistling. Paul decided it was way too damn early to be in that good of a mood.

He tapped his fingers on the steering wheel. Ethan ate quietly next to him, watching him watch everything else. Paul shifted in his seat, looking out the windshield, the driver's side window, Ethan's window, the back windshield, then facing forward and doing it all over again. His legs felt jittery with the urge to simply move and to keep moving.

There would be more.

More like Tony.

Everywhere he went.

And if there wasn't someone like Tony, it would be Chac Mool.

Paul ran a hand over his face. His knee began to bounce. He checked the back windshield again, saw the attendant still at the pump, still fucking whistling. Seeming to sense Paul watching, the guy ducked his head down and looked in at him. He waggled his fingers at him.

Paul faced forward, gritting his teeth. Finally, he heard the gas pump shut off. He hit the button to lower the window a few inches.

A snake of cold air blew in.

Ethan's fork scraped against the Styrofoam take-out container. There came the *tick-tick-tick* as the gas cap was screwed back on.

Paul looked into the rearview mirror, watching with a frown as the attendant stopped at the corner of the car and dug something out from inside his coat.

Snow crunched abruptly as the attendant exploded into motion. He launched himself at Paul's side of the vehicle, appearing at the window like a jack-in-the-box. The gun he aimed in at Paul was small but deadly and whereas Paul had originally thought this guy had looked around high-school age, now he didn't. His face was hard, lined, and flat, filled with a purpose that screamed amateur. If he'd truly known what he was doing, he would've approached Ethan's side of the car. Because then Paul wouldn't have been able to defend himself.

Like now as he jerked the car door open, slamming it into the guy's chest. Ethan made a strangled noise of surprise and Paul vaguely hoped he wasn't choking on his pancakes. Paul clambered out of the car as the gun went off, sending a bullet thunking into the back tire.

Paul clambered out, grabbing the K-bar from the hip pocket of his pants. He rushed forward as the guy tried to regain his footing, slipping in the snow and ice. Paul didn't hesitate as he drove the blade into the guy's neck. Blood erupted like a geyser, spraying like liquid candy all over the ground and across Paul's coat.

He jerked back. The guy's eyes were huge and surprised, a horrible wet burbling sound coming from his throat as he tried to scream or speak or both. His gun hand came up and Paul pulled the weapon from his fingers as the man fell to his knees, his body jerking and twitching like he'd touched a live wire. Paul wrenched the knife from the guy's neck and danced back a few steps as blood-slicked hands made a grab for him. The man's face thinned and stretched as his hands grabbed at the rip in his throat, flapping wildly like red birds. He tipped backward, turning his hate-filled gaze to the sky.

Paul turned away and re-sheathed the knife, swearing under his breath when he saw the back tire of the SUV flat and sagging on the pavement. He leaned into the open driver's side door.

"Come on. We're getting out of here," he said to Ethan.

He grabbed his bag as Ethan scrambled to close up the food containers.

"Leave the food," Paul snapped. "Let's go."

Ethan was out of the truck a split second later and the two of them raced across the street. The sounds of snow crunching and breaking beneath the clerk's body as he died pounded in Paul's brain and he resisted the urge to look back. He tore off his blood-splattered coat as they darted between a general store and a bank that had yet to open for business for the day.

"Who—Who was that?" Ethan panted as they ran. "Why—"

"Keep running," Paul shot back as he flung his coat to the ground.

The cold made it impossible to breathe as they ran. It burned Paul's lungs and tore at his eyes. It wasn't long before Ethan began to slow down. Paul scooped him up and kept moving. He had no idea where he was going or what the fuck he was supposed to do now. The town was waking up, people were looking out of their windows, leaving their houses to go to work and to no doubt investigate where that gunshot had come from. It wouldn't be long until one of them found that guy lying in the snow, in a pool of his own blood.

Not to mention the guy in the bathroom at Mel's Diner.

Paul mentally drew together a string of curses. He darted through backyards and alley ways, looking for something but not quite sure what. He just knew he had to keep moving.

Hole's getting deeper and deeper.

What little civilization the town had gradually tapered off into houses that were quite a distance apart and after that were thick, dense woods that did nothing to make Paul feel any better about the direction he was going in. He stopped beneath a huge pine tree, sucking in frigid air and wincing as his sides began to cramp. He set Ethan down and leaned against the tree.

"Shit," he muttered, panting for breath.

He closed his eyes for a second, trying not to think about his arm that throbbed or the snow that leaked into his boots or the world of shit that he was burying them both in. Shuffling his thoughts into some kind of order, he opened his eyes. The woods were thick and uncompromising. Going back into town was suicide, for them as well as for any innocent bystander who got in the way.

"Shit," he said again.

The hush of morning was stark and complete, allowing him to hear Ethan's teeth chattering. He looked down at him. He was standing a little ways to his right and staring at something in the distance. It made Paul push away from the tree and stand next to him.

"What is it?" he asked.

"Ed—Edna's," Ethan stuttered out.

"What?"

"Edna's. Over there. The place that Mel was talking about."

Paul looked at the white farmhouse that stood on the other side of a large field and thought *peach cobbler*. But he said, "How do you know that's Edna's? It could be anybody's house."

"Mel said that it was by the woods."

"I'm sure there are lots of places by the woods."

Ethan looked up at him, his lips turning blue.

"All right, all right. Point taken."

They trekked as quickly as they could across the field. Paul kept Ethan close to his side, his eyes constantly moving around them. There was no discreet way to get to the house but crossing this open field made his insides itch. He quickened his stride or tried to as the snow became deeper and deeper with every step. The snow was up to mid-thigh now and he swung Ethan up into his arms when the snow hit his chin after he lost his footing.

"Goddamn snow," Paul muttered. "When we get out of this, we're going to the beach."

"I've n—never been th—there," Ethan stammered, burying his face in Paul's shoulder.

"Gonna love it," Paul panted, his leg muscles burning. "Nice and hot, sand between your toes. Water's gonna be around your ankles and the sun's gonna be frying you to a crisp. Absolutely love it."

He felt Ethan nod, his body trembling.

"It's great. Relaxing, listening to the frigging waves, building some sand castles, make a fucking *fortress* with a moat and everything. Win some kind of contest or something."

In response, Ethan curled his legs around Paul's mid-section and Paul tried not to think of how familiar that was becoming. He clenched his jaw, forced himself to keep moving. God, it was so cold, it hurt and all he wanted to do was stop and catch his breath.

For just a minute.

Surely he could be spared that, right?

Only after what felt like hours of not gaining any ground, they arrived at the back porch. He came to a staggering halt at the bottom of the steps, looking up at the door, wondering if he would even have the strength to get up there, wondering if he would have the fucking energy to walk away if this house turned out not to be Edna's.

Suddenly the back door banged open.

"What in the name of all that is holy are you doing out here with no coat on, boy?"

Startled, Paul instinctively tried to shuffle back. But the snow at the back of his knees locked him in and he could only stare up at Mother Goose as she pointed a double-barreled shotgun at his chest.

"Tongue frozen? Reckon it might be after the trek you made across my property. I suggest you state your business before I leave you out here like a popsicle."

She glared down at them and the no-nonsense tone of her voice made Ethan squirm until he could look over his shoulder at her. Her big, brown eyes grew bigger.

"And with a child too! There's at least four feet of snow out here, moron. You nuts or something?"

"I'm—We—We're just looking for Edna's place," he said carefully, hoping to any divine being that would listen that this wouldn't turn into the third goddamn attempt on his life within the last half hour.

He was pretty sure he'd never live it down in the afterlife if he was taken down by Granny.

"Well, you sure found it."

Paul licked his lips, wincing as they stung from the cold. "Don't suppose you could let us—"

She let out an indignant huff as if he was a dog who'd just pissed all over her rosebushes.

"Great, another one who thinks I got some kind of open-door policy. You wouldn't believe how many folks come sashaying up to my door, asking for a place to stay, knowing goddamn well that you need to make appointments for these kinds of places. I mean you just can't *expect* to get food and a bed. No way of knowing if I got vacancy or not 'less you call in advance. You see what I'm saying, son?"

"Well, I—"

"Do I look like someone who takes on charity cases?"

Paul's brain was too numb to come up with any kind of response.

"You think I should feel sorry for you or something and just *allow* you into my bed and breakfast because you're out here wandering around like some ass clown without a damn coat? That's your own stupid fault, you know, and I only take people in if they got an appointment and a brain. So now tell me, son. Do *you* have an appointment?"

Paul tried to keep up with her whip-crack flow of words that didn't seem to require any oxygen. He gave her a quick cursory look. Small, thin-framed, surprisingly big, brown eyes and white-blonde hair done up in pink curlers. She held the shotgun with an ease that spoke of experience and the cold didn't seem to bother her as she stood at the top of the steps in a pink, flowered robe and pink, fuzzy slippers.

"You gonna answer me some time this century?"

Her voice brought his eyes back to her face. Paul shifted then slowly bent over to set Ethan on the steps. The kid stood on shaky legs, looking up at him with glassy eyes before turning his head to look at the woman. Her gaze sharpened as it snapped from Paul to Ethan and back again.

"You armed?" she said, raising an eyebrow.

Paul weighed his answer, looking at the gun in her hands before meeting her eyes. "Yes. But not for the reason you think."

"And what reason might that be?"

"That I'm here to rob you."

"And are you?"

"No, ma'am."

"Am I supposed to believe you because you're dragging a child along for the ride?"

"No, ma'am."

"Then why should I believe you?"

"There's no reason why you should but if I was going to rob you, I certainly wouldn't come onto your property where you could plainly see me."

One side of her mouth twitched. Paul wasn't sure if she was fighting a smile or if she was annoyed.

"No, you certainly wouldn't. You'd probably wait till you were safely inside before tying my old, wrinkly ass to a chair and—"

"No way, ma'am. I would never tie a lady to a chair. Unless she asked me to."

Her eyes began to sparkle. "Lovely. I have a sweet-talker at my door."

Paul gritted his teeth. He seemed to be unintentionally amusing this woman.

"Ma'am, please—"

"You call me *ma'am* one more time and I'll drop you right there. You call me Edna, got it?"

Paul shut up, his eyes moving to the shotgun. Edna eyeballed him, taking her time as she took him in from head to foot before moving onto Ethan. Her face didn't soften as she looked the kid over. If anything she only began more suspicious. Paul could feel himself balancing precariously on her scales.

"Let me see what you're armed with," she demanded after several moments of tense silence.

Ethan shifted his weight from one foot to the other, hunching his shoulders as Paul carefully unzipped his bag. The metal zipper hurt like hell and set his fingers to a painful tingling. Wincing, he held the bag up for her to see. The corners of her mouth turned so far down, her mouth resembled a horseshoe.

"What else?"

He bit back a sigh.

"Easy. Slowly now," she advised him as he took out the nine-millimeter from behind his back.

Holding it loosely in his palm, he held it out and looked up at her. But she wasn't looking at the gun. She was looking at him, giving him a long, assessing look. It resembled the kind of looks that Ethan had given him on more than one occasion. They didn't make him feel any better coming from somebody else.

"What kind of business you mixed up in, son?" she said quietly.

Paul lowered the gun to his side. Something hot welled up inside his chest.

"All due respect, Edna, you asked for weapons, not information."

She made a rude sound. "If I'm letting you in here to use up my heat and my water then you best start talking."

He shook his head. "It's for your own safety."

"Bull," she snapped. "If you were that concerned, you wouldn't even be on my back step."

He glanced down at Ethan. His eyelids were turning an alarming shade of blue.

"You don't need to worry about me and my safety," Edna informed him. "I'm a grown-ass woman, born and raised in this rotten town where everyone knows your business, knows what's going on, but refuses to do anything about it, no matter how bad it is. I was married three times and they were the meanest sons-of-bitches you'll ever meet. I stabbed one and shot the other two while they slept. Police still ain't having any luck finding their remains so don't you tell me about my safety. Got it?"

Paul momentarily forgot about the cold that had taken permanent root inside his bones.

"Now," Edna said, squaring her shoulders. "It's rather clear that you and your boy got nowhere else to go, half-frozen jack-asses that you are. So why don't you move yourselves up these steps. I'm freezing my own ass off and my curlers will end up stuck to my head."

He hesitated. "All right, but we won't be staying long—"

"Put a stop to that nonsense right now and just get on up here, will you? I promise I won't kill you 'less you give me a reason."

Moving stiffly, Paul zipped up his bag and guided Ethan up the stairs. As they neared the top, Edna maneuvered the shotgun until it was pointed at the roof. He watched her as they came to the top. She came up to his elbow. He suddenly felt like laughing. She craned her neck back, unfazed.

"You're as big as a house, boy. What you been eating?"

"I—"

"Don't even think about trying to eat me out of house and home. I'll give you a bed and three squares and that's it. You raid my fridge without my permission and I'll take you grocery-shopping, at gun-point if I have to before you leave here. Sound fair? That sure as hell sounds fair to me."

Paul cast a quick look over his shoulder at the woods then back down at Edna.

"Look, I appreciate this but like I said, we won't be staying for—"

Edna's brown eyes drilled into his head. It wasn't the invasive look that Paul was used to. It was more of a don't-fuck-with-me kind of a look which, considering how short she was, was quite an accomplishment.

"This is my house. I decide who stays and who goes. You don't like it, you can turn your ass back around and freeze to death out here."

Paul pressed his lips together. He saw Ethan hovering in the door-way of the house, as close as possible to the warmth inside without actually going in. Paul gave a nod, jerkily like it hurt.

Edna nodded in return. "Okay then. In you go."

CHAPTER 38

Paul wasn't sure if he should be annoyed or grateful at this turn of events. Granted, they were out of the cold. The warmth of the house was god-like but it was distracting and Paul didn't want to be distracted. Just because they were inside didn't mean they were safe and they sure as hell weren't safe with Ms. I-Killed-All-of-My-Husbands either. There were too many windows, too many potential entrances that a bullet shot from a long-range rifle could make and send his brains exploding across the pretty flowered wallpaper in Edna's kitchen. For the one hundredth time, as she shut the door behind them, he berated himself silently for coming here. But at least Ethan's blue eyelids were returning to their normal color.

Stashing the shotgun, Edna led them through the kitchen. Paul looked around. Being a big, old farmhouse, it held a lot of rustic charm. Wide wooden floorboards; plenty of windows and furniture that, despite being worse for wear, looked comfortable and solid. The air smelled of sawed wood, heat, and, as Paul suspected, peach cobbler. It was too warm, too cozy, amplifying the exhaustion that was ready to pounce and drag him under at any second. As they passed through a large dining area, Paul heard the floorboards creak from above. He froze, grabbing the back of Ethan's coat. The boy looked back at him, eyes wide. Edna kept walking then stopped when she realized they weren't following her. She turned with an irritated, "What?"

"How many people are staying here right now?" Paul asked quietly, eyes on the ceiling, as if waiting for it to open up.

Edna rolled her eyes. "One couple. Very nice people from Connecticut. They're on their way down to North Carolina. Would you like their social security numbers? How about I get you their license plates?"

He lowered his head to look at her and it wasn't entirely friendly. Her eyebrow twitched.

"I'm being paranoid for good reason," he snapped.

"I don't doubt that at all. But don't you think I would know if I had unpleasant people staying under my roof?"

"I'm not sure. Would you?"

"You're damn right I would. I can read people, son. They're like open books, and you and your boy as well as those folks upstairs are no exception. You're in some kind of trouble. I get that, and it's gotten so bad that now you're jumping at shadows. Well, the shadows in this house are nothing but that. Shadows. Now you best start relaxing or you'll end up dead before you get a chance to eat my food and use my electricity, got it?"

Without waiting for a reply, she turned around and headed out of the room. Paul glared after her, feeling his nerves fray at her condescension. He chewed on the inside of his cheek then looked back over his shoulder. His instincts demanded that he keep moving, that he not stop or slow down or pay attention to some crack-pot woman who ran a fucking charming bed and breakfast. He didn't want to be digging into a dish of peach cobbler only to have his face blown off. He didn't want to be sleeping in what he was sure was going to be a very comfortable bed only to have someone sneak through the window and cut his throat, and he wouldn't feel a thing because he would be sleeping too fucking deep. And then he would be dead.

And so would Ethan.

Then Edna would find them dead in their beds and not only did they use her electricity and hot water, but they ruined her bed sheets, and probably the walls too, depending on how bad the blood sprays were. There was a certain kind of hopelessness to this situation. It sat in the pit of his stomach like a lead ball and when he looked down at Ethan, the lead ball seemed to enlarge until its jagged edges grazed his lungs and breathing suddenly became a problem. He forced himself to let go of Ethan's coat and the kid turned to face him.

"Won't we be safe here?" he murmured so softly that Paul barely saw his lips move. "For a little while, at least?"

Paul hesitated. "I'm not sure. Probably not."

But where else are we going to go?

The question was unspoken but as loud as a banshee's wail in the middle of the desert.

"Hey." Edna's sharp voice interrupted them. "You coming or not?"

Paul's mouth moved with no idea as to what was going to come out of it when another voice cheerily interrupted, "Good morning, Miss Edna!"

A middle-aged couple trooped down the narrow, creaky staircase that stood at the other end of the dining room. Paul felt his heart do triple-beat at the appearance of more people and *holy shit* if he wasn't hard-pressed to dig a gun out of his bag right now.

Just as a precaution, of course.

Watching the couple carefully as they cleared the stairs and walked toward them, Paul just barely stopped himself from taking a step backward.

"That bed you have up there is to die for," the woman said, smiling.

She was tall, pretty, with smooth, flat features, red hair, and sparkling green eyes that sadly reminded Paul of Kelly. The man she was with was dark-haired, graying at the temples, with a kind, open face, pale eyes, and a mouth that looked to be smiling even when he wasn't. One hand was busy rubbing sleep from behind his rectangular-shaped glasses and the other held the woman's hand as if he were blind and she was leading him along.

"Oh, man," he yawned. "It sure was. Excuse me, I don't mean to be yawning so that you can see my tonsils but I haven't slept that good in ages."

"I didn't feel you toss and turn once," the woman teased him. "And the blankets were still on the bed when we woke up."

Edna laughed pleasantly, the perfect hostess. Paul looked at her. Apparently Ethan wasn't the only one who could turn it on and off.

"I'm glad to hear that, folks. I just replaced those mattresses, too. Had a man in here not too long ago, he woke up with the worst backache ever. Barely got himself downstairs, and granted he had walking problems to begin with, but that damn bed just made it worse. So anyway I figured it was high-time for new mattresses. Can't have my guests limping on out of here like they'd just been shot in the foot, you know what I mean?"

"Absolutely," the woman agreed. "My aunt was having sleeping problems and for the longest time, we all thought it was her mattress. It turned out to be sleep apnea."

"Oh, my," Edna replied. "That's not good. That the one where you stop breathing in your sleep?"

"The very one. Dangerous too from what I was told. So she got herself one of those breathing machines and viola! Hasn't had a problem since."

"Well, good for her. And speaking of sleep, I need to get these two on upstairs. They've had a hell of a morning and the sun ain't even all the way up yet."

The woman turned to Paul and smiled apologetically at him. She held out her hand.

"Hello there. Sorry to keep you here with all my yammering. I'm Allison and this is my husband, Jensen."

Turning to Paul, Edna threw a quick, sharp smile up at him before dragging his bag out of his hand. He nearly went after it as she stepped back and he bit the inside of his lip as annoyance flared through him. Forcing himself to smile, although it felt more like a snarl, he awkwardly shook her hand, then Jensen's.

"Nice to meet you," he said. "Paul and this is…Ethan."

"You guys look like you've had a rough morning," Jensen observed, putting his arm around his wife's waist. "Car trouble?"

"Car trouble's an understatement," Edna jumped in breezily. "Poor boys nearly froze to death walking over here."

Allison winced in sympathy. "The weather here is brutal, isn't it? We're on our way to North Carolina and I can't *wait* to get there. No offense to your hospitality, Miss Edna," she added with a wink.

Edna beamed a smile.

"Yeah, it's, uh, It's pretty cold," Paul said, shifting his weight from one foot to the other.

"So where are you headed?" Jensen asked.

Paul narrowed his eyes at him, suspicion rearing its ugly head. Jensen blinked, immediately sensing that he was toeing a line that he hadn't known existed until now.

"Well, you know if—if you were going in the same direction as us and if you're having car problems—" Jensen said, stammering.

"Oh, honey, I forget how sweet you can be sometimes," Allison cooed at him, laughing.

Jensen chuckled, looking away from Paul with a slight blush to his cheeks. "I have my moments."

"Okay, now, I think that's enough chatter," Edna said. "Why don't you two head on into the kitchen while I set these guys up in a room? There's coffee waiting for you, nice and hot."

"Perfect," Allison said. "It was nice meeting you."

Paul tipped his head. "Likewise."

Jensen smiled, rather uneasily before following his wife into the kitchen. Edna waited for them to leave the room before turning an annoyed look up at Paul.

"What?" he asked.

"Can you make it any more obvious?" she whispered harshly at him.

"What—" he started to exclaim then immediately lowered his voice. "What the hell are you talking about? I was civil."

"You were glaring at that man like you wanted to rip out his tongue through the back of his head."

Paul gave her a flat look. "That would be anatomically impossible."

She made a rude noise. "Impossible or not, try not to scare away my customers okay? I have a living to make."

"You shouldn't have taken my bag."

She raised her nose into the air. "I'm the hostess. It's what I do."

Without another word, she led them up the staircase that groaned and creaked beneath their weight. Paul cast backward glances to the kitchen as they ascended. Sure, fine, they were a nice couple but the kid at the gas station was nice too and look what happened to him. Mentally shaking his head, he half-listened as Edna went on about meal times and the bathrooms at either end of the hallway and kindly stay the hell away from the third floor because that's *her* floor. No guests allowed up there, thank you very much.

They went down a wide hallway, their feet sinking into plush chocolate-brown carpeting. The walls were a rich cream color, adorned with bronze sconces. There were rooms on either side, the doors open to show different motifs and styles but radiating the same country charm and aromas of pine and fresh sheets. Paul looked inside every single one.

"No boogeymen," Edna sniped at him as she stopped in front of the last door on the right.

He took his bag from her without a word and stepped into the room. Two comfortable beds, a night table, a bureau, and a wall of windows that were covered with sheer white curtains that only intensi- fied the blinding snow from outside. The walls were a deep burgundy color and there was one painting on the wall that looked like a five- year-old had gotten his hands on a can of bright yellow paint and gone to town.

"Is this acceptable?" Edna asked from the doorway.

He nodded.

"The bathroom is across the hall from you," she replied. "Towels and soap are in there, too. If you need anything else, let me know."

"Thank you."

She gave him one of those assessing looks before nodding at Ethan and closing the door after her. Paul stared at the door for a few seconds before turning around and looking at Ethan who had perched on the edge of the bed furthest from the door.

Kid's catching on quick, Paul thought to himself then said, "Look, I'm going to take a quick shower. I want you to stay here, okay? Lock the door behind me and don't open it for anyone but me, got it?"

His little teeth chewed on his lower lip. "What about Edna?"

"What about her?"

"What if—"

"That crazy woman isn't coming back up here anytime soon. I don't want you leaving, all right? Just stay put."

He nodded. Paul took a gun from his bag then pushed the bag under the bed with his foot.

The shower was heavenly and Paul was sure he could stay in there all day. Leaving his clothes on the floor, he shrugged into a cream-colored terrycloth robe and went back to the room to find Ethan in the same place that he left him.

"It's all yours," Paul said, shoving his wet hair back from his face. "When you're done, just head on downstairs and get something to eat, okay?"

Ethan tucked his hair behind one ear. Not sure how to interpret such a gesture, Paul pointedly stared at him until Ethan stuttered out, "A—are y—you—"

"I'll come down, too, all right? Just go."

Ethan went without another word, leaving Paul to sink down onto the bed, nearly groaning at how soft it was and before he knew it, his eyes were closing. When they opened, the sun was high in the sky and he bolted off the bed. He scrambled recklessly, still in his bathrobe, looking for his clothes before realizing they were still in the bathroom and *where the fuck was Ethan?*

He dashed into the bathroom. It was empty and his clothes were gone.

Panic exploded into his gut. Grabbing his gun, he jammed it into the robe pocket, not caring how obvious it looked as he bolted downstairs.

"Ethan?" he shouted. "Ethan! Ethan, where the hell—"

Paul came to an abrupt stop in the doorway of the kitchen.

Ethan was staring up at him from the table. His eyes were wide and shocked and a chocolate-chip scone was inches from his open mouth. Edna stood at the stove, spoon poised above a pan of scrambled eggs. The look in her brown eyes matched Ethan's at Paul's chaotic entrance.

"What in the name of—" she started to say.

"Where—What—" Paul tried to form a coherent sentence but the sight of everything in front of him being so calm and collected while his heart raced and his mind in pieces, had him nearly collapsing to the floor.

Ethan shot to his feet, scone slipping from his fingers. He was dressed in a similar robe as Paul except his somehow fit his small frame.

"I'm sorry," Ethan immediately began to say. "I didn't—"

Paul shook his head, leaning heavily against the doorframe. "No, no," he panted. "No, it's—Jesus, I fell asleep and—"

"Jesus on a cracker, boy, sit down before you fall down," Edna interrupted in bewilderment as she shooed Paul into a chair. "You, too, Ethan. Go on now, it's all right. This man's obviously in the mood for giving people heart attacks today, that's all."

Moving jerkily as if his limbs didn't quite work, Ethan sat down. Edna put a mug of hot tea in front of Paul and proceeded to stare at him as well. He could practically *feel* her wanting to berate him for such a display but he must've looked like he couldn't deal with it, and he couldn't, because she stayed silent.

She turned back to the stove. Paul picked up his cup, feeling his wrist nearly break at how heavy it seemed. He took a sip, feeling it burn a hot trail down to his stomach.

"Where are my clothes?" he asked after a suffocating moment of silence. "Where're Ethan's?"

"Oh, I put them in the wash." She looked at him. "They smelled like they needed it."

He closed his eyes, trying to get his heart rate back to a normal rhythm. His eyes slid open to find Ethan still looking at him, somehow ignoring the tasty-looking scone in front of him. There was a cup of hot chocolate at his elbow.

"Go ahead. Eat," Paul said softly.

Ethan's mouth twisted and he turned his head slightly to one side. He looked so young inside that robe, it made Paul's chest ache harder than when his heart had been knocking against his rib cage.

"Are you all right?" Ethan murmured.

Paul bit the inside of his cheek, forcing himself to nod. He took big sip of tea so he wouldn't have to say anything, wincing as it seared his tongue.

Two plates of scrambled eggs and cheese were set on the table followed by two glasses of orange juice. Paul glanced up at Edna who was watching him reproachfully.

"Thank you," he said, hoping it would appease her at least a little bit.

Of course, it didn't as her mouth turned down even farther at the corners.

"What the hell is going on with you, boy? You trying to give me more gray hairs?"

"Please don't call me boy. My name is Paul," he said wearily, rubbing his forehead with his fingertips.

"Oh, *excuse* me." She took a step back. "*Paul.* What the hell is going on with you?"

"Nothing."

"Bullshit. Pardon my language, Ethan," she added, looking over at him with a quick smile.

Paul scowled. "Nice to know you two have been bonding."

"Well, there was nothing else for him to do while you were upstairs, dead to the world. Now are you going to explain to me why the hell you ran into my kitchen like you were being chased by a pack of wild dogs?"

"You don't need to know."

There was a moment of silence and Paul kept his eyes on the table top, ignoring the eggs. At least he was trying to as his stomach growled and protested to be fed.

"Is there someone after you?" Edna asked, her voice low.

Paul's jaw flexed.

"I suggest you tell me right now if there is. Because if someone's going to come crashing through my front door or my back door or any of my windows, I want to be ready."

Paul shook his head, a humorless chuckle slipping out of him. "What, with your shotgun? Like that's going to stop any of them?"

"So there's more than one?"

He clenched his teeth and finally moved his head back to meet her eyes. "Most likely," he finally admitted.

Edna squared her shoulders, trying to look tough but only succeeded in looking more fragile without her curlers and robe. She was dressed now in a pair of gray slacks with a bulky white sweater. White fluffy slippers decorated her feet.

"And when do you think they'll come a-knocking?"

"Look, Edna, don't try to be a hero, all right? Something happens, you run like hell."

"I'll have you know that I—"

"Yeah, I know, you killed three men and they all happened to be your husbands but this is different."

"How is it different?"

"Your husbands weren't expecting you to kill them and they sure as hell weren't trained to make someone disappear."

"I made them disappear," she insisted. "I told you the police are still looking for their remains."

Paul squeezed his eyes shut briefly, taking a moment to listen to Ethan chew his food.

"I get the impression that you're not taking this seriously."

"Of course, I am," she exclaimed, indignant. "Listen, whatever's going on, I can handle it. You just keep your boy safe, you hear? That's all and any that you need to be worrying about."

He glanced at Ethan who had stopped chewing. Edna seemed to sense something because she left the room, only to come back with Ethan's clothes, fresh from the dryer.

"Here you go now. Upstairs with you and change, okay?"

Ethan paused then gingerly took the clothes. Paul nodded minutely at him as Ethan looked over at him as if for confirmation. Then he slid from his chair and Paul saw him dip his face into the clothes and breathe deeply.

Edna slid into Ethan's unoccupied chair, waiting for him to leave the room before stating, "I didn't let you in here blind, Paul," she said. "I want you to know that."

Paul fiddled with his fork, pushing it through the eggs. "You should've said no."

"And then what? Make it easier for those sons-of-bitches to get a piece of you? Do you think it would've been more noble to freeze to death? It's human nature to seek shelter and you found it here. It's worked in your favor so far, wouldn't you say?"

Paul looked at her, really looked at her, allowing her to see the man whose face was the last people saw before they died. It irked him somewhat to see that it didn't seem to have any effect on her. He shook his head. "You should've turned us away."

"I have a feeling that you're used to that."

"You don't know anything about me," he snapped without meaning to but honestly, a psych exam was the last thing he needed right now.

"I know enough," she said sharply, letting her hand fall with a dull smack to the table. "Regardless of what you might think or say, *boy*, you're not that hard to read."

The anger that boiled into his bloodstream felt good and fresh. He jumped to his feet so suddenly Edna shot back in her seat, staring up at him with wide eyes.

"My clothes," he gritted out. "Now."

Her jaw clenching, she moved to her feet and left the room. When she returned, she all but threw them at him. He caught them and stalked out of the room, his head buzzing.

He stormed up the stairs, grinding his jaw hard enough to break bones. He slammed open the door of the bathroom and jerked off his robe, leaving it where it lay crumpled on the floor. There was a metallic *clink* as the gun, still inside the pocket of the robe, hit the tiles but he didn't hear it. The compulsion to break something, to fling knives at human targets was terrible in its shake down his arm. Hell, even his broken arm wanted to get in on the action. He wiggled his fingers experimentally and gasped, gnashing his teeth as pain set the limb on fire. His left hand flew into the wall and he left it there, struggling for control.

His eyes squeezed shut of their own accord, presenting visual aid for his thoughts that he didn't need or want. Who the fuck were these people who thought they knew him? Who thought they had the fucking right to pry his head open and stick their bony fingers inside, trying to stir something up? Jesus, it was none of their goddamn business.

'But it is my business,' Aaron had told him once, smirking as only he could. *'Everything inside is mine. Every thought that flies through your head, every beat of that heart in your chest. Now you'll probably run across people who will think that they know you better than you do or even better than I do. They'll try to find your weak spots, the right buttons to push, and they might succeed, and it'll probably piss you off to no end. I know it'll piss me off but no worries, Paul. Because they won't ever know you the way I do. They can't and you won't let them. Will you?'*

No.

No one.

Not Jakob.

Not Edna.

Although Ethan had been coming closer and closer without even trying.

Paul took his throbbing hand away from the wall and wiped it over his face. Somehow managing to get dressed, he padded across to his room and opened the door.

CHAPTER 39

His brain actually misfired twice before processing what the hell he was looking at.

Mel.

The big jolly Santa Claus look-alike.

Owner of Mel's Diner, a *fabulous establishment.*

Was in his room.

Laughter bubbled up the back of his throat because this was completely and totally ridiculous and there was absolutely no reason why this cheerful motherfucker could be in his room holding a knife to Ethan's throat. But then his eyes found Ethan's and they were strangely composed, as if this kind of thing happened all the time. His nostrils flared as the knife angled his head back against Mel's torso, his hair bunching up around the top of his head like a halo. Mel's free hand was huge and too tight against Ethan's shoulder.

"Hello, good sir!" Mel said. His voice no longer held that carefree thunder but something rubbery and oil-like. "Glad I didn't have to wait that long for you."

"What the fuck is this?"

Mel beamed a smile and it was full of things that drove a spike of ice through his chest. "This is a time to collect. Sorry to be busting in on you like this but this little guy is way past his due date."

The spike of ice shattered, exploding outward so that shards of it pierced Paul's heart and lungs. Something shuddered through him, sending hooks into his brain, hooks that sank in and tore it clean apart. He tasted blood in the back of his mouth, wondering if he could get any more stupid because while he was having a fucking crisis in the bathroom just now, Ethan was getting cornered and manhandled. And Paul doubted Edna would've given Mel free reign to wander up here, small town or not.

Jesus.

"Past his due date," Paul repeated, swallowing past the dryness in his throat. "I wasn't aware he had one."

Mel sneered and it sat wrong on his red, cherry face. But yet, it didn't. It actually seemed quite well-suited. "Oh sure," he cooed. "They all do."

Paul was sure if he gripped the doorknob any tighter, he'd break it clean off the door. That would really give Edna something to bitch about. His face tightened.

"Edna let you in?"

"Sure, she did. Edna and I go way back."

"Doubt she'll let you leave with him."

Mel's smile was all teeth. "She has a lot of spunk, I'll give her that. But I kind of doubt she'll be able to stop me."

"Wouldn't count on it."

"Like the old broad, do you? Wouldn't have pegged her as your type."

"No?"

"Nope," Mel shook his head then raised his large hand off of Ethan's shoulder to ruffle his head.

Paul nearly bit his tongue in half.

"But this little man? Oh yeah. Definitely more your type."

If Paul had had a gun in his hand—*and he probably would have if he'd freaking remembered the damn gun still in his robe pocket*—he would've easily landed a bullet right in the middle of his fat face. He kept his breathing easy, calm because there was *no way* that this situation was leaving this room.

"How would you know that?" Paul forced himself to say.

He wanted to look over his shoulder to see if there was someone standing behind him but he didn't dare take his eyes off Mel.

"You're famous, my man," he replied with a dirty grin. "You have no idea how famous. In fact, I'll let you come with me if you want. There's someone dying to see you again." He paused. "Hell, I'd probably get first dibs on the fresh meat if I do bring you so why don't you help me out, huh?"

Just hearing him say the words was a clue as to how badly Paul had misjudged him.

"Who is dying to see me again?' he asked in favor of launching himself across the room.

"Now, I can't tell you that. That would be cheating."

"Aaron?"

Mel's smile faltered a bit at the edges. "Aaron? Who the fuck is Aaron?"

A light went on in the back of Paul's brain. An image of those three punks sailed through his mind, surrounding his car, taunting Ethan through the glass.

'Come on, Twinkie, open the door.'

'We just wanna talk to ya.'

'Let us in, ya little faggot. Fucking cold out here. Think you're bet-ter than us, sitting inside this car? How many dicks did ya suck for that jacket? Ya know Jack's gonna be pissed when he hears about this.'

Jack.

The name was like a blade through the top of his head and he in-stantly pulled away from it, hard enough to slam it back into the dark-ness of his mind before it could blast its way out.

Mel's nasty laughter skated down his spine. "You remember now?"

Paul stared at him, feeling his insides settle and turn blank. "You're not leaving this room."

"The hell I'm not. Come on, Lefty, you think you can stop me with one hand and no weapons? You think this little morsel is going to lis-ten to you now that he knows how fucking *pissed off* he's made every-one by disappearing?"

To accentuate his point, Mel pressed the blade into the thin flesh of Ethan's throat until a narrow line of red appeared. A small sound es-caped from him.

"Paul!" a voice suddenly shrieked from somewhere downstairs.

It was the distraction Mel needed as the big man tossed Ethan aside and rushed at Paul like a freaking runaway train. He took most of Mel's weight against his broken arm and he screamed through his teeth as he was run back into the wall. Landing punches as quick and as hard as he could with one hand, he felt Mel shift as he dug his meaty shoulder into Paul's torso. Paul thrashed against him, trying to shove him off. He felt rather than saw Mel's knife hand come out for a side strike and with a painful grunt, brought his knee up into the side of Mel's rib cage. Mel staggered, dropping the knife but he stayed on his feet. It was like trying to kick a human-shaped Jell-O mold. Mel bought his head up suddenly so he could look Paul straight in the face. His eyes sparkled with malice and something too sick to name.

"I'll get even more praise if I bring your head back with me," he seethed against Paul's face, barely struggling to keep Paul pinned against the wall. "I'll get to pick from all that sweetness Jack has working for him and you know I'm going to pick that little cocksucker behind me. You know what they call him? Huh? Do you?"

Paul let out a half-growl, half-scream as he pushed and twisted be-tween Mel and the wall, his blood on fire in his veins.

"They call him Twinkie," Mel went on, his voice dropping to an unnerving half-whisper, his lips so close they brushed against Paul's cheekbone as he spoke. "Did he tell you that? Twinkie. And I *love* Twinkies."

"Motherfuck—" Paul spat out, trying to bury his fist in the center of that sneering, sick face.

Mel wrapped a meaty hand around his bicep, slamming it back to the wall near Paul's head.

"So soft," he murmured. "Soft, spongy, and so, so sweet. I can gobble him up in one—giant—bite."

"Sick—fucking—"

"Hey, hey, that's not nice," Mel cut in smoothly with the ease that Jakob used when Paul was being *unreasonable*. "A little appreciation would be nice, Paul. It was always because of people like me that you were kept alive. You were kept safe so that you didn't end up with your ass shredded or left for dead in a ditch somewhere."

The disbelief must've shone on Paul's face because Mel smiled and it was barely a shadow of the man who'd first greeted them at the diner.

"It's true. The money paid for Ethan, for others like him, *for you*, even though I've never had the pleasure, keeps a roof over their heads, man. Keeps food in their stomachs and clothes on their backs. Or in some cases, not so much." He grinned, pressing his bulk against Paul, grinding him into the wall. "You ever miss it, Paul?" He sighed. "Hm? Do you? If you say yes, I might think about sharing."

"Fuck you," Paul snarled.

Mel laughed softly. "No. You're a tad bit too old for me—"

He suddenly jerked back, letting loose a howl of pain. Paul shoved him and Mel stumbled, collapsing to one knee. The room seemed to shake as he landed. Paul looked down to see one of his knives sticking out of Mel's calf. Ethan was backing up against the bed, his eyes wide and seething, shiny with tears—or was it anger?

Mel twisted around to look at him. His eyes blazed. Spit gathered at the corners of his mouth, his face twisting into something nearly inhuman.

"You fucking little shit. You're going to wish you'd never done that. I'm going to make sure Jack lets me have you and when I get you under me, I'm going to shove my cock so far—"

Paul stepped behind him and grabbed Mel's head with both hands, gritting his teeth against the pain that shot up his arm. With something like a scream spilling from his throat, he gave a sharp twist and the sound of Mel's neck snapping went off like a cracked whip.

CHAPTER 40

A ir whistled in and out of Paul's chest as he stared down at Mel's unmoving body, half-expecting him to shake off a broken neck the way you'd shake off a mosquito bite. Seconds passed then minutes and Paul dragged his eyes back to Ethan, who was slouched on the edge of the bed, looking strangely…blank.

Paul knelt down in front of him, waiting for those gray eyes to find his. It took a few moments but when they did, life seemed to seep back into them like water flowing into a bowl.

"Okay?" Paul asked, touching the boy's chin lightly to move his head up and back to inspect the narrow line of blood. It was sharp and bright against the white of his throat. "You okay?"

Ethan gave a shaky nod, his little jaw tight. Paul continued to stare at him, waiting for him to either start to cry or scream or both. When nothing was forthcoming, he asked again, "Ethan? Are you sure you're okay?"

Ethan's stare became so intense that Paul almost backed away. Then it flicked to the dead man at their feet. A shiver went through his small body.

"He said he—he said he'd take me b—back," he stammered, his voice so soft, Paul could barely hear him. "And Jack—when he gets mad, he—" He paused, swallowed, then tried again. "He likes to—"

"It's okay," Paul cut in. "Ethan, it's okay. You're not going back. I'm not fucking allowing that, all right? Huh? Look at me. All right?"

Ethan's watery gaze came back to him. Paul gave him what he hoped was an encouraging nod.

"Paul!"

There came another shriek of his name, the same voice that had distracted him the first time. He shot to his feet and went out into the hallway.

Edna was limping her way toward him, using the shotgun as a cane. Her mouth was bloody, her hair tousled. She looked like someone had knocked her flat on her ass. "Christ, are you all right?" he said, looking her over.

Her eyes were wide but snapping with anger. "That lousy son-of-a-bitch broke down my back door."

"Are you *okay*?" he insisted, gesturing at her split lip.

She glared up at him. "I'm fine. I'm walking and talking, aren't I? Where's that asshole at? I'll show him to punch a poor, defenseless old woman."

Paul's eyebrows twitched and he suddenly wanted to laugh. "In my room."

He watched as she hobbled over to the doorway then promptly froze in place. Paul waited for a reaction, resisting the urge to scuff his feet like a kid about to be scolded. After a few moments of silence, she held out one hand. Ethan appeared in front of her, moving slowly like he always did when he wasn't sure what Paul's position was.

"My lord," Edna breathed.

She searched Ethan's face, gently cupping his chin. She didn't miss the flinch he gave at the contact. She let go then turned sharply to Paul.

"You boys need to get out of here. As in right the hell now."

Paul nodded, moving around them to go back into the room. He slipped his feet into his boots. He bent over to get his weapon bag out from under the bed, when Edna gave him a firm shove onto it.

"What the—"

"Sit there. Let me tie them boots."

Paul flushed. "What? No, it's—"

"You want to be on the run with untied boots? How far do you think you'll get before you do a nice face-plant into the sidewalk?" She hunkered down slowly at his feet and Paul swallowed hard as he remembered Jakob doing this very deed.

At least this didn't have a million innuendos behind it but it was still embarrassing. He snuck a look at Ethan who was hovering in the doorway. His mouth was twisting ever so slightly. Paul scowled. He thought he saw the edge of a smirk grace Edna's bloody lips as she angled her head down to quickly and tightly tie up his boots.

"What are we going to do about the body?" Paul said, trying to get the attention away from the blush in his face.

"Who cares?" Edna snapped as she finished and pushed to her feet.

She snatched a hair tie off the night table. Paul opened his mouth to protest but she glared him into silence.

"What do you mean, who cares?" he said, frustration evident in his voice as her fingers scraped his hair back from his face. "Are you crazy? There's a corpse on your bedroom floor with a broken neck. I would love to hear you tell the cops about this one."

She tied his hair back too tightly. It felt like his face was going to split down the middle.

"You're not going hear anything because you're not going to be here. Now get your shit and get moving." She was already walking out of the room.

"Edna—" he called after her then muttered, "Goddammit." He got to his feet, grabbing his bag. Turning to Ethan, he paused for a moment then held out the bag. "Here. Take this. Follow Edna downstairs, all right? I'll be down in a minute."

Ethan took the bag, the weight of it nearly bowling him over. Casting one last unreadable glance at Mel, he left the room. Paul skimmed a hand over the top of his head then over his face. He looked down at the body and let out a long breath. He went over to the windows, letting his mind get a grip for a second because this was a sucker punch of enormous proportions and if the noise inside his head could cool down for just a second...

He pulled the curtain back. The sun was halfway to the tree-line and the shadows along the back part of the property were already deepening. He wasn't looking forward to going back out into the cold. God, just the thought of walking made his feet throb. Vaguely he wondered if Edna was feeling magnanimous enough to let him borrow a set of wheels.

Borrow.

He forced himself to use that word.

He'd return it.

He'd make damn sure.

Leaning forward, he pressed his forehead to the glass. It was cold and slick against his forehead. His eyes flicked down, able to see the back steps, his footprints where he'd stood, shaking, numb, and so fucking desperate for Edna to let them in and Christ, look where it got them all. And that look on Ethan's face...

He shut his eyes, his breath fogging up the window. When he opened them, his vision tunneled and he saw Ethan's footprints in the snow, when Paul's arms had felt like they were going to snap off at the shoulders from carrying him, and the kid had barely been able to stand as he forced himself around that tree and up the steps into the warm house and—

Paul's sluggish thoughts came to a halt and he blinked, hard.

What tree?

He blinked again at the large dark object that was sprawled across the back steps. His hands gripped the edges of the window.

No.

His brain raced, his eyes seeing but not, pulling the image into the gray matter in his head and sending off a screaming message that yes indeed, it was a body.

A body with no head.

Blood, fresh and wet, seeped from the open neck, looking like someone had spilled paint on the bright white snow. There was a trail of blood splotches leading away from the steps and a part of his brain could almost say, *Hey, follow the trail, Hansel and Gretel*! But his stomach lurched and he tore away from the window, leaping over Mel, and thundering down the steps.

Edna was cleaning up the cut on Ethan's neck as he barreled past them and nearly slammed into the back door.

"What the hell's the matter?" Edna started to ask, coming toward him.

"Stay there," Paul demanded, holding his hand out behind him, not bothering to look at her. "Just…don't come over here."

"This is *my* house, I'll have you know—"

"Edna, dammit, just…stop a minute, all right?" he exclaimed as he searched the back porch through the window pane.

He couldn't see the body from this viewpoint for which he was thankful because Edna appeared at his side, stubborn as a freaking cat on cat-nip.

"What? What're you looking at?"

Paul ignored her, staring hard enough to break the window. Nothing moved, nothing breathed beyond the glass. He was vaguely aware of Ethan shifting closer behind him.

"Stay there," he growled.

Taking a deep breath, Paul nudged Edna out of the way and eased the door open. The cold bit into him and he winced. He opened the door just wide enough to squeeze through and shut it behind him, muffling Edna's, "Hey!"

He stood still, eyes moving restlessly. The sun burned coldly, the color of butter. The snow began taking on a bluish tinge and, again, Paul couldn't fucking *wait* to go to the beach.

It almost hurt to move as he edged to the top step. His breath puffed out slowly as he breathed evenly even though the blood was pounding through him, in a rush to get nowhere.

He was sure Mel had come alone so he was hoping that the body on the steps was nothing more than a hallucination. Glancing around again at the tree line, knowing it was beyond stupid to be out in the open like this, he kept moving. He saw the blood first, but the scent of meat quickly followed.

Staring down at the body, he tried to look past the purple-red-white stump of the spine but Jesus it was so slick and shiny and the bile that roiled around in his gut made him close his eyes. When he opened them, he heard his breath shake. The body was dressed in black camouflage. There was a gun holstered at the small of his back and two different-sized knives sheathed to each leg.

Then Paul noticed something that he wished he hadn't.

The flesh around the neck, where the head had been sliced away was flat and smooth, indicating that a very sharp blade had been used.

And the head was nowhere around.

Just moving his eyes, Paul followed the blood trail that he'd seen from the upstairs window, tracing it around the side of the house. He swallowed hard, feeling the cold stabbing at the back of his throat. This wasn't making sense. This poor bastard was obviously here for him or maybe for Ethan or both—who the hell knew anymore?—and now he was dead.

So what the hell was going on? What did this mean?

It would be too much to hope for that every asshole out to get him would kill each other first instead of him because he was pretty sure that the amount of money offered for his head was substantial. But why would they take the head from this poor bastard? What would be the purpose aside from it being some kind of twisted trophy…his thoughts trailed off and he stumbled back.

No. Oh, no…

His hand fumbled for the doorknob but the door opened of its own accord and he came into the kitchen nearly ass-first.

"What is it?" Edna asked immediately as she shut the door after him.

Paul whirled to Ethan. "We need to go." He turned back to Edna. "Now."

Her lips tightened in a thin white line and he thought for certain she was going to demand that she come along too. She left the room, still using the shotgun as a cane.

"What is it?" Ethan said quietly. "Is it someone else—"

"No, well, maybe," Paul replied, willing his voice not to shake. "I—we just need to get out of here. All right?"

Ethan nodded then looked toward the back door like something had caught his eye. It made Paul turn to look and the bottom dropped out of his stomach.

Someone stood at the edge of the property, back by the trees. It was a shadow of a person, dark and straight like the trees behind it. Paul's hand twitched, a spike of cold fear inserting itself through the back of his neck. The fear came as a surprise to him and it wasn't only because he'd just been out there and hadn't seen anyone. It was because he knew exactly who this was.

He could see the jade-green eyes from here.

"All right, here," Edna announced, coming back into the kitchen.

He jumped away from the door and spun around. "Wh—What?"

She was holding out a black garbage bag that was crammed full. He pressed his lips together and took the bag without saying a word.

He turned back to look outside again.

Chac Mool was gone.

Paul sucked in a sharp breath, half-expecting him to pop up in the window.

"Hey, you want to get going, I suggest you stop the sight-seeing," Edna snapped.

Paul met her eyes then glanced down at the bag as if it had just appeared in his hand. He cleared his throat.

"You want me to take out the trash before we leave?"

"That's stuff you're going to need," she replied, rolling her eyes. "Oh and here." She handed him a thick wool coat she had draped over the back of one of the kitchen chairs. Ethan was shrugging into the one from Irene and Jakob's.

"Edna—"

"Don't thank me. I'm just doing what I was raised to do."

"I was just going to ask if there was any chance we could borrow a vehicle."

She glared at him and it only made him feel a *little* bit like an asshole. "You're lucky I like you." She tossed him a set of keys. "In the garage. Go out through there." She pointed at a door off to the kitchen.

Paul tugged on the coat. "I'll return it."

"Please," she scoffed.

He looked her in the eye. "I will."

She returned his stare then nodded once.

"You look after him, okay?" she said to Ethan, passing a hand gently over his head.

Ethan nodded up at her, the corners of his mouth twitching. He gave a slight jerk as if he wanted to move forward and hug her. He settled on another nod and Paul hustled him to the door. Once there, Paul hesitated and turned back.

Edna frowned at him and flapped her hands at him. "Just be careful, for crying out loud," she griped. "It's bad enough I'm surrounded by dead bodies but I don't need your sorry ass littering my property before you even make it out of the damn driveway."

Paul looked down at her then reached out to squeeze her arm. "Thank you."

Her eyes softened a notch but only a notch and when she opened her mouth she said, "Get the hell out of my house before I call the cops."

Paul bit back a smile and they left with the smell of peach cobbler lingering in the air.

CHAPTER 41

A 1970 Pontiac Bonneville.

Dark green, two-door, sparkling whitewalls and enough chrome to make a gangbanger jealous.

It was not what Paul had been expecting when he entered the garage but, man, it was gorgeous.

And it ran, actually, it *purred.* And when Paul stretched out behind the wheel, he could've groaned. He couldn't help but smile at Ethan who was kneeling gingerly in the front passenger seat as if he didn't want to get the cream-colored upholstery smudged with his fingerprints. But he met Paul's gaze and a small smile flickered across his mouth.

They drove around the outskirts of town, staying away from prying eyes, taking Edna's directions back to the highway with minimal fuss. Ten minutes in, Ethan was asleep and Paul checked and rechecked the rearview so many times, it was a wonder he was even driving in a straight line.

In the quiet warmth of the car with his backbone curving delightfully into the soft seat beneath him, his mind made a brave attempt to wander aimlessly, to not think at all, to plainly drift because he was sure that was all the mental energy he could spare. But there was just too fucking *much* crowding him.

He wished there was a way to blast it all back so he could at least breathe a little but there were too many potentials, too many problems, and not enough solutions.

How long do you think you'll be able to keep running?

Just about everyone had posed that question to him and that was before he even figured Chac Mool into the equation, stalking them like some kind of jewel-eyed jungle cat.

He'll kill you before anybody does, Paul thought to himself. *That's why he decapitated that poor bastard on Edna's back porch. He doesn't want anyone else to have you.*

Reluctantly, Paul decided it could possibly be helpful having another pair of eyes at his back. He didn't want to think about what that man—now headless—would've done to Edna if he'd gotten in the house. It probably would've been a lot worse than the split lip Mel had given her.

Night was falling and he flicked on the headlights. The two-lane highway was dark, the trees on either side darker. There was no one behind him or in front of him and he settled back into his seat a little more. He knew they would have to stop for the night. As much as he wanted to, there was no way he'd be able to drive all night. He didn't like the way his vision was beginning to blur around the edges.

Miles and miles of silence and dark flew by before he passed a place that rivaled the Bates' Motel. Not seeing any other choice and feeling himself rapidly succumbing to the kind of exhaustion so acute that his bones ached, he pulled in. There were a few other cars in the parking lot and flickering red and blue lights read "Vacancy." He killed the engine and reached over to shake Ethan's shoulder.

"Hey, wake up," he said quietly.

"Hm?" Ethan mumbled.

"Come on, we're crashing here."

Ethan sat up slowly and peered out of the windshield, rubbing his eyes. Paul ignored the tightening warmth in his chest.

"Here?" the boy asked, his voice rough from sleep.

"Not up to your standards?" Paul demanded with a raised eyebrow.

Ethan looked over at him for a minute then something flashed across his face, something like amusement. "Unless you're Norman Bates."

Paul surprised them both by laughing. He climbed from the car to keep himself from doing something cheesy like ruffling the kid's hair. He glanced around out of instinct, shoving his Smith & Wesson into the back of his pants as they strode toward the front office. The place wasn't very big but it had definitely seen better days. Even in the half-lit parking lot, he could see the sagging steps, the splintered doors with half the numbers missing, and the badly-peeling paint. Definitely Norman Bates.

He went into the front office, Ethan tight to his side. The man behind the desk was half-asleep and half-drunk. Paul felt the knot between his shoulders ease up. Unless the guy was a good actor, Paul didn't think he would have to worry too much about him trying to make a stab at his throat while he slept. Still, after securing a room, Paul backed out of the office, listening, watching perpetually for anything and anybody.

Ethan tried to be on alert as well but he kept rubbing his eyes and yawning, basically not being a very good side-kick.

Dragging the garbage bag and his weapons from the backseat of the car, they made their way swiftly to their room—Number nine, all the way at the end. Their footsteps dragged along the half-rotted wooden planks, breath frosting in the air in front of their faces. The breeze was gentle but biting and the room was warm when they went in. Paul locked it behind them, flicking on the lights and wincing at the dark orange shag rug; ugly orange, gold, and white wallpaper; and two full-sized beds, one of which was propped up on a couple of cinderblocks. It smelled dusty but with a tinge of disinfectant and Paul hoped to hell that he wouldn't wake up covered in bed-bug bites or cockroaches.

You've had worse, the voice in the back of his head sneered.

He ignored it then snapped the curtains closed. Settling on the bed, he opened the garbage bag and nearly laughed out loud. "We'll have to send Edna a thank-you card," he told Ethan as he dumped out the contents on the bed.

Ethan chuckled tiredly as he looked over the extra clothes, the bathrobes, bottles of shampoo, bars of soap and, Paul noticed with a raised eyebrow, a number of plastic spoons and forks. Then he dug deeper into the bag and took out a small mountain of Tupperware containers filled with food.

"Holy shit," Paul whispered in amazement as he pried open a lid of one container and nearly melted at the sight of spaghetti and meatballs. Tired or not, they dug in and it was easily the best meal on the planet. All but licking the sauce from the inside of the container, Paul sat back, belching loudly and humming in contentment. He watched through half-lidded eyes as Ethan speared the last meatball.

The kid paused and glanced up. There was a question circling in his gaze.

"What?" Paul grumbled.

Ethan held out the meatball. Paul smiled a little and shook his head. "You eat it."

Ethan polished it off in three quick bites.

"You should get some sleep," Paul advised.

"I slept in the car."

"Yeah, well, you need more."

"What about you?"

"What about me?"

"Aren't you going to sleep?"

"As much as I want to, probably not."

Ethan looked away, playing with the fork in his hands. His hair fell in front of his face but Paul could see the furrowed brow. There was something coming and any chance Paul had for relaxing at least for a little bit was getting ready to fly right out of the window. The kid had an uncanny knack for hitting too close to home with all his fucking questions and observations.

But the soft, "I'm sorry" wasn't what he expected.

"For what?"

Ethan gave a half-hearted shrug, not looking at him. Paul rubbed at his eyebrows, debating whether or not to push this.

You don't really want to know, do you?

No, he didn't. He didn't want to know because he knew the kind of thoughts knowing would invoke. But then he thought of the look in Ethan's eyes when he'd stabbed Mel in the leg, giving Paul the time he needed to snap the bastard's neck. There was something bubbling right beneath the surface and for all Paul's tap-dancing, it was getting harder and harder to ignore. So he forced out, "What, Ethan? What are you sorry for?"

"I should've gotten out of the car when you told me to."

Paul frowned. "What?"

"At the church."

Paul's breath left him in a rush.

Jesus.

He leaned forward, resting his elbows on his knees. "Ethan—hey, look at me. Come on, look at me."

It took a far shorter amount of time than usual for Ethan to make eye contact and when he did, it was like looking into a mirror. His eyes were old, ringed with red, and exhaustion, the skin around his mouth tight and thin and, if they didn't get killed, the fucking exhaustion was going to put them in the ground instead.

Paul ran a hand over his mouth, his shoulders sagging heavily. "Do you think it would've made a difference if you had gotten out of the car?"

Ethan turned his head like he wanted to look away but his eyes stayed on Paul's face. "Yes."

A large part of Paul's brain gave an indignant huff and he found he had to hold himself back a bit because, *Jesus Christ* the things he'd done, that he'd opened himself up to in order to keep this fucking kid alive and now he was saying that he never should've been there in the first place after he'd pleaded and begged to stay with him.

Paul gave himself a mental shake, forcing his thoughts away from that dangerous road. He took a deep breath. "You could be right," he said carefully. "But there's no way of knowing now, is there?"

Ethan shrugged again and stared at the wall beyond Paul's shoulder.

"What if…What if I just went back? On my own?" Ethan suggested in a small voice.

Paul's shoulders stiffened as he stared at him.

"Do you want to go back?" he asked, his voice squeezed tight.

Ethan floundered a bit.

"Do you?"

His small hand clenched around the plastic fork. "I think it'll help."

"That's not answering my question."

Ethan's mouth moved soundlessly as he tried to find the right words. Then he said, "If—If I went back then maybe there—won't be as many…" His voice trailed off under the force of Paul's glare.

"You're dead if you go back," Paul stated plainly.

Ethan gave a little shake of his head.

"Yes," Paul went on. "You won't be doing either of us any favors."

"B—But you'll be able—"

"What?" Paul cut in harshly, ignoring the cringe Ethan gave as his voice filled the room. "I'll be able to what? You think this, all of this, will suddenly become easier if you're not here? You think I'll be somehow safer if you're not here, that *you* will be safer if you're not with me?"

Ethan shifted in his seat, looking a little helpless now in the face of Paul's mounting frustration.

"I just thought—"

"Forget it," Paul snapped, letting his eyes drill into the kid's head because seriously he was going to understand this if Paul had to beat it into him. "I'd still be running, Ethan. I'd still be running and you'd be dead so it really won't help either of us."

Ethan gave that odd little shake of his head. "I wouldn't be dead."

"Oh, no?" Paul asked, practically growling. "You think you're going to be welcomed back to wherever the hell you came from with open arms and doughnuts?"

"But Mel—Mel was going to take me alive."

"So?" Paul snapped. "Mel's dead. And he may have wanted to take you alive but there was no way you'd be alive once you got to wherever he was taking you."

"You don't—I—how do you know that?" he stammered.

"Christ, kid, why would you even think about it? Don't you know how the game works?"

"It's not a game," he said shakily. "It's my life."

The words hit harder than he thought they would and Paul wanted to scream. God knew that this kid had given him a different path to go down even without meaning to. His mere presence had sparked a shift, perhaps as deep as Paul's own genetic make-up. The weight of that crushed the relative ease it would've taken to tell Jakob, Irene and Aaron to *fuck off*, thereby earning himself a bullet in the head. The simplicity of saying *no* and facing those consequences would've been so much easier than scraping to stay alive.

Simple, easy, and perfect.

Paul would've gladly done it. He knew that now.

But then Ethan came along and it was suddenly like trying to staunch the blood flow from a gut-shot. He was there, all the time, in every corner of Paul's mind, staring up at him, curling into him, trusting that he would protect him even if he never believed that Paul would come back for him but hoping, always hoping somewhere down deep, that he would. And Paul gave him reason after reason to hope because if there was at least one person he could give a life to after all the death he delivered, it was Ethan. It had to be him. Paul knew it as sure as the sun rose and he wasn't about to lose it under a mountain of what-ifs and coulda-woulda-shouldas.

Ethan broke eye contact, leaving Paul to stare at the top of his small, blond head, words at a jumble on the tip of his tongue.

Aaron gave you to me to save you. He just didn't know it at the time.

Silently he reached over and plucked the fork from Ethan's hand. When Ethan looked up at him, Paul avoided his gaze by getting to his feet.

"Try to get some sleep," was all he could say.

He busied himself with the task of cleaning his weapons, his back to Ethan's bed, listening with half an ear as Ethan settled down and his breathing evened out. He quietly got up and went to take a shower. When he came back out, Ethan was gone…

CHAPTER 42

He was walking through a forest of lush green so thick and vivid it was like being lost inside an emerald. Golden sunlight splashed across the trees, rustling leaves whispered and spoke, tinkling like wind chimes. Beautiful and quiet, he walked in the sun, trailing fingers against the rough, warm bark of the trees and the smooth surfaces of leaves.

Safe.

It was safe here.

Something sharp pricked his finger. Startled, he looked down to see the leaves he was touching turn brown, the edges curling inward like burnt paper. It trailed upward, eating away at the trees like a disease, turning them into black splintered spears like railroad spikes.

"No…No!" he tried to shout, backing away as if the distance he put between himself and the blackening trees would somehow save them. But it spread viciously and the air smelled like rot and decay. The ground crunched beneath his feet, split open, dry and dead, fanning outward like a shockwave from a bomb blast. Dead leaves swirled around him, blackened tree branches, shriveled and disintegrated, bent like skeletal arms, coming toward him as the sky darkened and ash and blood filled the air, shot down his throat like a hard burst of water, choking him, making him gag …

❧❧❧

Paul jerked awake, blinded by darkness, scrambling upward, his legs shooting out only to be brought up short as his head slammed into something. Groaning, he collapsed back, his heart hammering in his chest. He blinked. Darkness persisted before his eyes. He bought his hands up to his face with a dry moan, feeling the duct tape around his wrists tighten and pull against the delicate skin. His head throbbed and his cold fingers felt for blood. When he found none, he let his hands fall and he lay still for a moment.

The sound of his breathing was erratic and it took him a minute to realize that he wasn't even attempting to calm himself down. And why the hell should he? Why should he even fucking bother when all he kept seeing was the empty motel bed through the steam as he'd opened the bathroom door? The small Ethan-shaped imprint on the blankets and then the all-encompassing hysteria, something he hadn't felt since he saw Melanie disappear into that van all those years ago, and he knew then that he would never see her again and, acknowledging it, that it was a possibility that it could happen to him twice in one life-time had Paul nearly swallowing his tongue in panic. The cold had stung his skin, still damp from the shower as he rushed outside, his breath streaking in front of him as he shouted Ethan's name like the fucking curse and cure that it was.

The hush of the night was as blatant and quiet as the *fuck you* he'd heard a second too late from behind him and then he was collapsing in the snow, head lit up with pain and stars, eye-level with two pairs of boots before hands grabbed him and hauled him up. Another blow to the head and he'd lost consciousness. And now here he was, trapped in a car trunk that stunk of gasoline and something else that had died very recently.

His eyes burned, his throat felt like it was stuffed with cotton as he tried to breathe past it. He choked and sputtered, glad he wasn't gagged but then thought *wouldn't that just be a bitch when they came around to pop the trunk only to find me already dead?*

He almost laughed.

Almost.

Because then at least he wouldn't have to keep hearing Ethan's last words echoing in his head like a schoolyard taunt.

'It's not a game. It's my life.'

Biting back a groan of anger and something close to helplessness, he shifted his body. His senses began to bleed through the wall of pain that had set up shop around his cranium. He could barely make out the faint glow of tail lights and the purring of the engine grated on his pounding head. He wondered vaguely if he had a concussion and if he did, he hoped he would have the opportunity to puke on the sons-of-bitches who'd caught him. As he lay there, he found that he was a hundred percent sure that Ethan hadn't been taken, that he'd left of his own accord and there was a part of Paul that was glad for that. At least this way, he would have a goal, something to keep him going, some-thing that would prompt him to survive, even if the kid cutting out on him pissed him off to no fucking end. He only hoped that the damn pain-in-the-ass stayed alive long enough for Paul to get to him.

And just where was he anyway? What the hell did he do, hitchhike?

Paul let out a slow breath and squeezed his eyes shut. He tried to ignore the pain in his head and his right arm—*God*—which was next to useless. The duct tape was tight enough to nearly cut off the circulation to his hands and the mending bones of his right forearm were *not* pleased. He felt around him, searching for a weapon of some kind. He tried not to breathe through his nose. The smell in here was making him light-headed.

The car stopped and rocked as people got out.

Paul still had a faint memory of two pairs of boots. He really hoped it was only two. Any more than that and he'd be screwed. Footsteps came then faded, and there was nothing but silence. He lay there, waiting, breathing in steadily through his mouth. The footsteps came back and before he could brace himself, the trunk lid popped open. He reared up, hands grabbing at whatever and whoever he could reach.

"Whoa, easy tiger," a voice laughed from above him.

Eyes watering and his head furiously protesting the sudden movement, Paul felt hands grab his flailing limbs and yank him from the trunk. His feet caught on the edge and he went face-first to the ground. Biting back a groan as the gravel bit into his knees and elbows, he waited for his eyes to adjust to the light and for the world to stop dipping beneath him.

"Fuck—you—" he managed, coughing through the road dust.

"Oh, kitty, I like it when you're feisty," that same voice said.

"You always like the feisty ones," another voice commented and Paul could almost hear the eye-roll that went along with it. "Feisty ones have a tendency of clawing your eyes out."

"True. But not if you rip their claws out first."

Paul held back a shudder as he was pulled to his feet. His eyes came open almost involuntarily and he blanched as the world spun around him.

"Aw, come on, I know I didn't hit you that hard." A hand slapped at his cheek. "Did I? I don't think I did."

"You probably did. You've never quite grasped the concept of your own strength."

"Yeah, well, concept or not, it's saved your ass a bunch of times."

A pause then, "I won't deny it."

"Okay, come on, Paul, we've got to walk. You can walk, right, because seriously I do *not* want to carry your useless ass."

Paul blinked blearily, finally focusing on who was holding onto him. Jesus, both men had Aaron's stink all over them. He pulled weakly at his arms but their fingers bit hard into his biceps. He fixed his eyes on the man to his left, saw a long face; a wide flat nose; and beady, coal-black eyes. He was only an inch or two shorter than Paul but the strength in which he held Paul's arm was enough to convince him that short did not mean weak.

The man grinned as if reading Paul's mind. "How you doing, Paul?" he quipped, flashing a cold smile. "The name's Mark and this is Simon."

Paul moved his eyes over to the right to see Simon, a brute of a man who stood too close with a smile that came too easy. His thin lips were wet and cherry-red beneath a nose that looked to have been broken more than once. Quick green eyes stared Paul down and he felt a prickle of uneasiness trip its way down his spine.

"It's nice to finally meet you," Simon said.

There was a strange gleam in his eyes and Paul attempted to take a step back away from him. But the action only pulled Simon closer, close enough for Paul to see his pupils.

"Not sure I can say the same," Paul rasped, wincing as his own voice seemed to explode inside his head.

Simon's smile was wet and unpleasant, the presence of crooked, yellow teeth notwithstanding.

"You're a hard one to find," Mark said. "Almost as hard as finding Aaron."

Paul looked at him, waiting for the blurred edges to morph into something more solid so he could say, "Aaron?"

Mark smiled as if he were a kitten. "You wouldn't happen to know where he might be, would you?"

Paul blinked as his brain unhelpfully conjured up an image of a leaking picnic basket. He swallowed back a wave of queasiness, struggling to clear his head. "No idea."

Mark's smile didn't waver but it was hard enough to cut glass. "Well that's not very forthcoming, is it?"

Mark's eyes cut to Simon and by some unspoken signal they began to move, half-carrying, half-dragging him. Paul's head lurched and bile burned up the back of his throat. He tried but failed to keep his feet under him. It felt like an elephant was standing on his head.

Fuck it, he thought and let himself go limp.

He listened with half an ear at the muttered curses and labored grunts as Mark and Simon were forced to take all of his weight.

Good, he thought. *Let the fuckers drag me. They think they're going to kill me, might as well make them earn it.*

"Fucking asshole, you better not puke on me," Simon grunted.

Mark scoffed in his other ear. "If he does, it'll serve your stupid ass right. Christ, man, how hard did you hit him?"

"Might have a concussion," Paul mumbled or at least he thought he did because nobody answered him.

A prickly darkness stabbed at the edges of his vision.

"…didn't hit him that hard, for Christ's sakes," Simon was griping.

"Well, then, why the hell can't he walk?"

"How the hell am I supposed to know? He's probably fucking faking it."

Oh, how I wish, you fucking—

He never got to finish the thought as he was let go and fell to his knees.

The change in latitude did not help and he bent forward until his forehead was inches from the cold ground. The pounding of his heart took over his hearing, drowning out his screaming instincts to get up and fight, to get free before he was *killed*. But God, if everything would just shut the fuck up for two minutes and stop moving and swirling, he'd be able to assess the goddamn situation. He was pretty sure it wasn't a lot to ask for.

'*Wanna bet*?' Aaron's voice was suddenly in his ear, in his head, as real as the last time Paul had heard it. '*You're dead, you hear me? You're so fucking dead. You and that little whore I gave you, wherever the fuck he is. Your bodies will never be found. No one will ever know you've even been alive, that you ever existed. No one will miss you, either. It'll be like you were never born and you might as well not have been, you ungrateful little fuck-up. After everything,* everything *that I've done for you, everything that I've given you, this is how you repay me? This? You on your goddamn knees in the dirt and my head in a fucking basket? You better hope there's no afterlife, you fucking coward, because there's going to be nothing that will keep me from you.*'

Paul squeezed his eyes shut, letting the shivers travel through his body. From far off, he was aware of his arm throbbing and he realized that he'd began, almost subconsciously, to twist his wrists back and forth in an attempt to loosen the duct tape. The pain lifted the fog a bit and he allowed his eyes to crack open. His bound hands filled his vision, the gray of the tape so close, it was almost black. He eyeballed it, following the tight stretch marks it made around his wrists like the lanes of a racetrack. A trick of light caught it, making it flash more silver than gray and it made him think of Ethan's eyes. It jolted him or maybe it was just Simon, nudging him hard in the ribs with his foot.

"Shit," Mark muttered.

Simon didn't seem as sympathetic as he kicked him again. "Come on, get up, you piece of shit."

Gritting his teeth and getting a whiff of shoe polish from Simon's shiny black shoes, Paul's mind started to whirl and conjure all sorts of interesting ways to knock out every fucking tooth in this guy's mouth without getting shot. He wasn't sure how to actually get the strength to do it but after the third and fourth kick to the ribs, the anger that boiled through him was enough. Clenching his jaw hard enough to break his molars, he lunged up, watching with glee as Simon's green eyes widened with the classic *oh-shit* look. He was about a hair's breath away from jabbing his bound hands into Simon's smug fucking mouth like a battering ram before his legs were kicked out from under him. He barely registered the ground beneath him before he was rolling to his feet, sparing a second to quickly squeeze his eyes shut as his head swam in agony.

Then there was the cold press of a gun barrel against the back of his head.

He stilled, his breath harsh and heavy in his lungs.

"Ease down there, kitty," Mark said calmly from behind him. "I don't think you want me to do this prematurely."

Paul bit back a snarl, jerking his head away. The gun neatly followed. "How about not at all?"

There was a pause as if the man was actually considering it. Then he said, "That'd be a bit of wishful thinking."

"Just a bit."

"We're not exactly here to make things easy for you, Paul," Simon said, sliding his hands into his coat pockets.

"Just do it, okay?" Paul snapped. "I think I've been talked at enough."

He just barely stopped himself from flinching when Mark was suddenly pressed into his side, putting his mouth right next to Paul's ear.

"Don't make me rush this, Paul. I want to remember every detail."

"I'm sure your kids will appreciate this as a bedtime story."

Mark chuckled, low and deep. "Oh, not my kids. Yours maybe."

"I don't have any."

"Sure you do," Simon smiled and again, it wasn't pleasant.

Paul humored him. "Yeah?"

"Yeah. That little cocksucker. The blond one, what's his name? Allen? Igor?"

"Ethan," Mark said helpfully.

Paul felt a flush work its way across his face. He blinked at Simon, fighting to keep eye contact even as his skin colored. His chest felt like it was being crushed. "He's got nothing to do with this," he forced out through gritted teeth. He turned his head to look at Mark, his hands twitching.

"No," Mark replied. "But he might be a bit more cooperative than you."

"Meaning?"

"He could tell us where Aaron is."

"And why do you think he would know that?"

"He was with you, wasn't he? Riding around, bonding, doing whatever. He must've seen or heard something."

"He didn't."

"I think I'd like to hear from him. Where is he anyway?"

"You'll only be wasting your time. You won't ever find him."

"Paul, I'm hurt that you would think us to be so incompetent."

"Incompetent is a nice way of putting it."

"The man doubts us," Simon said.

"Well, he *has* been through a lot," Mark countered.

"Which could've been avoided," Simon smirked.

"True. But he decided to make things hard on himself, didn't you, Paul? I don't think I'll ever understand why people do that. Instead of just doing what it's expected of them, they try to be all high and mighty. They try to be *different* and it never works out, man. Never. It's ridiculous, and even more ridiculous to watch."

"Maybe people do it because they're bored," Simon guessed.

"You think so?"

"Sure. Their lives become tedious, predictable, and they need a way to spice things up."

Mark made a thoughtful sound. "Is that it, Paul? Were you bored? Is that why we had to go on this wild fucking goose chase because you wanted to become a mailman or something?"

"That doesn't sound very exciting," Simon said. "And mailmen don't make nearly as much as we do."

"No way. Even if it is a government job." Mark sighed, his breath warming the side of Paul's face. "Should've stuck with something a little tamer, Paul. Like jumping out of an airplane."

"Or hiking through the Alps," Simon offered.

"Or the Amazon."

"I think I'll take the Alps."

"Nah, too cold."

"You'll sweat your ass off in the Amazon."

"I'd rather sweat to death than freeze."

"Really?"

"Yeah."

"How about you, Paul? Alps or the Amazon?"

Paul glared. "Neither."

"Oh come on," Mark chided. "You have to choose."

Paul didn't reply, simply willed for their heads to explode.

"Which do you think Ethan would like?" Simon asked.

Paul's eyes snapped to his face. Simon grinned.

"We'll have to ask him when we find him."

"You won't," Paul snapped.

Mark's lips curled slowly, a just-barely there smile that sent a spark of understanding tripping down Paul's spine.

"Care to make a small wager on that?"

Paul curled his lip at him, his hackles rising at the confidence in Mark's tone. *No. No, no, no, there was no way that these two morons knew the first place to look*, he told himself fervently. *There's not a chance in hell.*

He turned his gaze away from Mark's sparkling eyes, only to find himself looking at Simon, which wasn't much better. Something shone in his eyes, something that sparked that uneasy feeling again. It wasn't amusement or triumph or even cruelty. It was a sickness, a fierce, hungry infection that was eating its way through his easy, watery smile. Something dark and there was a part of Paul that recognized it. His stomach twisted.

"Just leave him alone."

Simon's grin widened. Mark's breath touched his ear. "Come on. Let's take a walk."

Giving an almost gentle nudge with the gun, he had Paul march in front of him. Simon was to his right, just outside of arm's reach. He didn't appear to be armed but Paul knew that he was. He spared a thought to his bag of weapons and wished he'd put that wire pick in his hair.

Gravel crunched underfoot. The air was cold but there was no wind. He did a cursory glance around, noting something familiar about the construction site he was being led through. It looked like condos were being put up—their metal and wood skeletons rising from the barren earth like the bones of ancient beasts. The morning sun lit the stark scars that heavy machinery had carved into the ground and Paul wondered if he was going to be buried in one of them.

They herded him inside one half-finished condo. Huge plastic sheets hung everywhere, moving gently in the air. Bare wooden beams crossed over their heads. Metal scaffolding lined the outer edges of the room, reaching up until it disappeared into dark blue shadows. No walls or doorways had been erected so everything was big and spacious. Climbing a wooden staircase had Paul wondering if they were going to push him off the landing to make it look like a suicide. But then they reached the third floor and it was laid thick with layers of plastic sheets. Paul's step faltered but Mark pushed him along, urging him to stand in the center of all that plastic. It crinkled beneath his feet, like dead twigs snapping. That was when he looked out and saw the familiar skyline.

They bought me home.

He turned to face them, catching sight of the workbench over to his right. Across the top of it lay his weapons, meticulously laid out like they were being shown off at an auction. His heart lurched. For the first time since they'd pulled him from the trunk of the car, he thought that there was a very real possibility that he wasn't going to be alive for much longer.

He waited for a cold rush of panic but it never came. He waited for a frenzy of emotion to bog his mind until he thought he'd collapse under the weight of it. But it never showed up. Neither did the will to beg, to offer these two idiots something in order to spare his life. The thought of what this might mean—*the end*—confused him. He could only watch as Mark took a stroll up and down the bench. He let his fingertips trail lightly, touching a gun here, caressing a knife there, his eyes moving slowly, almost delicately until he raised them to Paul's face. There was something like admiration in his eyes.

"Pretty impressive, Paul, really."

Paul allowed a stiff shrug. He looked around the large room, at the swaying sheets of plastic, at the dark collection of shadows in the far corners, at Simon who stood in front of him, looking at him like he was something he wanted to dissect and study. Uncomfortable once more under the man's scrutiny, Paul glanced away.

After a second, he looked back.

Simon still stared.

"What?" Paul asked.

"What's it like inside your head right now?"

Paul frowned at him. Out of the corner of his eye, he saw Mark do the same.

Simon waited expectantly for an answer. "I'm serious. I want to know."

"You want to hear my confessions?"

Simon rolled his eyes. "Do I look like a priest, asshole?"

"The question you just asked me sounded like it could've come from one."

"Or from a shrink," Mark chimed in.

"Come on," Simon said impatiently. "It's not a hard question at any rate. Just tell me what it's like inside your head right now."

Paul's attempt to square his shoulders and stare him down was not going well so he bit off, "Not so good."

Simon's lips gave an unhappy twitch. He stepped forward until the toes of his shoes were at the edge of the plastic that Paul stood on. Mark stopped in his sight-seeing expedition of Paul's weapons to watch, his hand hovering in mid-air above a serrated hunting knife.

"Come on, Paul. Tell me. Tell me what it's like," Simon repeated, his voice soft. "Tell me what it's like to be you because quite frankly, from my point of view, it looks like it's pretty fucking awesome."

Paul raised his eyebrows widened at the admission.

"I mean think about it," Simon continued. "You're trained for all types of situations: fighting, recon, weapons, everything you would need to survive from a bar-brawl to the end of the fucking world. You've got it all stashed in that brain of yours. You've got a real advantage over people, man. You have to admit. You're pretty lucky."

There was something lurking in the bright depths of his eyes, circling, coming closer. Paul cleared his throat, shifting slightly. "Yeah, lucky, which is how I ended up here."

Simon waved a dismissive hand. "This doesn't matter, Paul. All that matters is how you got here."

"So you approve of then?"

"Absolutely."

Paul said nothing. It was like he was talking to Tony all over again. His silence seemed to irk Simon and his face tightened with annoyance. "And you don't, I suppose, huh? It was good enough for you fifteen years ago and now it's not?"

"That's none of your business."

"The hell it isn't."

Darting forward, Simon suddenly was in his face, the plastic sheets crunching beneath his feet. Paul moved back but a wicked-looking knife was placed at his jaw, halting his retreat. Simon glared at him, his eyes hot and wild.

"You are one ungrateful little fuck."

"Simon," Mark called over with a warning in his voice. "Simon, what're you doing?"

Paul's eyes went to Mark, holding absolutely still as Mark made his way slowly, too slowly, like a handler who didn't want to spook an unbroken steed, around the workbench, toward Simon.

Hurry up and get this crazy motherfucker away from me! Paul wanted to yell.

"No," Simon said tightly, a vein beginning to pulse in his forehead. "No, fuck this and fuck *you*." He spat the last part in Paul's face. "What the fuck is so special about you, huh? What is so goddamn special that I, that *we*, had to spend all this time tracking your traitorous ass down?"

"Simon—" Mark said, his tone placating and careful.

Simon snarled in response, never looking away from Paul's face. "Everyone seems to think that you're worth something. But for the life of me, I can't think of a single thing that makes you worth this much of my fucking time."

Paul stared at him.

"Then why don't you just shut up and kill me?"

Simon's jaw flexed. The knife moved, inching its way into the thin flesh of Paul's throat. He tried not to flinch when the skin broke open.

"I want to," Simon breathed. "I want to so badly you have no idea. Wasting Aaron's protégé. What a treat. Even if you are a fucking traitor."

"But first," Mark said soothingly, finally making it to Simon's side. He stared hard at Simon's profile, as if mentally willing him to keep his cool. "We should find out if Paul knows where Aaron is."

Simon didn't seem to notice that Mark was even there. It made Paul wonder how many times Mark had to pull this man back from the edge. The silence that followed was halting, ticking down a countdown that was oppressive and ominous.

Paul tried to breathe but the air was too thick, too cold, too everything. "I don't know where he is," he tried to say without moving his jaw too much.

"Don't fucking lie to me!" Simon screamed.

Paul and Mark jumped. Paul felt the knife slip harder into his neck. His eyeballs burned. Mark shifted closer to Simon, his hand out as if to touch him.

"Simon—"

"Don't lie to me," Simon repeated, softer now but his was voice no less harsh. "It's already not going to end good for you, Paul. I don't think you want to make it worse."

"Come on, Simon," Mark said. "Come on, just calm down, all right? We're going to find him. He'll tell us where he is, just relax, okay?"

It should've been reassuring but the fact that Mark still had a gun in his hand didn't make Paul feel any better. Simon gave a hard nod of his head, leaning closer to Paul.

"Yeah. You tell me. You tell me right now where he is and then I'll calm the fuck down."

Paul pressed his lips together, not getting a chance to respond when Simon started talking again. "He was a great man, Paul. You probably don't agree. You probably don't give a shit, but the man's knowledge was boundless. Anyone was lucky to train under him. But because you turned out to be a whiny little bitch, all that knowledge, all that greatness is gone. You have no idea what we've lost because you couldn't keep your head in the game."

"You're acting like he's already dead," Paul said.

"Because he is," Simon snapped. "You won't tell us and you probably never will, no matter what we do to you and for that, I'm going to take you apart." His hand tensed around the knife's handle.

"Simon, not yet. We can get it out of him—" Mark started to protest.

"Bullshit," Simon cut him off, barely sparing him a glance. "We're just wasting our fucking time with him the same way Aaron did."

"What kind of a life do you think I had under him?" Paul asked.

Mark raised an eyebrow at him. Simon narrowed his eyes with a sharp, "What?"

"What do you think it was like, being trained by him? You think it was fun? You think I had a blast being under his thumb all the time? What kind of man do you think he is?"

"Please," Simon sneered. "Don't give me this shit about how horrible it was, how awful it must've been to be coached by him. He did you a favor and you're too much of a pussy to appreciate it."

Paul's jaw muscles bulged. "If you admired him so much, why the fuck didn't you train under him?"

Simon's face turned dark and he probably would've drawn the knife across Paul's throat if Mark hadn't gripped his shoulder. Simon froze under the touch, nostrils flaring.

"He would have," Mark cut in quickly. "And he wanted to but…"

"But then Aaron found you instead," Simon finished for him. "He saw how easy you would be to break, to mold, to shape. Me? He said I was too…unpredictable."

And apparently you still are, Paul thought then said aloud, "Tough luck for you, I guess."

Mark shot him a reproachful look as Simon growled, "You fucking—"

"What, you want me to say I'm sorry? I'm sorry that he chose me instead of you? I'm sorry that he wasted his knowledge on someone who took it all for fucking granted? I'm sorry that you never got the opportunity to work with him?"

"That'd be a start."

"Fuck that," Paul stated harshly. "Fine, he had knowledge, he had plans, he could probably rule the world if he wanted to but you—you have *no* idea what it was like with him. Not a fucking clue. If you had worked for him, I can guarantee you that—right now?—our positions would be reversed."

"See, that's where you're wrong," Simon said, his voice calm now. "I know very well what kind of man Aaron is…was. I would've made it. I would've survived. And I'm not expecting you to say that you're sorry, Paul." He smiled suddenly, nasty and ice-cold. "But I am expecting you to beg. Just a little."

The blade pressed into his throat. Paul's breath caught. Mark stepped back away from him, cocking his head to one side as he gave Paul a thoughtful, almost sad look.

"Sorry, Paul."

"Fuck you."

Simon's fingers flexed around the knife handle like big fat white worms. His slippery smile filled Paul's vision, just this side of manic. Paul wondered how long it would be before Simon turned that smile on Mark. Staring into that ugly face, his mind buzzed with three words.

Ethan, I'm sorry…

CHAPTER 43

An infinite pause dragged and scraped like scruffy shoes over linoleum. Simon's dark chuckle circled slowly like a vulture, punctuating this strange hesitation with an overwhelming feeling of slowing down to an absolute stand-still. It kind of sucked actually because Paul wanted it to be quick. He always thought death would be more agile, sneaky like a black cloth would simply drop over his head from behind and he would go blind, deaf, and dumb except for a small flicker of pain and then silence, full and complete. There was no reason for it to last except that Simon, the sadistic fucker, was waiting for him to beg.

Keep waiting, you unbalanced asshole, Paul thought to himself then wondered if he would have the time, within this strange slow-stop world he was suddenly in the middle of, to ram his fingers straight into Simon's triumphant, laughing eyeballs.

There was a flicker at the far corner of the room. It drew Paul's eyes like a hanging diamond used by a hypnotist.

The darkness was gathered there.

It was *moving* and the world was no longer still.

Something came hurtling out of all that darkness, so fast he could barely track it with his eyes. But it was flying in his direction and he instinctively jerked back.

Mark shouted a warning. Simon turned with a snarl and suddenly he was staggering back like he'd just been hit by a wrecking ball. He fell, heavy and flailing, against Paul. Paul grappled with him, grunting as the back of Simon's head connected with his chin. Simon twitched and jerked like he was being run through with electricity. Paul braced himself, holding the man up, trying to see what the hell was happening.

"What the f—" he started to exclaim then he froze.

Something long and horribly familiar-looking was protruding from Simon's chest, nearly pitting him. Paul felt the blood drain from his face.

There was a soft *click* from somewhere in front of him.

He looked up. Mark was pointing his gun at him. His face was white with anger.

"You motherfucker," he growled.

Paul shook his head uselessly.

Simon gave a hard twitch against him, a stifled scream making its way out of clenched red teeth. Spots of blood flew from his mouth. His hands fluttered in the air, grappling at the spear—*oh Jesus, no*—in his chest, slicing his palms open as he tried to pull it out. Blood was everywhere. Mark's gun shook and Paul's vision tunneled as he saw his finger tighten on the trigger.

Muttering a quick prayer in his head, he jerked Simon up, using him as a shield as the gun went off again and again. He felt more than heard Simon try to scream, could almost feel the blood filling his mouth and gushing down his chin like fruit punch. His body danced and shuddered as the bullets struck the meat of his body. Paul tried to make himself as small a target as possible but a twinge of pain blossomed across his lower leg. He ignored it, concentrating on keeping Simon up and in front of him. He was sagging though, rapidly becoming dead weight as Mark kept shooting. Gritting his teeth, Paul almost didn't hear Mark's gun click empty through the ringing in his ears. He chanced a quick peek over the top of Simon's shoulder. Mark was panting heavily, hands fumbling over the weapons on the table.

Shit.

Paul heaved Simon's body to the ground, knowing that he wouldn't stand a chance if Mark got his hands on more ammo.

He ran for the stairs.

From behind him, Mark reloaded.

Paul's heart thudded in his ears. He could feel the aim between his shoulder blades as surely as the duct tape around his wrists. He heaved himself toward the staircase when a cut-off scream erupted from behind him.

Paul whirled around. Saw the gun fall from Mark's hand as he spun in a wild circle, blood spraying everywhere from the knife sticking out of his neck. Paul froze, watching the man struggle and thrash as if under a spell. The sounds that came from him were frantic and hopeless.

Mark's eyes met his. They brimmed with pain and hatred. He collapsed to his knees, trembling, the whimpers fading into gasps that fought for every breath. His eyes remained on Paul, drilling into him with the intensity that only the dying had. Each inhale became shorter, each violent jerk of a limb became a soft twitch. Finally—dear God, finally—Mark fell to the floor, barely moving now, eyes seeing nothing. Only then did Paul dare to look away. His knees refused to hold him anymore. He sank to the floor, breathing heavily through his mouth.

Slowly, his gaze landed on the handle of the blade that was buried in Mark's neck.

It was made of stone, carved with intricate artwork and hung with beautiful colored feathers that were drenched and shiny with blood. Paul's breath came out of his body with a gasp and he tried to pull himself to his feet but only sank again to his knees.

"Oh—shit—" he choked.

Movement caught the corner of his eye.

Chac Mool was standing just a few feet away, half-hidden by a hanging sheet of plastic, watching quietly. His green eyes glowed hungrily, bright with a power that made the air evaporate in Paul's lungs. Paul shook his head, trying to shake away the sight of him. "What're you—How—I don't—"

Taking a few deep breaths, he managed to pull himself to his feet and say with some degree of coherency, "You—You were at Edna's. I saw you. At the edge of the woods."

The headless body in the snow.

The trail of blood—so bright…

Chac Mool gave a slight nod. "Your death is mine, Paul. I've told you that before and I meant it. It would do me no good to have your life ended so—" He paused, flicking his eyes over the spreading pools of blood. "—crudely."

His eyes came back to Paul.

Paul swallowed against a dry throat. "So you don't want to share, huh?"

It was a sad attempt at humor if Chac Mool's dead-pan expression was anything to go by. Every muscle in Paul's body tensed as Chac Mool moved, gliding like water over rocks. He side-stepped the smears of blood and bent over Simon's bullet-riddled body. Paul found himself watching with mounting horror. *Oh God, if he decides to cut his heart out in front of me…*

Chac Mool put one foot against Simon's shoulder. He gripped that fucking spear with one hand and pulled it free with one viscous yank. Without pausing or looking at Paul, he turned to Mark. He bent over at the waist, curling his long fingers around the blood-smeared handle and wrenched the knife from Mark's neck. Paul winced at the wet, squelching sound.

Chac Mool straightened, his eyes catching Paul's once more. "No, Cortez. I do not share."

He started toward him, a weapon in each hand, dripping with blood, looking very much like the warrior with a collection of hearts and skulls. Paul belatedly realized he should've been arming himself rather than watching Chac Mool do the same. His eyes darted to the table where his weapons lay in plain sight and how ridiculous would it be if he was killed while all his guns lay well within his grasp?

'*Idiot*,' he could hear Aaron sneer.

"You have quite a following," Chac Mool said now, drawing Paul's attention away from his weapons. "How many more will there be?"

He lifted his chin toward the dead men near his feet.

"They'll keep coming till I'm dead," Paul replied.

Something close to a smile flitted across Chac Mool's features. It looked a lot like triumph. "So then why don't I save them the trouble?"

Paul looked at the workbench again, desperately.

"Would you like to arm yourself?" Chac Mool asked and the humor in his voice was like something with very sharp talons.

"That would be fair, I think—"

"There is nothing here that is fair," Chac Mool interrupted smoothly. "Only what is owed. But if it will make you feel better, then by all means." He gestured toward the workbench. "Go on," Chac Mool insisted patiently. "I will wait."

Paul swallowed hard, his pulse thudding in his throat. Chac Mool was still moving toward him, slow but steady. Paul took an unbalanced step back, felt the heel of his boot sink too low and almost fell. A quick glance back and he saw he was at the top of the stairs. They were steep and narrow, something he hadn't noticed on the way up. The possibility of escape itched through his brain. He wondered how far he could get if he ran, skipping down the steps, two, three at a time.

Nope.

Dead before he reached the bottom, run through with the spear like poor, deranged Simon.

Then how about hurtling himself down the staircase, ass over tea kettle, in the hope of breaking his neck enough to die with all parts of his body intact?

Risky but a better probability of success.

Chac Mool was just out of arm's reach now. His eyes were unwavering but gleamed with a certain understanding as if he'd read Paul's mind somehow.

"You have a debt to be paid, Cortez," Chac Mool's voice hissed at a demented sing-along pitch. "Anything short of that would be…unwise."

"Can't blame a guy for trying."

"You stole from me. You willingly stole from me. You knew there would be a price to pay."

"Yeah, well I didn't expect you to come back from the frigging dead to demand payment."

"You took something that was very powerful, Cortez. A simple arrow in the back would not have stopped anyone, much less me, from going after it."

Paul was somewhere between skepticism and disbelief. "You *died*, man. Are you in denial or something?"

Chac Mool gave a dismissive shake of his head. "We've discussed this before, Cortez, and got nowhere. Let's not waste more time on the subject."

"Right, because we have so much more interesting things to do," Paul couldn't help but say.

But Chac Mool only waved him toward the workbench. Paul let out a sigh. "Impatient, huh?" he said as he began to move around Chac Mool, giving him a wide berth. "Never would've pegged you for it. How long have you been following me?"

"Long enough—" Chac Mool stopped abruptly, pinning Paul in place with a stare. His bright eyes began to narrow.

Oh shit, what now?

A beat of silence passed. Then, "There is only one of you. Where is your child?"

Paul's blood turned to ice. "What?"

"Your child. He is not here."

Not the first time since he'd been pulled from the trunk of the car, Paul was insanely glad for Ethan's absence.

"Where is he?" Chac Mool demanded.

Paul could only answer honestly. "I don't know."

Chac Mool glared at Paul through his eyebrows, his gaze unearthly. "Where is he, Cortez?"

Paul treaded carefully, aware of the ice, thin and fragile beneath his feet. "You don't need him. You have me."

"He is part of your debt."

The words were crushing. *In more ways than one.*

"He's just a kid."

"All the more worthy."

Silence stretched between them, taut and waiting, broken only by Paul's attempt to get past the lump in his throat.

"Okay, look, I, uh, I have a rough idea of where he might be. I just need some time. Then—Then you can have us both."

His brain barely processed Chac Mool's movement until he was right in his face. The point of that goddamn spear was pressed threateningly into his chest, right above his heart. Paul gaped in shock when he felt a small but increasingly steady stab of pain.

"Do you find me so gullible?" Chac Mool asked, his voice quiet despite the anger that swirled in his eyes.

Paul began to move back but Chac Mool raised his other hand. He set the bloody knife against Paul's throat, the edge feather-light but there. It was wet and cool and Paul fought back a shiver.

Deja-fucking-vu. He wondered if this was what a pin cushion felt like. "Hey, wait," he tried to placate. "Just wait—"

"Quiet."

Paul shut up, struggling with the effort to remain still.

"You're lying."

"No—"

"You've hidden him. You've hidden him and now you're trying to buy more time."

"More time for *what*?"

Chac Mool leaned impossibly close. "To run from me."

It made sense. It really did and it was a good plan. But Paul wasn't that smart and being separated from Ethan, willingly or not, had never been an option when Paul knew who was after them.

"No," he tried to say. "No, that's not what happened."

Chac Mool's jaw clenched and unclenched. "Do not lie to me, Cortez."

"I'm not," Paul insisted. "I'm—"

"Tell me where he is."

Paul's brain scrambled for a shut-down but the words were coming from his lips before the shut-down sequence could be initiated.

"He ran away. All right? I was taking a shower, I came back out and he was gone. He…"

He trailed off when he saw Chac Mool's face become calculating.

"He just left without any provocation."

"Yes."

Liar.

"He wouldn't have left you without a reason." The green eyes burned into Paul's forehead, sure and arrogant and it pissed Paul off.

He raised his bound hands as if to push Chac Mool away. "You don't know him."

"Apparently neither do you. What did you say to make him leave? Did you tell him that if the two of you split up, you would be safer? That it would be harder for me to find you?" He added pressure to the weapons that kept Paul at sharp attention.

"No," Paul said, wincing. "No, I—you're not the only one after us. There are people after me and there are people after him. Two different brands of assholes, okay? Ethan wouldn't have lasted an hour if he went off by himself."

"Which he did anyway. Or maybe that was your plan all along."

"Christ, what is your problem?" Paul nearly shouted. "He's just a kid! I was—I was just trying to keep him safe. That's all I've been doing. And he—" his voice caught and he blinked hard. "He th— thought that if he went back, it would make things easier for me."

He barely finished speaking before a well of emotion rose up in his chest, nearly succeeding in cutting off his air supply. Guilt was a jagged ball that went from his throat to his stomach, shredding its way through, sticking in and then tearing out chunks of tissue and innards to lay in crumpled, bleeding heaps. He tasted the tang of copper in the back of his throat, mingled with the sacrifice that Ethan had made, to leave him, to go back to the horrors that awaited him.

"Went back where?" Chac Mool inquired softly.

Paul looked helplessly up at him. "To…a place that's not so good."

"And he was willing to do that. For you."

"Maybe, yes, I don't know," Paul murmured, suddenly wanting nothing more than to lean into the spear and have it stop his heart once and for all. It probably wouldn't even hurt all that much.

"Will you find him and bring him to me?"

Paul could only stare at him. "Yes."

Chac Mool tilted his head to one side. "Even when you know what I will do?"

"Yes."

"And why?" He sounded like he already knew.

"Because what you're going to do is better than what he's doing right now."

Chac Mool smiled. He eased the spear downward, cutting through the duct tape around Paul's wrists.

"Now you understand."

Bleary-eyed, Paul pulled at the tape. "It won't be easy."

"Why?"

"Those men over there?" Paul nodded at Simon and Mark. "There'll be more of them."

Chac Mool's smile deepened. "I'll be watching."

CHAPTER 44

He was stuck in morning rush hour. The normalcy of it was staggering. Sitting stoic and stiff behind the wheel of Mark's Lincoln town car, Paul was sure he was going to throw up. He blasted the air-conditioner, triple-checked to make sure he'd grabbed all of his weapons off of that goddamn workbench, looked at all the cars grid-locked around him, trying not to scream at the honking symphony that rattled his back teeth. His coat collar was saturated with cold sweat, his palms sticky and freezing. His head pulsed, the inside simmering with things that were frantically beating a path to the forefront of his brain. The struggle to keep Ethan as his primary focus was deteriorating and he half-hoped he'd have a panic attack or something like it in the car instead of the place he knew he had to go. And oh sweet Jesus, he did not want to go. For the hundredth time since Chac Mool left him, he thought of how easy, how *done* he'd be if he had just let the son-of-a-bitch cut out his heart when he had the chance.

You know what's waiting for you if you go back.

He rubbed his eyes.

The car behind him leaned on its horn. He jumped, flipped the guy off and inched forward to cover the two-foot-wide gap between his car and the SUV in front of him. The car honked again in retaliation and Paul thought the sound was more like a scream.

"Shit," he muttered.

He contemplated walking but his legs twinged at the thought. Besides, he'd be shit-out-of-luck if he walked all the way there only to discover that the place was abandoned. Although he was pretty sure it wasn't. It would take nothing short of death to make Jack close up shop.

Jack.

Jesus, the thought that the man was even alive after all these years was both horrifying and amazing. No one had killed him, no one had turned him in, and if Ethan's reaction to the man was anything to go by, he was still running the business the same way. Paul's stomach churned unpleasantly.

Traffic finally began to unclog and he drove as fast as he dared. It was a lot like coming home. A very depraved home but home nonetheless.

He took a route around the city limits, back roads, and short cuts that he was surprised he even remembered. When he was halfway through the sticks and turning down a desolate gravel road, he felt an agonizing jolt. The road was one-lane, which was fine because not too many people knew the house was back there. At least, not the decent kind of people.

A stone dropped through the center of his gut when he saw the overgrown, neglected driveway leading up to the crumbling house. His worst fear was recognized, blazing bright in front of his eyes. He pulled up to the front door, moving slowly as if trapped in a bubble. Putting the car in park, he stepped from the vehicle, holding onto the car door with a white-knuckled grip. The smell of pine and dead leaves was a familiar punch in the gut and Paul had nowhere to turn to get away from it. Every exhale ended with a whimper and it was hard to tell if it was from the past or the present. Nausea washed over him and he bent over, trying not to be sick. He shook violently, feeling the pane-less windows gaping at him, burning into him, remembering him, and crucifying him in ways he couldn't bear to think about.

Jesus. God...

The lemon-scented floor wax, lace curtains in the windows, the pitter-patter of running feet, forced laughter, and dead smiles in the daytime. Could almost be a kid when the sun was up, could almost be normal. Until it started to get dark. Then the headlights would appear in the distance, glowing pairs of eyes coming closer and closer and the laughter would fade away to silence, the dead smiles would sink like rocks through a pond.

Welcome to Bushmann's Orphanage for Young Boys. Here for your pleasure and servitude. Youngest are in the upper levels of this magnificent mansion. Oldest down below. Please watch your step.

The echo of the greeting that he'd heard night after night, filtering up to his third-floor room that was one below the attic while beneath him, there was the robust, excited laughter of men, thick with anticipation and quick money exchanges. Cash only, if you please. No need for the wife to see the charges on the credit card bill.

Ten minutes later, his bedroom door would open.

Paul bit the inside of his cheek until he tasted blood. Straightening slowly, he forced himself to turn around, his movements jerky like his strings were tangled.

The sign above the door was weather-beaten and faded but he could see it as clear as day. Just like he could see the bright white double doors at the top of the front stoop, free of dirt, grime, and chipped paint that did nothing to hide the warped wood. There had been promise here, such safety. He'd followed a group of boys here, no older than himself, and they'd all seen the same thing.

Shelter.

Protection.

After countless weeks of wandering the streets, it seemed too good to be true.

And after the first night, they all realized that it was.

Some stayed, some left, some were brought back for a night and then never seen again. It was all so confusing because there were warm beds here and hot food, toys and video games to play with, teachers who would teach math, English, and history. It was run like an honest and true orphanage.

Except that it wasn't.

And Jack...

Jack knew exactly what he was doing. What he offered, what he could take away because surely this was better than kneeling on cold concrete, blowing a man in an alley somewhere. It was a business and it was protected. By any means necessary.

Paul blinked, realized that he had somehow worked his way up the steps to the front door. He stared blindly at the rusty door handle. He reached for it, his hand cold and trembling. Pressure was building in his ears, at the opposite side of the door, inside, waiting, breathing.

He could feel it smiling at him.

The door handle crumbled beneath his touch.

The smile grew wider, the breath more rancid.

The door opened a crack and the air rushed out in a dusty scream. It clogged his lungs, filled his head until he couldn't, couldn't, dammit, *breathe*!

He snapped the door shut.

Something whimpered from behind it.

Ethan's gray eyes filled his vision.

Paul staggered back, clutching at his chest like he was having a heart attack. Tripping over his feet, he flew back to the car. Without another glance, he sped away, kicking gravel up from under spinning tires.

He's not here, he's not here, he chanted through his head.

His hand tightened on the steering wheel.

He wasn't here.

But Paul knew where to look anyway.

CHAPTER 45

Cruising Wal*Mart's parking lot without looking suspicious was tough. So he parked the car in a spot that had a good view of the store's entrance. And he waited, eyes scanning through the people, the cars, everything. He was still shaky and he knew he was pale but at least he wasn't dry-heaving anymore. He drummed his fingers against the steering wheel, thinking of Kelly. He hoped he wouldn't see her this time.

Twenty minutes crawled by before he saw them. Three of them, looking as exhausted and skittish as the first time Paul had had the dubious honor of meeting them. They came around the far corner of the store, moving like a trio of hyenas, walking close enough to be construed as a group but far away enough to keep an eye open in every direction. Paul honed in on Kyle, remembering his slight lisp and cold blue eyes. He wasn't wearing a skull cap now. His hair was blond and short, a little more than a buzz-cut, and most likely, it wasn't by choice.

The boys huddled in their coats before going into the store. Paul ran a hand over his jaw. He needed to get Kyle alone, to talk to him, to bribe him, anything to get the information he needed. And he couldn't do it with one arm and trying to fend off three punks. These kids were a lot like crack addicts, unpredictable and borderline crazy.

The doors slid open again and Kyle came back outside, alone. He lit a cigarette, shoulders hunched against the cold.

Paul gripped the door handle.

Kyle turned and started to walk back toward the corner of the building. Paul watched him then opened the car door. The store doors whooshed open again and a man came out. Paul thought nothing of him until the man stopped and began to fiddle with something inside his coat pocket. He was middle-aged, gray-haired, and wore a long, dark coat. Paul's heart lurched when the man turned his head and looked at Kyle's retreating back.

Paul held his breath.

The man began to follow.

Paul forced himself to wait, thinking that maybe he was jumping to conclusions. Kyle disappeared around the corner. The man followed without missing a beat, without looking back.

Cocky. He's been doing this for a long time, Paul thought resentfully.

He pushed away from the car. Adrenaline was already halfway through him. Approaching the corner of the store, he slowed his step then stopped. He peeked around the corner. A chain-link fence ran down one side of the parking lot before turning sharply and barring off the area where Wal*Mart held their plants and outdoor supplies during the warmer months. There were only a few cars parked along the fence and Paul saw no sign of where Kyle and the man could've gone.

Paul sucked in a deep breath then went on at a normal pace. Sunlight glinted off the car windshields, brightening the surrounding piles of snow to an almost blinding pitch. He squinted as he moved down the line of cars, trying unsuccessfully to loosen the knot between his shoulders. The fact that he knew exactly where this was going to lead made him queasy all over again. Forcing in deep breaths, he came upon a big, black SUV.

Snow crunched on the other side of it.

Voices came, talking, murmuring.

He went to one side of the vehicle and hunkered down to peer beneath it.

On the other side was a pair of shiny black shoes that unfortunately reminded him of Simon. The shoes shifted apart and suddenly there was a pair of sneakers, facing the shoes, standing very close. Then the sneakers disappeared, replaced by a pair of knees.

Paul straightened to his feet.

He came around the SUV, low and fast, in time to see two sets of eyes swing toward him, one surprised and the other angry. He focused on the surprised ones—wide, brown eyes belonging to an average-looking man dressed in an average-looking suit, with a wedding ring on one finger and his cock out.

A startled, "Oh my God!" came from the man as he tried to stumble away which was hindered by his pants around his knees. "I'm sorry! I'm so sorry, oh—"

Paul gave the man's head a hard shove. He fell to one knee, his hands scrambling to do up his zipper.

"Get the fuck out of here," Paul growled at him.

The man's face was beet-red and he scurried away, tripping and gasping.

"Hey, what the fuck, man?"

Paul spun around.

"What the fuck is wrong with you, asshole?" Kyle demanded. "That was—"

"I need to talk to you."

Kyle's blue eyes flashed violently and his breath puffed in short angry clouds. "Oh, you need to talk to me? Well, take a fucking number, shithead 'cuz you can't—hey!" He let out a painful *oof* when Paul shoved him into the car.

"I need to talk to you now," Paul said, bracing himself.

Kyle came away from the car, swinging. Paul dodged his white fists, like little comets flashing across his field of vision. He grabbed Kyle by the bottom half of his face and caught a glimpse of shock and barely suppressed rage before Paul threw him backward. The impact of his body hitting the car seemed to echo and for a moment, Kyle sagged there, his eyes unfocused. Paul waited, watching him closely. He took a cautious step forward.

Kyle flew at him again, spit flying from his lips, his features trembling. Paul grabbed the front of his coat, pushing him back until he was pressed against the car. Kyle flailed, squirmed, and fought, shoving frantically at Paul's chest. "Fuck you, get off me!" Kyle hollered.

"Will you wait a fucking minute—" Paul demanded.

"You fucking douchebag—"

"Shut up—hey!"

Kyle placed a well-aimed kick to Paul's shin and it was hard enough that Paul loosened his grip. Kyle threw himself to one side but he only went two steps before Paul hauled him back.

"Get off!" he howled, twisting and pulling, his feet scraping on the icy concrete.

Paul shoved his face into Kyle's. "I will give you twice as much as what that asshole was going to give you if you shut the fuck up and listen to me."

Kyle gave him an ugly sneer. "Oh, well, I'm all fucking ears. You want me to put on some coffee?"

"I want some answers."

Kyle's nostrils flared. "Do I look like *Dear Abby*?"

"You don't want me to tell you what you look like after seeing you on your knees with someone's dick in your mouth."

It was a low blow and Kyle's struggling ceased. His eyes burned into Paul's face, the level of hatred in their blue depths deep and staggering. His fist came up and out, lashing toward Paul's nose. Muttering a curse, he ducked. The only thing saving him was Kyle's lack of momentum since they were standing too close together.

"Fuck you," Kyle panted angrily.

Paul pinned his body, feeling it quiver with tension and rage. The air whined from his lungs as he squirmed. "I want answers," Paul repeated.

"Congratulations," the kid snapped back, still straining against him.

Paul tried not to roll his eyes, his patience already in tatters. "Did you forget the part where I said I'd pay you double?"

Kyle looked up at him and for a minute, Paul was sure he'd tell him to fuck off again and then one more time for good measure. Several seconds of silence went by before something shifted in Kyle's eyes. Violence or not, this was still a business transaction.

Bit by bit, the fight went out of the kid, dribbling slowly like water through a cracked cup. But Kyle still remained taut and on-edge. Paul could feel the tension singing through him like struck piano wires. But then Kyle gave him a lazy smile that belied his physical state.

"All right, tough guy. You want answers. Show me the fucking money."

"How much?"

"Fifty for the question. Another fifty for the answer, if I can give it."

"Driving a hard bargain, huh?"

"Competition, man, especially when I got assholes like you fighting over me." He laughed but it didn't sound like he found it funny.

Almost reluctantly, Paul released him and stepped back. He didn't take his eyes off him as he pulled out the money. Kyle's smirk deepened, brimming with arrogance. Steadying his resolve and his patience, Paul held out a fifty. It barely saw air before it was plucked from his fingers and pocketed. Kyle pushed away from the car, making a show of straightening his coat. He eyed Paul expectantly, obviously waiting for whatever he had to ask him but the words were sticking in Paul's throat.

He could only stare at Kyle as if hypnotized and when Kyle realized that nothing was being said, he allowed himself to grow more and more relaxed. Even his face had softened as the tip of his tongue appeared, candy-pink, to touch the corner of his mouth. But Paul wasn't seeing Kyle. He was seeing Ethan in the back of his head, remembering the way he'd reacted to Paul's scrutiny, like a flower to the sun and it jarred Paul away from the sick feeling that was rising in his chest.

"Where's Jack?" he demanded point-blank.

There was a flicker of something across Kyle's face before it closed down completely. His face hardened and his cockiness morphed into something like disgust as if Paul was the scum on the bottom of his shoe. "Fuck off."

Paul blinked. Kyle shouldered past him with a snarl. Paul rushed to catch up with him.

"I wouldn't consider that an answer to my question."

Kyle answered by quickening his step and hunching his shoulders.

"What about the other fifty?"

"Shove it up your ass," was thrown over Kyle's shoulder.

Paul gritted his teeth, very aware of the time slipping through his fingers. He reached out and grabbed his arm.

"Get the fuck off me, man!" Kyle snapped.

"Not until you give me what I'm paying you for." He couldn't believe how easy the words came from his own lips.

"Fuck you. How's that for a quality purchase?"

"Not bad but not quite what I'm looking for."

Kyle yanked hard on his arm but Paul held him tightly. He could feel the arm beneath his fingers, so fragile and thin compared to the fight that was in him. Like a bulldog trapped inside a poodle.

"Dude, come *on*, fucking quit it," Kyle demanded.

"No," Paul replied, tightening his grip when the kid feinted to the left then went right.

Kyle tried to hold back a wince but Paul could see the tightening of his eyes, knew that his grip was bruising him.

"Tell me where Jack is."

"Not telling you shit, asshole."

"Bullshit," Paul shot back through gritted teeth as Kyle unknowingly bumped against his broken arm. "You'd tell me everything if I paid you enough."

That made Kyle fight harder. Paul couldn't understand why he was antagonizing him. Everything that came out of his mouth was something that he *knew* would piss Kyle off because he himself had had the same things said to him at one point in his life and it was no picnic.

But it got people what they wanted.

And right now, Paul wanted what Kyle had and he wanted it *now*. Even if he had to turn into some asshole-shitbag. He'd worry about feeling guilty later.

"Fuck you, man," Kyle was spitting out. "You don't know shit about me."

Paul snorted. "Sure I don't."

"I—"

"Was he the first customer of the day?"

Kyle pulled harder, ramming his fist in Paul's chest. "You shut the fu—"

"Did he offer to pay you extra to have you blow him outside? Just a few yards from a fucking store, where it'd be so easy to get caught?"

Kyle's eyes were murderous and his mouth moved, screwing up to say something scathing but Paul talked right over him.

"Probably didn't take him long to get hard. Adds to the excitement, knowing that anyone could see at any time. Easiest twenty you'll ever make."

"Yeah, until you came along and fucked it up."

"Oh, please." Paul rolled his eyes. "It won't take you long to find another one—and another one and another one and another one…"

Kyle's face was red now, either from the cold or something else. He turned to look over his shoulder, still tugging ineffectually at his arm. His eyes came back to Paul and a little desperation had leaked into them.

"Let me go. I'll—I'll scream my fucking head off, I swear to God, I will and what're you gonna tell everyone then, huh?"

Paul shrugged. "You won't scream. You know no one will help you."

"How the fuck do you know that? We're at *Wal*Mart*."

Paul leaned down close to him. The movement stopped Kyle's struggle as if someone had put a gun to his head.

"Odds are, you've screamed before," Paul said quietly. "And no one ever came. So why should now be any different?"

Something shifted in Kyle's eyes, something broken and lost and for a just a second Paul could see the despair. It was bone-crushing and awful. Paul gave him another year before he either killed himself or let someone else do it for him.

When he gave Paul another shove, albeit weak and half-hearted, Paul let it carry him back a few steps and he released Kyle's arm. Kyle wiped his nose on his cuff of his coat. He threw nervous glances around the parking lot, suddenly appearing a lot younger.

"Tell me where I can find him," Paul said softly.

Even though he didn't say Jack's name it was enough for Kyle to flinch. He looked down at his shoes.

"No."

"Tell me."

"*No.*"

"Yes."

Kyle's head came up. "You got any idea what would happen to me if I told you? People can't just show up at his door like fucking strays. You got to be invited."

"I don't have time to get sent an invitation. I need to know now. And how the hell would he even find out you told me anyway?"

Kyle's eyebrows drew together in a frustrated frown and he looked away again.

"He'll find out. He always does."

It sounded final but Paul wasn't about to give up. "He won't find out."

Kyle scoffed. "Yeah, okay."

Silence followed.

Paul waited him out.

He counted to thirty before Kyle began to fidget.

"Why you want to see Jack anyway?"

"It's business."

Kyle rolled his eyes. "Yeah, business. Sure, I get it."

"Do you?"

"Yeah. You want certain things, certain...people that you can't find in fucking Wal*Mart. You think Jack'll give you what you need. Business." There was a sharp edge to his voice now, something that was old and bitter.

Paul pressed his lips together. "You're right. Jack does have something I need."

Kyle chuckled.

"But it's not what you think."

"Sure it isn't."

"Jack has someone I want."

Kyle gave him a skeptical look. Paul took a deep breath, wondering if he should—then thought *fuck it*. If Kyle's going to put his ass on the line and he would if Paul had anything to say about, then it might as well be worth his while.

"Twinkie."

Confusion flashed across Kyle's face before recognition flowed over. Which in turn unleashed awful, braying laughter. He doubled over, slapping his leg.

"Twinkie? *Twinkie*? Oh my—Oh my fucking *God*, Twinkie! Yeah, okay, man, I thought you looked familiar." He dissolved into laughter again.

Paul bit his tongue, waiting for the laughter to wear itself out.

"Here—Here I am thinking you—oh man, shit, this is—frigging funny. Wow! Twinkie and you, ah, you want him back. Sounds like a bad movie." He laughed again, wiping at his eyes. "Wait 'til I tell Gavin about this, man. He was so pissed that night you almost broke his arm. He's gonna lose his shit when I tell him about this."

"Yeah," Paul said tightly. "Hysterical, isn't it?"

"So what's the deal, man?" Kyle said breathlessly, finally getting himself under control. "You find Jack, go in with guns blazing, rescue Twinkie then the two of you ride off into the sunset together?"

"It's not like that."

"Oh, no?" Kyle smirked cruelly. "Then what's it like? You love him? You tell him that you'd never hurt him? That he's special? That no one will ever come between you? That no one else even comes *close*?"

Paul glared. "Actually, no."

"No?"

"I tell him to keep him clothes on because I don't want to see some motherfucker's fingerprints on his shoulders. I tell him to sleep in a separate room and to eat chocolate chip pancakes and drink chocolate milk. I took him shopping because I didn't want him wearing what he had on the night my boss thought it'd be funny to give him to me as a fucking present. I tell him to eat at my kitchen table instead of kneeling on the floor. I tell him to call me by my name because it makes me fucking sick to be called anything else."

By the time he took a breath, he had backed Kyle up into the chain-link fence and he was so close to the kid he could see the clear outline of his pupils. Kyle wasn't smiling anymore. He stared up at Paul much the same way Ethan had when Paul had demanded that he sit at the table to eat breakfast. It seemed like years since that had happened. Several beats went by before Kyle asked, "And did he?"

"Did he what?"

Kyle's jaw flexed as if he were thinking. "Did he call you by your name?"

"Yes."

The look on Kyle's face was unreadable and Paul didn't have it in him to figure out what was going on behind those old blue eyes. So he waited, watching as Kyle pursed his lips and tried to put some space between them. But the fence wasn't going anywhere. Kyle's hands flexed, trembling slightly as if he wanted to push Paul away but didn't want to touch him. "You know he might not even be alive, right?" he finally said in a forced matter-of-fact tone. "Especially since people had to come looking for him."

An unwanted picture of Mel poped up in his brain. "Does that happen a lot?"

Kyle's mouth twisted. "Sometimes. Depending on how big the client list is."

"And is the client list big?"

The look on Kyle's face turned sour. "What the fuck do you think?"

"You tell me," Paul replied. "If the client list is that big, then there's no reason why you would be out here."

Surprise lit up Kyle's face but it disappeared quickly. "You don't know what the fuck you're talking about."

"The hell I don't."

"Please," he scoffed. "You think you know how the business works because you're in some profound fucking relationship with a piece of ass?"

"I'm pretty sure it's not hard to figure out. Just like it's not hard to figure out that the only reason you're out here, in the freezing-ass cold, is because you need to play catch-up."

A tic jumped beneath Kyle's right eye. "There's nothing—" His voice caught and he cleared his throat to try again. "There's nothing wrong with earning a little extra."

Paul nodded. "Right. Extra that you need to accrue in order to make up for the fact you're getting too old for most of your clients."

The tic became more pronounced. A small noise came from Kyle's throat as if something had grabbed his balls in a tight, hard grip. "How—How do you—are you—are you a cop or something?" he demanded, his voice trembling now. "I—I don't—"

He broke off, floundering, suddenly looking so confused that Paul felt the first stirrings of sympathy. He softened his voice. "I'm not a cop. I—"

"Then how do you know this?" Kyle exploded. "Christ, how do you know that I've been—that I've been trying and—and Jack—God, he just wants more all the time and I'm out here for fucking hours and—"

"Take me to him," Paul insisted. "Please. If you want to be done with this, please, tell me how to get there."

"Done with what?" Kyle said harshly. "Done with—shit, I've been doing this for so long, I don't—I don't fucking *know* anything else, man. What the fuck am I supposed to do? I can't—"

"You can tell me where he is."

Kyle suddenly laughed and it was hollow, full of rusty nails. "Oh yeah, what a great fucking idea. I can tell you where he is and suddenly all will be right with the world." He gave him a nasty leer. "You think it'll be that easy, tough guy? I tell you what you want to know, you go swooping in like a goddamn superhero and then what?"

Paul stayed silent, since he hadn't quite worked out that part of his plan yet.

"It gonna be like a smash-and-grab or something? You break down the door, demanding that Twinkie be turned over to you? Or better yet, you put a gun to Jack's head, sure, because threatening him will surely get you what you want." Kyle shook his head. "You don't stand a fucking chance, asshole. But hey, I'll give you an A for effort."

Paul stared at him, unmoving. He couldn't think of a damn thing to say because everything the kid had just said was right. He didn't even have a plan. He looked away from him and ran a tired hand over his face. He half-heard Kyle light a cigarette.

"Don't look so glum, man." He chuckled. "You're not the first person to be Prince Fucking Charming."

Paul looked at him. "No?"

"No." Kyle shook his head. "But since I'm probably going to be dead soon, anyway, here."

He took a business card from his back pocket.

Paul took it, flipping it over to read the embossed gold lettering. Silently, he met Kyle's eyes through a haze of smoke.

Kyle smiled.

CHAPTER 46

To maintain some kind of dignity, Paul slipped Kyle a hundred-dollar-bill. The kid had taken it with a knowing smile and sauntered off, as if he hadn't just been bullied into giving out information. Paul made it back to the car, where he all but collapsed behind the wheel. The card crinkled between his fingers and he let his head fall back against the headrest. He closed his eyes, feeling nauseous. Surprisingly, Kyle's presence had kept it mostly at bay but now in his absence, reality was an ice-cold shock of what lay ahead.

Kyle's derision rang in Paul's ears and he couldn't shake its effect. He felt like he was being slowly crushed. Every inhale of breath was a struggle, and he vaguely wondered if maybe he was having a heart attack. He fought to open his eyes, blinking away the gritty feeling beneath his eyelids. His instincts, far-away and poking at the back of his brain like a child's curious fingers, demanded that he snap out of it and come up with some kind of a goddamn plan because right now, he was falling into a fog. A shiver ran down his spine like an insect. He clenched his hand around the steering wheel and pulled himself up straighter in the seat. He ached. Every bone, every muscle was coated with wet cement and all he wanted to do was—

"Cortez."

Paul jumped, letting out an embarrassing shout loud enough that he was glad the windows were shut. He jerked around in his seat to find Chac Mool sitting, no, lounging in the back seat. He was draped in a long, black, wool coat with the collar turned up to frame his face, black trousers, and shoes. One leg was drawn up onto the car seat and his hands were in his pockets. He honestly looked like he was posing at a photo shoot. But his eyes, green and fiery, drilled into Paul's face and Paul could only stare stupidly at him.

"What are you doing here?"

The look he was given was entirely too much like a well-fed lion.

"Checking for progress."

Paul frowned, peering out through all of the windows before meeting his gaze once more. "I don't need a babysitter."

"No? That was quite a confrontation you had with that boy."

Paul felt his face flush. He wasn't sure if it was from the way he'd treated Kyle or if it was the fact that Chac Mool was watching him.

Making sure no one snuck up on his prize.

His teeth clenched hard and he glared at him. "Do you really give a shit about that?"

Chac Mool raised an eyebrow. "Of course I do. I have quite a bit invested in you, Cortez. It would be a shame for me to wait for the chance to take you only to have you fall victim to some senseless tragedy."

"Your concern is touching."

Chac Mool's eyes sparkled. "You were antagonizing him."

"Excuse me?"

"You were. Deliberately, I might add."

Paul's eyes narrowed.

Chac Mool chuckled and it held the slightest edge of danger. "I saw you. I heard the words you spoke. You knew what kind of effect they would have on him."

Paul's flush deepened. He blinked hard then spat out, "It was the only way to get what I needed."

Chac Mool moved his head in a half-nod. "And perhaps a good way to cheat me."

"What? What're you—wait, are you insinuating that I started a fight with *a kid* on purpose so I could get myself killed?"

Chac Mool gave a strange smile that made Paul acutely aware of how small the car was.

"He wasn't even armed."

"Perhaps you were hoping that he was."

"Look," Paul snapped before this got completely out of hand. "If I wanted to cheat you, I would've blown my own head off by now. Or slit my wrists or jumped off a goddamn bridge. I gave you my word. Remember? I don't really appreciate you accusing me of doing otherwise. I told you I needed time and I'm using it the best I can. I'd probably be making a lot more *progress* if I didn't have to participate in these little chats with you. So seriously, just back the fuck off, let me take care of this and then you can use my head as a fucking lampshade, all right?"

In hindsight, Paul would say it was pure mental exhaustion taking temporary control of his vocal cords. Could anyone really blame him? He was going four or more days without sleep, trying to find this fucking kid who had eluded him while he took a shower, not to mention being shadowed by a man who apparently found it fun to keep reminding him that his days were numbered. There was no mistake, however. Paul was scared shitless of what was to come. But right now, at this

very moment, he was just too damn tired to care. He was almost positive that Chac Mool wouldn't kill him here, in broad daylight in the
parking lot of a retail store. But telling this man to fuck off probably
wasn't the smartest thing to do, if the look in his eyes was anything to
go by.

As if pulled by strings, Chac Mool drew himself in and slid forward to the edge of his seat. His eyes were bottomless and steadfast
and, despite the heat of his impromptu rant, Paul felt himself growing
smaller and smaller. The steering wheel dug into his side and he was
suddenly not so certain that Chac Mool wouldn't kill him here.

"Are you attempting to anger me on purpose?" Chac Mool asked,
his voice dropping to that strange, vibrating hiss so that it was like a
torrential downpour had taken up residence inside the car.

"No, no," Paul found himself answering in a wilted voice.

"No?"

Paul held his breath as Chac Mool continued to stare at him. His
long fingers appeared on top of the headrest, lightly caressing the material.

"I think you are," he murmured. "I think you want me to kill you
now."

Paul's nerves frayed, his throat went dry.

"I think you want me to take your head now in order to save your
child—"

"*No*—"

"—but please know that even if you will not bring him to me, I
will surely find him."

"That's not what I'm—I'm trying—"

"Your sacrifice would surely be in vain," Chac Mool continued,
talking easily over Paul's stuttered words. "But if that's not your intention, the only other reason I can think of is that you don't want to find
your child at all—"

"Of course, I do!"

"—for the simple fact that you fear what you will have to face."

Paul's protests stuck in his throat. He sagged back against the car
door, emitting a choked sort of whimper. Curiosity lurked in Chac
Mool's eyes. Paul's brain sizzled out.

Jesus.

"Am I right?" Chac Mool said quietly.

Paul stared at him, feeling something deep inside lift up under his
gaze. He struggled to force it back down. "Don't psycho-analyze me,"
he said, trying for conviction.

Chac Mool only slid closer. "Tell me."

Paul jerked his head in a weird kind of nod, wanting to look away from the probing green depths but finding he was unable to. A million things began to tumble through his head, as if erupted from a broken levee.

"There's—nothing to tell," he whispered.

That strange balloon feeling swelled against his rib cage and he took a few panicked breaths, keeping it quelled. The look in Chac Mool's eyes was earnest now and Paul tried again to look away, swallowing hard.

"Tell me," Chac Mool whispered. "Tell me what you fear."

Paul felt the words against his face, felt them brand his skin.

"I will listen," Chac Mool was saying now, his voice like melted butter, like smooth chocolate, coaxing and soothing.

Paul looked sharply at him, blinking hard against the heat that was pressing against the backs of his eyeballs.

"I will listen."

The swell rose through his chest once more and this time, it broke through savagely and Paul was helpless to contain it. Looking into the ever-reaching green of Chac Mool's eyes, where everything seemed silent, serene and still, where it called to him, Paul let it all bubble forth in an uncontrollable tide.

Everything came out—his parents' deaths and him running, running, running until he became ensnared in a violent, depraved web created by Jack, which in turn led to the hell conducted by Aaron. He left nothing out and he didn't understand why, *why* it was coming so easily. He was unloading his entire life on a man who wanted to *kill* him, who wanted to take his vital extremities and add them to his collection, who wanted to make his death as worthy as his life wasn't.

The words tumbled over one another, shaking and clipped, like starbursts in the air. There was a river of faces, voices, hands that coursed through his mind, singing darkness and pain. It was easy to become immersed in it but strangely, Chac Mool's presence was an anchor, holding him firmly in the present, not letting him or unable to let him get washed away. He didn't know how long he spoke. By the time silence fell between them, his voice had grown rough, his throat sore and parched. He licked his lips, waiting for a feeling of relief to come over him, like in all the movies he'd seen. Talk and everything will be fine. Life will go on and you'll be happy.

But the feeling never came.

In fact nothing came except for more silence. The faint noises from outside the car worked their way in, sounding weirdly normal. He turned his head and looked at his backseat passenger.

Chac Mool was staring hard at him, his face blank. He didn't even appear to be breathing. Paul contemplated snapping his fingers in his face but thought that might get his fingers chopped off. Then Chac Mool moved, sliding back into the seat, his coat scraping against the upholstery. His eyes never left Paul's face. "I don't believe you."

The words were like ice water and for a moment, Paul could do nothing but gape at him.

"Which part?"

"All of it."

"Are you serious?"

"Do I not look serious?"

Shaking his head in disbelief, he said, "I don't—You wanted me to tell you."

"Yes."

"And you don't believe me?"

"No."

Paul fixed him with a sharp look. "And just what the hell were you expecting?"

"The truth."

The words were cold, indifferent and Paul couldn't help but feel like he'd just been played, very, very badly. He sucked in a deep breath. Disbelief was morphing into an indignant anger and it was inching across his skin like a bad sunburn. He fought for calm, tried to see it from Chac Mool's point of view. "Okay, look, I can see how some parts of it may seem kind of—fucking fantastic or something," Paul forced out. "But why would I make any of this up?"

"To hide."

"Hide? Hide what? I've laid everything out for you."

"This story—"

"It's not a story," Paul cut in sharply. "Jesus, my imagination is not that good or that perverted and, as you know, I'm running out of time to play games."

Chac Mool looked down his nose at him. "You will play games for as long as it extends your life."

Paul's hands trembled. "You son-of-a-bitch. What the *fuck* do you think is going on here? You're going to kill me. I am going to die. By your hand. I already know that. I have no fucking reason to lie to you. And after everything that's happened—"

"And what has happened?" Chac Mool demanded, his voice like hot metal. "I've seen you try to steal from me. I've seen you working with people who hoped to rob me. I've seen you spin your words, try-ing to find some loophole so I won't do what I've done to dozens before you who thought they could out-smart me. And now you give me this tale, this *farce*."

Paul flinched back as if he'd been struck.

"People who have come from stories such as yours take their own lives, Cortez," Chac Mool hissed at him, his eyes blazing with cold fury. "They do not know how to function in society. They can't survive. It's a proven fact, one that I've seen countless of times. But yet, here you are, a grown man, one who has risen above all this turmoil and pain." He shook his head, his upper lip curling with disgust. "No, I do not believe it and I do not believe you. You have fought me so hard to stay alive and why? After supposedly being through so much, how can you *want* to live?"

Paul's mouth moved mutely.

Chac Mool gave him an ugly smile. "Death will be a reprieve for you, Cortez. You'll be at peace. You and your child."

He flung open the car door and climbed out. The blast of outside air made Paul jump. Chac Mool leaned back in, his face tight against the cold but the smile was still there.

"You have until sundown, Cortez."

He slammed the door before Paul could even think to respond.

CHAPTER 47

Exhausted, Paul could do nothing but helplessly close his eyes and allow himself to sleep. It was uncomfortable, cramped, and the visions that his brain manifested were horrifying, snapping him awake after a half an hour.

He decided to start moving. Any more time spent sitting in this Wal*Mart parking lot and someone was liable to call the cops. He drove aimlessly, clenching the steering wheel as if it were Chac Mool's neck.

That fucking asshole.

The frigid disbelief, *Jesus*, it was excruciating, making him think of so many people who looked upon him, who acted out upon him, thinking it was okay to fuck a child, to ram their cock down his throat because he was simply *here* and if he was here, there was a reason for it and the reason was that he *obviously* liked it because if he didn't like it, why would he be here? And there had a been a few, a precious few who wanted to *know*, who had looked at him the same way Chac Mool had—all serious compassion, revered sympathy, ready to listen while their cum cooled on Paul's inner thighs. And he had told them and when he was finished, the looks in their eyes had been the same.

Disbelief, incredulity, doubt and a certainty that he might be a little bit nuts.

Anger flooded through his veins and he welcomed it. He would need it for where he was going.

He wanted to wait until full dark to do this. It was safer, easier to hide—*from everyone, even the angels*—but that wouldn't do. Not if that green-eyed son-of-a-bitch had anything to say about it. So Paul drove, stopping for food and gas. It was nearly two in the afternoon when he decided to head for hell. He read and re-read the address, making sure he knew where he was going. It was beyond the reaches of the city, in the sticks. Always in the sticks. He recalled coming out here on assignment once. The target had been an avid hunter and Paul had left his body for the animals.

The woods were thick, bare, and unwelcoming. The pothole-filled road barely accommodated his vehicle as he bounced and rolled, his teeth jarring with every dip. He was sure the bottom of the car was going to drop out at any minute. Tree branches scraped at his windows. Snowdrifts were skidded with dirt and dead leaves. It was a barren wasteland and it made him wonder what mode of transportation Kyle used to get out of here and into the city. It was at least a two-hour car ride.

Anything for the almighty dollar.

'*Park your car before you get to the bridge,*' Kyle had reluctantly told him. '*It's about a half mile to the farm. You'll have to walk if you don't want to be seen.*'

The farm.

Paul could just hear the sales pitch: *Where we harvest the solutions to your deepest desires*!

His stomach roiled and he tasted the hamburger he'd eaten for lunch. The bridge loomed ahead. He braked, gaping a little uncertainly through the windshield. It was a covered bridge for Pete's sake, painted a rich red and complete with sturdy wooden beams crossing the ceiling. It was something straight out of *Little House on the Prairie*.

Homey.

Comfy.

You'll be safe here.

He pulled off the road. There was no going back now. With hands that shook too much, he armed himself to the teeth.

Guns, extra clips, knives, a wire pick, a small pair of binoculars, and small strips of clothes for make-shift tourniquets. He hoped he wasn't forgetting anything.

'*There's security,*' Kyle had advised with a grim look. '*They're pretty good too, loaded with just about everything. Might want to change your mind and bring a small army with you.*'

'*How many?*'

Kyle had hesitated long enough that Paul thought he was dodging the question. Then he realized that Kyle was mentally counting.

'*Between twenty and thirty.*'

Paul wasn't worried. His instincts were in full-combat mode, giddily happy to be doing something productive for once. Taking a deep steadying breath, he climbed from the car. The air was still but bitingly cold. He thought about leaving his coat in the car since it would probably hinder his movements. But one whiff of the frigid air and he knew he'd probably drop of hypothermia before getting anywhere near his destination.

He crossed the bridge. His footsteps echoed like hollow gunshots. As he came out the other side, he was abruptly aware of the air smelling different. It was just as cold but there was a strange tense feeling of *waiting*. Like the moment of stillness before a tiger pounced.

It was silly, he thought but the farther he walked, the thicker it grew.

Heavy, heavy anticipation.

He wondered if his mind was playing tricks on him.

But then just as suddenly as he'd registered the difference in the air, there was movement behind him, rushing and sudden.

A switch flipped in his head.

Squatting low, he spun and kicked his leg out. Air whined over his head and he caught a long flash of silver. A black-clad figure hit the ground in front of him then rolled back up as if on springs. Paul took a quick step back, keeping himself just outside of arm's reach.

"Who are you?" the man barked. "You're trespassing."

His face was flushed red from the cold. He looked to be around Paul's age with blond hair cut close to his scalp and quick, assessing blue eyes. His jaw was hard and square like a block of granite. Paul had no doubt that he'd probably break his hand if he tried to punch him. He regarded Paul with blatant mistrust if the machete clenched in his hand was anything to go by. Paul blinked at it in surprise.

Jesus, what kind of place is Jack running here?

It could only mean one thing.

Jack had come too close to getting caught.

Paul gave the man a quick once-over, noting the holstered gun at one hip and a walkie-talkie at the other.

"You're trespassing, shitbag," the man barked again.

Paul held his hands up, schooling his face to appear harmless. "Okay, okay, man, look, just calm down, all right? I think I might be lost or something—"

"No shit, Einstein. You happen to take a look around?"

"I know, I know," Paul said, blinking innocently. "Could you help me out or something? You got a phone? My cell phone died and my car—" He lashed out with his hand, catching his fist on the man's nose.

The man dropped the machete and fell back as blood sprayed from his nostrils, his cry muffled by his hands flying to his face. Paul hit him again and knocked him out, laying him flat on his back. The man sprawled, limbs every which way, blood leaking steadily from his busted nose. Paul squatted next to him, casting quick glances around. He eyed the walkie-talkie, guessing that the man must've relayed his position before making his move to take Paul down.

With a freaking machete.

Shaking his head, he looked down at the long blade that winked in the weak sunlight. He could've been taken out with a gun but the man had chosen the knife instead.

Because it was quieter. Messy but quieter.

In the woods, in the middle of winter, gunshots carried for miles.

He took a deep breath and grabbed the walkie-talkie.

Then he began to run.

CHAPTER 48

Taking the road was suicide but the snow was too deep on either side of him. It would take him twice as long through the snow but he would have cover, at least. Paul glanced up through the trees, watching the sun sink lower and lower in the sky. His breath pushed out in front of his face in a long cold exhale.

To hell with it.

Trotting silently along the side of the road, he found an open channel on the walkie-talkie, allowing him to listen in on security's conversations. So far, there was no panic, no mention of anyone not checking in, no demand for an update about a supposed trespasser. But it was only a matter of time before that changed. Paul increased his pace, stopping every thirty or forty feet to duck behind a tree and use the binoculars. They were high-powered and clear as a bell. He easily spotted three men to his right who he wouldn't have been able to see with his naked eye. There was one man straight ahead, taking a smoke break against the base of a huge pine tree. Two more to his left at nine and ten o'clock.

Paul chewed on the inside of his cheek, weighing his options.

He put the binoculars away and turned the walkie-talkie volume all the way down before shoving it into his coat pocket.

Keeping low, he ran at a half-crouch at the very edge of the road. He dodged and leapt over the enormous potholes, now thinking that they were probably put in on purpose to wave off anyone curious enough to drive down here. The shadows were getting longer, deeper in some places.

He caught a whiff of cigarette smoke on the wind. He slowed down, darting behind a huge tangle of fallen tree branches. Through the binoculars, he could see the man, at least forty feet away, leaning against the tree now, smoke in hand, eyes at half-mast like he was trying to stay awake.

Paul hurried forward, moving through the snow as quietly as he could. He carefully pulled out his Smith & Wesson, creeping closer.

He was nearly on top of the man before his presence was finally realized. But by then it was too late and Paul had pistol-whipped him into unconsciousness.

No sooner had the body settled to the ground when there was an eruption of shouts from behind him. Without even looking, Paul took off at a sprint, hitting the road and running full-out. The volume of shouts intensified, carried in the wind like the curses and omens Chac Mool had spoken about. Paul caught dark flashes of movement from the corner of his eye, streaking toward him like missiles. Something whizzed past his ear, thrumming into the bark of a tree as he stormed past it. He flinched as something else brushed the side of his head like the touch of a hand and he saw an honest-to-God arrow striking a snow bank on his right. He wanted to say that he was relatively lucky that they weren't shooting bullets but they were still shooting at him and their accuracy, while not very good, wasn't terribly bad either.

He kept moving. He still had his gun in his hand, slick with blood but he wasn't going to try and take aim. It would only give them a better chance of locking in on him. He ran faster, nearly tumbling headfirst into a two-foot wide hole in the road. He hurled himself over it.

Glancing up, he saw someone running perpendicular to him, striving to cut him off at about twenty feet ahead. Paul saw the crossbow in his hands, saw the way he bounded through the snow like a deer.

Paul took aim and fired without breaking stride.

The gun blast ricocheted up toward the trees where a flock of birds took off with a huge, collective protest.

The man went down with a cry and Paul tore past him.

"Shots fired! Shots fired!" came from far too close.

There was a break in the trees and he saw what looked like a huge silo, rusty from disuse, but rising tall and proud through the tree canopy.

Thunderous footsteps were gaining. He reached deep, searching for that extra bit of energy that would pull him ahead but *dammit—no*, his legs wouldn't respond.

A half-strangled sound came from his throat. His heart felt ready to burst, his lungs ached. *Just a little bit farther, just a little bit...*

Someone shrieked from behind him and the sound was so close, Paul ducked his head. He braved a glance over his shoulder.

Then tripped and went down, face-first. The ground was as cold as the air and his chin smacked against it, hard enough to send his teeth through his bottom lip. The world went white for a second or two. Blood gushed down his chin and with a breathless grunt, he managed to push himself up on all fours. The hard-packed earth and gravel bit into his palms and knees. He heard feet scuffling frantically from be-hind him, the sound propelling him to his feet. He staggered, wiping at the blood on his face with the back of his hand.

The sudden hush around him pierced his ears and he turned.

The temperature was dropping. There was ice already forming along the edges of the blood that was splashed across the road.

The men, Paul counted seven, who had descended upon him like a swarm of jackals, lay strewn about like dolls left on the floor after playtime. The nearest one was four feet away from Paul's right boot, face-down, a white, white hand reached above its head, fingers curled into the road, reaching for a knife that lay just beyond its reach. Blood was moving sluggishly out from under the head, slowly filling in the imperfections of the road like hot, melted macadam.

Paul raised his eyes to the trees. The sun had disappeared but the sky was still light. He could feel frost forming on the inside of his coat collar. A twig snapped off to his left. He knew who was out here with him.

He ran.

CHAPTER 49

He was going in blind.

It was the worst kind of scenario but there were no other options and he was out of time. The farmhouse came into view like a postcard. A sprawling, two-story, pristine-white structure with a wrap-around porch, red shutters, and hills that rolled on forever. It didn't appear to be a working farm, at least not in the way it normally meant, but there was still a hint of manure, mud, and animal lingering in the air. A big horse coral was set up next to the house and beyond that was the giant silo that Paul had seen from the woods. The road led to a two-car garage and a path was shoveled to the front steps.

Paul shot the three men who were coming out of the front door. Chills chased down his spine when he heard more screams from behind him. But he didn't dare turn around to see Chac Mool working his particular brand of magic.

Drawing closer to the open front door, Paul felt his heart try to jump from his chest. The darkness beyond the threshold tugged at him like wires caught around his limbs, cutting deep into his flesh. He went quickly, willingly, crossing into that darkness, feeling it lift up then close behind him like the lid of a coffin. He stepped over the bodies that lay half on the front porch and half in the foyer, blood leaking, limbs twitching ever so slightly.

He ignored them, coming to a stop and roaring at the top of his lungs, "Ethan!"

The house was dark, lit only by the fading daylight through the windows and upon his entry, had stopped breathing. He stood there, snow leaking onto the hardwood floor from his boots, his muscles on fire, listening. And he knew, he *sensed* that those who occupied this house were listening too. Without moving any other part of his body, his eyes cut to the left where a double set of wooden doors shielded a room from view. This he knew would be the viewing room. A room that a client was taken to in order to see what his choices were that matched his criteria. To his right, a set of French glass doors stood open in welcome, inviting him into a room with a stone hearth that crackled comfortably with a fire, wingback chairs, shelves of books that reached to the ceiling, and several different cigar boxes on the coffee table.

And the whiskey decanters in finely-cut crystal.

It was a regular gentlemen's club.

Directly before him was a curving staircase and there was a door beneath the steps, cracked open slightly, revealing a soft, flickering light from beyond. It drew Paul like a moth to flame.

A floorboard creaked overhead.

He stopped, looking up. Then he glanced back down at the door. The light glowed warmly.

It's safe here.

He backed away and made for the stairs.

He took them two at a time. The shadows deepened, clogging the corners and the ceiling. It seemed to grow darker the higher he climbed, the air hotter and thicker. It made his fingers flex around the gun in his hand. He made it to the top step and that was when the smell hit him. His eyes watered from too much Pine-Sol and ammonia that did nothing to cut the underlying stench of stale sweat and sex. He blinked the sweat out of his eyes, feeling it bead along his scalp as he quickly rounded the first corner he came to.

Keep moving, keep moving, he chanted to himself. *Do not stop and think about this. Just keep going.* The hallway stretched about thirty feet in front of him before it veered sharply to the right. It was dusty-gray with shadows, dim from lack of light. Wall-mounted sconces were unlit. The window at the far end was painted black. He ventured forward, carefully as if wading through unchartered waters. Holding the gun out in front of him, he slid quietly to the next corner. He stopped, ears strained.

It was still.

Too still, like the house was waiting for something to happen. Like Paul was waiting for something to happen. Sucking in a chemical-laden breath, he ducked around the corner. He halted about five feet down, back pressed to the wall, listening and watching once more. There was another window at the end of the hallway, covered with black paint except for a small diagonal strip in the center, allowing only the faintest of light inside. It was enough so that Paul could see, through the murky gray, the doors on either side of the hall.

Six on each side.

All the doors were closed and each one had an eye-slot cut into it. High up, at about Paul's height. A wire mesh screen covered it from the outside. A trickle of sweat, cold and slow, inched its way down the side of Paul's face.

'Come on. Come on, put on a nice show for the nice gentleman here. He just wants to watch you, okay? No big deal. Come on. Yeah, that's it, turn around. A little more—a little more...'

He swallowed hard, feeling the trembling in his skin, down to his bones. Pushing hard against the memories, he approached the first door on his right. He gave the doorknob a hard twist.

Locked.

Reluctantly, he felt his gaze pulled to the eye slot, to the little push-handle and he stared against his will, feeling entranced as if trapped by a poisonous snake.

Oh my God, man, come on, you don't want to see this, do you? Why the fuck are you torturing yourself?

He slid the slot open, surprised at how noiseless it was. He looked inside.

His lungs shook, ready to close up shop and get the hell out of dodge. A strange noise came from his throat that was a half-laugh, half-something broken.

Soft light came from a small lamp perched on a pink nightstand. It stood next to a twin-sized bed, adorned with pink sheets, lace-edged pillows, and a thick comforter covered in white and purple butterflies. The walls were a pale pink that seemed to shimmer depending on what way you moved. A huge dollhouse took up one corner of the room while a low table with two chairs took up another. A pink plastic tea-pot sat on the table top alongside two pink tea cups. It was adorable. Adorable and so sick. He stared at the room until his eyes were ready to bleed out of his head. He pulled himself away from the door when he saw the furry pink manacles hanging from the bed post.

Sickness crawled up his throat like a swarm of angry bees. His brain was already screaming as he went to the next door, peering in through watery eyes. Again the room was empty but there were Star Wars posters on dark blue walls. A bean-bag chair made to look like a soccer ball lay in one corner. A desk covered in drawings in the other, drawings of happy, smiling stick figures and running dogs.

A tube of lubricant sat on the night table next to an Ewok alarm clock.

Paul squeezed his eyes shut hard enough to see spots. His chest constricted so tightly, he couldn't breathe. He tripped over his feet, running down the hallway, wanting to see but not, needing to see but unable to give a reason why, burning the controlled, sick fantasies into his mind—the video games, the pajamas laid out neatly, the ballerina outfit, the little dresser filled with make-up and plastic jewelry, the soccer cleats, the baseball glove, the easel with watercolors arching across the papers in rainbows, daises and sunshine.

Then he came to the last room at the end of the hallway. His whirling, screeching thoughts hit a sudden brick wall with a loud, painful, wet-sounding *splat*.

Oh, Jesus.

The room was lit by a single bare bulb hanging from the ceiling. The walls were barren, earth-toned, splattered with the faint outlines of stains that no amount of ammonia could get out. Darker splotches dotted the floor around the solitary wooden chair that sat in the center of the room. Black leather straps hung limply from the arm rests. More straps snaked across the floor from the chair's front legs. In front of the chair was a low wooden table. White lines cut grooves into its surface and it only took Paul a second to realize that they were fingernail scratches. A beat-up wooden cabinet stood in the far corner, its doors slightly open. He could see the edges of a bull-whip. He wondered if it was the same one Jack had always been so fond of using.

This was the core of it. This was where it was laid bare to anyone with the gift of sight. This was where monsters were created, where they destroyed, where they broke the weak. There were no happy pictures here, no fantasies, no dress-up. This was for the ones who knew damn well what they were doing and didn't care. They didn't try to hide it with gifts and toys and ice cream. This was where the darkness was, omnipotent and cruel in its entirety and judging by the darker stains on the floor, irregular-shaped, dried, and brown, almost black, very few could harness it. Very few could survive it.

He took an unsteady step back. Teetering on a knife's edge, he howled, "Ethan!"

Rage pulsed, abrupt and loud, inside of him. He turned in an endless, frenzied circle, the need so great now to find him, to get him away from all of this, to get himself away from all of this that Paul nearly missed the small voice from behind him.

"Hello."

He spun wildly, almost blind with anger. His finger tightened on the trigger of the gun in his hand and he almost squeezed off a wild shot. Through his reddened vision, he saw the door in front of him, saw that the eye-slot was still open. It was a room full of fairies, the walls painted like a meadow. Little twinkling lights hung from the ceiling and he'd been pretty damn sure that the room had been empty when he first looked inside.

He hit the door with a soft gasp and peered in.

A little girl, no older than nine, sat on the bed, facing the door. She smiled at him, open and trusting. Her big brown eyes sparkled with youth and humor. Her brown hair was pulled back into a ponytail; wispy bangs hung in front of her smooth white forehead. She was dressed like a fairy, complete with shimmery wings, tights, and a dress that shone with blues and violets. The sight of her made him want to fall to his knees, the anger that had nearly consumed him just seconds before, crumbling beneath the weight of this small, fragile creature locked inside of a nightmare. She seemed to ripple as he stared at her like he was looking at her through plastic film. Paul wiped at his eyes, squinting, wondering if perhaps she was nothing more than a hallucination. Maybe she was something that his overtaxed brain had conjured up to keep him from making the wrong move. Her small, slippered feet swung freely above the floor, lightly bumping the side of the bed. The twinkling lights from above illuminated her smooth white arms. Her skin seemed to sparkle.

Fairy dust, he thought numbly.

He started to think that there was something familiar about her but then she asked him in a voice high-pitched, innocent and so fucking young, "Would you like to come in and play with me?"

He had to try several times to find his voice. "Uh, no, no honey, that's all right."

"But isn't that why you're here?"

He took a painful breath. "No. I'm—I'm looking for someone."

She gave him a curious look. "Are you playing hide-and-seek?"

Jesus, God. Paul felt like his heart was about to break.

"Kind of. Listen, sweetheart, could you—"

"Melinda."

"What?"

"That's my name. Melinda. You can call me Melinda if you want to. What's your name?"

He swallowed. "Paul."

She giggled. "Your voice sounds funny. You're not nervous, are you?"

"I—no."

She nodded. "Good."

The look she gave him was heavy and expectant. "If you want to come in, you'll have to find Uncle Jack so he can unlock the door."

Paul's fingers bit into the small mesh screen covering the eye slot. "Uncle Jack? Do you know where I can find him?"

"He's probably at the silo."

"The silo?"

"Yup. He always goes there before it gets dark."

"What's in the silo, Melinda? Do you know?"

She shook her head. "Only the bad kids go there."

His heart lurched. "The bad kids, huh?"

"Uh-huh."

"Why only the bad kids?"

"Because, silly, they don't follow the rules."

"What kind of rules?"

She swung her feet harder now. "You have to eat your food, do your chores, smile for everyone, and never, ever run away."

"Really?"

"Yup. 'Cuz then you go to the silo."

Paul leaned back, biting his lip. Then he said, "Okay, look, Melinda, I'm going to go to silo, find Uncle Jack and then come right back here and get you out. Okay? How's that sound?"

A small frown graced her features. "Why?"

"What?"

"You don't have to get me out. You come in here. I don't come out there."

"But—"

"This is where I belong. You leave. I stay."

He blinked. "But don't—don't you want to go home?"

She flinched as if he'd struck her. "Home is bad. I get hurt at home."

"Don't you get hurt here?"

She brightened. "Nope. I get lots of ice cream here. Chocolate chip, too. It's my favorite. I get it all the time because I'm a good girl."

Her eyes were almost fever-bright as they drilled into his and Paul found himself backing away under the force of it.

He half-stumbled, half-ran back the way he'd come.

"Hurry up so we can play," followed him down the steps and out onto the porch.

Bile rose in the back of his throat. He leaned over the railing and vomited.

CHAPTER 50

The silo rose, massive and sinister into the air. Paul stared up at it, still tasting the vomit in the back of his throat. It was kind of surprising how easily he threw up nowadays. He was never the puking type. Sure, he'd upchucked after his first few blowjobs, even had a wicked stomach virus when he was eight and couldn't keep anything down, not even his mother's chicken soup, but as an adult? Never puked once, not even after washing blood and bits of brain matter out of his hair or picking someone else's flesh out from under his fingernails. Now, however, it didn't seem to take much.

Hell, *he* didn't think he could take much more of anything. Especially not this silo.

'*Where all the bad kids go.*'

The words circled in his head like a bad nursery rhyme. He was only ninety-eight percent sure that Ethan was inside. The other two percent, he didn't want to think about. Glancing around, he saw that dusk had almost completely settled, turning the shadows into deep shades of purple. The tree line was a ways off, pushed back to the edge of the farm, where the trees stood like frozen soldiers, silently looking on from their chilly posts, unable or unwilling to offer any form of comfort or aide to what he had to do. The silo stood, front and center, like the iron-fisted commander of a tired, somnolent army that was too exhausted, too fatigued and too disenchanted to offer up much of a salute. Paul was willing to bet that ol' Uncle Jack had soundproofed this structure, finely tuned it to be ground zero for his thriving business. There hadn't been a silo when Paul had been under his watch.

But there had been a basement.

Something soft and light touched the hollow spot behind his ear. He turned and saw Kelly…

‰

'*Come back to bed, babe,*' she murmured from beneath the covers.

The silver light of the moon glowed on her smooth bare shoulder as she held out a hand to him. He leaned down, pressed his lips to her sleep-warm skin.

'*I won't be long,*' he murmured.

Her hand slid away, disappearing back under the shadows of the blankets, cocooned in warmth. A small frown of disappointment creased her pretty face before smoothing away under the advancement of sleep. The heated taste of her skin burnt his mouth and when he swiped his tongue over his lips, he tasted…

☙☙☙

…cold air and dry, cracked skin.

He shivered again, blinking hard as his vision blurred.

He was going to die here.

And it wasn't going to be by Chac Mool's hand.

The surprising presence of a scream jumped up the back of his throat and he was barely of conscious mind to shut it down before it could make its way out of his mouth. He pulled himself, shaking, toward the steel-enforced doors of the silo. He was so used to running away from things that crippled him with fear and pain. Never had he run toward it so willingly.

Swallowing hard enough to hurt, he eased open one of the doors and slid inside. The blast of heat nearly made him stagger back outside. Christ, it was like a goddamn sauna in here. Sweat sprang from his forehead and his skin seemed to shrivel like shrink-wrap onto his muscles under the abrupt transition. Wincing, he slowly, carefully eased the door shut behind him. He felt almost bereft of the cold as the heat enveloped him, sucking the air from his lungs. Not two seconds in and he felt like he was cooking. He forced himself to take a deep, steadying breath then almost choked on the musty, heavy air.

He smelled sweat, human sweat, dirt, blood, and pain and it was thick, hanging in the air like some kind of parasite. He leaned back against the door, trying to balance himself, to take stock of his surroundings, to frigging *calm* himself. Breaths coming in deep and slow with a slight twitch of his gag reflex, he forced his eyes around, following the path of the curving walls, covered in soundproof padding, rising up and up to the domed ceiling. Narrow metal beams crisscrossed randomly and a few of them had lengths of chains draped over them. There was a dirt floor and he could hear the hum of portable heaters. The light source he was sure came from gas lanterns. He could smell a hint of the kerosene and judging by the way the light flickered and danced along the walls, there were a lot of them. Directly in front of him, blocking his view of the center of the space was a wall, about seven feet up and five feet long. It was made out of some kind of cork material. Confused, Paul stared at it.

Then he heard something heavy hit the other side.

The wall shuddered then went silent. He heard a quiet voice, a man's, murmuring and soft then there was a sharp, high-pitched keening sound that made Paul want to crawl out of his skin.

He suddenly remembered with horrifying clarity what the wall was.

One of Jack's arsenals. Most of his favorite toys were mounted on that wall, everything from whips to belt buckles, dildos to knives, ball gags to blindfolds and probably some new things he'd acquired since Paul's absence. He always kept it hidden from view when he first dragged you into a room like this. That way he would have you securely within the soundproofing system before you started screaming when you saw what he wanted to use on you.

Paul's pulse thundered in his throat. The keening sound broke off to sobbing, choking, and breathlessness.

A child.

Paul's brain began to vibrate with the sound and the gun in his hand suddenly felt very, very warm and solid. And then his feet were moving and he was around the wall and—

He was sighting down the barrel of his gun and that was when his vision skewed, like he was suddenly hanging upside down. He blinked hard, trying to focus, straining for clarity, the noises in front of him getting louder, more abrasive as if scrubbing the inside walls of his brain with a steel brush. He felt blind but there was a nightmare alive in his eyes. He could smell it in the thick air, the displacement of it as the whip tore through, and into, the fragile flesh of the boy who was trussed up in that stall, so much like cattle and less like a human. Paul's finger was twitching heavily under the weight of the trigger and the force of it was grinding, crushing, pushing through his veins and shrieking in his ears until he thought he would scream. He wiped at his eyes, thinking wildly that he just had some dust in them because *Christ* they were runny.

He was suddenly too fucking close and he could *smell* the anguish, the hurting and the pain coming off the kid. The arousal and the sweat and the power from the man who held the whip stung Paul's nostrils and he was panting as if he were the one tied up. He watched a welt of blood appear as the skin parted like paper. He watched as a finely-boned jaw clenched, teeth digging into the leather gag, eyes squeezed tight behind the blindfold and the chains that held the thin, thin arms stretched so tightly above his head, elongating that poor, broken body until it just about snapped. *Not yet, not yet,* he told himself feverishly. *Don't lose your mind yet. Now is not the fucking time.*

Something whizzed by his ear and he heard the whip crack. Suddenly there were words piercing the fog in his head, snapping him back from his turbulent thoughts.

"Here comes another one! You like that, don't you? Yeah, this is what you get for being bad. Oh, yeah, here we go, yeah, damn, this looks good on you."

Paul blinked and very suddenly realized that what he was seeing before him was like striking gold. Those words, so close, so familiar, snarling right in his ear and he had the means to end them. It was unbelievable. It was fate. It was meant to fucking be and he squeezed the trigger with such exuberance, such superiority, he thought for a second that *he* should be worshipped, that *Chac Mool* should get down on his fucking knees and thank the gods that—

His ears popped.

He choked on his saliva, coming back to himself as if he'd been in a trance. But that couldn't be because the screaming was still there. It hadn't stopped.

He glanced down.

There was a man on the ground, hollering in pain, clamping both hands around his bloody thigh. A bloody coiled whip lay in the dirt next to him like a dead snake.

"Ah, you motherfucker!" the man shouted. "What the fuck is wrong with you? Jesus Christ, you fucking shot me—"

Paul blinked several times, took an unsteady step back.

It wasn't Jack.

He looked up at the kid dangling from his wrists.

It wasn't Ethan.

"...gonna have your ass, you fucking cocksucker. You won't have any balls left when I get done with you..."

Shaking off the vibrant, *What the fuck?* that rang in his ears, Paul squatted and jammed his gun beneath this asshole's chin, effectively shutting him up. Leaning down into his face, Paul hissed, "Shut the fuck up."

The man's face trembled, his dark eyes wide with pain, fear, and something else. Something that had to do with getting caught. He was a middle-aged man, stocky, average-looking—they were always average-looking—except for the gleam of sickness in his eyes. He wasn't wearing a shirt but his torso gleamed with sweat and smudges of blood and other bodily fluids. Blood gushed between the fingers that he held over his leg. The blood didn't spurt so Paul knew he hadn't hit anything vital but he knew without medical attention soon, he'd most likely bleed out. He found that he wasn't particularly worried about that.

"Who are you?" the man asked as best he could with a gun keeping his mouth shut.

"Don't move," Paul advised.

He got to his feet and turned toward the kid.

"Oh! Oh, oh, okay, I get it," the man suddenly laughed from behind him. "Yeah, you're some kind of fucking vigilante, right? Some do-gooder type? Here to save the children? My ass, you self-righteous dick. You have any idea about these kids? It's what they're made for. I'm doing a public service here—"

Paul whirled and fired at him. The bullet struck the ground, inches from the man's head. He screamed, flinching away.

"I will shoot you in the fucking head if you don't shut your mouth."

"You're fucking crazy!"

Paul aimed between his eyes.

The man threw an arm up. "Okay, okay! Jesus!"

Paul went over to the narrow stall, stopping at the entrance. It was something farmers used to raise veal. Planked stalls just wide enough to allow something inside but to hinder any kind of movement.

Nowhere to go.

Nowhere to hide.

The kid's back was an awful bloody mess. A mass of deep red, purple and black, whip marks, cuts, and bruises, gaping and bleeding freely. Blood saturated his pants that were barely clinging to his narrow, bony hips. He was somehow still on his feet, his wrists, rubbed raw and bleeding under the metal cuffs, stretched over his head and it was then that Paul realized that the width of the stall didn't allow for him to even sag properly.

Swallowing hard, Paul said softly, "Hey. Hey, kid."

The kid didn't move, didn't flinch, nothing.

Paul sucked in a hard breath then stepped up into the stall. His boot made a heavy fall on the wooden planks and the vibration of it made the kid come alive. Paul nearly jumped back as the kid twisted and moaned through the gag, his cries muffled. Paul wanted to reach out but knew that would only make things worse.

Then he saw the plugs in the kid's ears.

He shoved his gun into the front of his pants, took a deep breath and waded in. The kid's struggles grew more intense as he felt Paul draw near. Paul had to try several times to get a grip on the kid's head in order to tear away the blindfold and yank out the ear plugs. The kid twisted around and Paul found himself face-to-face with Kyle.

"Kyle!" he gasped in shock. "Kyle—holy shit…"

His face was lost under blood, snot and swollen flesh. One eye was forced shut under a shiny bubble of red and black. Blood leaked from his nose and there was a bright bruise on one side of his face from temple to chin. His good eye flickered in recognition and a weak *unf* came from behind the gag.

"Jesus Christ," Paul exclaimed. "What the fuck? Oh Jesus, what the fuck, Kyle? How did you—oh, shit—shit…"

His words trailed off as he pulled the gag away. Blood followed in glistening red strands. Paul shook his head over and over again, fumbling with the metal cuffs until Kyle fell free. He sagged against Paul, a small, hurt sound crawling out of him as Paul hooked his arms around him and dragged him carefully out of the stall. He was so slippery with blood that he nearly slid right out of Paul's arms. Paul tightened his grip, earning a whimper before he laid him gently on the ground, on his side. Then he sat back.

Fuck, fuck, fuck, fuck.

Paul stared at Kyle, words failing him.

'*I'm probably going to be dead soon anyway.*'

He leaned back over him, his hand hovering uselessly over Kyle's chest. His chest that was amazingly smooth and free of blood. Paul laid his hand gently over his heart, feeling it thump slowly, oh so slowly. He stared into his face, feeling blame, hot and clogging, settle deep in his chest like fire-laced phlegm.

This. This right here. This is because of me.

"Kyle, I—I'm so sorry," he whispered. "I'm sorry—I didn't—I thought—"

Kyle looked up at him blankly, his breathing uneven and painful-sounding. His good eye rolled in its socket, glazed and unfocused. Paul hung his head. The buzzing in his ears ceased long enough to allow Kyle's words to echo. '*I've been doing this for so long, I don't—I don't fucking know how to do anything else.*'

No truer words had been said in jest and Paul knew exactly what it meant. It was everything that could make him hate and despise his existence yet not give him the strength to do something about it. He stared down in Kyle's battered face, felt the kid's heart struggle under the palm of his hand and tried to find the power he *needed* so badly right now to finish this.

To finally put an end to it.

A single tear squeezed itself down the bruised flesh of Kyle's face, tracking a path through the blood. Paul followed it with his eyes, feeling his own vision blurring. His fingers curled against the fever-hot skin of Kyle's torso. He leaned in close, his voice hissing out in a forceful whisper.

"Kyle, Kyle, listen to me. You need to stay awake. I'm going to get you some help, all right? Hey? All right? Buddy, you pass out, you're not gonna wake up. Come on, stay awake."

"You can get me some help while you're at it, asshole."

Paul looked over his shoulder. The man was struggling to his feet, gasping as he tried to put weight on his injured leg. Paul straightened to his own feet, slowly. Dirt clung to the man's skin, his dark hair sticking out in all directions, his face a mask of pain and ugliness.

Paul strode up to him and gave him a shove. His arms pin-wheeled and he crashed back to the ground.

"Hey!" He flopped onto his back like a turtle. "Listen, asshole, you want to rescue the kid, fine. I was just about finished with him anyway. But that's no reason to—"

"Where's Jack?"

He glared up at Paul. "What?"

"Jack. Where is he?"

The man's jaw tightened and he didn't respond. Paul shot him in the other leg.

"You're fucking *nuts!*" the man screamed.

"Where's Jack?"

The man panted so heavily, each breath was like a sob. It was kind of like how Kyle had sounded, trussed up and gagged, but not as broken, not as fearful. If Paul had it in him, he'd string this sick fuck up by his ankles and whip him within an inch of his miserable life.

"I don't—I don't know."

Paul pointed the gun at his forehead. The man flinched back, scooting back a few feet across the dirt.

"Come on, man."

"Tell me where he is."

"If I tell you—"

"This isn't a fucking negotiation," Paul spat at him.

"Please, I was allowed to do it! I was! Ask him! Ask that little fucker! He wanted me to do it! Jack said—"

Paul didn't bother holding back on the anger that bled into his voice. "Jack said? *Jack* said? That's your excuse for killing a kid?"

"He's not even dead!"

Paul shot him in the shoulder. "Not yet, you fucking scumbag," he growled over the man's howls.

"Oh my God, oh my God," the man whimpered, his hands fluttering, not knowing which wound to tend to. "Oh—please, man, please, please, don't kill me, oh my God—"

Paul curled his lip in disgust and waited.

The man stared up at him, tears leaking from his eyes. "He's—He's at the house. Oh my God, he's at the house, all right? Please—"

Paul shot him in the head.

CHAPTER 51

Paul covered Kyle with his coat, tucking it gently around him. Kyle had looked at him, his eye brimming with things to say, his mouth moving soundlessly before passing out. Paul touched his fingers to Kyle's throat to ensure a pulse and he could feel it, faint but steady. He left the silo.

The cold air froze the sweat on his body. Gasping a little, he secured the doors behind him. It wouldn't take long for the local wildlife to scent out the blood from the mess inside.

He made for the house.

Darkness had finally settled like a hesitant suitor. There was no moon, barely any wind. The snow provided some illumination but not nearly as much as the farmhouse did. Just about every window was ablaze with light and it really did look like a postcard. Inviting you in for hot apple cider after a long trek through hell. Paul's step continued on.

He glanced out into the woods, half-expecting to see headlights cutting through the trees. It was about that time after all. Let the games begin.

But he was the only thing that moved as he went up the porch steps. He didn't bother keeping quiet.

Jack knew he was coming.

The front door was closed. Paul was pretty sure he'd left it open.

Someone was definitely home.

The bodies had been removed but the bloodstains were still there. Paul could see them like black ink spills on the floorboards. He stood at the front door, staring at it.

'*Don't be a pussy. Just do it,*' Aaron sneered in his head.

Paul swung the door inward.

Warmth and light filtered around him. The foyer that had been so dim and shadowed when he first arrived was now awash in soft lamplight. Gleaming, hardwood floors, earth-tone paint on the walls, comfortable, sturdy furniture that looked tempting enough to sink into and never get up.

Safe.

He stepped inside and shut the door. The doors to the viewing room were still shut and the bodies from the porch were stacked in front of it like broken dolls, limbs askew, blood pooling across the floor. He turned away.

Through the french doors, he saw that the fire was still roaring with a vengeance. Shadows leapt around the room, glinting off the cigar boxes and the crystal glasses on the table. He took a hesitant step inside the room and looked around. It looked empty but it wasn't. There were a lot of ghosts in this room and Paul felt like one of them, floating, rootless, where one strong wind could sweep him away. His breath stuttered when he saw the big oak desk in the corner, across from the fireplace. The worn leather chair was empty, pushed away from it as if he'd gotten up while in the middle of doing something. Paul could almost see the outline of him, pushed into the material and the creaks that the chair would make as his weight shifted and moved and how it never seemed to take long for his arm to reach across the mile-wide desktop and grab...

Paul turned away, feeling his body grow unpleasantly warm. Realizing he was standing right in front of the fire, he started to take a rather unsteady step back when the picture frames on top of the mantel stopped him.

There were ten frames, each spaced exactly six inches apart, each holding a picture of a child. He tried to swallow but a rock seemed to have lodged itself in his throat.

A blonde girl, around seven, beamed out at him, a mile-wide grin pocked with missing teeth.

A boy with a mop of black curls stared solemnly at the camera, a slight upward tilt of his mouth.

A set of twin redheaded girls, arms locked around each other, both looking uncertain but smiling nonetheless.

Paul noticed with a jolt that one frame held Melinda, without her fairy costume, brown hair blowing back from her face, a fading bruise on one freckled cheek. He stared at her, at all the pictures, unable to comprehend this, unable to decide what the hell this was.

Some kind of shrine? Some kind—

The thought died in his head because he then saw the last picture, all the way on the end. The flash of white-blond hair in the photo was unmistakable, pulling him toward it like a magnet. His fingers bit into the edge of the mantel as he stared down at the picture of Ethan, looking terrified and small, staring up at the camera like it was the barrel of a gun. Paul felt an invisible boot in his gut and it only burrowed farther in when he saw another photo tucked into the edge of the frame. It was smaller, older, faded and worn around the edges.

His knees nearly buckled. The fire suddenly felt way too hot. The air around him choked and clawed at his throat.

He stared at the picture of himself.

Eleven years old.

He remembered that picture being taken. He remembered the relief, the gratitude of having a place to live. He remembered how eager he was to do everything right, to make sure Jack never regretted bringing him under his roof. He remembered smiling for the first time in months when he first heard Jack's voice because it was so soft, so *understanding*, a replica of his mother's voice, layered with hope and the support he needed to move forward, thus finally allowing himself to weep for her and his father. In his eleven-year-old mind it had been like coming home. It had been like starting over, fresh and new.

Until it wasn't.

He stared until his eyes burned, until the two faces blurred together. It was no coincidence that his picture was alongside Ethan's. He reached with trembling fingers, skirting the edge of the photographs.

Please be alive. Please…

The air moved behind him and he spun around with a scream locked hard in his throat.

"Hello, Paul."

CHAPTER 52

Facing Jack, no matter how armed to the teeth he was, was not something Paul could ever be prepared for. The physical presence of the man was so jolting, so incredibly numbing that Paul could do nothing but gape at him.

What're you gonna do? You break down the damn door, demanding that Twinkie be turned over to you? Or better yet, you put a gun to Jack's head, sure, because threatening him will get you what you want.

Yeah, right.

Paul's entire body felt like it was encased in ice. Even with the fire at his back, he felt cold and what made it worse was that time had done surprisingly little to Jack. Paul had expected—*wanted*—to find a sloop-shouldered bag of wrinkles or a glass containing a set of false teeth. But there was none of that. Not even hair shot with silver. Instead, all that stood before him was a man as powerful and prevailing as he'd been since the last time Paul had seen him. A well-worn plaid shirt hugged the well-formed muscles of his chest and shoulders, faded blue jeans clung to lean legs. The only thing missing was an axe and he could've been a lumberjack in the woods somewhere in Montana. Floppy brown hair fell across his high, tanned forehead. The smooth planes of his face were etched with smile lines and his eyes were a brown so pale, they glowed almost yellow. He didn't look a day older than Paul and it was disarming enough that Paul wondered if he'd somehow stepped into a time machine, waking up to discover that he was still eleven years old and the last decade and a half had been nothing more than a bad dream.

Paul blinked at him.

Jack smiled, dimples cutting into his cheeks. "It's been a long time."

His voice—*God*—it was as soft and melodious as a lullaby, worming gently into Paul's skin, pecking and nibbling, incessant and insisting that he fall to his knees *now*. His brain trembled in confusion, at war with his body, which somehow knew what to do in this situation because if that little voice in the back of his head got its way, he would be on his knees in an instant and wouldn't that make things so much easier?

'*I've been doing this for so long, I don't—I don't fucking know how to do anything else.*'

Paul used to think the same thing. But there was a line drawn now. Things were different. The puzzle pieces were the same but they no longer fit and the picture as a whole was different. And he was here, facing down Jack, facing down his past, everything, to get a boy who would *not* suffer the same fate. Even if he was leading him to Chac Mool , it was better than being on his knees for the world.

Sucking in a slow deep breath, Paul returned Jack's stare. It was hard, harder than he ever thought, but he maintained eye contact. Jack's eyes twinkled golden in the firelight, amused.

"Yeah," Paul replied, his voice small but steady. "Long time."

Jack moved his head back a little, letting his eyes move deliberately down Paul's body then travel back up to his eyes.

"My, how you've grown."

"I didn't think you'd remember me."

Jack's smile deepened. Paul felt his skin twitch.

"Now why would you think that?" Jack walked around him, brushing his shoulder with his as he passed.

Paul felt the contact burn through his shirt and corrode the flesh beneath. Jack's stride was easy and unhurried. The way he moved was like lava, fluid, slow and scorching, taking down everything in its path and burying it, smothering it. He stood in front of the fireplace, casting a shimmering shadow of himself across the floor, dark and empty. His eyes moved over the picture frames. One hand came up to lean against the edge of the mantel.

Paul watched him, his heart pounding. "Like I said, it's been a while since we last saw each other."

With his back to him, Jack murmured, "You left me so suddenly, Paul. I didn't think you'd ever come back."

"That makes the two of us."

He saw Jack's head turn a little. "I don't think I need to ask why you're here."

"Probably not."

"Did you think you could just come in here and take him?"

"You're not exactly busy tonight."

Jack shot him a look over his shoulder. His smile had vanished and a cold, calculating look had taken its place. It was a look that Jack rarely showed and seeing it now made Paul's fingers twitch, ready to go for his gun. Jack's eyes flicked down to it, tucked securely in its shoulder holster then back up to Paul's face. He seemed unworried but the skin around his eyes was tight.

"I've had to cancel tonight's activities, Paul. As you can see, a little clean-up was in order."

Paul felt a strange rush of satisfaction. "Yeah, there's a bit of a mess in the silo you might want to take care of, too."

Jack pushed away from the mantel, turning to face him. Paul braced himself. "Letting the clients do your dirty work now, Jack? I'm surprised."

"Business has expanded in the time you've been gone, Paul. It's important that I evolve and change along with it."

"I doubt this business has changed that much."

"You'd be surprised."

"Is that why you're using security?"

Jack tilted his head slightly to one side, giving Paul a searching yet disturbing look. "My employees aren't quite what they used to be, Paul. I can only do what I can to ensure that they don't take advantage of my hospitality and good will."

Paul's jaw flexed. "In other words, you have them shot on the spot if they try to make a run for it?"

Jack shook his head, the corners of his mouth twisting downward as he appeared to give this some thought.

"Well, I don't like to encourage force but I will make sure that they've given this a fair chance. You know, stick it out and see if they like it rather than deciding after only a day or two that it's 'not for them.'" He chuckled to himself as if it were something unheard of.

Paul swallowed against a sudden surge of bile in the back of his throat. "Is there any...employee that actually likes doing any of this?"

Jack's eyes crawled with a darkness that had nothing to do with the shadow and light that played around the room. "You did once."

The words struck deep, their implication even deeper. For one horrible second, an uncontrollable swell of doubt swept over Paul. His eyes burned, his ears ringing with far-away echoes of cries and pleas and demands and human flesh bent and twisted in ways not ever meant to be. Paul stared at Jack, at the just barely-there smile that pulled smugly at the corners of his mouth. He shook his head belatedly, loathing the sound of Jack's laughter.

"Oh, sure you did," Jack chuckled. "Why else would you have stayed with me for as long as you did?"

"I was barely with you for a year."

"And within that time, you were my best employee. You were the one everyone wanted. You were the one with the most promise. So excuse me if I find it a little hard to believe that you weren't happy here."

Despite himself Paul felt his face flush. The praise was shameful and it made him break eye contact. It was obviously the moment Jack was waiting for because he came toward him, slowly, steadily. Paul shuddered weakly, feeling something old settle onto his shoulders, pushing his head down in a bow.

The tops of Jack's boots came into his line of vision and Paul immediately moved away from him.

"You know, Nicky wasn't quite the same after you left."

Paul froze, bringing his eyes back up to Jack's face. He'd stopped moving toward him, *Thank God*, but the smugness was still playing with the edges of his lips.

"Nicky?"

Jack nodded. "You remember him, don't you?"

Paul nodded numbly. Jack pursed his lips as if trying to remember something.

"Wasn't he the one who brought you to me?"

The question was like a dagger being inched into his back, just behind his heart.

"Y—yeah," he stammered.

"Hm. Yeah. He was quite a soldier, that one. Took a shine to you, too, didn't he?"

"You know he did."

"I do. I also know he was your only friend and you left him behind."

Paul swallowed hard and almost choked. "No."

"Yes," Jack insisted. "He was so crushed when you left, so heartbroken. You wouldn't believe the pain he suffered."

"No. He—He was the one who helped me get out."

Jack laughed a little, the sound sharp and low. "Did he? You mean to tell me that he *wanted* you to leave him behind?"

"He was supposed to meet me. He was supposed to—"

"Oh, a rendezvous." Jack laughed again. "Guess that didn't quite work out, did it?"

"You made sure of that."

Jack's eyes sparkled. "It was bad enough I lost you, Paul. I couldn't afford to lose him, too."

He moved toward him again. Paul felt his skin jump as he backed away. Amusement flared in Jack's face. Shadows slid around him like smoke as he moved.

"Is he dead?"

"You know he is."

The dagger pushed in a little deeper and Paul's next words came out as if he'd been punched in the gut. "He was loyal to you."

"He was but he was more loyal to you." Something flashed in Jack's eyes. It took a moment for Paul to see it as irritation. "I gave him everything. Food, a warm bed, clothes and he was willing to forsake all of that to follow *you*." He shook his head, his smile hardening like ice.

"He was doing this far longer than I was," Paul said. "Maybe he just wanted out."

"No. He didn't want out until he met you."

Paul frowned.

"I thought I was the only one who knew just how special you were but Nicky knew it too. I think deep down, he always regretted bringing you here. I saw it in his eyes when he first presented you to me. I think that was why he fought so hard that last night. I had to re-tie him to the frame two times because he kept getting away." He chuckled softly in remembrance.

Paul snapped, his mind screaming *monster* and he went for his gun, feeling the glorious weight in his hand. But Jack was suddenly *so fast* in his face, curling hot fingers around his wrist and forcing the gun out to the side, away from him. His other hand clamped on the back of Paul's neck, his grip like a talon-tipped vice. Paul nearly shrieked as the contact, burning and slicing, sent paralysis shooting down his spine. He tried to push away but his arms wouldn't cooperate and he could only let Jack guide him backward, half-stumbling, half-walking until Paul collided hard with the desk, the edge of it digging into the back of his legs. Jack loomed over him and the sudden proximity, the achingly familiar closeness blinded Paul with unadulterated panic. His body seized and he sputtered uselessly as Jack came closer, leaning into him, his breath pouring over Paul's mouth like honeyed poison.

'*Just relax. I won't hurt you. You want to stay here, don't you*?'

'*I do b—but—please, don't do this.*'

'*Shhh, I won't hurt you. You'll like this, I promise.*'

God, he could hear it. He could feel it as clear as day, as if it were happening all over again. The rough pull of fabric being torn away, Jack's too-hot fingers ghosting over his rib cage, the desk's edge biting into his hips and the cry that fell from his lips, thick with tears, his own voice, young and pleading, torn because it was *wrong, so, so wrong* but also because of the repercussions if he didn't follow through. Paul fought to turn his face away but it was all around. It was all there in the forefront of his brain, real and loud and invasive, shining in the spotlight and impossible to ignore.

"You make people do crazy things, Paul," Jack said now as he tried to bear him down on top of the desk. "Things they would otherwise never do."

Paul was pushed farther back onto the desk. Jack eased his knees apart so he could stand between them, his eyes shining with something dark and dangerous. Paul arched weakly, trying to gain some leverage but Jack was too strong. He was always too strong. Sweat ran down his neck to pool in the hollow of his throat. A small, broken sound crawled out of his chest as he felt Jack's lips brush against the side of his neck. Hysteria was rabid in the center of his body, making him shake and he wondered if this is what it felt like to be thrown head-first into madness. To be trapped, cornered with no one to help you but your own brain, screaming and screaming because for some reason your vocal cords weren't working but the words were so fucking loud in your head, over and over again, looking for a way out, sounding something like, G*et off me*! *Oh my God, get off me*! *Get the fuck off me*! *Now, please, just stop please I can't, no, stop please, not again, not ever again, I can't—*

"Get the fuck off me!" tore from Paul's mouth so suddenly it was like the earth had careened out of orbit and crashed silently into the sun.

The look in Jack's eyes was murderous and his hands tightened on Paul's neck and wrist.

"You're going to look so good spread out on my desk," he hissed into Paul's face. "Better than you looked the first time I had you."

He released Paul's neck then grabbed his broken arm, slamming it once, twice into the side of the desk. Paul howled in pain, rolling away as Jack finally let go. He fell to the floor, gasping.

"You come into my home, armed and you don't even shoot me," Jack sneered, his voice fading in and out as pain throbbed through Paul's arm. "You know how much I hate these things."

Paul heard his gun clatter across the floor. He hadn't even realized he had dropped it. He struggled to his knees, cradling his arm to his chest. "Where's Ethan?" he wheezed.

Jack let out a surprised laugh. "Excuse me?"

"Where's Ethan?"

"You ballsy little piss-ant," Jack fumed, his face twisting with rage. "Who the fuck do you think you're talking to?"

Paul pushed himself to his feet, wincing and trembling. "Tell me where he is."

Jack's lips turned into a thin white line across his face. "So this is what you left me for."

Paul bit the inside of his lip until it bled.

"This is what you've become. Some kind of fucking savior." He took a step toward Paul, his eyes snapping with barely leashed control. "It makes me wonder if this is what Aaron had in mind when he took you in."

Paul froze.

Jack curled his lips in something that could've been a grin but came out looking more like a snarl. "Oh, yes. Aaron and I go way back. How else do you think he found you?"

Paul sagged heavily against the side of the desk.

"*What*?" he managed to croak.

"What?" Jack said sharply. "You think your life happened by chance? You think it was some kind of fate that led Aaron to you? Come *on*, Paul. Catch the fuck up, will you?"

Paul could only stare helplessly at him. Jack stared back, little by little, gaining his calm back. It was like watching the ocean pull the tide back. He rolled his shoulders and came toward Paul again, a hard gleam in his eyes.

"I never had any intention of handing you over to him. I wanted to keep you too much."

He stopped and smiled a little, the movement like a snake slithering over his face. Paul tried to move away. But the desk behind him wasn't going anywhere. Jack moved closer.

"But when I found out that you were gone and I offered you up to him. It was a moment of weakness, I know and I was so pissed off. I didn't think you'd ever have the balls to leave. But you did, and when Aaron arrived, I thought this would be my opportunity to teach you a lesson."

"Lesson?"

"I thought maybe you would finally be able to see that there were worse things out there than working for me."

"Like Aaron," Paul whispered hoarsely.

Jack nodded. "Like Aaron. He was always a mean son-of-a-bitch. Figured you wouldn't last a day with him. Not a lot of kids could. There'd been quite a few times when he came by to collect some for work and those that survived found their way back to my doorstep, begging to be let back in."

"What—What would he use them for?"

Jack shrugged. "Some of them were used in recon jobs, you know, distractions, things like that. But most were used for target practice."

Paul would've keeled forward if Jack hadn't been standing in front of him. "Did you—" He stopped, swallowed, tried again. "Did you know what he had planned for me?"

"Oh, no," Jack said with a shake of his head. "I had no idea he intended to make you into some fantastic fucking killing machine." He raised an eyebrow. "Or some avenging angel."

Paul shook his head, feeling sick.

"I kept waiting for you to come back to me," Jack said, his voice growing softer. "But you never did. Until now."

"How did you know where to send him to find me?"

Paul nearly jumped when gentle fingers touched his chin and turned his face up to Jack's. Jack's eyes were too close and there was so much, too much there that Paul didn't want to read. He tried to move his head but Jack's fingers tightened. Paul could feel the threat and he forced himself to go still.

"Paul, don't you know me by now? I know a lot of time has passed but I haven't changed that much. I have eyes and ears in places far and wide. No one can hide from me. Not even you. Especially not you."

His gaze became tangible, like he was touching him with more than just his fingers on his chin. Paul fidgeted, trying to pull away but Jack's grip was deceptive, like velvet-covered steel.

"Did Aaron ever come back to you after you told him about me?"

"After I told him about you, he didn't come back for years. Not until recently anyway."

"Ethan."

Jack laughed and shook his head. "Imagine my surprise when I opened the door to see his smug, shit-eating grin on my front porch."

He gave Paul's chin a squeeze before letting his hand drop. He watched Paul, expectantly, waiting for his laughter to finish echoing through the room. Paul looked at him.

And there it was. The sad, pathetic truth that was once again thrown in his face like acid, that everything, *everything* that made up the seconds, minutes, days, years of his life and not a single solitary moment of it had ever been *his*.

Come on. You're honestly not surprised by this, are you?

No, he decided. No, he wasn't.

And he wanted to be angry about it. He wanted to be so fucking pissed off that he couldn't see straight. That he would go blind and savage and when and if he ever came back to himself, Jack would be nothing more than a bloody lump on the floor at his feet. But there was nothing.

Nothing but exhaustion.

Or maybe on some level, it was acceptance. Things had never been in his control. He bounced seamlessly from Jack to Aaron, two men who had ruled him with pain, threats, and fear. It seemed rather fitting that they had worked together, that they were two kings on a chess board with only one pawn. And what could he do about it now? Everything was over. Everything was upside down and unrecognizable. Aaron was gone. The life that had been predestined for him was finished and Jack—Jack was never going to let him leave here alive. In that moment, it all seemed amazingly cut and dry. It had seemed so complicated before. Now, it wasn't.

Very anti-climatic, Paul thought to himself.

Numbly, he straightened, pushing himself away from the desk. It put him closer to Jack. Paul licked his dry lips, ignoring the way Jack's eyes followed the movement.

"Where's Ethan?"

Jack tilted his head to one side. "That's all you have to say? After everything I just told you?"

"What were you expecting?"

"I don't know. Tears, an angry rant or two, something other than this."

"This?"

"Yes, this calmness you've got going on."

Which was funny because Paul felt like anything but.

"I'm not," Paul found himself saying. "I think I'm just finished."

"Finished?"

"Yeah. With you."

Jack's smile vanished. In one quick stride he was in Paul's face, his eyes flashing. "You'll never be done with me, Paul. I'll always be around. Even if by some fucking miracle, you make it out of here, with or without Ethan, you'll never forget me. Never."

Paul stared into his eyes. "Maybe. But then you'll never forget me either."

Jack's hands were instantly wrapped around Paul's neck like a fleshy, too-tight turtleneck. Paul cried out in surprise as he was pushed back onto the desk.

"I haven't forgotten you, Paul," Jack spat in his face, his fingers tightening painfully. "How could I? Especially when I have Ethan to entertain me."

Paul clawed at his hands, gurgling, feeling the blood freeze in his face.

"Oh yes," Jack went on, almost conversationally as if he weren't choking someone on top of his desk. "All the stories he told me of his time with you. All the times that you resisted him, that you practically cried like a fucking baby at the slightest touch." He leaned down into Paul's face, his breath hot and quick. "Even if I don't have you in the flesh, Paul, I'll always have your memory and that's enough for me on a cold night."

He peeled one hand away from Paul's neck and went for his belt. Paul flailed at him, pushing and kicking, grunts of pain and panic mingling, pouring out of his constricted throat. Jack laughed, his teeth flashing in the semi-darkness, his face contorted like some kind of demon as he popped the button on Paul's pants.

"Yeah, that's it, fight me," Jack taunted him cruelly, his eyes gleaming. "Struggle, you know how I like it."

Wildly, Paul swung at him but couldn't get leverage. The screams that wanted to come out of him were trapped inside his head, so loud he thought he was going to go deaf. He managed to get a foot up onto the desk, intending to use it to push himself up and away. Something rough rubbed against his ankle. He thought that it was Jack's hand and tried to kick it away. But the roughness followed.

Then he realized with a jolt, *That's my knife*. He wrenched his hand away from the side of Jack's face, where it had been trying to gouge out his eyes, and reached down, fumbling.

"Should've done this the second you walked in here," Jack was saying, yanking Paul's zipper down. "Should've shoved my cock down your throat just like I used to—"

As if he'd been side-swiped by a sledgehammer, the anger was suddenly *there*. It snapped through him like lightening, hot and untamed, boiling through his blood. His brain felt like it was imploding. The knife was in his hand and the screams finally found their way out as he brought the blade back and plunged it into the side of Jack's throat. He held onto the hilt, pushing it in, hot blood hitting his hand as he screamed wordlessly into Jack's face.

Jack's eyes bulged. A shocked gurgling sound came out of him as his hands flew up to his neck. Paul held on tightly, drawing in breath after breath, scream after scream, almost dizzy with the force of his rage. Blood arched, pouring down Jack's neck, splashing onto his shirt, glowing black in the firelight. Jack tugged desperately at Paul's arm, his eyes wild, his face a mask of blood splatters and shock. Paul let go, shoving him backward.

Jack staggered, twisting this way and that, like a puppet whose master had epilepsy. His eyes rolled wide and then they found Paul and the hate that filled them was awful and huge. Paul rolled off the desk as Jack stumbled toward him, horrible, angry babbling sounds following in his wake as he tried to speak. Blood showed on his teeth, spilling from his lips, slicking across his chin like a cheap whore's lipstick. Paul backed away, stumbling along the wall. His legs failed him and he slid down to the floor. Jack followed suit, collapsing to his knees, his eyes locked on Paul's. His head moved back and forth, shaking, trying to deny what was happening. His hands fluttered around the hilt sticking out of his neck. Then he pitched forward, one hand slapping down on the floor to hold himself up.

His eyes never left Paul's face.

Paul pressed back into the wall, the power of Jack's gaze like a massive hand on his chest, keeping him pinned. The room took on a strange look, walls bowing out, the ceiling caving in, the floor bursting upward like there were monsters beneath it. Jack remained in the center of it, his body rippling, blood surrounding him in lopsided puddles. Paul's head throbbed and he felt parts of himself float in and out of focus. It took him a moment to realize that he was watching a part of him die.

Convulsions hit Jack hard, sending him crashing face-first to the floor, finally breaking the awful eye contact. Paul felt an excruciating jab in the center of his rib cage like someone was digging through his body to get at his organs. He watched, made himself watch, as Jack trembled and quivered, body knocking against the floorboards. His head jerked as if he were trying to twist around to look at Paul.

Then he went still.

Paul stared, his breath moving noisily in and out of his mouth. He was surprised to find tear tracks on his face. He hadn't even known he was crying.

CHAPTER 53

Blankly, he watched as blood spread from beneath Jack's body. There was so much of it. Even after all his years of killing people, it never failed to amaze him how much blood the human body contained. The edge of the blood pool crept slowly toward Paul's boots, giving him plenty of time to get out of the way. But he couldn't move. He stayed slumped against the wall. Pieces of himself lay shattered, beyond any hope of being put back together the right way, littered around him like leftover confetti from a party. He sucked in a few deep breaths. When he glanced down at himself, he was only vaguely surprised that he wasn't sporting any wounds. Just bruising and blood splatters from Jack's severed artery.

But then he saw his open pants and he leaned over and vomited all over the floor.

He wiped at his mouth and pushed himself to his knees, fumbling to do up his pants, one-handed.

The blood was creeping closer. He finally scooted away from it then stopped. A line appeared in the center of the blood as if someone had cast a fishing line through it. The line ran along the floor for about two feet before disappearing underneath the desk. Frowning, Paul followed it with his eyes then he exploded to his feet. He threw himself against the side of the desk, pushing frantically at it.

"Ethan!" he shouted. "Ethan!"

For an instant, the heavy desk refused to move. Paul heaved and shoved until finally with a grating screech, it moved, inch by inch until it slammed into the wall, dragging bits of wooden floor and blood with it. Paul dropped to his knees, hand scrambling until it hit a metal ring bolted into the floor and then he saw the hinges.

A trapdoor.

He grabbed the ring and yanked the door up. He let it slam back against the floor and gagged at the smell of earth, mold, and feces. Putting a hand to his nose, he saw the splintered ladder that led down into darkness. Swallowing hard, he barked out, "Ethan? Ethan, you down here? "

His voice echoed, bouncing back at him, lonely and shaking. He looked up at Jack's unmoving body. His body shivered at the thought of going down there.

"Ethan?" he tried again. "Come on, answer me! Ethan!"

Fuck.

He wondered if Ethan was alone or if there were more down there with him.

Or if he was down there at all.

Paul peered down into the gloom. It was enough to break anyone, being thrown into a hole. It didn't matter how old you were. Locked in darkness, for an infinite amount of time with no contact except maybe for the rats, no food, no water, no sound, you either retreated deep inside your own mind or you started screaming.

Ethan would never scream, Paul thought. *He would never make a sound.*

Paul got to his feet and scooped up his gun that had been thrown to the other side of the room. Shoving it into the back of his pants, he came back to the trap door. Putting a foot down on the first step of the ladder, he almost fell headfirst. His muscles locked and he stayed frozen to the spot, staring in the dark until spots danced before his eyes.

Movement caught his eye.

Blood was still seeping through the cracks in the floorboards, glistening for a moment in mid-air before disappearing into the earth. He swallowed hard, trying not to think about his own time spent in a deserted basement, alone with only the spiders for company.

It's not about you, a small, reasonable voice whispered from the back of his mind. *It's about Ethan and you need to get him out, right the fuck now.*

His breath trembled, echoing around him as he slowly lowered himself down the ladder. The darkness swallowed greedily around him, pressing in until he thought he couldn't breathe. He kept going, moving carefully, lest he miss a step and break his neck on the way down. He couldn't see how far the ladder reached but as long as there was another step, he kept descending.

His foot hit the ground. Loose dirt by the feel of it under his boot. He glanced up. Christ, the trapdoor was at least fifteen feet above his head. The light that came from above was just enough to light the area in which he stood but not much else. He felt like he was on stage in a spotlight with an unknown audience just beyond, watching him. He inched his foot forward, out of the light and reached a hand out in front of him.

Something knocked against his forehead.

He jumped, biting back a sound that would've been a lot like a scream if he hadn't rooted his mouth shut. He looked up, his fingers swiping. Heart in his mouth, he could see the faint outline of a hanging light bulb. Breathing a sigh of relief, he pulled the chain and the bulb flared to flickering life, throwing dirty yellow streaks of light across an earthen floor, walls and a ceiling that wasn't much higher than his own head.

A cave.

It was the only word to describe what he was standing in the middle of.

Squinting, Paul turned in a quick circle.

It wasn't very big; maybe ten by twenty and the light didn't reach the far wall. Paul focused on that. He took a tentative step forward.

"Ethan?" he said, making sure his voice carried. "Ethan, come on, buddy. You down here?"

Dead silence pierced his ears. Paul waited, forcing himself to be patient. He sucked in a deep breath, almost gagged, and tried again.

"Ethan, it's Paul."

A faint scuttling came from the shadows at the back of the room. His heart leapt into his throat and he took another slow step forward, straining his eyes to see through the thick shadows.

There was a dragging sound, followed by scraping.

Paul froze. "Ethan? If you're there, answer me."

The quiet was thick, oppressive.

"Come on, buddy. I'm getting you out of here. You want to get out of here, right? And I don't mean just out of this hole but away from here completely. Away from Jack. He can't hurt you anymore, man. He can't and he won't."

He moved forward again. He skinned his lips back over his teeth. Cold sweat trickled down his spine.

"Ethan?" his voice cracked. "Ethan—please. I'll take you for pancakes. Chocolate chip. You can have as many as you fucking want. Please, just—just come out so I can see you, okay?"

Something moved in front of him and Paul came to a halt once more. There was movement just beyond the edge of darkness, close enough so that he could just barely see it. Then a small pale foot came into view, followed by an ankle, a calf, a knee.

Ethan stepped timidly into the light, flinching and eyes cast downward. His white-blond hair was filthy, falling around his face in tangles and knots. He was naked. His thin body was covered in smears, dirt, blood, and other things that Paul didn't want to think about. His hands were balled into loose fists at his sides and there was a metal cuff around one ankle. The length of chain lay in the dirt behind him, leading a path back into the shadows. Paul looked at him, eyes trailing over him from head to toe. His shoulders sagged with something like relief and he came forward, hand outstretched.

"Ethan."

Ethan's hands curled into tight fists, so tight, his arms shook. His entire body stiffened and his head moved farther down until it was bowed. Paul stopped. A fine tremor went down his own body and he suddenly wanted to climb back upstairs and plunge that knife into Jack a couple more times.

He went toward him, moving slowly, making noise so Ethan wouldn't be startled.

"Ethan?"

No answer.

"Ethan, it's Paul. Remember me? Huh? You remember me?"

Again no answer.

Paul moved to his knees, just outside of arm's length. "You remember me? We went out for pancakes and they were really good because you had them with chocolate milk. Remember?"

There was a slight twitch but nothing more than that.

Paul moved his head back. He had to get him out of here. He scooted closer, moving around to Ethan's left side. Ethan didn't move but Paul thought he saw his eyes follow him, a glint of silver tracking him through his dirty hair. Paul pulled his gun, aimed carefully at the chain and fired. The blast was deafening but it worked.

A surprised scream came out of Ethan and he darted to the wall, hunching down and covering his ears with his hands. Paul followed but carefully kept his distance.

"Sorry about that, buddy. Ethan, I'm sorry. I had to free you, okay?"

Ethan huddled closer to the wall, not looking at him. Through the grime on his body, Paul could see finger-shaped bruises on his hips, sprinkled across his back. More bruises decorated his legs and his shackled ankle was swollen and raw. He closed his eyes briefly. Holstering his gun, he gently touched Ethan's shoulder.

He flinched away.

Paul clenched his jaw. At this rate, they were going to be down here all night.

He stood up and grabbed Ethan by the arms, swinging him up and wrapping his arms tightly around him. It wasn't the best idea but for now it was going to get the job done.

A cry came from Ethan's lips and he trembled hard against him, not fighting but not totally submissive either.

"Shhh," Paul whispered as he strode toward the ladder. "Shhh, I got you, buddy. We're getting out of here. We're getting out of here right the hell now."

Ethan hung onto him, limp and unresponsive as Paul climbed the ladder. He cleared the trap door, slamming it shut with a loud bang. Ethan jumped, his trembling intensified.

Paul stepped around Jack's bloodied body and set Ethan down in front of the fire. There was a blanket thrown across one of the couches. He picked it up and wrapped it tightly around Ethan's quaking shoulders. He didn't look up, didn't say a word. Paul stared at him, at a loss.

"Stay here, all right?" he said, wiping a hand over his mouth. "Just stay here. I'll be right back."

He strode from the room then came back in. He stopped and looked around.

His eyes found a phone on top of the desk. He frowned at it then made a decision.

CHAPTER 54

It was the strangest thing. Paul had never called the police for anything in his entire life. He always figured that if he just kept running or if he just kept doing what people told him to do, he would be fine.

And look how well that had turned out.

He found a key in Jack's pocket that allowed him to take the cuff off Ethan's ankle. With its removal, Ethan seemed to sag lifelessly to the floor as if his strings had been severed. Panicking a bit, Paul felt for a pulse. It was strong under his fingers. He scooped Ethan up and searched for a bathroom. He hosed him down gently, careful not to touch him too much or too hard. Ethan stood with his eyes closed, not fighting at all, just allowing Paul to maneuver him wherever and however he needed. He dressed the kid as if he were an invalid, finding clothes in a chest in one of the rooms upstairs after he'd shot his way through the door.

He heard children crying and he shouted that the police were coming. The crying died down to sniffling. Paul wondered if Melinda would be happy about this turn of events.

Probably not.

As he gathered Ethan into a heavy coat, he noticed him staring down at Jack's body. Paul guided him out onto the front porch then left him there to go back to the silo.

Kyle was still breathing but appeared to be unconscious. Paul knelt next to him, tucking his coat around him more securely.

"Kyle, the police are coming."

Kyle moaned weakly.

"You're going to be fine, man, all right? Jack can't hurt you anymore. You're going to get away from all of this and you're going to have a real fucking life, you got that? A real life. Not this shit. Not ever again." His voice caught and he swallowed hard.

Kyle's good eye came open a little, focusing blearily on Paul. Words fluttered out of his mouth, breathless and faint.

Paul left the silo in a daze.

He hotwired a blue SUV that was in the garage. Buckling Ethan into the passenger seat, he drove away, replaying Kyle's words over and over again in his head.

It could've been delirium. He'd lost a lot of blood, been beaten within an inch of his life. There was no way he knew about a green-eyed man. How could he?

Underneath the coat, Kyle's more serious wounds had been cleaned, disinfected somehow, the blood wiped away.

It didn't make sense.

As he pulled out onto the main road, Paul heard police and ambulance sirens coming from the opposite direction. Red and blue flashed in the rearview. He kept driving.

He glanced over at Ethan who was staring out of the window, huddling in his coat.

They drove for miles before Paul pulled into the parking lot of a roadside diner. It looked a lot like the first diner Paul had taken Ethan to. He cut the engine.

"Cortez."

He whipped around in his seat, screaming a loud, "Shit!" as he went for his gun.

Chac Mool was in the backseat, inches from his face, his hand clamping around Paul's wrist. Ethan curled into a ball against the door, whimpering softly. Chac Mool's green eyes burned brightly.

"Christ, where did you come from?" Paul gasped.

"I was with you when you left that place," Chac Mool said.

Paul looked at him, really looked at him. He seemed disturbed which was a strange look for the usually unflappable man. Paul frowned at him. Before he could say anything however, Chac Mool said softly, "I am sorry I doubted you, Cortez."

Paul's eyebrows hit his hairline. "What?"

"I was so certain that you were lying, that you concocted that story to save yourself. But then I saw…" He trailed off.

Paul swallowed, twisting farther around in his seat. "You helped Kyle."

Chac Mool nodded once. "His wounds were in danger of becoming infected."

"Why? Why did you—"

"It is not of importance," Chac Mool interrupted harshly. "Your debt to me is paid. You and your child."

Paul's eyes widened. "Wh—"

"Neither one of you are worthy."

Paul blinked. "Uh—"

"And by worthy, I mean that you have not fulfilled your lives. You have spent it with such pain, such fear and brutality. It will take you a long, long time to compensate for that. Until then I cannot follow through."

Paul could only gape at him. "I—I don't—"

"You have a lot to make up for, Cortez. Perhaps one day we will meet again."

Without waiting for a reply, he slid from the car, shutting the door softly behind him.

Silence settled and after a few moments, it was like he had never been there. Like Paul had simply hallucinated. He looked out the window, just to make sure Chac Mool didn't change his mind. Ethan shifted on the seat next to him. Paul looked over.

Big gray eyes stared back at him.

"Paul?" Ethan asked, his voice a whispery rasp.

Paul pressed his lips together. "Yeah?"

"Could we get some chocolate chip pancakes?"

The urge to laugh was unexpected, the hot rush of tears that followed even more so.

"Yeah, buddy. Chocolate chip pancakes sound really good."

THE END

About the Author

Melissa Groeling graduated from Bloomsburg University with a degree in English. She lives, reads, and writes in the Philadelphia region and wherever else life happens to send her. She is a hardcore New York Giants fan and loves chocolate.